DELORES FOSSEN

A TEXAS KIND OF COWBOY

HQN

ISBN-13: 978-1-335-62399-7

Recycling programs for this product may not exist in your area.

A Texas Kind of Cowboy
Copyright © 2023 by Delores Fossen

Breaking Rules at Nightfall Ranch
First published in 2023. This edition published in 2023.
Copyright © 2023 by Delores Fossen

For questions and comments about the quality of this book, please contact us at CustomerService@Harlequin.com.

HQN
22 Adelaide St. West, 41st Floor
Toronto, Ontario M5H 4E3, Canada
www.Harlequin.com

Printed and bound in Barcelona, Spain by CPI Black Print

CONTENTS

A TEXAS KIND OF COWBOY

CHAPTER ONE

LORELEI PARKMAN WAS actually hoping this was a wild-goose chase. Or rather a wild-butt chase since she couldn't see the face of the man in the photo.

In fact, she couldn't see much of anything because he'd been on his stomach when the shot was taken. Added to that, he'd had his arm bent at such an angle that it'd covered his face, ear and most of his hair. The photographer had captured only a portion of his neck, back and that rather superior butt. Said butt had a longhorn tat just above the right cheek.

Those little "identifying" tidbits were hardly a detailed description to determine exactly who he was, but she'd have to work with what she had. Because Lorelei had to know the truth of whose butt was in the picture even if, in this case, the truth wasn't necessarily going to set her free.

Maybe just the opposite.

It could turn her life into a seriously tangled mess.

A lot was riding on IDing the butt's owner, and if the owner turned out to be rodeo star Dax Buchanan, then... well, she wasn't going there just yet. She'd hope for this being a wild-goose chase and start with trying to confirm or disprove it was Dax's butt. Then she would figure out the next step.

Tucking the photo in her purse, Lorelei pulled on her lightweight jacket and tried to tamp down her nerves. Tried not to chicken out, either, as she made her way out of her office and into the storefront of the Glass Hatter. Her shop.

Her baby.

It had been a good chunk of her focus before a real baby had come into her life nearly a year ago.

Lorelei recalled a quote from the town's founder, Hezzie Parkman, that no one put on their tombstone that they wished they'd spent more time at work. She wasn't sure she'd fully bought that until she had become a mom. Now, her daughter, Stellie, was her life, but Lorelei still managed to have plenty of love for the shop. It was just no longer her top priority.

She walked past one of the displays of delicate blown glass art that her sister Nola had created. It always fascinated and boggled her mind that Nola could create such things from fire, glass, breath and imagination. Each one of them was a little masterpiece.

Lorelei had personally arranged this display of the pieces with wings—angels, butterflies and birds—on the spotless floating shelves so they'd catch the morning sun just right. She'd done the same to the others. The vases, bowls, paperweights and whatnots that Nola thankfully created on a regular enough basis to earn them both good livings.

Even now, even with so much weighing on her mind, Lorelei took a moment to adjust a lavender and mint-green centerpiece sculpture before she went to the front display window. Her assistant, Misty Bennington, was there setting up an arrangement of glass spring flowers in clear tall vases.

"I need to run an errand," Lorelei said, trying to make it sound as if it were routine. Even though it wasn't.

Since it was nine in the morning, the shop wouldn't be open for another hour, and Lorelei hoped she'd be back by then. Of course, depending on how this visit with a hot rodeo star went, she might not be in any mental shape to return to work. Because if it was his butt, then she'd have to deal with that. If it wasn't his, then she'd have to keep searching. There wasn't exactly a reliable database to search guys with great butts and longhorn tats.

"There's nothing wrong with Stellie, is there?" Misty asked. She was Lorelei's age, thirty-five, and they'd known each other all their lives. That was probably why Misty had no trouble picking up on the worry vibe Lorelei was no doubt sending off.

"Stellie's fine," Lorelei assured her. Her nearly eleven-month-old adopted daughter, Estella, AKA Stellie, was with the nanny, and they no doubt had a wonderful, fun day planned.

Lorelei focused on that, on the fun and wonderful, on her precious daughter as she took out the photo to show Misty. "Without reading anything into it or asking me why I'm showing you this, could you tell me if you recognize that?"

Misty took the photo, blinked, then laughed. "You want me to ID a hot ass?"

Yes, this was a long shot. Especially long since even though Misty was attractive, her love life was even less lover-filled than Lorelei's.

Lorelei waggled the picture, urging Misty to take a longer look. She did. No laugh this time, but she made a sound of yummy approval.

"No, I don't recognize it," Misty insisted. "Please tell me your errand involves getting a look at the butt's owner."

It might, indeed, but Lorelei reminded herself that it was a good thing she'd struck out with Misty. If and when she struck out with Dax Buchanan, she'd next show the photo to her sisters. Not that they were big butt experts, either. But the more people who ruled out knowing the butt's owner meant he was likely some random stranger she would never be able to find.

Which would suit her just fine.

For now, though, the ruling-out had to continue.

Repeating that to herself and steeling herself up, Lorelei went out of the shop and to her car in the parking lot. The morning March wind had a bit of a chill to it, but it wouldn't last, not in this part of central Texas. Despite the fact that it wasn't officially spring yet, the temps would climb into the eighties by early afternoon.

She drove through Last Ride, the hometown she knew like the back of her own hand. Past the shops and businesses that were unique to a unique small town. For Heaven's Cake Bakery and Once Upon a Time antique and art shop. Fowl Feathered Friends was having a sale on birdseed.

Normally, she would have driven slower to take in the ever-changing displays of the storefronts, but today wasn't about savoring the sites. She headed out of town and toward Sunset Creek Ranch.

It felt a little as if she were heading to some kind of showdown like a gunfight at the O.K. Corral, but it was possible it might be nothing more than a very short, perhaps embarrassing, encounter with Dax Buchanan. If she struck out with him and his butt, then she would go to the next phase of her search—maybe even hire a PI. She couldn't breathe easier until the search was over and done and her life felt righted again.

Lorelei took the turn to Sunset Creek Ranch and drove through the massive wrought iron gates that were thankfully open. Then, she got a look at the ranch itself that was just as picturesque as its name. Acres of lush green pastures, white fences and three barns. The sprawling two-story stone-and-pine house had been well maintained, a reminder that Dax wasn't just a rodeo star but that he'd also made a fortune off endorsements and the sales of the prized rodeo bulls that his team of ranch hands bred and raised.

Since Dax's brother Wyatt was married to her glass artist sister, Nola, that meant they had a family connection. It also meant Lorelei was privy to the gossip about Dax. Lots and lots of gossip. About his chaotic, unconventional lifestyle and the equally chaotic reputation he had with women.

About the longhorn tat he had on his butt.

Yes, people in Last Ride gossiped about such things, and Lorelei had heard plenty of giggled whispers about having seen the tat. Of course, a tat sighting like that would have likely happened during sex. Or in her case, a photo.

Lorelei made her way up the porch that ran across the entire front of the house, rang the bell and waited. And waited. Because of that family connection with his brother Wyatt, she knew Dax wasn't away at some rodeo event since the night before, he'd hosted a bachelor party for his good friend, Sheriff Matt Corbin.

After the nanny had arrived to tend to Stellie and Lorelei had left for work, she'd seen Wyatt at the diner in town. Wyatt would have definitely been at the party so she'd figured if he was up and about, then so was Dax.

But she was possibly wrong about that.

She rang the doorbell again, waited some more and was ready to go looking out back for him when she heard the sound of what appeared to be someone dropping or bumping into something. Male muttered profanity followed. Then, hobbled footsteps. And a naked Dax Buchanan finally opened the door.

Well, almost naked, anyway.

All he wore were black boxers that dipped low on his

hips. So low that if they dipped even slightly lower, then she was going to get an eyeful. Or perhaps even a look at the infamous tat if he turned around.

Of course, the eyeful had already happened with the rumpled dark brown hair, the dreamy green eyes and the body. Yes, that body. Toned, lean. Perfect, like one of those calendars filled with hot guys for each month. And the face. Mercy, oh, mercy. He'd clearly gotten some amazing genes that blended together to create that equally amazing face.

A definite eyeful.

It was easy to see why so many women had wanted to take Dax for a spin. Even if that spin had a shorter shelf life than an already-ripe avocado.

"Yeah?" he said, rubbing his knee, swearing and yawning at the same time.

There was a red splotch on the knee that he'd obviously banged. Beneath the splotch was a white scar that appeared to be from a surgery.

"Oh," he added when he fully opened his eyes. "Lorelei."

Of course, he knew who she was. He'd known her for years, since Dax and his brothers had moved to Last Ride when he was a kid. Other than the family link with Nola and Wyatt, there was another "connection," too. Once when she'd been sixteen and Dax had been eleven, Lorelei had sort of babysat, or rather supervised him, when she'd worked in the after-school program.

Thinking about that now made her feel old and somewhat icky. Not icky enough, though, to quit noticing that he was hot.

And confused.

Since this was the first time she'd ever been to Sunset Creek Ranch, that probably accounted for the confusion she saw in his eyes. Maybe a hangover was playing into this, too, because she seriously doubted it'd been a no-booze bachelor party.

"I need to talk to you," she said to get her mouth working again before drool could accumulate.

"Yeah," he repeated, and he scrubbed his hand over his chin, which was sporting plenty of stubble. "Look, if this is about the red panties and the stripper, I didn't invite her. Tiffany Carver just heard about the bachelor party and thought she'd provide entertainment. I didn't manage to get her out of here, though, before she shoved red edible panties in Wyatt's jeans."

Lorelei just stared at him. "Uh, I'm not here about that." And she had no doubts, none, that Wyatt had resisted both the panties and the stripper. Nola and he were soul mates. Well, soul mates with complications, anyway, but they'd finally worked out their path so they could be together.

"Oh," Dax said, yawning again. He stepped back, motioning for her to come in. "Is this about Wyatt and Nola?"

"No," she answered, stepping inside. Though that was a good assumption since Wyatt and Nola were expecting a baby, and there'd been talk of maybe doing a joint family baby shower with both the Parkmans and the Buchanans. "It's something else."

Dax didn't question what that something else might be. "All right, then hold on while I locate some clothes. Help yourself to anything in the kitchen, and if you want to take mercy on me, please make some coffee."

With that plea, he headed toward a hall, and with his exit, Lorelei got a really good look at his back and shoulders. Since she was a woman with normal eyesight, normal urges, too, she had to get past the kick delivered by all that testosterone. The man threw it off like a high-powered lawn sprinkler. Setting testosterone and toned muscles aside, she tried to compare his backside to the photo, but the best she could manage was maybe it was a match.

Lorelei stayed put a moment and glanced around. Since this was an open-concept floor plan, she had no trouble seeing the living room, dining room and kitchen. She'd expected to see tables and counters cluttered with beer bottles and party debris, but it was surprisingly clean.

She made her way to the kitchen, located the coffeepot. Not one of those single-serving machines that she'd imagined a guy like Dax would have because of the convenience of it. This one was the old-fashioned drip sort. Lorelei found the coffee in a nearby cupboard and got a pot started while she continued to look around.

No red panties.

In fact, nothing like the bachelor-cave vibe that she'd expected, but she saw a "vibe" of a different sort. There were three flyers on the counter. Apparently, mock-ups for the Last Ride Charity Rodeo that Dax had hosted for the past couple of years. This year's rodeo was due to take place in about six weeks.

Talk had it that Dax did the event so he could bring in his drinking, womanizing pals under the guise of doing something good for the town. Other talk claimed it was Dax's attempt to make amends for his wild and rowdy past. Lorelei knew that many went just to get a look at the hot rodeo star in action.

And speaking of hot rodeo stars, Dax came back in while the coffee maker was still sputtering out the brew.

He'd pulled on a shirt that he hadn't bothered to button and jeans he hadn't fully zipped. Apparently, he was a man accustomed to being only partially dressed around women. Or maybe he simply didn't see her as a woman he wished to impress.

That made sense since she so wasn't his type.

Even though he was thirty, barely—she'd checked that on his National Rodeo Association profile—talk was that he went for women in their early twenties. Buckle bunnies and those fresh out of college. Lorelei was thirty-five, and while that was only five years older than Dax, she was pretty sure there was a generation of difference between them and that showed in their dating habits. Her occasional boyfriend, Alan Sandoval, was nearly fifty, technically old enough to be Dax's father.

"Sorry, but I need this," he muttered, taking out a huge cup with a bucking-bull logo and Sunset Creek Ranch printed on it.

He put the cup beneath the still-perking coffee and grabbed a much larger mug from the cupboard. He filled that mug from the pot, added an ice cube from the fridge dispenser to cool it down some and started drinking while he poured her a cup.

"Cream's in the fridge. Sugar's there." He tipped his head to a cartoon bull sugar bowl on the other side of the pot.

Lorelei didn't especially want any more caffeine since she already felt wired and edgy, though she sipped some, anyway. She opened her mouth to speak, but Dax held her off by lifting his finger in a "wait a second" gesture. He finished that mug, refilled it and went through the ice-cube routine before drinking more as if it were the cure for whatever ailed him.

"All right," he finally said. "I'm human now so tell me why you're here."

Dax opened another of the cabinets, pulled out a twin pack of strawberry Pop-Tarts. He offered her one, and when she shook her head to decline, he bit into both of them at once. When he finally stopped moving and leaned against the counter, Lorelei knew that was her cue to spill why she was there.

"Do you know about the Last Ride Society?" she asked.

More surprise flickered through his eyes. Then, realization. Then, concern. "That's the cemetery-drawing deal, right?"

Lorelei nodded. That was, indeed, an accurate if not somewhat thin description of it.

"The Last Ride Society was formed decades ago by the town's founder and my ancestor, Hezzie Parkman," she explained and went into the spiel she'd heard since childhood. "Hezzie wanted her descendants to preserve the area's history by having a quarterly drawing so that one Parkman would then in turn draw the name of a local tombstone to research."

Research that required the Parkman who'd drawn the name to dig into the deceased person's history, take a photo of the tombstone and write a report for all the town to read. Well, for all the town who was interested in reading such things, anyway. Which was apparently more than one might think. Lorelei didn't have the stats of those doing the reading, but there was always enough chatter about it to indicate dozens if not hundreds did.

"My brother's name was drawn last year," Dax muttered.

Yes, and that was the reason for the concern in his eyes. His brother Griff had ended his own life, and that had come out in the research. Lorelei was hoping that would stay the big bombshell of all future drawings. She definitely didn't want another revelation this time around.

"I won the drawing this quarter." Lorelei put *won* in air quotes. "And I drew Dana Smith's name."

She watched him carefully to see if there was any recognition. There wasn't. He just ate more of the Pop-Tarts and kept his gaze leveled on her.

"I'm guessing you think I can help you with the research on this Dana Smith," he said. "But I didn't know her. Who is she?"

Relief washed over Lorelei. Temporary relief, anyway. Since Dax didn't know Dana, that should mean he wasn't the naked guy in the photo she'd found in Dana's things. *Should mean.* But if Dax had slept around as much as the gossips claimed, then maybe he didn't know all the names of his lovers.

"No one knows a lot about Dana," Lorelei explained. "She moved to Last Ride a little over a year ago, and right before she died, she was living in one of the cottages behind the library."

Definitely not a cheap rental since it was just one block away from Parkman Row, a street with some of the most expensive homes in Last Ride. Lorelei lived on that street because her mother had given her the house that she'd once shared with Lorelei's late dad.

"Dana was a jewelry artist and kept mostly to herself," Lorelei went on. "Unfortunately, she died giving birth just a couple of weeks after she arrived in town."

"Oh, yeah. I remember my brothers talking about this. No one could find her next of kin so you adopted the baby."

Lorelei nodded. She had, indeed, adopted Stellie after fostering her as a newborn the day she'd been released from the hospital.

Even though Lorelei had already been vetted and approved for both foster care and adoption, the process still hadn't been easy. It had involved the sheriff's office sending out missing person's requests and posting Dana's name and picture through police channels. After eight months,

Child Protective Services had finally given Lorelei the green light to adopt the baby who'd felt like her own right from the start. Ironically, she'd signed the final papers just yesterday morning.

And a couple of hours later, Lorelei had found the picture.

It had felt as if fate had given her a hard jab in the stomach.

"Anyway," Lorelei continued after she dragged in a long breath, "as I said, I drew her name for the tombstone research, but when I couldn't find anything on her, I asked Sheriff Corbin if I could take a look at the things Dana had left in the cottage. There wasn't much, mainly jewelry-making supplies and a few baby things."

No nursery to speak of, which was a little odd. Just a newborn onesie and a blanket. Still, the doctors believed that Stellie had been born three to four weeks early so maybe Dana just hadn't gotten around to it yet. But it was troubling. Most women would have set up a space for the baby they were expecting. Then again, most women wouldn't have moved to a new town during their last trimester.

And that ate away at Lorelei.

Had Dana been on the run from someone or something? Sheriff Corbin had sent in her fingerprints and DNA, and there'd been no matches in the databases. That meant Dana hadn't had a criminal record. But people could and did run for other reasons, and the bottom line was that Dana Smith was probably an alias since there was no DMV or birth records matching her age and description. It was as if the woman hadn't existed before she'd driven into town.

Dax shook his head. "Sorry, but I'm still not sure how you think I can help with this." He stopped, his eyes meeting hers. "You think I hooked up with Dana?"

"The thought occurred to me," Lorelei confirmed.

But it was a thought she totally wanted to be able to dismiss in the next couple of minutes. Dax was her top candidate right now, but rather than ask for him to bare his butt cheek, she went with a different approach.

She took out her phone and pulled up a photo of Dana. Not an especially good one because there were no good photos of her available. Well, none other than the morgue shot that the sheriff had sent out when searching for her next of kin. Lorelei hadn't wanted to look at that, though. The one she showed Dax was a picture of Dana taken outside Once Upon a Time where several of her handmade jewelry pieces were being displayed. Unfortunately, Dana hadn't been looking directly at the camera when the shot was taken.

Dax moved in for a closer look, and she watched as his gaze slid over the petite pregnant brunette with a pixie haircut, shy eyes and lowered chin. According to the ID Dana had used during the short time she'd lived in Last Ride, she was twenty-six, but she looked younger.

"No, I don't think so," Dax said, still studying the photo. "But it's hard to tell. Got a different photo of her?"

Oh, she had a different photo all right. Just not of Dana. It was time to deal with the butt.

"There weren't a lot of personal items in the cottage where Dana was staying," Lorelei went on. "But as I said, the sheriff allowed me to go through them. I found a concealed compartment in her purse. I have the same one so I knew it was there. It's a small sleeve at the bottom of the bag meant to hold a credit card or cash." She paused, swallowed hard. "And this was in it."

Her fingers were trembling a little when she took out

the photo. Her heart and stomach were trembling a whole lot more than just a little.

"I figure it's a long shot for this to be you, but..." Lorelei just let that trail off, and she handed him the photo.

Like the one on her phone, Dax moved in for a closer look, but he didn't take a long study of it. No. He uttered one word that caused Lorelei's heart to drop to her knees.

"Hell."

CHAPTER TWO

DAX FORCED HIMSELF to breathe, and he wished he hadn't wolfed down those Pop-Tarts. His stomach was already churning, and looking at this picture sure as hell wasn't helping.

He'd never seen a picture of his backside, but he was almost positive that he was looking at his own butt. The tat was the same, anyway, and it was his usual habit to sleep facedown, which would have given the photographer a decent shot at capturing his back and ass.

Since the photographer was perhaps this Dana Smith who'd died during childbirth, Lorelei had obviously played "connect the dots." Dots that had led her straight to him. She was staring at him now, clearly waiting for him to say something, and he didn't think it was his imagination that she looked ready to do some puking from a churning stomach as well.

"Okay," he finally managed to say. "Let's work this out." And he needed to work it out in a way that confirmed that even though that was his ass, it had nothing to do with Dana Smith and the child she'd had. "Was there anything in Dana's things to make you believe she knew me?"

And, of course, that was "knew" in the biblical sense of the word.

"Just the photo," Lorelei answered. There weren't tears in her big blue eyes. Not yet, but along with the possible puking, Dax thought she might be on the verge of doing some crying.

"Okay," he repeated while he tried to gather his thoughts.

He kept his voice as steady as he could manage because if Lorelei lost it, he would have to calm her down before they could get to the bottom of this. Thank merciful heaven that Lorelei didn't have a reputation as someone who often lost it. Nope, her rep was more that of a rock-steady, responsible, dignified and polished person.

In other words, his polar opposite.

The only time Dax felt rock-steady was when he was on the back of a pissed-off bull that wanted to toss him up in the air and then stomp the crap out of him.

"Okay," he said for a third time. "Let's start with some basics. How old is the baby?"

"She's nearly eleven months," Lorelei instantly provided in a way that made him think she could have provided the days, hours and maybe even the minutes of the child's age.

She started to pull up something on her phone that she was still holding in a death grip. Maybe Lorelei had been about to show him a photo of the child, but she seemed to change her mind about that. Perhaps because she didn't want to spring it on him yet that the child was his spitting image. Both of them would need more than a moment or two to level out before handling that.

Dax did some quick mental math. "Eleven plus nine would be twenty months ago." He dragged out his own phone from his pocket and tapped onto the calendar that he was diligent about keeping up-to-date so he wouldn't miss a rodeo event or important meeting. He scrolled back those twenty months and felt relief wash over him. "I was laid up most of that month with an injury I got in a ride up in Fort Worth."

He expected that to perk Lorelei right up. It didn't.

"Stellie was born a little early," she muttered, some of the color blanching from her face. "The doctor thinks she was born at thirty-six or thirty-seven weeks."

That was certainly *not* the news he wanted to hear, but Dax held on to hope and counted forward another four weeks on his calendar.

And the hope vanished, whipped away like thin smoke in a really gusty wind.

"By then I'd recovered from my injury." A bad one that had required a boatload of pain meds and even some physical therapy. No way had he had sex during his recovery. He'd barely been able to walk. "Let me see the picture of Dana again," he tacked on to that.

Some of Lorelei's trademark rock-steadiness disappeared as quickly as his hope had, and with her hand trembling a little, she showed him the photo on her phone again. Dax tried to focus on just her face, but the angle was off so that he could only see one cheek, a portion of her forehead and the profile of her nose.

Still… Crap… Still, it could be her. That is, it could be Dana if she'd changed her hair.

"You recognize her," Lorelei blurted out on a sharp rise of breath. "You recognize her." Groaning, she went to one of the stools by the counter and dropped down onto it as if her legs had given way.

Dax was right there with her on that particular response. He was feeling wobbly in a lot of places right now.

"I *might* recognize her," Dax emphasized, and he intended to hang on to that *might* as long as he could. He wasn't a big fan of denial, but there was that wobbliness and puking potential so he needed to keep as steady as possible. "But if it's really her, she was a blonde, and her hair was long, well past her shoulders."

It wasn't hard for him to mentally pull up that image of her when he'd first seen her eyeing him. A stunner with sad eyes. The looks had made him want to chat her up. The eyes had made him want to offer her a shoulder.

"You probably don't remember her name," Lorelei muttered.

Because there was a firestorm of emotions going through him right now, Dax flicked off the insult. And it was, indeed, an insult. Despite what people thought of him, and he knew they didn't think very much, he made a habit of learning a woman's name before he took her to bed.

"Valerie Foster," Dax provided, still looking at the picture.

Hell. Had he gotten Valerie pregnant? He'd used a condom, always did, *always*, because he didn't want to be a father.

But had that happened?

Dax just didn't know so he tried to work through the details of her that he remembered. Not just her stunning looks and sad eyes, but what she'd said. "I met her after a ride at a big rodeo event in Fort Worth. It was the first night of the event, and I was due to be there for three days. She'd been crying but was trying to hide the fact she'd been crying if you know what I mean. We talked for a while, and then we went for a drink and something to eat."

Lorelei made a sound of agreement and then swallowed hard. "You had sex with her?"

This time, Dax didn't just flick away the insult. "Not then and there," he grumbled, giving her a flat look. "When I see a sad, crying woman, my go-to response isn't to drag her to the ground and have sex with her."

She didn't apologize, didn't seem to react to his annoyance. "But sex eventually happened." Her voice was a shaky whisper.

Dax nodded, causing Lorelei to groan. All right, so the basics matched up with the possibility of Valerie getting pregnant that one time they were together, but it still didn't make sense.

"Valerie had my number," he said, going back over that night they were together. "I told her to call me. And I tried to call her," Dax added before Lorelei could hit him with another zinger that implied his casual attitude toward his sexual partners. "But she didn't answer. I left her a message, two of them in fact, and when she didn't return my call, I figured it'd been a one-off for her."

Strange, because he hadn't picked up on that when he'd met her, and he usually had a good radar for buckle bunnies or those on the hunt for a one-nighter with someone they considered a celebrity. Not that he was totally opposed to that because he'd had his own share of one-nighters. Too many. And that's why people would never think of him as rock-steady or responsible when it came to relationships.

Or anything else for that matter.

But by the time he'd met Valerie, Dax had been trying to, well, be more responsible. Because he'd learned that even one-offs came with a high price tag, and they didn't lead to anything other than one and off. He wasn't opposed to having a good time, but he supposed he'd been looking for the "more" that so many of his friends and even his brothers had found.

More came with a high price tag, too, but he was betting it wouldn't leave him with this hollow feeling he'd carried around for as long as he could remember.

"So, it could be you in the photo," Lorelei said, yanking his attention back to her. "Do you recall her taking it?"

This was an easy answer. "No. No recollection of it whatsoever, but I have been accused of sleeping like the dead." He winced because, hey, they were talking about a woman who'd died.

Cursing himself, he took a harder look at the photo of his backside. Since it had a grainy texture, it appeared to have been printed not on a professional printer but a "home office type" machine. So, it was possible Valerie had taken the shot with her phone and then printed it out later.

But why?

As a memento of their one night together? If that was it, why hadn't she just taken a picture of his face or done a selfie with them together? Unfortunately, she wasn't around to explain any of that. Nor was she around to explain why she'd changed her name. Or why she'd perhaps given him a fake one. People didn't usually do that unless they had something to hide.

"Why had Valerie been crying when you met her?" Lorelei asked. She was obviously trying to work out some explanations as well.

Dax dug through even more memories of that night. "She wouldn't say, but I think she might have been going through a divorce or broken engagement because there was an indentation on the finger of her left hand where she used to wear a ring. I did ask her if she was married, and she said no."

And none of this was helping either of them. Lorelei looked even closer to not being able to stave off those tears, and Dax's stomach was trying to wring itself into a tight knot.

"Let me see a picture of the baby," he insisted. "Of Stellie," he added, remembering that's what Lorelei had called the child.

Lorelei certainly didn't jump to do that, and he totally understood her hesitation. He was dealing with the possibility that he'd gotten a woman pregnant. A woman who'd died giving birth. But Lorelei was dealing with the fear that there was a birth parent out there. Or rather a birth parent right here in Last Ride. That had to give a hard slap to any insecurities she had as to her legal claim to the baby.

When she finally started scrolling through the photos on her phone, he could see there was a slew of them, maybe multiple ones for every day of the child's life. Lorelei finally settled on one, and she lifted the screen again to show him a picture of a smiling round-faced baby with dark brown curls. She looked like one of those cute babies in ads and commercials.

He stared at all that cuteness but didn't feel any kind of jolt that he was looking at his DNA offspring. Was that the way it worked? An instant love and connection triggered by primal instincts so you'd protect the child and therefore continue the human race?

Maybe.

But maybe that only happened when you knew for sure this was your kid, and he didn't see any "jump right out at you" resemblance to Valerie or him. Stellie just looked like a cute, happy baby.

So, another strikeout in that he couldn't confirm he was her father, but there was still nothing definitive, either.

"I could do some searches for Valerie's name," he said, going through the contacts on his phone. "Because if she gave me her real name, there'll likely be something on the web about her." Dax paused, though, and reconsidered. "But I'll have Sheriff Corbin do that."

Matt Corbin was a longtime friend and would get right on this. Especially since he recalled Matt working hard to find the woman's next of kin after she'd passed.

Before he could press Matt's number, though, Lorelei caught onto his hand. She opened her mouth, clearly about to protest, but after a few moments, she closed her mouth and eased her grip off him.

"I might not be the baby's father," he reminded her. "But if Dana truly was Valerie, then she might have relatives looking for her."

"I know," Lorelei whispered, and here the tears came.

Oh, man. Talk about the absolute worst thing he could have said to her. He might as well have found a thousand paper cuts on her and poured lemon juice on them. Cursing under his breath, Dax reached for her, but Lorelei dodged his attempt and moved away from him fast. She didn't go far, just into the living room.

"Call Sheriff Corbin," she finally said with her back to him.

Well, he could add honest and even brave to Lorelei's list of attributes. If any other woman had been in her proverbial shoes, she might have begged him to keep this all to himself. Then again, she had come to his house to show him a photo of his naked butt so it was obvious she wanted to know the truth. Then again, maybe she'd just hoped that it wasn't his butt, his one-off with Valerie/Dana, his baby.

Dax was especially hoping for the latter, that Stellie wasn't his. Because he was so far from being daddy material that it wasn't even a blip on a distant radar. There had to be some-body else better out there who could fill that daddy role for her. If it needed filling, that is. After all, there could be a good reason, perhaps a troubling one, why Valerie hadn't spelled out to someone in Last Ride whose baby she was carrying.

It was especially troubling if he'd been that man.

Dax pressed the sheriff's contact number, and Matt answered on the second ring. "No, I didn't arrest Tiffany Carver for crashing the party and stripping," Matt said right off.

"Well, good." Dax hadn't wanted the woman arrested. He'd only wanted her to leave, and when she wouldn't, Matt had stepped in to convince her. Dax had gladly let him handle it.

"I'm calling about something else," Dax went on. Oh, but how to say this. He went with a very abbreviated version. "It's come to my attention that Dana Smith might have been a woman named Valerie Foster." Of course, it was possible that was an alias, too. Just as possible that Valerie and Dana were two different people. "I was thinking you could run a background check on her or something."

Matt didn't jump to volunteer to do that, and Dax could practically feel the cop's brain at work. "I can do that, sure. You want to tell me why?"

"Not yet. Long story." Well, not that long, but Dax didn't want to go over the possibility he'd knocked someone up while Lorelei was still here. "I'll fill you in, though, of course, if it turns out that Dana Smith was actually Valerie."

"All right," Matt finally said after a really long pause. "Give me any other details you have on her other than her name in case I get more than one hit."

"I'll have to ballpark the age. Mid-twenties. Height, about five-two with a slight build. Blond hair. A natural blond," Dax added, figuring that Matt wouldn't ask him how he knew that little tidbit.

"Accent, birthmarks, tats or anything else distinguishing?" Matt pressed.

"No real accent, no birthmarks or tats that I noticed." Now it was Dax who paused, and he recalled something that had struck him about her. "She sounded high-end, like maybe she came from money. She talked about traveling abroad and was wearing an expensive-looking necklace."

Her underwear had been silk. Black silk. But again, he'd save that detail for a private conversation with Matt.

Matt apparently, though, wasn't finished with his cop's questions. "And when was the last time you saw her?"

Since Dax had just done the math for Lorelei, it was still fresh in his memory. "A little over nineteen months ago." Using his calendar, Dax gave him the date of the Fort Worth rodeo.

"Hell," Matt muttered. He'd apparently done some math, too.

"Yeah," Dax verified. "Let me know what you find out."

He ended the call, downed some more coffee that would in no way help his stomach and then he went into the living room to face the music. Or rather to face Lorelei. Yeah, the tears were still there, and even though he'd seen her dozens of times, he'd never seen her like this. It was as if she were about to shatter into a million little pieces.

"You've adopted this baby?" he asked. "I mean, you're not in the middle of the paperwork, right?"

"I adopted her. The process was finalized yesterday." She swiped away the tears as if disgusted that she had not managed to stop them. There was no way he'd mention that in the swipe she'd smeared some mascara and now had a black streak on her cheek. "I'm not sure the legalities, though, if Dana did have any next of kin."

Dax didn't know the legal stuff, either, but Lorelei had to

be thinking that someone with that next of kin connection might challenge the adoption. Or accuse her of not showing him the photo twenty-four hours earlier so that he or Dana's family couldn't somehow interfere with the final adoption papers. He didn't want her going there just yet, though, because there might be much ado about nothing.

"Certainly, somebody in town knew Dana and heard her talk about her baby's father," he threw out there.

Lorelei shook her head, her perfect blond hair moving with the gesture. "Dana was only in Last Ride a couple of weeks before she went into labor. She died a few hours after giving birth. A blood clot," she added in a murmur.

Dax felt that stab of grief and did another "don't go there yet" reminder. He had too much to learn and get through before he could tackle the guilt and grief.

"But Dana, Valerie or whoever she was would have talked to someone in those two weeks," he pointed out.

She nodded and blinked hard at the tears. "A few people. Millie Parkman had several pieces of Dana's jewelry in her shop so they'd had a couple of brief conversations."

Since Last Ride was the very definition of a small town, that meant Dax knew Millie as well, and Lorelei and she were distant cousins. The Parkmans were *the* family in town, most of them loaded with old money, and spent their days on the various society committees and clubs. Not Millie and Lorelei, though. They both owned businesses. Ditto for Lorelei's twin sisters, Nola and Lily. Nola was a glass artist and Lily ran a horse ranch where his brother, Jonas, was the foreman.

Again, this was a small town where people and things just coiled and coiled around each other, often with only one or two degrees of separation at most. Dax was so hoping, though, that one of those coils wasn't about to come back to bite him in his tattooed ass.

"So, Dana made jewelry?" he asked.

Best to fill in as many blanks as possible, and he couldn't recall Valerie mentioning anything about that. Maybe because they were talking about two entirely different women here. Just because Dana was in Last Ride, didn't mean she was Valerie.

"Yes," Lorelei verified. "Millie said the pieces were very good, that they were modern takes on antique pieces. They worked with the other inventory she has in Once Upon a Time so she agreed to try to sell them."

That filled in another blank. Well, maybe it did. Dana probably wouldn't have gone to Millie had she not needed money. Of course, she might have just been an artist who wanted others to be able to buy and wear her art. Again, that matched with nothing that Valerie had said, but he did remember that necklace she was wearing. Very distinctive with dark red stones set in silver. He wasn't a jewelry expert by any stretch of the imagination, but that piece seemed to fit the very definition of a modern take on an antique.

And that caused Dax to do some more muttered cursing.

"FYI, I always use protection when I have sex," he let her know in between some of those curse words. "*Always*, even when my partner says she's on the pill."

That was something he recalled Valerie saying. She was also the one who'd initiated sex. Considering that she'd had those tear-reddened eyes, Dax had figured it would be just a talk/dinner date. Something he would have been fine with, but Valerie had wanted more.

Or rather like she'd *needed* more.

Maybe to forget whatever or whoever had made her cry in the first place? People had sex for all kinds of reasons, and while he was pretty sure Valerie had enjoyed her night with him, that didn't mean she'd been searching for anything other than enjoyment. In fact, if that butt photo hadn't been connected to a possible pregnancy and baby, Dax might have considered that she'd taken the photos to sell to some gossip site. It certainly wouldn't have been the first time that'd happened. And that led him to another question.

Were there more photos?

If so, had she shared them with anyone instead of just hiding one in her purse?

"What about Dana's phone or computer?" Dax asked. "Certainly, she had those things, and there must have been something on them to prove or disprove who she was claiming to be."

Lorelei dragged in a weary breath. "Nothing. All of this came up right after Stellie was born because Sheriff Corbin was trying to locate any next of kin. Dana was using a prepaid cell, and the only calls she'd made were to her doctor's office here in Last Ride. There wasn't anything of use on the computer. She didn't even have an email account set up, and there was nothing personal in her car. The car was a long-term rental, and she'd used the name Dana Smith to get that."

Well, crap. That didn't sound good, and his first thought went in a really bad direction. That maybe Dana had, indeed, been on the run from someone.

And that someone could have been him.

Perhaps because she hadn't wanted him to know she'd gotten pregnant? But that didn't make sense since she'd obviously come to Last Ride. Why would she have done that if she'd been trying to avoid him?

She wouldn't have. Which meant he had to move on to theory number two.

"I'm about to say something that has a big *what-if* in it," he started. "Keep that in mind because, again, this could mean nothing. But what if Dana came here to let me know she was pregnant?" That tightened the knot in his gut again. Because it could be the spot-on truth. "I'm always in and out, going here and there for the rodeo events so maybe she was waiting for the right time to come to tell me."

Lorelei stayed quiet a moment. "Look at your calendar again. For the end of March and the beginning of April last year. She died April thirteenth so it would have been the two weeks before that."

Dax did look and then realized it shot a big hole in his theory. In this case, it was a good hole and a bad theory. One that he definitely hadn't wanted to be true, and the dates confirmed that it wasn't.

"I was here in Last Ride and at my ranch for eleven days of the two weeks prior to April thirteenth," he verified.

He'd been dealing with a new buyer for the rodeo bulls so he hadn't even made that many trips into town. In other words, if Dana had wanted to talk to him, she could have come to his ranch. Everyone in Last Ride knew he owned Sunset Creek. So did plenty of others since there'd been magazine and newspaper articles written about him and the ranch.

"I'm sorry," Lorelei muttered, drawing his attention back to her.

That's when he saw her swipe at another tear. Now she had two streaks of mascara on her cheeks. Since he seriously doubted she wanted anyone to see her like that, he went into the powder room, grabbed some tissues that his housekeeper thankfully kept stocked there and handed them to her when he came back.

"No need to apologize," Dax assured her. "I tend to have a lot of chaos in my life, but I'm betting you don't."

"No," Lorelei quietly agreed. "I own a glass shop where one wrong move can destroy fragile pieces of art so I keep the chaos to a minimum. It's the same for crying. I keep it to an absolute minimum because I hate it," she added. "It solves nothing, makes my eyes red and clogs my sinuses."

"Yeah, it does that, but sometimes it just can't be helped."

She looked at him as if he'd just told her a whopper. Or sprouted an extra ear. Dax had no intention of filling her in on what might or might not have led him to do some crying because it went back to a time where he just couldn't go. Mean bulls were a piece of cake compared to some stuff.

Dax heard the sound of a vehicle approaching, and he glanced out the window to see his brother pull his truck to a stop behind Lorelei's car.

"It's Jonas," he told her.

That got Lorelei frantically swiping at her face with the tissues, along with muttering some G-rated profanity. At least he thought what she said qualified as profanity. He heard her say *Son of a Baloney Eater*. Maybe she'd switched to that kind of talk because she had a kid around. Jonas had done pretty much the same when he'd become a stepfather more than a dozen years ago.

Since she hadn't been successful at removing the black smears, Dax took one of the tissues, and using the moisture from her tears, he wiped away the mascara. Then, he went Honest Abe with her.

"Jonas isn't blind so he'll see you've been crying," Dax pointed out. "Unless you want to get into a discussion with him about that, why don't you just hang back, and I'll get rid of him?"

She didn't even hesitate. "Thank you," she said, adding a nod.

"No problem." He wanted to add that soothing women was sort of his specialty, something he was darn good at, but considering the circumstances of another woman, Valerie, who he'd soothed and maybe gotten pregnant, he just went to the door.

Jonas had already lifted his hand to knock, but he stopped when Dax stepped into the doorway. "Figured you'd need some help cleaning up after the party," his brother immediately said, and then he hiked his thumb to Lorelei's car. "What's Lorelei doing here?"

"No help needed. Couldn't sleep after everyone left so I took care of it." Dax paused, leaned in closer and lowered his voice to a whisper. "Could you do me a favor and not ask anything about Lorelei?"

Jonas cursed, not the G-rated crap, either, and Dax could see where his brother's mind was going. His obviously very dirty mind.

"No," Dax assured him. "Just no. That's not why she's here. I'll fill you in when I can."

Jonas studied him. "It's bad?"

"To be determined." But, yeah, it could be a whole crapload of bad.

Since Jonas was the big brother of the family and therefore the self-appointed fixer of all things Buchanan-related, Dax could tell he wanted to hang around and, well, try to fix something. But thankfully, Jonas didn't push to come inside, and when Dax's phone rang, that was apparently his brother's cue to get moving.

Jonas would put his curiosity and concern on hold, but it was only a temporary reprieve for Dax. Soon, Jonas would want assurances that he wasn't dicking around with Lorelei, and that included dicking around in every sense of the term.

"It's Matt," Dax relayed to Lorelei as he shut the door. Since she would no doubt want to hear every word of this conversation, he put the call on speaker. "FYI, Lorelei's listening," he warned Matt right off.

Judging from Matt's silence, he might have wanted to do some real cursing, too. Maybe because he had things to say that he knew Lorelei wasn't going to like. But that didn't stop Matt from jumping straight into business.

"Valerie Elise Ford," Matt threw out there. "I'm texting you her DMV photo now. I've compared it to her morgue shot, and even though the hair colors don't match, it's the same person."

Well, hell. Valerie Ford was damn close to the name of Valerie Foster, and since Matt was certain that Dana and Valerie Ford were one and the same, then it wasn't looking good for the outcome Dax wanted. The outcome where he hadn't gotten a woman pregnant and then she'd died in childbirth.

"Tell me if it's the woman you met in Fort Worth," Matt instructed.

Dax waited for the ding to indicate a text and had a look at the picture. A thousand words went through his head. Really bad words. At the moment, it was the only thing his brain could manage. He certainly wasn't going to be able to come to terms too quickly with what this all meant. That's why Dax started with a simple answer to Matt's "not so simple" instruction.

"Yeah, that's the woman I met in Fort Worth," Dax managed to say.

Lorelei hurriedly moved to Dax's side. Shoulder to shoulder with him, and even though it was barely audible, he heard the hitch in her throat. A hitch to let him know that she wasn't disputing what the sheriff had just said and that she was experiencing the same crap storm of emotions as he was.

"All right," Dax said, taking in a few much-needed breaths. "Tell me about Valerie Elise Ford."

Matt took a long breath of his own before he started. "She was twenty-six when she died. No criminal record. Her folks are Miriam and Greg Ford from St. Louis. Real estate moguls with plenty of money. Valerie was their only child, and they reported her missing right around the time you hooked up with her in Fort Worth. They withdrew the missing person's report a couple of days later, which is why her name didn't come up when we were searching for her next of kin."

"Parents," Lorelei muttered, and just as he'd seen the dirty thoughts go through his brother's mind, Dax could see the worried ones go through hers. Because these people would be Stellie's grandparents.

"There's more," Matt said.

"Bad more?" Dax wanted to know when Matt didn't continue.

"Yeah." Another pause. "She was married, Dax."

Shit. Shit. Shit. Dax didn't hold back on the cursing because his number one rule was not screwing around with a married woman. Number two was not getting a woman pregnant. It was possible, likely even, that he'd managed to bust both of those rules at once.

"Her husband's name is Aaron Marcel," Matt went on. "He lives in St. Louis as well, and I'll be calling him shortly to do a notification of his wife's death." He paused a heartbeat. "Lorelei, are you still there?"

"Yes," she muttered.

"I'm not sure what Mr. Marcel is going to tell me, but I'm looking at the dates, and it's possible that he's Stellie's biological father," Matt informed her. "Depending on how he takes that news, he could be paying you a visit very soon."

CHAPTER THREE

LORELEI NO LONGER cared if anyone saw her crying. No longer cared if the gossips had a field day with speculation as to why she'd screeched to a stop, bolted from her car and was running toward her sister's glass workshop in the center of town.

She needed family, and she couldn't go to Stellie like this because it might upset her to see her mom crying and near hysterics. No. She had to get control of herself and then she could go home and be with her daughter.

Her daughter.

The words repeated like a mantra in Lorelei's head as she hurried into Nola's workshop. "Shut the door," her sister called out without even glancing back to see who'd come in. It was her standard greeting/scolding when she was blowing because it was the heat from the furnace that kept the glass from cooling too fast.

"My timer's about to go off," Nola added, still not even giving Lorelei a glance. "Doctor's orders that I can only be in the heat for ten minutes so I have to hurry to finish this."

A very pregnant Nola was seated on a small stool in front of the roaring glory hole furnace. She was turning a pipe, shaping the hot glass at the end. If this had been different circumstances, Lorelei would have oohed and aahed at seeing the beautiful azure blue sculpture that was coming to life right before her eyes. But this wasn't different circumstances, and she burst into a fresh round of tears that she couldn't hold back another second.

Nola's head whipped up, her gaze zooming across the workshop to land on Lorelei. Instant alarm went through her sister's eyes. She dropped the pipe, the sculpture shattering, and she hurried to Lorelei.

"What's wrong?" Nola demanded, taking hold of Lorelei's shoulders. "Did something happen to Stellie?"

Lorelei tried to answer, tried to tell her that Stellie was okay, but she couldn't speak through the sobs. Obviously, Nola was shocked because she'd never seen her big sister like this. That's because Lorelei had never been like this, and that was saying something, considering everything she'd been through.

As much as her pregnant belly would allow, Nola wrapped her arm around Lorelei and led her across the workshop to an area set up with industrial-sized cooling fans. Again, that was part of the doctor's orders since the prolonged heat wasn't good for the baby. Her sister got a cup of water from a cooler and handed it to her.

"Drink," Nola instructed, having a cup herself.

Nola didn't press her with more questions. She just waited until Lorelei had had a few sips of the water and put some semblance of a chokehold on the emotions that were threatening to crush her.

"It was Dax's butt in the picture," Lorelei blurted out.

She could instantly tell from the blank look in Nola's eyes that she had to back up again as she'd done with Dax.

Lorelei sighed and gathered her breath. "When I was doing research for the Last Ride Society on Dana Smith, I found this picture." She pulled it out of her purse to show Nola. "It's Dax. He confirmed that. He also confirmed he was with Dana. Except her name wasn't really Dana. It's

Valerie Ford Marcel." Lorelei's voice cracked. "God, Nola. She was married and has parents."

Nola looked at the picture, and her face definitely wasn't blank when she lifted her gaze to meet Lorelei's. "Well, crap." She paused, obviously trying to wrap her head around this, and she muttered those same two words several more times. "What's going to happen?"

Lorelei knew what the worst-case scenario was but she couldn't go there, not yet, anyway. For now, she just focused on what she did know. "The sheriff is calling her next of kin to notify them of her death." She had to pause and take another sip of water before she finished. "The husband might be Stellie's bio father."

Lorelei left it at that, but Nola was no doubt mentally filling in the blanks. The parents and the possible bio father would almost certainly come rushing to Last Ride. Well, they would unless they were horrible people who hadn't cared about their wife and child.

But Lorelei rethought that.

Maybe Valerie/Dana had been the horrible one and her family had been glad to see the last of her. Even if that were true, though, that didn't mean they'd feel the same way about the baby. All three of them could want Stellie.

"Oh, crap," Nola repeated, her voice coated with her own experiences with adoption.

That's because when Wyatt and Nola had been sixteen, they'd had a baby together, a daughter they gave up for adoption. Then, seventeen years later, just as Nola had found out she was pregnant with the baby she was carrying now, the daughter, Marley, had arrived in Last Ride so she could get to know her bio parents. That was a good thing for Wyatt and Nola, but Marley was practically an adult who could make her own decisions about such things. Stellie was just a baby.

Her baby.

Lorelei couldn't even bear the thought of losing her to someone solely because they shared DNA. Heck, she couldn't bear the thought of losing her, period.

"All right," Nola said as if trying to steady herself. Trying to steady Lorelei, too. "So, the husband might be the biological father, *might*," she emphasized, "but it's possible that Dax is?"

Lorelei nodded. "The timing fits."

And Lorelei didn't know what to wish for. That Dax was the father or the husband was. Of course, it was possible neither was, and that was about the best Lorelei could hope for here. That another man would be Stellie's bio father and that he wouldn't want to make any kind of claim on her.

"The adoption is final," Nola reminded her. "We're celebrating it when we have Stellie's first birthday bash." Their mother, Evangeline, and Lorelei had spent weeks planning it.

"Yes, the paperwork is final, but what if Valerie's family accuses me of withholding info that would have prevented the adoption?" Lorelei asked. "I didn't know they existed, but they might not believe that."

Nola didn't immediately dismiss the possibility of such an accusation. "You should talk to Sophia Parkman since she was your lawyer for the adoption. She might be able to put your mind at rest."

Lorelei had already considered that. She liked Sophia, but going to her would feel as if she'd taken a step to fight for Stellie. She didn't want to have to fight. She just wanted the life with her baby that she'd had before she'd found that blasted photo in the purse.

The door practically flew open, and their sister, Lily, came rushing in. She was wearing her usual ranching clothes. Jeans, a work shirt and mucky boots. And her gaze zoomed across the sprawling industrial space to locate them.

"What's wrong?" Lily immediately asked. "I was at the feedstore, and I got three texts and two calls saying that Lorelei came running in here and that she was crying." Lily looked at Lorelei. "You *are* crying," she said in disbelief as she hurried toward them. "What the heck happened?"

Since she was, indeed, sobbing now, Lorelei motioned for Nola to fill Lily in. "I'll bottom line this," Nola volunteered. "Dana Smith was a woman named Valerie, and she had a husband and parents. Also, Dax might be Stellie's father."

Lily's mouth dropped open. Nowhere near her usual expression, either. Along with being a rancher, she was the single mom of a teenager, and she didn't shock easily. Or curse. But that was what she did right now.

"What the hell is going to happen?" Lily asked.

"Nothing for now," Nola assured her, but Lorelei saw right through Nola's calm, steady voice and the empty assurance. Yes, it might be nothing for now, but it could be a Texas-sized something after the sheriff did the notification to Valerie's husband and her parents.

Which he was probably doing at this very second.

The door opened again, and this time it was their mother who hurried in. As Lily and Lorelei had done, Evangeline had to pick through the dim lighting in the workshop before she located them. She ran toward them, taking hold of Nola.

"Bright blessings," Evangeline said, throwing out her usual greeting. A greeting that was laced with worry that their mother was almost certainly trying to tamp down. "I thought you'd gone into labor." She was breathing hard and had likely run here after getting multiple calls and texts that something was wrong.

"No," Nola assured her, and she gave their mother the same bottom-line explanation as the door opened for a third time.

It was Wyatt.

He certainly didn't issue any "bright blessings" greetings, and while he wasn't running exactly, he didn't waste any time getting to the little huddle they'd created. He brushed a kiss on Nola's mouth before turning to Lorelei. Not a kiss of relief. It seemed to be one of reassurance for Nola, but it was still coated with worry for what he no doubt realized was some kind of trouble.

"I would ask if you're okay, but I can see you're not. Dax called me," Wyatt tacked on to that.

So, no bottom-line explanation was needed for Wyatt. Of course Dax had called him. Had probably phoned his other brother Jonas as well because this had almost certainly knocked him for a loop just as it'd done to Lorelei.

"Oh, dear," Evangeline muttered. "How is Dax?"

Evangeline slipped right into her counselor's voice, which was pretty much her norm since she was, indeed, a counselor. One who worked long hours with little pay and would give anyone the shirt off her back.

Lorelei dearly loved her mother, but she didn't think she could handle Evangeline's eternal "rose-colored glasses" approach right now. She needed to wallow in the sickening dread for a little while to try to get it out of her system before she went home to see Stellie who was there with the nanny. She definitely wouldn't be going back into the shop today. No way. The gossips would just show up wanting tidbits and their questions would hash and rehash every-thing she was feeling.

"Dax is, well, Dax," Wyatt said in answer to Evangeline's question. "In other words, I don't know how the hell he's doing, but I suspect he's trying not to panic right about now."

Panic. Yes, Lorelei was dealing with some of that, too, but she thought hers was a whole lot different from Dax's. He might be in the mindset of "get the heck out of Dodge" or "deny it until he had proof." Whereas Lorelei wanted to take Stellie and run far, far away from anyone who might think they had a claim on her.

"Well, we can talk this through," Evangeline said, causing Wyatt, her sisters and her to groan. "Or not," her mother amended. "I just wanted to try to reassure everyone that all of this will work out."

Yes, Lorelei silently agreed, it would work out, but whatever happened might not end up in her favor.

Lily checked her watch, muttered some more profanity that caused Evangeline to give her a scolding glance. "I'm supposed to pick Hayden up from school to take her to a dental appointment, but I can cancel," her sister offered.

"No," Lorelei insisted. Hayden was Lily's fourteen-year-old daughter, and Lorelei knew the girl had been having trouble with a loose filling. "Go, I'll be fine."

All of them knew that *I'll be fine* was a lie, but thankfully Lily also knew there was nothing she could do to help at this moment. Lorelei had no doubts that once the dental appointment was finished, Lily would be back to lend whatever support she could.

"Go," Lorelei repeated, kissing Lily on the cheek.

Lily issued an apology, muttering about texting her as

soon as the dental appointment was done, and she hurried out.

Since it would likely take more than a loose filling to get the others to go back to their normal day, Lorelei searched for her "big girl" panties and mentally started putting them on. She also dried her eyes, again, and took out her small cosmetic bag from her purse to repair her makeup. One look in the mirror, however, and she ditched that idea. It was unrepairable, but at least she wasn't still sobbing.

"Thank you," Lorelei told them. "After I check on Stellie, I'll call Sophia to let her know what's going on."

"I can go with you," Evangeline immediately volunteered.

But Lorelei shook her head and muttered a heartfelt thanks for her mom's concern. She probably hadn't run completely out of tears, but she was going to hold it together for Stellie. However, Lorelei had barely made it a single step when the door opened yet again.

And Dax came in.

The first thing Lorelei noticed about him was that he'd zipped his jeans and buttoned his shirt, but he was still sporting the same harried expression as when she'd left his house over a half hour ago.

Dax definitely wasn't doling out any of his customary cocky grins or speed sprinkling any testosterone. Well, maybe some testosterone but nowhere near his usual levels.

His gaze skirted past the pile of broken glass in front of the furnace, and his attention focused on Lorelei. He held up a blue and white box, and as he walked closer, she saw the picture of the man and a little boy on the front. Saw the name, too.

Dependable Paternity Results.

Mercy. There went the hold she'd managed to clamp over her roller-coaster emotions. This was moving way too fast.

"It's not a blood test," Dax quickly told her. "Just a cheek swab. I've already done mine, and I want to go with you to do the swab on the baby. On Stellie," he added as if speaking her name around a sudden lump in his throat. "Once I have her swab, I'll have a courier pick it up and take it to the lab in San Antonio. I've already called the courier, and he'll be here in just a few minutes."

Lorelei couldn't answer. That's because her throat had clamped shut. She'd never had an anxiety attack, but she thought she might be on the verge of one now. However, no one else in the workshop must have realized that because they didn't rush toward her. Maybe because they had their attention nailed to Dax and that little box he was holding.

Dax was the only one staring at her, and she thought they might have that anxiety attack together. Still, he managed to look, and sound, a heck of a lot stronger than she felt.

"Once the test is at the lab," Dax went on, "it'll take twenty-four hours to process. By tomorrow morning, we'll know whether or not the baby is mine."

CHAPTER FOUR

DAX TRIED NOT to dwell on what he'd just said to Lorelei, that by morning he'd know if he was a dad or not. No, he couldn't dwell on it. This was a situation where he just had to go through the motions, one step at a time and not think about the possible "big picture" outcomes.

Sort of like a bull ride.

He mentally went through those steps now to keep himself grounded. Climbing into the chute and onto the bull, wrapping his hand in the rope and going through the routine of getting a solid grip. Leaning forward. Positioning and bracing himself. Then, holding the hell on.

This DNA test was sort of like climbing on the bull, a maneuver where Dax was still full of hope that his ass would stay on the non-ass-friendly fifteen-hundred-pound bull from hell for the entire eight seconds. Now, he was full of hope that his DNA wouldn't be a match to Stellie's.

Of course, if he didn't match, that would be the end of the need for his grounding steps. But it would leave Lorelei with a puzzle and perhaps a whole crapload of trouble from Valerie's husband. If that happened, then Dax figured she was going to have to come up with some grounding steps of her own.

"Well?" Dax prompted when Lorelei didn't respond to what he'd just said. He waggled the test box again because she looked like a woman who'd just slumped into a deep trance. Or maybe she was in shock.

"Yes," she finally said, which in no way answered anything. However, she also added a nod to it, which gave him hope that she might soon get the rest of herself moving, too.

In his mind, the sooner they got this DNA test done, the better, but Lorelei might not be ready to face that just yet. Unfortunately, she wasn't going to have the luxury of putting her head in the sand because that *sooner* was almost certainly going to include some kind of communication from Valerie's family once Matt told them about her untimely death. If Lorelei didn't have paternity tests ready, the husband and her parents would no doubt order it to be done.

"I can go with you to do the swab on Stellie," Evangeline offered.

"Me, too." That came from Nola, which meant Wyatt would also be in on it since he wasn't likely going to let his pregnant wife out of his sight until he knew she wasn't stressed out about this.

"It's all right," Lorelei tried to assure them. "It'll be Stellie's nap time soon so it's probably best if she doesn't get overstimulated with visitors."

Dax wasn't sure if Lorelei included him in that visitor's status or not, but then she motioned for him to follow her. "I can drive," he offered, mainly because she didn't look steady enough to do that.

She apparently didn't feel steady enough, either, because Lorelei didn't nix the idea. Nor did she suggest they walk even though her house was only about four blocks from Nola's workshop. The last nixing had likely been because she hadn't wanted to face people and their questions during that short trip. In Last Ride, you could run into a lot of people in four short blocks.

Dax was right there on the same page with wanting to avoid running into people. He didn't want to talk about DNA, paternity or the way this could turn both Lorelei's and his lives upside down and inside out. So, he stayed mum on the way to his truck.

Lorelei, however, didn't.

"Do you have any children that you know of?" she asked, her question tentative, as they got into his truck that he'd parked right outside Nola's workshop.

Another zinger, and Dax knew this was payback for all those years of screwing around. "I could answer that with a simple no or say that no, I don't have any children that I know of because my go-to response during sex isn't to knock someone up."

"The first response is fine," she remarked.

And there it was. The "ice princess" tone. Of course, he'd provoked it, but this was the Lorelei he knew. Well, sort of knew. Most of what he knew about her was through her reputation, which meant the info might be as skewed for her as it was for him. Past deeds and reputation were the gifts that just kept on giving. In his case, people thought the worst about him. In her case, people thought she was uppity.

Since there wasn't a normal everyday reason for the two of them to be in a truck together, they no doubt created a whole bunch of speculation from the folks who watched them drive away. Tongues would be wagging a mile a minute, and while Dax had no intention of spilling squat about this, it would get around.

"I'm sorry," she murmured. "I know I'm being rude, but I can't seem to stop myself. I'm just so…so…terrified."

Dax figured she could have filled in that particular blank with some other words. Like *pissed off*. *Sick to her stomach*. But *terrified* definitely worked, and it reminded him that he needed to cut Lorelei some slack. His part in this might end with the DNA results if they came back without a match, but it would be just the start for her. Maybe a very ugly start that could get uglier if Valerie's family objected to the adoption.

"434," Dax threw out there. He was speaking more to himself, but he thought it was a stat Lorelei might want to know, and it could possibly give her a little peace of mind that he wasn't Stellie's father. "I dated a grad student once who was researching the odds of a guy knocking up a woman."

That got her attention. Lorelei angled herself in the seat so she could look at him. "And it's 434?"

"According to her, it is. Condoms are ninety-eight percent effective when used properly so I sure as hell learned to use one properly. Then, there's the timing of a partner's ovulation. Six days out of the month, which means one-fifth of the time. Anyway, the grad student said a man could have sex 434 times before the odds were optimum for getting a woman pregnant."

Lorelei stayed quiet a moment. "Are you saying you think Valerie might have been the 434th?"

"No, I'm saying I haven't reached that 434 number." Which, of course, was stupid logic since pregnancies happened after having sex just one time. Still, the odds were on his side that the condom hadn't failed and it'd been the wrong time of the month for Valerie.

And, yeah, he was trying to convince himself of that.

Dax took the turn onto Parkman Row, passing the houses that managed to look both massive and claustrophobic at the same time. The one exception was the small fairy-tale looking cottage that Nola owned. She no longer lived there since after their marriage she'd moved in with Wyatt at his

ranch, but Dax doubted she'd sell it because it had once belonged to her father. He'd heard her say she might give it to
their daughter, Marley, so she'd have her own place when
she came to Last Ride for visits. That would keep the cottage in the family.

He parked in front of the other house that had also once
belonged to Lorelei's parents. From what he'd heard, it had
been where Evangeline and her husband lived at the start
of their marriage, but once Lorelei had finished college,
Evangeline had given it to her and moved into the apartment
space above her counseling office. Apparently, Evangeline wasn't into massive houses or those on Parkman Row.

Lorelei's house definitely wasn't an apartment or cottage but rather a two-story white Victorian that looked as
put together as Lorelei usually did. Dax wasn't sure how a
person could breathe, though, with so many houses within
spitting distance, but apparently it suited her since she'd
been here for over a decade.

"Stellie might be scared of you," Lorelei muttered as
they made their way to her front door. "She's going through
this stage where she cries when a stranger tries to talk to
her."

All right, so he'd hang back since he didn't want to have
to deal with a crying baby any more than he had to deal
with her crying mother. Thankfully, Lorelei's eyes were
dry for now.

"I try to introduce Stellie to people by name," Lorelei
went on. Not quite babbling but close. "I know it might not
sound logical since she's just a baby, but she's learning to
talk, and I think it's important for her to understand that
people have names just like things such as toys and books.
Anyway, would you like me to introduce you as Dax, Mr.
Dax or Mr. Buchanan?"

There was only one of those options that worked for him. "Dax is fine."

She made a sound of acknowledgment and unlocked the door. They stepped into the cool marble foyer that was surprisingly cluttered with a stroller, a baby seat, a diaper bag and a basket filled with little hats, windbreakers and sunscreen.

"Hilda?" Lorelei called out. "It's me."

Hilda Barney, the nanny. Dax knew her because her son, Will, also did the rodeo circuit. Another example of those minimal degrees of separation.

"Back here," Hilda answered, and the woman came out while drying her hands on a dishcloth.

She was in her early fifties and had salt-and-pepper hair that she'd pulled back in a ponytail. She offered them a thin smile that showed nerves. Which meant someone had already texted her that there was a problem with Lorelei.

"Stellie fell asleep while I was reading to her so I went ahead and put her in the crib," Hilda said, her attention volleying between Lorelei and him. "What's wrong? What happened?"

Lorelei opened her mouth and then closed it. She sighed. "Keep this to yourself for now, but Dax is here to get a DNA swab from Stellie." She paused. "He, uh, knew Dana Smith."

"Oh." Hilda's eyes widened, a reaction Dax figured he'd be getting a lot in the next couple of days. Because despite Lorelei's request for Hilda to keep this to herself, word would get out. And folks wouldn't be using the word *knew*.

Swallowing hard, Lorelei turned to him. "Do you think we can do the swab while she's asleep?"

"Sure," he said, though he didn't have a clue if that was true. He knew squat about sleeping babies. But he also wanted to get this over and done since the courier would be arriving any minute now and texting Dax for instructions.

Lorelei nodded, not looking at all convinced of, well, anything, and she led him through the main living areas of the house. Again, there was lots and lots of baby stuff. Toys, activity mats and a playpen filled with even more toys.

When they reached a back hall, Dax spotted what he thought was the main bedroom on the right, and directly across from it was the nursery. Since the door was open, he had no trouble seeing the baby sleeping in the crib. Each wall of the room had a different theme. One for outer space that had some astronauts, another for a construction site and one for an artist studio. The fourth had a ranching theme, complete with cowboys, cowgirls and livestock.

"I wanted to expose Stellie to lots of possibilities," Lorelei muttered when she saw his attention sliding from one wall to the other.

"Well, you managed it," he muttered back, keeping his voice at a whisper.

Dax figured the ranch wasn't because Lorelei had sensed the baby had any connections to that particular profession but rather because her sister Lily was a ranch owner.

He didn't move closer to the crib until Lorelei did, and he peered down at the baby for a closer look. Of course, he was combing over that little face to see if she resembled him. She didn't. Well, other than the dark brown hair, but lots of babies had that.

"Her eyes are green," Lorelei whispered.

Okay, that was a bit of a gut punch since that meant Stellie and he had hair and eye color in common. Again, that meant nada. He hoped.

Dax wished his hands were a little steadier when he took out the swab. He moved it closer to her mouth, pulled back and tried to figure out the best way to do this. After a few moments of his awkward fumbling, Lorelei took the swab from him, eased it into Stellie's mouth and rubbed it around. The baby stirred, her forehead bunching up in a gesture that nearly made Dax smile.

Nearly.

But then he remembered this visit wasn't about admiring a cute baby with a cute expression. This was about learning if it was his DNA that had helped create all that cuteness.

Once Lorelei had finished, she handed him the swab and leaned down to brush a soft kiss on Stellie's forehead. Then, she brushed her hand over the halo of little brown curls. Since it seemed like an intimate mother-child moment, Dax busied himself with putting the swab in the plastic bag that had come with the kit. He sealed it up and then texted the courier with Lorelei's address.

"The courier will be here in about ten minutes," Dax relayed when he got a response.

Lorelei nodded in a resigned kind of way, and after kissing her daughter again, she led Dax back out of the nursery. He was trying to figure out what to say to her when the doorbell rang. No way could it be the courier that soon so he didn't go to the door. Hilda did, and he heard the woman have a short, muttered conversation before she came back to Lorelei and him.

"It's Derwin Parkman," Hilda explained, her attention on Lorelei. "He says he has to see you."

Lorelei groaned and pushed away a strand of her long blond hair that had landed on her cheek. Dax was groaning, too, because he knew that Derwin was head of a group called Sherlock's Snoops. Detective wannabes with way too much time on their hands.

"Derwin wants to volunteer, again, to help you with

the research on Dana Smith," Hilda added. She rolled her eyes, and it was obvious the woman didn't approve of this kind of intrusion, especially since her employer was clearly having a hard time.

"Tell him no," Lorelei grumbled, and the temper lit in her eyes. Temporary temper, but then she must have rethought the being rude approach—which Dax approved of. "Wait, tell Derwin that I'm not available."

"He'll just want to know when he can come back," Hilda pointed out. "You know what a pest he can be."

Apparently, Lorelei did know because there was another spark of temper that she expressed in some muttered profanity. Dax was surprised. This wasn't the G-rated stuff at all and not what he'd expected from "typically calm and collected" Lorelei.

"Derwin's already been digging into Dana Smith," Lorelei murmured to him. "And he and the Snoops found nothing. Derwin wants to keep rehashing that nothing because it's the only active case the Snoops have right now."

Her voice cracked, probably because it hit her that there was, indeed, something to research now that they knew Dana was actually Valerie. Once the Snoops latched on to that, they would continue to bug Lorelei. Dax figured he could nix some of that just by having a chat with Derwin. Not now, though. Now wasn't a good chatting time.

"Well?" Hilda prompted. "What do you want me to tell the pest?"

"Tell him that I might have a highly contagious disease and he'll catch it if he comes near the house again." Lorelei stopped, sighed and let go of the temper once again. "All right. Just tell him I'm not available."

Hilda sighed and shook her head, probably because she'd wanted her employer to add some more bite to that, and the woman walked away, no doubt to deliver the wishy-washy excuse. Derwin or one of the other Snoops might try to pay him a visit, too, but as a general rule, most people treated him more or less like a rock star. A local celebrity who shouldn't be bothered. Of course, that hadn't applied to Tiffany Carver when she'd shown up at the party doling out those edible red panties.

Lorelei stayed put, but at the front of the house Dax could hear Hilda giving Derwin a polite "get lost."

"I should be doing my own dirty work of getting rid of him," Lorelei grumbled. She kicked the baseboard. "But if I burst into tears again, Derwin will make sure everyone in town knows."

"True," he confirmed.

But he didn't point out that Derwin likely knew about her crying already and would spread that around, anyway. Along with pestering Lorelei about Dana. Dax suspected the man had gotten wind that Dana had something to do with Lorelei's crying, and that it had something to do with Dax and his trip to her house.

It wouldn't take long for the speculation to go in the most obvious direction, especially since Dana hadn't named the father of her child before she'd died. And that speculation would be that he was the father and that he was breaking Lorelei's heart because of the claim he'd have on the baby.

The baby who might or might not have his eyes.

And his hair.

And damn it, possibly his coloring.

Since Lorelei hadn't buried her head in the sand, she could no doubt see all of those things, too, and it was breaking her heart. Dax sure as hell wasn't immune to that.

"Look, no matter how this turns out," he said, "if there's

anything I can do to help just let me know. I sort of owe you."

Her eyebrow lifted. "How do you figure that?"

Dax shrugged, pulling up a childhood memory that he wished he hadn't had to pull up. "When I was eleven and in an after-school program that my guardian forced me to go to, you stopped some of the older boys from picking on me."

Lorelei certainly didn't ask him what the heck he was talking about, and he could tell from the look in her eyes that she remembered, after all. "The boys were being idiots."

"Yeah, they were," he agreed, "and the trio of idiots had been taking both verbal and physical jabs at me because I'd been trying to make friends with Kayla Dayton. The trio claimed I had no right to talk to her and that no girl would ever want me. You heard what was going on and told them you were my girlfriend." He grinned. "That shut them up."

Her face relaxed a little, but her smile was way too weary. "I probably shouldn't have said that, but I didn't like what they were doing to you."

"Yes, I didn't care much for it, either, and that's why I owe you. You really made them green with envy."

Dax wouldn't spell out the other details about this trip down memory lane, but that act of kindness had given him a serious crush on Lorelei. Her looks had helped with that. All that blond hair tumbling past her shoulders, and she'd had that amazing curvy body.

Still did.

No. There was no need to spell out those kinds of details especially since that crush was long gone, and their lives had gone in two entirely different directions. Except maybe their two entirely different directions had circled around to put them on the same path again.

"Thank you," she said. "You're trying to make this easier for me, and I appreciate it."

He nodded, worked up a smile and was beyond thankful to see that she was starting to steel herself up. The steeling went south, though, when the doorbell rang again. No anger this time. Just the bone-deep weary sigh of a person who couldn't take anyone or anything else adding to that weariness.

"It's probably just the courier," Dax reminded her.

So that Hilda wouldn't have to deal with that, he headed to the front door just as the nanny was opening it. But it wasn't the courier. It was Matt, and judging from the sheriff's serious expression, this wasn't a social visit.

Hell.

Apparently, Lorelei was going to have to face another addition to the weariness, after all.

"How bad is it?" Dax immediately asked.

"Not sure," Matt answered, scrubbing his hand over his jaw. He glanced down at the test kit Dax was holding. "How bad it is for you?"

"Not sure." Dax looked over his shoulder to see Lorelei walking toward them. "But it'll be worse for her."

Matt made a sound of agreement, causing every muscle in Dax's body to tighten. "Lorelei," Matt greeted. "I spoke to the Fords and to Aaron Marcel. They want to talk to you. And see Stellie."

"Do they have a right to demand to see her?" Lorelei asked, and the tremble was back in her voice.

Matt nodded. "I sent them a photo of Valerie, and all three of them made a positive ID." Matt paused, shook his head in what seemed to be frustration. "They'll be here in Last Ride first thing in the morning."

CHAPTER FIVE

LORELEI SAT ON the hardwood floor of the nursery and let the worry and darkness wash over her. Something that had been going on most of the night and was now deep into the wee hours of the morning. Something that might continue since she seemed to have no control over it.

Eventually, she had managed to quit crying, mainly because dehydration had kicked in, leaving her exhausted and with a throbbing headache. But even the headache and fatigue hadn't dulled the grief she was feeling. *Grief*—yes, that was the right word for it—because the perfect life she'd tried to build for Stellie had been shattered.

And now she might have to fight to keep her baby.

Even if Valerie's husband and parents didn't try to take Stellie, they would always be out there. A looming threat, and the grandparents would be able to give Stellie something Lorelei never could. A DNA connection to the woman who'd conceived her, carried her and died giving birth to her. In contrast, Lorelei had wanted her, loved her and signed some papers. She wasn't sure that would be enough to tip any legal or moral scales if it came down to it.

She pressed her fingers to her mouth to silence the fresh sob that was bubbling up in her throat. Stellie was still asleep, and Lorelei didn't want to wake her. It was only four in the morning, which meant it'd be at least two and a half more hours before her usual waking time. Once Stellie was up, Lorelei could feed her, rock her and try to hang on to every minute she had with her. It might ease some of the worry just to be able to hold her in her arms.

Lorelei had silenced her phone, but the screen flashed again with another text. It was from Lily this time, but throughout the previous day and now through the night and early morning, every member of her immediate family had contacted her and come over.

Multiple times.

It had taken Lorelei a while to get rid of them by lying to them when she said she was going to get some sleep. Obviously, though, they hadn't bought that lie because of the nonstop attempts with the texts to make sure she was okay. Since she wasn't okay, Lorelei had just quit answering, but in a few hours she would owe them reassuring conversations that she'd made it through the night and was doing as well as could be expected.

She jolted when she heard the tapping sound, and her gaze flew to the crib. Not Stellie. She was still sacked out. But Lorelei followed the sound to the window and nearly had a heart attack when she saw the man's face peering through the glass. Because of that near heart attack and her throbbing head, it took her a moment to realize it was Dax.

What the heck was he doing here?

As if in response to her unspoken question, he popped out the screen from the window and then leaned down to retrieve something from the ground. He lifted two large to-go cups and a "stuffed to the brim" white bag.

Lorelei wanted to shake her head, declining whatever he was offering, but when he continued to motion toward the cups and bag, she got up and went to the window to raise it. She would have snapped out her "what the heck are you doing here" question aloud, but Dax spoke before she could say anything.

"I didn't want to ring the doorbell and risk waking Stellie, but I figured you'd be up," he whispered as if that explained why he was tapping on the nursery window at four in the morning.

He thrust the cups and bag at her and then climbed through with all the agility of a cowboy cat burglar. Maybe because he was a pro at hopping onto the backs of bulls. He landed with far more grace and agility than she would have ever managed, and he immediately glanced in the crib.

"Good. She's sleeping like a baby," he commented, taking one of the cups and the bag. "I always wondered if that cliché was true."

"It's not," she assured him. "Stellie didn't sleep through the night for the first six months." And since this felt way too much like a casual conversation, Lorelei nipped it in the bud. "Why are you here?"

"Couldn't sleep. Thought you probably couldn't, either, so I brought you some coffee and sugar stuff to get you revving."

Lorelei didn't want to rev. She wanted to be alone in this particular pity party, but again he spoke before she could tell him that.

"Don't ask me to leave," Dax murmured. "It's best if neither of us is alone right now."

She wasn't so sure of that at all, but then she remembered Dax was no doubt going through his own pity party and that turmoil of not knowing what was looming on the horizon for him. Added to that, the coffee smelled good, and the caffeine might help her headache.

"Is that where you've set up base camp?" He tipped his head to the area on the floor where there were several empty water bottles, a small mountain of tissues, a half-empty bag of Oreos and an empty bottle of wine that she'd shared with Lily at some point during the past twelve hours. No glasses since they'd taken turns drinking straight from the bottle.

Lorelei made a sound to confirm that was, indeed, base camp, and she went back to it despite there being a rocker and another comfy chair in the room. "Nothing adds to a pity party ambience like sitting on the floor," she muttered.

He didn't argue with her on that, and he sank down next to her while she took the first sip of coffee. It was hot, fresh, and she could almost feel her body sigh with a thank-you. Her stomach got in on the pleasure, too, when she caught a whiff of sugar and cinnamon.

"I wasn't sure what you liked so I got an assortment," Dax explained. "Cinnamon rolls, bear claws and glazed donuts. Your coffee is black because you didn't add anything to it when you had it at my place."

It surprised her that he'd remembered that since he'd been in the haze of a hangover, but Dax was a textbook charmer so he likely made a habit of recalling things like that about women. Even if in cases like hers, he didn't see the women as potential conquests.

"Where'd you get all of this?" she asked, peering into the bag he handed her. "The café and bakery aren't open yet."

"I know one of the bakers at For Heaven's Cake. She owed me a favor so she came in a little early."

Lorelei looked at him, frowned and wondered if the baker owed him because of the multiple orgasms he'd given her.

The corner of Dax's mouth lifted in that grin that she suspected was a big gun in his arsenal of charming and seducing. "Not that kind of favor," he said as if reading her dirty mind. "I got her tickets to the sold-out rodeo in San Antonio."

Since Lorelei knew both bakers at For Heaven's Cake and knew they were both stunners, she thought maybe an orgasm or two had also been involved. Still, she bit into a cinnamon roll—mercy, it was still warm—and she let the sugar rush begin. Dax opted for a bear claw.

"We should have the DNA test results later this morning," he said. "I asked the lab to text me as soon as they're done."

Lorelei held back on the second bite of the roll and glanced over at him. He'd said that so casually as if it were more small talk, but since he was here sitting on the floor with her, there wasn't anything casual about it. She wanted to ask what he would do if the test came back that he was the father, but she wasn't sure she wanted to know. No. Best not to deal in what-ifs here, especially since no scenario was going to give her the peace of that picture-perfect life that she'd planned with Stellie.

It wouldn't be the same for Dax. Once he had those test results, he'd have a clearer path. Well, *a* path, anyway. He could celebrate a non-match and go back to his charming ways and use this as a cautionary tale to make sure he practiced safe sex. A match, however... Well, that was straying into what-if territory so Lorelei clamped down on that.

"You know that favor I did for you when you were eleven doesn't mean you owe me anything now," she commented as they ate.

He nodded. "But it was a big favor." He paused a heartbeat. "I saw you at the hospital that day when Nola and Wyatt had their daughter."

Of all the things Lorelei had expected him to say, that wasn't even on the conversational radar. He was talking about the child that they'd had to give up for adoption. And yes, Lorelei had gone to the hospital the day Marley had been born. She'd sneaked in to get a peek at her niece even though Nola had insisted on not seeing the child.

"I remember," Lorelei admitted. "You were on one side of the hall of the hospital nursery, and I was on the other."

Dax and she had both "borrowed" scrubs to try to blend in so no one would ask them to leave before they got that peek. No one had even though they likely hadn't fooled anyone with their sneaking around since she'd been barely eighteen and Dax had only been thirteen.

"That's when I knew I wanted to adopt a baby," Lorelei admitted.

And here came the flood of emotions that went with that date seventeen years ago. Nola had been emotionally broken right to the ground. Every part of her sister had been a train wreck. Wyatt hadn't been faring any better. But even though they were just sixteen, they'd known they couldn't do what was best for their little girl. So, with their selfless, heart-wrenching decision, they'd handed her over to someone who could.

"I wanted to be the person who could give a child the best when his or her parents couldn't," Lorelei explained.

She'd thought that's what she had done with Stellie, and she had to hold on to the hope she had been right about that.

Dax made a soft grunt, maybe acknowledging that he understood. "I just thought somebody in the family ought to see the kid," he admitted. "I knew Nola and Wyatt couldn't, so I did." He shook his head. "It didn't make me want to adopt or have kids, though." He'd tacked on that last part as sort of a haha, light addition, but it didn't work.

"Thanks," she muttered for his attempt. "For the coffee,

the sugar carbs and the conversation, but there isn't anything that can cheer me up tonight."

He made another of those sounds. "Sometimes, a rider draws a bull that's a big ball of nerves. I mean, you can just tell that he'll buck the hell out of you simply because he doesn't know what else to do with himself."

Lorelei was certain she gave him a confused look because she was, indeed, confused. She had no idea what this had to do with paternity tests or maybe losing a child she couldn't lose.

"Are you comparing me to a bull?" she came out and asked.

He grinned again. "Well, there's one similarity in a general kind of way. You're a big ball of nerves, and that means you'll be ready to buck the hell out of Valerie's family when they show up here in a couple of hours. That's probably not the best approach to take with them."

"Oh?" And, yes, there was a tinge of anger and annoyance in her voice, which probably proved his "ready to buck" theory.

"Not the best approach," he confirmed, setting his coffee aside. "They need to see that you're Stellie's mom, that you're doing one hell of a job raising her. That she's in really good hands. Because you are and she is."

Lorelei wanted to argue with all of that. She wanted to snap, snarl and, yes, maybe even buck. Again, it proved Dax's point.

"To stand a chance of getting that best approach," he went on, "you should try to relax. This is how I settle a revved-up bull."

She would have laughed if he hadn't touched her. Before Lorelei could bat him away, Dax slid his hand onto her back, inching her away from the wall.

"I don't want you to do this," she snapped.

But her demand was somewhat counteracted by the sigh that immediately followed when Dax curled his hand into a fist, and applying pressure with it, he used his little finger to stroke her spine.

He must have located some kind of chakra or a spot on her body that she'd been totally unaware of because the stroking and the pressure seemed to slide right through her. Much the way heat and lust could. Except this didn't arouse. This was more like a "Dax fist" sedative.

"Normally, I sing the bull a little song," Dax went on, his voice as soothing as his magic finger. "Something like 'Grandma Got Run Over by a Reindeer.' Hard to stay snorting mad when hearing that. Sometimes, I go with 'Frosty the Snowman.'"

She frowned or rather did that mentally because it was difficult now to move her slack jaw. But Dax sang stupid Christmas carols to a bull? That definitely didn't mesh with his "hot rodeo star" image, and it made her wonder what other mysteries lay beneath all that too charming, too good-looking hotness.

Despite the fresh hits of sugar and caffeine she'd just had, Lorelei felt her eyelids start to drift down. She also made a few more sighs and moans. She wanted to tell Dax that he had the magic touch. That it was no wonder he was a rodeo champion, what with this particular skill set. But she couldn't form words.

Apparently, her head was too heavy to stay upright as well because it lolled down onto Dax's shoulder.

"I can't sleep," she managed to mumble.

But Dax proved her wrong.

CHAPTER SIX

DAX STIRRED WHEN he heard the sound. Stirred but stayed in that half dream state where his body was waking up but his brain would have to play catch up. No one would ever accuse him of being raring to go the moment he woke up. It was always a long, slow process.

Much like sex.

And speaking of sex, his body registered the fact that he was with a woman and that her breasts were against his chest. Strands of her hair were also tickling his face. It also registered that his left shoulder was throbbing like a toothache. Actually, lots of places were throbbing, and even though it meant giving up the "chest to breasts" contact, he rolled off his side and onto his back to get some relief.

The throbbing got worse when his bum shoulder smacked against a hardwood floor. Emphasis on hard. Hell's bells. He was aching in too many places, and even the stirrings of a morning hard-on weren't overriding the pain.

He heard the sound again. A sort of cooing, and he wondered if the woman he was with was waking up as well. He lifted one eyelid, silently cursing when he glanced around. Not his bedroom. Not his house. So, how the hell had he...

His question skidded to a halt when he saw the woman with the breasts was Lorelei. And there was a baby staring at him. She was standing up in her crib, her pudgy little hands gripping onto the railing, and she said, "Goo." Then, she grinned, a big toothy grin as if she'd just seen her most favorite person on earth.

"Stellie," Lorelei mumbled, no doubt reacting to the sound of her daughter's voice.

Groaning, Lorelei sat up, and in the same motion, she shoved the now wild tumble of blond hair from her face. She conjured up what seemed to be an automatic smile that she aimed at the occupant of the crib.

But then the automatic stuff stopped.

Lorelei gasped when her gaze landed on Dax, and he could practically see her mind whirling, trying to recount how and why they were here together. Her gasp, though, turned to a groan—the kind of groan that usually accompanied a hangover or really bad news—when she looked at the debris on the floor. The cups of coffee, leftover food and tissues.

She opened her mouth, and he would have bet the tat on his ass that she intended to snap out the question of why the heck was he there. But she must have remembered. Not just his coming through the window with items to induce caffeine and sugar highs. But she also must have recalled the back rubbing and soothing. Yep, the very back rubbing and soothing that had caused her to drift off to sleep so she could then wake up on the floor next to him.

"Goo," Stellie said again, flexing her legs as if ready to jump right out of the crib. Thankfully, her tiny feet stayed firmly grounded on the mattress. Her little green eyes, however, stayed fixed on Dax.

Apparently, Lorelei didn't have bum shoulders or knees because she leaped up without making a single sound of pain or discomfort, and she hurried to the crib. "Good morning, sweet girl," she murmured, giving the baby a cheek kiss. "I'm betting you're wet and hungry."

Stellie babbled out another "Goo," but the inflection was somewhat different this time. It seemed to be a yes, and kissing her again, Lorelei lifted her from the crib to take her to a table-like deal where she proceeded to change the diaper, all the while cooing and talking to the little girl. There were some apologies mixed in with the talk, and from the apologies Dax gathered that Lorelei was usually up, showered and dressed before Stellie even woke.

He checked the time, not quite seven in the morning, and while he didn't usually start his day before eight o'clock, he would since he was already up and stood no chance of getting any more sleep. He'd drive back to his ranch, do some paperwork, check on how the training was going for a new bull and then wait for Valerie's husband and family to arrive.

And wouldn't that be fun?

Lorelei might need another night of soothing and such if that turned out bad. Hell, he might need a night of soothing as well. After all, he just might to have to fess up that he'd had a one-off with the wife and daughter whose death they were now likely grieving.

"I'll have to make a pit stop in one of your bathrooms before I head home," he commented, picking up the tissues and empties and putting them in the trash can tucked in the corner.

"There's one in the hall," Lorelei said without even looking back at him.

Dax headed in that direction but made a detour to the kitchen first so he could dump out the remains of the old coffee and put the pastries on the counter. The bag was splotched with oily spots now, which definitely cut down on their appeal, but Lorelei might need the sugar hit to get herself revving. Then again, she seemed like the "always on the rev" type.

He made that pit stop in a dainty powder room that was the color of lemons and smelled like flowers. There were some toys in here, too, making Dax recall the challenges of being a single parent. Not firsthand knowledge but rather from his oldest brother, Jonas, who'd married a woman with a baby. A woman who'd died when the kid had been just a toddler, and since the kid's father hadn't been in the picture, Jonas had taken over raising the boy. Apparently, single parenthood meant solo pit stops weren't always possible.

Dax groaned when he glanced in the mirror as he washed up. He looked exactly as he'd expected after a pisser of a day before and then sleeping on the floor. In other words, he looked like crap. But it was the pisser of a day that was weighing the heaviest on him, and he wished he could believe that Lorelei and he had already been through the worst of it. And maybe for him, that was true. Lorelei, though, might need a couple more late-night calls to soothe her.

Not his bull, not his rodeo, Dax reminded himself. Except it darn sure could be if that paternity test came back a match.

When he came out of the powder room, he heard Lorelei, and he followed the sound of her voice to the kitchen where she now had Stellie in a high chair. The kid had a little sippy cup in one hand and was plucking Cheerios off the tray while Lorelei stirred something in a bowl.

Lorelei was still wearing the same skirt and top she'd had on from the night before, but she'd changed Stellie's clothes. No more footed pj's with little pink bunnies on them. She was wearing purple overalls and fuzzy matching socks.

The kid repeated her "Goo" greeting to him and grabbed

a handful of the cereal bits to offer him. Dax obliged, ate the now soggy ball of oats, and the kid giggled.

Lorelei gave him a weird look. Well, weirder than the usual ones she gave him. The ones that made him feel as if he were pond scum with the morals of a really horny alley cat.

"Stellie sprinkled those with formula from her sippy cup," Lorelei informed him.

Dax just shrugged. "Could be worse. Could have been breast milk."

Which in hindsight just wasn't a good thing to say. For one thing, it reminded him that Lorelei did, indeed, have breasts. The very ones that'd spent a couple of hours against his chest. It also no doubt reminded her that since she'd adopted the kid, she hadn't gotten to do that particular motherly deal.

She finished stirring the stuff in the bowl that looked like lumpy goop to Dax, and when she turned to go to the table by the high chair, that's when Dax saw the greasy spot on the back of her pale blue shirt. The exact spot where he'd "bull lulled" her. Clearly, there'd been bear claw gunk on his fingers when he'd been doing all that rubbing.

"Sorry about that," he said, motioning toward her back.

Of course, she tried to look, but since it was in the center of the shirt, there was no way she could see it. That's probably why she twisted the top, tightening it against those very breasts of hers that he was pretending to be blind to and not notice.

She muttered something he didn't catch when she finally got a look at the silver-dollar-sized spot. "It's okay," she concluded. "My clothes don't have a long shelf life around Stellie." She hadn't said that as if it riled her but more like a shrugged statement of fact.

Lorelei sat down across from the baby to start feeding her. Apparently, Stellie didn't object to goop because she stopped eating the soggy cereal to gobble it up.

"Thank you for last night," Lorelei said, glancing up at him. "Or rather this morning. The rubbing really helped."

Judging from the little wince she made, she'd realized that sounded too raunchy. And that was his cue to head out. His cue to quit having dirty thoughts of this woman and her ample breasts.

"You're welcome," Dax told her. "Mind if I leave out the door instead of the window?" he tacked on to that just to try to lighten her mood.

It worked. Lorelei smiled a little, and even though she kept it short, his work here was done. He headed for the front door and was only a few steps away when there was a knock. He glanced back at Lorelei and saw the alarm on her face. Obviously, she wasn't expecting anyone this early.

"It's probably one of my sisters or my mom," she muttered, and volleying her attention back at Stellie, she went to the sidelight window and peered out. "It's Hilda," she said, opening the door to the nanny. "I'm sorry," Lorelei immediately told her. "But I won't be going into the shop today."

"I know." Hilda was doing some volleyed glances as well, but hers were over her shoulder. "Some people just drove up and parked right in front of your house," the woman said, hurrying into the foyer and shutting the door. "I don't know who they are, but I heard them checking to make sure they had the right address. They said your name, Lorelei."

Well, hell. This had to be Valerie's family. The visitors certainly wouldn't be local or Hilda would have recognized them.

"Oh, God," Lorelei muttered, and she went that sickly pale color again.

"What do you want me to do?" Hilda asked. "I can tell them you're not here."

Lorelei no doubt considered that, but she dismissed it with a headshake. "No, they're probably anxious to find out what I can tell them about Valerie. Anxious to see the baby, too," she added in a murmur that was drenched with fear and worry. "I'll talk to them, but could you please take Stellie to the nursery?"

The nanny didn't question that at all. She hurried to the kitchen, and while greeting the baby with a cheeriness that she in no way could be feeling, she scooped up Stellie and took her and the rest of the oatmeal out of the kitchen.

Just as there was a knock at the door.

There was a serious panicked look in Lorelei's eyes when she turned to him, but apparently just remembering he was there seemed to have her steeling herself up. Of course, he figured that was probably because she didn't want to lose it in front of anyone. She definitely seemed to be a more "suffer in silence" type.

"I need shoes," she muttered. "And I should brush my hair."

"I'd like to stay," Dax said, following her to the door of the main bedroom. Lorelei hurried in, scurrying around to locate those shoes and fix her hair at the same time.

There were a couple of reasons for Dax's request. He wanted to see these people and hear what they wanted. And they would almost certainly want something from Lorelei. At a minimum, information about Valerie's time here in Last Ride. They could be grieving, hurt and pissed, and they might try to take a metaphorical pound of flesh off

Lorelei. Not because she'd done anything wrong but simply because she'd be an easy target.

The second reason Dax wanted to be there was linked to that whole deal 'bout Lorelei being an easy target. She might look like a high-end ice princess, but he'd watched some of that ice melt when they'd been on the floor together. Depending on what these people threw at her, she could end up melting a whole lot more than she could handle. Whether she would admit it or not, she needed an ally right now, and he could do that for her.

Hopping on one foot while she put a pale gray high heel on the other, Lorelei nodded. Then she shook her head. The nod was probably because she truly didn't want to face this alone. The headshake because there might be speculation as to who he was and why he was there.

"They'll find out about me sooner or later," Dax reminded her. "But if you'd rather I not volunteer anything, I won't. I'd just like to be here."

Lorelei went through another mental debate while there was a second knock on the door. An impatient one this time, and the knocker followed it up by ringing the doorbell.

"Crap," she finally muttered. "Just play it by ear."

Lorelei tossed her hairbrush on the bed and straightened her skirt and top before she went to the door and opened it. Dax was right behind her, and he got his first look of the visitors as they stood on the porch.

Greg and Miriam Ford were in the front, and Dax saw an instant resemblance to Valerie. They looked to be in their mid-fifties and were dressed in conservative clothes that didn't scream the money he knew they had thanks to Matt's background check on them.

"Hello," the woman greeted. "I'm Miriam Ford and this is my husband, Greg." Her voice and expression were tentative, and judging from the dark circles under her eyes, she hadn't gotten any more sleep than Lorelei and he had. Ditto for Greg. Added to that, there were signs that both of them had been crying.

Aaron was a different matter, though. And Dax was sure this was Valerie's husband since Matt had also gotten his DMV photo. Aaron looked both rested and really pissed off, making Dax glad he'd insisted on staying.

Wearing a pricy indigo-colored suit with a white shirt and red silk tie that did scream money, Aaron stepped through the couple, like parting the Red Sea, and he faced Dax head-on.

"I'm Valerie's husband, Aaron Marcel," he snapped out like a bullwhip. He shifted his attention from Dax to Lorelei. "Are you Lorelei Parkman? Because if so, we have to speak to you right now."

Aaron didn't wait to see if Lorelei would verify her identity, and since Dax immediately labeled the man a dick, he didn't step back so they could enter. "I'm Dax Buchanan," he said, aiming the introduction at the parents who were looking pretty much thunderstruck by all of this.

"Dax Buchanan?" Greg repeated. The man did a double take. "The bull rider?"

Dax nodded and conjured up his trademark smile. It was genuine, mostly, though these days when he doled it out, it only reminded him that his days of doing what made him Dax Buchanan were nearly over. "That's me."

"Greg's a big rodeo fan," Miriam supplied, not sounding especially impressed but rather just someone on autopilot who was trying to say the polite thing. "I didn't know you lived here in Last Ride."

Dax nodded and would have continued to exchange a few nerve-settling niceties if Aaron hadn't huffed. "Just a few hours ago, these people learned their only child is dead," Aaron snapped. "And I learned I'm a widower. I want to talk to Lorelei Parkman."

That was interesting wording. A little thing, but Aaron hadn't said he'd learned his wife had died but had made it more about himself with his *I'm a widower*. Yeah, this guy was a dick all right.

"Come in," Lorelei said, stepping back and sounding a lot more inviting than Aaron deserved. She'd likely meant that milder tone for the parents because, yeah, they appeared to be grieving for the child they'd lost.

Dax's gaze connected with Lorelei's for just a second, and he could see the fight she was having to hold herself together. That's why he put his hand on her back and gave her a very short bull rub. It didn't work. No surprise there. She was wired now, and every nerve in her body had to be firing on all cylinders.

"I'm sorry about coming so early," Miriam muttered. "After Sheriff Corbin called us, we got the first available flight to San Antonio and then rented a car and drove here." The woman glanced around, no doubt looking for Stellie.

"It's okay," Lorelei assured Miriam. Again, she was going with the nice tone, but her voice was as strained as the woman's.

Lorelei led them into the living room, and Dax saw them checking out the place. Maybe looking for Stellie. Maybe assessing what kind of environment the kid had been in all this time. Apparently, whatever Aaron saw caused the muscles in his face to tighten even more.

"Are you the boyfriend?" Aaron came out and asked Dax.

Every word of that question caused Dax to bristle, even though Aaron hadn't specified if he meant Lorelei's boyfriend. Or Valerie's. Lorelei answered before Dax had to come up with an answer for that.

"Dax knew Valerie," Lorelei said.

That caused Greg, Miriam and Aaron to all give Dax long studying looks, and Dax didn't think it was his imagination they were all filling in the blanks as to what that meant. If Aaron's jaw got any tighter, his teeth might crack. But even though this guy was clearly a dick, Dax couldn't blame him. After all, Valerie had been married to the dick when Dax and she had had sex.

"Where's my daughter?" Aaron demanded. "I want to see her, and Miriam and Greg want to see their grandchild."

Lorelei certainly didn't jump to answer that time, and after several snail-crawling moments of silence, Dax stepped in. "Your granddaughter is fine," Dax assured Miriam and Greg before he even looked at Aaron. Dax didn't make it a habit of scowling and such, but he made an exception this time. "And it's very possible that the child isn't yours."

Oh, that pushed Aaron to the teeth-cracking stage, and the anger practically shot out in lightning bolts from his eyes.

"Valerie was my wife," Aaron said, enunciating each word as if Dax were an idiot. "So, the baby is mine. Bring her to me now because I'm taking her home."

Aaron made a move as if he might start searching for the kid, but Dax stepped in front of him. Greg took hold of his son-in-law's arm.

"I legally adopted Stellie," Lorelei informed him, and she'd obviously gotten back some of her steel because she, too, blocked the dick's path.

"You hid her from me so you could claim to adopt her,"

Aaron fired back. "Bring her to me now, or I start tearing this place apart to find her."

That apparently was not a good thing to say, and it was like dousing a gallon or two of gasoline on an already-hot fire. "You will not tear this place apart," Lorelei said, enunciating her words as well. "And you will not take her."

Aaron did a little swaggering movement with his head. A nonverbal *you and what army are going to stop me?* Dax was ready to explain to Aaron that he was about to get his ass kicked six ways to Sunday, but Greg's grip tightened on the man's arm.

"Aaron, you need to let me handle this." Greg's voice was one of reason and authority. The opposite of his son-in-law's.

"I want my daughter," Aaron snarled, and then he must have realized to get his way, he should probably tone things down a couple of notches. "She's all I have left of Valerie."

Aaron didn't quite manage to look or sound like an actual grieving widower or a father who loved a child he'd never seen. Nope. The assery vibe was still going on strong there.

"Valerie left you," Dax threw out there. "She came to Last Ride for a reason." He didn't spell out that he didn't know exactly why she'd done that. "She didn't go back to you. For a reason," he couldn't help but add, and he figured Aaron understood his meaning just fine. That Valerie had dumped this dick and then turned to him.

Apparently, that was like tossing a whole bunch of gasoline as well, and Dax got ready to do that ass-kicking, but Miriam stepped in front of her son-in-law.

"You're making things worse," the woman snapped, and she managed to sound like a scolding kindergarten teacher and experienced mom at the same time. "Take a walk around the block or something. Cool off. Then, we talk this out."

Because Dax was arm to arm with Lorelei, he felt her tense even more than she already was. Maybe because she, too, was thinking she might have to get involved in some ass-kicking if Aaron didn't do as his mother-in-law had advised.

Aaron stood there, firing furious narrowed-eye glances at all of them, and he must have decided to hit the pause button on trying to tear the place apart or blast out any more venom. Wise move. But the wise move didn't cool down his temper much.

"This isn't over," Aaron snarled, heading for the door. But he apparently had one last bit of venom in his arsenal, and he issued it as his threat from over his shoulder. "One way or another, I will get my daughter this morning."

CHAPTER SEVEN

LORELEI HOPED THAT Valerie's parents would follow Aaron out the door so she could fall apart with only Dax there to witness it. But Miriam and Greg stayed put. Dax, too, though he did go to the front door. He shut and locked it.

"Your son-in-law is a hothead," Dax remarked.

Neither of the Fords disagreed with that, and thankfully they didn't spew out any threats. However, their mere presence was a threat because Lorelei was betting if it came down to a fight, they'd side with Aaron.

But she was apparently wrong about that.

"Yes, he is," Miriam agreed, and her sigh was long and coated with weariness. "I'm sorry about that."

"I wish I could say it's just the heat of the moment that's stirred him up," Greg added, "but Aaron often acts like a jackass. I suspect that's the reason Valerie left St. Louis."

That eased some of the tension in Lorelei's stomach, but she had no intentions of relaxing just yet. "I can let you see Stellie, but I won't let you take her."

"Understood," Miriam quickly agreed. "We had our lawyers check the paperwork, and we know you legally adopted Stellie. Estella Elizabeth," she spelled out. The emotion was back in her voice, and fresh tears were watering her eyes.

Lorelei couldn't be coldhearted about those tears since she'd shed plenty of them herself. She motioned for them to take a seat. "Would you like some coffee or something?" she asked.

Miriam shook her head and dabbed at her eyes as she sat on the sofa with her husband. Greg held his wife's free hand and slipped his arm around her.

"I guess we're going to have to talk about some hard things," Greg started, shifting his gaze between Dax and her when they took the loveseat across from them. His attention settled on Dax. "Would it insult you if I ask if you were involved with my daughter?"

Dax drew in a long breath. "I was briefly involved with her. I met her at a rodeo in Fort Worth, but I knew her as Valerie Foster. And she never mentioned she was married."

Miriam nodded. "Valerie was miserable in her marriage, and Aaron can be controlling, especially when it came to Valerie's trust fund."

Well, that miserable part could have been the reason Valerie had cheated. "Why didn't she just divorce him?" Lorelei asked.

"Oh, I think it would have come to that," Miriam admitted. "But Aaron had worn her down. Browbeat her. I could see it going on, and I tried to stop it, but Valerie stayed with him." She paused, shook her head. "I don't know what happened to finally make her leave."

Lorelei suspected Aaron's temper had been a big factor. Maybe it had been a "straw that broke the camel's back" sort of deal. But that still left a lot of unanswered questions. Of course, one of the biggest of those questions was what the Fords intended to do now that they knew their daughter was dead and that they had a granddaughter.

"I filed a missing person's report shortly after Valerie left home," Miriam continued a moment later after she seemed to regain her composure. "But then she called to let us know she was all right so I pulled the report so the police wouldn't keep searching for her." Her voice broke with a hoarse sob. "If I hadn't done that, she might still be alive."

Lorelei's heart broke for the woman because now that she was a mom, she couldn't imagine losing a child. Even an adult one. Stellie would always be her baby, and Miriam no doubt felt the same way about her daughter.

"What-ifs can eat away at you," Dax offered. "But play this one out. Even if you'd kept the missing person's report in the system and the cops had found Valerie, they couldn't have forced her to go home. She was an adult, and she made her own choices."

Miriam made a sound of agreement, and another sob. "I didn't know Valerie was pregnant or in Last Ride."

Lorelei braced herself for Miriam to ask the million-dollar question. Why had her daughter been here? But then both Miriam's and her husband's attention landed on Dax. Even though they didn't come out and ask, they were clearly waiting for an answer.

"I didn't know Valerie was pregnant, either," he admitted, "but it's possible Stellie is mine. I'm waiting on the results of a paternity test." He paused a heartbeat. "How long had Valerie been gone from home before the rodeo in Fort Worth?" Dax rattled off the date, which he'd obviously committed to memory.

Greg's forehead bunched up while he gave that some thought. "She left about a week before that."

Lorelei's stomach sank. Because it meant Aaron could, indeed, be the bio father. It was ironic that less than twenty-four hours ago her biggest fear was that Dax had been the one to get Valerie pregnant, but Dax no longer felt as big of a threat as Aaron. Of course, that was maybe wishful thinking on her part. Dax might be opposed to fatherhood *now*, but that could change in a blink. Then, she could be battling him for custody.

"Did Valerie call or contact you any other times after she left St. Louis?" Dax pressed, maybe because he was trying to piece together where Valerie had been for the months in between the rodeo and when she'd come to Last Ride. Or maybe he wanted to know if she'd mentioned him to them.

Miriam nodded. "She texted me three other times. Just quick messages to say she was all right and for me not to worry about her. I tried to call her back on those numbers, but they were no longer in service. I think she did that so Aaron wouldn't know how to get in touch with her. Not that I would have told him," she quickly added. "But I think Valerie was just being cautious."

That meshed with what they knew about her. After all, Valerie had used a no-contract phone so she might have tossed one as soon as she'd used it to text her mother. She could have done that to avoid Aaron getting the number.

"I would like to see our granddaughter," Miriam went on after she wiped her eyes again. "But first can you tell me if Valerie suffered when she died?"

"No," Lorelei quickly answered. Now, here was where she could give grieving parents some peace because she'd asked the doctor the same thing. "It was very fast, just a couple of minutes after Stellie was born." Lorelei had to speak around the sudden lump in her throat. "Valerie got to see and hold Stellie."

Of course, the holding hadn't lasted long. Mere seconds before the blood clot that the doctor hadn't even known about ended Valerie's life.

Miriam managed a watery smile. "Good," she muttered. "So, she died happy."

Lorelei wouldn't go that far because she had no idea if

Valerie had wanted to have a child. In fact, it was possible she'd come to Last Ride to hand over the baby to Dax. That could account for why Valerie hadn't set up the nursery. Of course, it was equally possible that the woman simply hadn't had time to do that since she'd delivered Stellie several weeks early.

"May we see Stellie now?" Miriam asked, and her tone was the exact opposite of Aaron's.

Lorelei didn't want to say yes. But she couldn't say no, either. Yes, Stellie was her daughter in every way that mattered, but she was also the Fords' granddaughter, and these people hadn't done anything, so far, to warrant them being kept away from the baby. That's why Lorelei nodded and got to her feet.

To give Hilda a heads-up, Lorelei tapped on the closed door of the nursery. "Uh, we have visitors," she settled for saying and then waited a couple of seconds before she opened the door.

Lorelei couldn't help but smile when she saw Stellie and Hilda on the thick play mat where they had a stash of toys, including Stellie's favorite, a colorful cloth caterpillar with wings that rattled when shaken. Stellie was shaking it now and giggling even though it was something she'd done and heard dozens if not hundreds of times.

"Gak," Stellie immediately said, looking at Dax, and Lorelei wondered if her baby was trying to say his name.

Maybe.

And that caused Lorelei to frown.

Stellie had only started saying Mama a few weeks ago, and that was after much coaching from Lorelei and Hilda. Added to that, Lorelei hadn't said Dax's name much around the baby. Had she? Well, maybe she'd muttered it more than a couple of times when she'd been bathing Stellie and putting her to bed.

"Gak," Dax repeated back to her, causing Stellie to giggle as if he'd replaced the toy caterpillar as her favorite thing in the world.

Stellie crawled toward Dax, babbling the Gak sound, but Lorelei saw Dax's grin fade. Maybe because he preferred to admire babies from a distance. Of course, it could be that seeing a babbling, crawling baby drilled home that he might be Stellie's father.

"Oh," Miriam said with a world of emotions in her voice. "She's so beautiful."

"Thank you," Lorelei muttered, and then she frowned again.

Normally, she introduced Stellie to people, but she had no clue how to do that. She certainly couldn't say grandma or grandpa. Not yet, anyway. And if she called them Mr. and Mrs. Ford, they might get insulted at the formality. Lorelei settled for not saying anything.

Despite the fact she was wearing a dress, Miriam sank down onto the floor. She didn't scoop up Stellie, though Lorelei suspected that was something she wanted to do. Instead, she just sat there and watched as Stellie made her way to Dax, and demonstrating her new skill set, she latched onto the legs of his jeans so she could pull herself up.

"Gak," Stellie said, looking up at Dax.

Heck, did Stellie have some kind of primal sense that this was her DNA kin? Or maybe her daughter was just as enthralled with the hot cowboy as most females were?

Dax brushed his fingers over Stellie's curls, and to prevent him from having to do something he clearly wasn't comfortable doing—picking her up—Lorelei scooped Stellie up and brushed a kiss on her cheek.

With her husband's help, Miriam got back to her feet. "She looks so much like…Valerie," Miriam murmured. She'd probably stopped herself short of saying *her mother*. "Is she a good baby?"

"The best," Lorelei assured her. "I've had her since she was three days old. I brought her home from the hospital." Before that, Lorelei had spent every possible moment with her when she'd still been in the hospital nursery.

When Lorelei heard her words, heard the tone of them, she wanted to cringe. It was all true, but she sounded as if she were reminding them of the claim she had on the child. And she was. However, these people had a claim, too. Not custody. No. Not that. But they did have the right to see, and love, the child their daughter had carried and delivered. That's why Lorelei leaned in so that Miriam could take Stellie and hold her.

Stellie had never shown any fear of strangers, but her little girl didn't even look at the woman who was holding her. The woman who was crying over the bittersweet joy of holding her baby's baby.

"Hey there, Stellie," Greg said, lightly taking hold of the baby's hand to give it a little jiggle.

Hilda walked closer, volleying glances at Lorelei, Dax and their visitors. Lorelei made introductions but made no mention of exactly who they were. Since Hilda was no fool, she no doubt had already figured it out.

"I think I'll check the laundry," Hilda said after she gave Lorelei a long look. Probably to make sure it was okay for her to leave.

Lorelei nodded and managed a murmured thanks. A murmur because it was hard to talk now. Her throat felt as if it had filled up with broken glass, and there was a heavy weight on her chest as if her lungs were being crushed. She stiffened, though, when she felt Dax's fingers on her back. He'd launched into a discreet bull rub. Discreet because the Fords had all their attention focused on Stellie so they weren't noticing what he was doing.

Or rather trying to do.

Lorelei appreciated the gesture, but even a thousand bull rubs wouldn't ease the tension in her body.

When Greg's phone buzzed, he stepped back, looked at the screen and frowned. "It's Aaron," he relayed to them, and he stepped even farther away from Stellie to take the call.

Even though Greg didn't put the call on speaker, Lorelei could still hear Aaron's voice. Not the actual words but the volume and anger. Apparently, he hadn't cooled off after he'd stormed out.

Miriam tried to focus on Stellie, but she kept glancing at her husband. Kept sighing, too.

"We can discuss this later," Greg finally said to the man, and he ended the call. When he turned back to face them, Lorelei could tell he had not gotten good news in that brief conversation.

"Aaron's already contacted his lawyer," Greg relayed. "He plans to fight the adoption and try to get custody of Stellie."

And there it was. The "gut punch" feeling that nearly robbed Lorelei of her breath. "But the adoption is final," she muttered.

Greg nodded. "Aaron believes Sheriff Corbin and you didn't give him an adequate chance to claim his child and he insists he'll prove it." He walked closer to his wife but kept his gaze on Lorelei. "I believe the sheriff did try to find Stellie's next of kin. I don't believe you went into the adoption with fraudulent intentions."

Well, that was something at least, but it didn't help ease that tight ball of worry in her stomach.

Greg looked down at his wife, and it seemed to Lorelei that something passed between them. An entire unspoken chat. At the end of it, Miriam nodded and turned to Lorelei.

"Greg and I will have to fight Aaron's custody challenge," the woman said. Stellie reached for Lorelei, and she took her baby, pulling Stellie to her. "We know Valerie would have wanted us to do that."

Heck, Lorelei wanted them to do that. She didn't want Aaron's hands on the baby even if he did turn out to be the bio dad. But then Lorelei let the woman's words and the impact of those words sink in.

"You're going to challenge the adoption," Lorelei managed to say.

Greg and Miriam nodded. Not an anger-filled threat the way Aaron's had been. No. This was more of a painful resignation of what they felt had to be done.

"If we win custody," Miriam went on a moment later, "we won't keep Stellie from you. We'll give you generous visitation rights. Maybe even split custody."

Lorelei shook her head, fought the tears that were already burning her eyes. She didn't want visitation rights or split custody. She wanted to be a mother to her child.

"We'll be going," Miriam said. "But we'll be in town until all of this is settled. If you need to get in touch with us, we'll be at the inn on Main Street. So will Aaron. He got a room there as well." She brushed a kiss on Stellie's cheek. "See you soon, sweet girl."

Oh, God. This wasn't going away. *They* weren't going away. And neither was Aaron. It was all Lorelei could do to stop herself from crying, and the only thing that stopped her was she didn't want Stellie to see her and be upset.

Thankfully, Dax's feet weren't glued in place as hers seemingly were because he motioned for the Fords to follow him to the front door. Lorelei stood there, watching him usher out the couple, hearing their murmurs as they exchanged phone numbers. All very polite and civil.

While her own heart was shattering.

She heard Dax lock up after the Fords left, but he didn't make a beeline back to the nursery. Lorelei heard him go in the direction of the kitchen, and a few minutes later, he returned with Hilda and a cup of coffee.

"Hilda's going to play with Stellie while you drink this," Dax said, and when Hilda took the baby, Dax handed her the cup. "Irish coffee, heavy on the Irish," he informed her.

Lorelei didn't want booze, but she took the cup, and because there was no fight left in her body, she allowed Dax to lead her into the living room. Dropping down on the sofa, he had her sit beside him.

"Sophia Parkman's your lawyer?" he asked, and when she nodded, he took out his phone, scrolled through some contacts and called her.

Sophia didn't answer, of course. It was still too early for office hours, but Dax left a message to have her call Lorelei first chance she got.

"I use Curt Dayton for my legal stuff," Dax explained, "and depending on how things go, I can call him."

How things go. That was code for if this turned into the custody battle from hell. Of course, any custody battle fell into that "hell" category for Lorelei.

"You want to cry it out, talk or have me try the bull rub again?" he asked.

None of the above. Or maybe all three. She took a sip of the coffee and grimaced. Dax had been right about it being heavy on the Irish so she set it aside on the table. Best not to add getting drunk to everything else she was feeling.

"If yelling will help, go for it," he offered.

Tempting, but she didn't want to scare Stellie. "Just keep talking and swear to me that I'm not going to lose my baby."

Dax frowned, shrugged. "Can't do the swear part, but I can talk." He paused a moment. "I've been through sort of a custody deal myself."

Now Lorelei looked at him and frowned. "You have a child?"

"Hell, no." He said it fast, obviously without thinking, but then he obviously backtracked and rethought. "Well, I guess that's to be determined, but I was referring to a custody battle that took place when I was eight years old."

She thought of all the things she'd heard about Dax and his family. Not good things, either. His parents had died when he'd been a kid, and he and his three brothers had been forced to move to Last Ride to live with their cousin. An ornery woman named Maude Muldoon. If the gossip was true, Maude had inflicted a lot of misery on the Buchanan boys before she'd finally passed away.

"Someone challenged Maude for custody of you and your brothers?" she asked. Not to be polite. But because his talking did help. It wasn't quite as soothing as the bull rub, but Dax definitely had the knack with his easy drawl. Then again, almost anything that got her mind off Aaron and the Fords would help settle her.

"No," Dax answered. "This happened with Frankie Mc-Cann."

Lorelei knew Frankie as well. She was the owner of Ink, Etc., a costume shop/tat studio less than a block from the Glass Hatter. Added to that, Frankie was the sister-in-law to one of Lorelei's best friends and cousins, Millie Parkman McCann.

"Frankie is your age," Lorelei pointed out, "so how could she have challenged you for custody? She has a son, but his father is Tanner Parkman."

"Oh, this happened well before adulthood. Like I said, I was eight, and Frankie had a crush on me so she asked me to marry her. Since she brought me brownies with the proposal, of course I said yes. She wrote out a kid's version of a marriage license and had me sign it. Then, about a week later, she was crushing on somebody else, and she drew up divorce papers. Literally drew them," he emphasized, "with little yes and no boxes and a place for us to write our names."

Lorelei couldn't imagine this had anything to do with what was going on in her life, but it occurred to her that she hadn't been very imaginative in elementary school. Or since then for that matter.

"I was okay with the divorce," Dax went on, "but during our very short marriage, I'd started helping Frankie feed a stray cat she'd found hanging out behind the gym at school. We named it Baby and fed it some of our lunch. We both got attached to it, but when Frankie asked for a divorce, she wanted custody. She apparently knew what that word meant because she was in foster care and was waiting for her big brother, Joe, to turn eighteen so he could get custody of her."

Lorelei knew all of this, too. Hard not to know it in a small town, and while it was a sad story, right now it felt devastating.

"I don't want to hear about Baby being taken away by someone and put in a shelter," she let him know.

"Oh, that didn't happen, but Frankie and I weren't the

only ones feeding Baby. So was Miss Garza, the PE teacher, and Rizza Barker, the custodian. They wanted Baby, too. Heck, so did I. So, Frankie talked Curt Dayton into settling the dispute. He was sort of a tight-ass even when he was a kid but really smart, too, and he decided to have all of us line up, and the one that Baby went to would be the one to get custody."

Again, this felt devastating, and the look on her face must have told him that.

"This has a happy ending," he assured her. "Baby went straight to Frankie because she'd been the one to feed and love her right from the start. She'd been Baby's mama." He looked her in the eyes. "Just as you're Stellie's mom. In a metaphorical line-up, the Fords and even the asshole Aaron will see how much you love her, how much Stellie loves you, and bottom-lining it, that'll count for something."

"Maybe," Lorelei conceded, though she wasn't sure love would be enough to get them to back off. And the possibility of it wasn't enough to stave off this dark mood that was washing over her.

"Is Frankie the one who inked the longhorn on your butt?" she asked just to keep the conversation going.

"Yep. Long story about that, but I'll save it for another time," he added when his phone buzzed with a text.

He pulled his phone from his jeans, and much as Greg Ford had done earlier, Dax frowned. "It's from the lab," he muttered. "It's the result of the paternity test."

CHAPTER EIGHT

Dax had never thought of himself as a coward. After all, he rode bulls for a living. But he had a moment where he wanted to duck and run for cover. A moment where he didn't want to look at the paternity test results that he'd pressed so hard to get.

"What does it say?" Lorelei asked.

He looked at her, and he didn't think it was his imagination that Lorelei was going through a cowardly moment of her own. Rightfully so. Because this could change, well, pretty much everything.

Dax drew in a long breath just in case breathing wouldn't be as easy in the next couple of minutes, and he tapped the attachment for the test result.

And there it was.

Oh, yeah. Breathing got a whole lot harder. So did the "slam in the gut" shock. Of course, he'd known what the results could be since there was a fifty-fifty shot either way, but Dax realized he hadn't steeled himself up nearly enough for this.

"It's a match," he managed to say, though he wasn't sure how he got out the words.

Lorelei took his phone, looked at the screen. "99.9 percent accurate," she muttered.

He'd noticed that little tidbit, too, which meant he was definitely Stellie's father. Him, a father. To that cute little kid who called him Gak. A father to the child Valerie and he had made.

Because the bones in his legs had apparently dissolved, Dax didn't move. He just stayed there, trying and failing to level himself. Judging from the way the color had drained from Lorelei's face, she was dealing with the same thing.

"Uh, I'm going to need a little time here," Dax finally said.

Lorelei's nod was slow but definitely not hesitant. Nope. Again, dealing with the same thing.

"Uh," he repeated. "I'll be at my ranch for a bit. You've got my number, right, in case you need to talk?"

A slow shake of the head this time, and with her eyes wide and staring, Lorelei handed him her phone while Dax added himself to her contacts. He gave her his phone so she could do the same. Normally, this was what happened when he did a hookup with a woman, but this was a first. He now had the number of the woman who was raising his daughter.

His daughter.

Yep, that was going to take a bit of time to wrap his mind around. Alone time. But he immediately rethought that when he considered that whole deal about Lorelei being in this same boat with him.

"Will you be okay here?" he asked.

Lorelei didn't jump to answer. She swallowed hard. "I'll call my sisters or my mom."

Good. Family could help. It could help her, anyway. Dax just wanted to be alone in his house so he could… Well, he didn't know what the hell he was going to do, but whatever it was, it was best not to have an audience for it. He'd learned over the years that dealing with something big and messy wasn't a spectator sport.

The goodbye was awkward. No way around that since

they'd both gone into the "fewer words, the better" mode. Apparently, fewer steps, the better, too, because Lorelei didn't follow him to the door. Dax let himself out, went to his truck, drove away from her house.

And then he yelled every curse word he knew.

Hell in a son of a bitching handbasket headed straight to the hottest level of hell. How had this happened? Not the "making a baby" part. He knew the biology of that. But why for shit's sake hadn't Valerie told him? Why had she thought it was okay for him to go on not knowing they'd had a child together?

Maybe because she hadn't known it, either?

The idea slowly began to take hold of Dax as he drove to Sunset Creek. It was possible that Valerie hadn't known for certain he was the father, that she'd thought maybe Aaron was. Dax held on to that notion for several comforting moments before he had to curse again. If she'd thought Stellie was Aaron's, there would have been no reason for her to come to Last Ride.

Was there?

That question was eating and twisting away at him when he pulled into his driveway. And he cursed again after he saw his brother's truck. Jonas was already on the porch, kicked back in one of the rocking chairs. Clearly waiting for him.

In the rare instances when Dax actually locked the door, Jonas could have used the key Dax had given him to let himself inside. Apparently, though, Jonas had chosen the porch. Maybe because it meant there'd be no delays in seeing his kid brother when he drove up.

Groaning, Dax got out of his truck with the goal of making this a very short visit so he could get the hell on with more cursing. Maybe gathering a bag of rocks, too, to hit himself over the head with. Unconsciousness might be the best way to deal with this right now.

"I passed by Lorelei's house early this morning and spotted your truck," Jonas greeted, getting to his feet. "Does that mean you got the results back on the paternity test?"

Of course, Jonas knew about the test, not because Dax had told him but because Dax had told Wyatt who'd then apparently thought it was his sibling duty to pass it along to their big brother. Dax wouldn't have kept this from Jonas even if he'd wanted to do that, but he hadn't planned on telling him until he'd known for sure. Well, 99.9 was pretty damn sure.

"I screwed up," Dax grumbled. He opened the door and went straight to the kitchen to start a pot of coffee.

"You personally or the condom?" Jonas asked.

"Maybe both." And Dax had to take another of those deep breaths before he got out the rest. "I'm Stellie's father."

Jonas just sighed. Not in a "weary, holy crap" kind of way, either. No, it was more a "don't blow this out of proportion/calm down" kind of thing. Coming from the unrufflable Jonas, it wasn't just lip service, either, because he was the World Series winner of staying calm and not blowing stuff out of proportion. And since he was a widower and the stepfather of a teenager, Dax was certain Jonas had had bad stuff that had kneed him in the balls.

"Times like this, I wish I had a sister," Dax grumbled while he held a cup under the brewing coffee. "An overly dramatic one who'd rant and rage over this right along with me."

"Well, you don't have one. What you've got is me, and I'm here to give you a kick in the ass or lend an ear, depending on what you need."

No way was Dax ready to let go of the "really pissed

off" anger he was feeling. Anger all directed at himself. "Since you're not planning on actually cutting off your ear, I'm guessing you think talking about this will help?"

Jonas made a sound of agreement. "Talk can fix exactly nothing, but I figure it works like this. If you're talking, then you're not thinking, and thinking leads to worry. Worry, especially solo, can dissolve the lining of your stomach." Once Dax had his coffee, Jonas started filling a cup for himself. "What do you usually do when you're trying to deal with something tough?"

Dax didn't even have to think about this. "Shove it down as hard and deep as it'll go."

Jonas sighed again. "What do you usually do that doesn't cause high blood pressure?"

"Don't know. I haven't found that fix yet."

And Dax had looked. Man, had he. But the past could bite you in the ass when you were least expecting it. Like now, for instance. He was getting all the reminders of why he'd never, ever planned on being a father. Because plain and simple, he didn't have his own life together so there was no way he would have tried to help bring a new life into the world.

There was a knock at the front door, and Wyatt came in, his gaze immediately sweeping around until he spotted them. No sigh for him. Wyatt took one look at Dax's expression, cursed and shook his head. Apparently, Dax was wearing his heart or some such shit on his sleeve, or else Lorelei had already spilled to Nola, and Nola had spilled to Wyatt.

"I heard," was all Wyatt said. He went to Dax, took his coffee and downed some. "How are you holding up?"

"He wishes he had a sister," Jonas provided in a ribbing kind of way that only older siblings could have managed.

Wyatt repeated his headshake, drank more coffee and refilled the cup. "Don't expect me to sympathize with you for knocking up a woman when knocking her up wasn't the intention. I've done it twice."

He had, indeed, but that was different. "Yeah, but you knocked up the same woman twice, and she's the love of your life," Dax pointed out.

Wyatt made a sound of agreement, and even though he was obviously trying to fight it, he was smiling a little. Nola was that whole "soul mate" thing for him, and she was pregnant with his child. Their other kid, the one that Dax had gone to the hospital to see way back when, had been conceived when they'd been in high school. Despite the hell to pay that'd caused, Dax knew that Wyatt loved both of his children.

"Valerie's husband and her folks showed up at Lorelei's this morning," Dax went on. "The folks are okay enough, but the husband's a dick and claims Stellie is his."

"Then it might be fun to let him and his dick know he's wrong," Wyatt quickly reminded him.

True. But it would only be a couple of minutes of satisfaction to watch Aaron having to back down and back the hell off. After those few minutes, Dax would still be faced with the whole deal of being Stellie's father, and Aaron would leave to get on with his miserable life.

It twisted at Dax to think of Valerie having been with an ass like that, and Aaron had likely made her life so miserable that she'd gone on the run. Again, that was speculation on his part, but after spending less than ten minutes with Aaron, Dax thought that was the most logical reason for her to have left her home and family to show up in Fort Worth.

"Both the husband and the folks told Lorelei they'll fight her for custody of Stellie," Dax added, causing Wyatt to curse again. Causing Jonas to repeat his sigh and the shake of his head. "But now that I know Stellie's mine…" He trailed off, not certain at all how to fill in that particular blank.

Dax's phone rang, and figuring it was Lorelei, he banged his hand into the counter when he hurried to answer it. But it wasn't her. It was Matt. Considering it was still early, this probably wasn't a "catch up/friendly chat" kind of call.

"Let me guess," Dax said when he answered. "Aaron Marcel came by the police station to make some kind of complaint."

"He did," Matt verified. "He wanted me to go to Lorelei's and get his daughter. He insisted Lorelei and you had basically kidnapped her and had to turn her over to him."

Dax had known the guy would try to cause a stink. But he had a cure for this particular brand of stench. "Stellie's not his. I got back the results of the paternity test, and I'm her father." And, oh, he nearly choked on the words.

"Well, won't that be satisfying to tell him that?" Matt remarked.

"Wyatt and you are in agreement. Personally, I just want him to go away so he doesn't cause any more grief for Lorelei."

"Having the test results is a good start to having him back off because technically he did have a claim on Stellie. By Texas law, the husband is the legal father of any child born to the wife during the marriage. This is true even if the husband and wife were separated when the child was born."

Well, hell. Dax didn't want to know just how ugly this would have gotten had he not paid to get the expedited results.

"Anyway," Matt went on, "my visit with Aaron Marcel is only one of the reasons I called. Now that I have Dana

Smith's real name, I've been doing some digging, and I found a flag."

Dax was certain he frowned. "What kind of flag?"

"I'm not sure. It's possible she was under investigation for something. Possible, too, that she was helping the St. Louis PD in some way. Did she mention anything about that to you?"

"No, nothing," he said. "But she was vague about personal details, and obviously she lied when she told me her name."

Matt made a sound to indicate he was giving that some thought. "My plan is to call St. Louis PD later this morning and request whatever's buried under that flag. Then, I'll have a chat with her parents to see if they can help fill in any part of the timeline during the months she was gone. I'll need you to do that, too."

"I didn't have much of a timeline with her. Only about twelve hours." Obviously not his finest moment, but then he'd had other moments like that, too. He could see now that his attempts to outrun the hell going on in his head only created more hell.

"Did Valerie come on to you or vice versa?" Matt pressed.

Dax had already given those twelve hours some thought, so he didn't have to pick through the memories to come up with the answer. "She came on to me. She was waiting for me after I finished my ride and walked up to me."

And that hell-like feeling went up a notch.

"She knew stuff about me," Dax said. He glanced back at his brothers, realized they were trying to hang on to every word. "She knew my rankings, the names of the bulls I'd recently ridden. She quoted some lines from *Lonesome Dove*."

"Lonesome Dove?" Matt asked.

"Yeah, someone had posted a picture of me reading it on their social media page and tagged me. I figured that's how she knew I liked it."

Matt made another of those "cop thinking about that" sounds. "Did she seem to be hiding or scared of anything?" he continued.

"I could tell she'd been crying, but when I asked if anything was wrong, she blew it off. Why?" Dax tacked on to that.

"Just trying to get a complete picture so I can make the pieces fit. I'll let you know if I get any relevant details from her parents." Matt paused a moment. "When do you plan on telling the asshole husband that you're the baby's father?"

"Soon," Dax assured him. Well, soon-ish. He needed a little more leveling time first. "I'll go into town, locate the SOB and spill the news," he added right before they ended the call.

"You want one of us to go with you to confront this guy?" Wyatt immediately asked.

"No." Dax scrubbed his hand over his face and felt the serious need for a shave. Hell, a shower, too. "I'll do it in an hour or two. For now, I thought I might yell and cuss for a while and see if that helps."

Both Wyatt and Jonas gave him *that* look. The one accompanied by insults about him maybe having been dropped on his head when he was a baby.

"I don't know how to handle this," Dax admitted, pushing the brotherly moment aside. "Even by stretching it to some minor skill set I might have, neither one of you will say I'm daddy material."

They didn't jump to dispute that. Of course, Wyatt and Jonas were both good dads. Not by design, though. And

Dax latched on to that. Like him, neither had planned on fatherhood, and it had turned out okay for them.

Well, sort of okay.

Jonas was still trying to fulfill his late wife's wish by tracking down his stepson's birth father, and Wyatt no doubt had some bad memories of having to put up his daughter for adoption when she'd been born seventeen years ago.

"All right," Wyatt said, "call me if you need anything." He gave Dax a punch on the arm. Even though it wasn't a gentle punch, Dax felt the love behind the gesture. Both of his brothers were worried about him.

Welcome to the club.

Dax was worried about himself and everyone else in this tangled mess.

He watched Wyatt and Jonas leave, and he downed another cup of coffee before he headed for his bedroom for that shower. He was hoping the hot water would unfuzzy his brain, but he'd barely managed to strip down when his phone rang, and he saw Lorelei's name on the screen.

"Is something wrong?" Dax asked the moment he took the call.

"Yes," Lorelei answered just as fast. "Aaron came by, and he demanded to see Stellie—"

"Hell." He reached for his clothes. "I can be there in ten minutes."

"He's already gone," she said, stopping his frantic rush to get dressed. "I slammed the door in his face."

"Good." Dax still continued to dress since this had probably shaken her up.

"I slammed the door in his face," she repeated, "but not before I told him you were Stellie's father. He laughed, Dax."

That definitely wasn't a reaction that he'd expected the man to have. "Why?"

"Because he didn't believe it. He said we were lying to keep him from his daughter."

Dax groaned. Either Aaron was an idiot or else he thought they were idiots to do something like this.

"Aaron said he'd be back with his lawyer and a court order to get a DNA sample from Stellie. Then, he insists he'll send the results to the lab, and that this time, it'll be the results to prove that Stellie is his."

Everything inside Dax went still. "You think he'd try to falsify the test." Not a question because he thought that was exactly what the man would do.

But why?

He thought about what Miriam had said about Aaron being controlling when it came to Valerie's trust fund. A trust fund that her child might now have inherited.

Well, hell.

"Talk to your lawyer," Dax told her. "I'll talk to mine and Matt, and we'll figure out how to stop the son of a bitch."

CHAPTER NINE

DAX SLID DOWN into the chute and prepped himself to climb onto the bull that the trainers were calling Hell Raiser. It was a Brahman-longhorn mix that had a fairly even temperament until someone was stupid enough to climb onto his back.

This morning, Dax was the someone stupid enough.

Sunset Creek had a reputation for using prime breed stock and prime humane training to produce rodeo bulls that had the genes and inclination not to allow riders on them for long. Hell Raiser was no exception to that, but according to the trainers, he was an exception in that maybe he was the best bull they'd ever worked with.

Dax didn't doubt that high praise from the training team because he'd seen Hell Raiser in action, but the final assessment—as it was with all the bulls raised on the ranch—was what Dax called the "sore ass" test. If Hell Raiser could give him, a professional bull rider, a sore ass, then he was ready for the rodeo. If the bull didn't buck and battle enough to get what he wanted, then he wasn't ready for competition.

The moment Dax lowered himself onto Hell Raiser, the bull started to snort, and his massive muscles began to tighten, flex and ripple. Dax applied the black rosin and saddle soap mixture to his glove so he could slide it over the rope. Quick hard strokes that soon turned the mix into a sort of adhesive.

Once he had the grip the way he wanted, he adjusted his hand so he could try the finger bull rub. Hell Raiser wasn't having any part of that, though, and the snorts and rippling only revved up. Ditto for the bull not settling down one bit when Dax sang him the first verse of "Jingle Bells."

That was both good and bad news.

It meant Hell Raiser wouldn't fall for similar ploys by other riders, which meant both rider and bull would put on a heck of a show for the competition. But it was bad news for Dax because it meant he was almost certainly getting a sore ass out of this.

Dax gave the nod to his head trainer, Mike Espinoza, who lifted the gate. Hell Raiser didn't hesitate. The bull charged out, already bucking before he cleared the chute, already trying to get rid of this nuisance on his back.

This was the moment that drew Dax back to the ride time and time again. That sharp slam of raw adrenaline. Being on that razor-edge where he was positive that he would win despite the overwhelming odds against him doing just that.

Considering the rodeo bulls won about seventy percent of the time and managed to toss the rider before the eight seconds were up, it was somewhat delusional for Dax to believe he'd win every single time. But that belief was strong.

And in this case, wrong.

Mike wasn't verbally calling off the "holy grail" eight seconds aloud, but Dax could hear them in his head, and at the five-second point, Hell Raiser dipped his massive head and slung his body. At the same time, he kicked up his powerful hind legs, creating the perfect slant. A really bad angle for a rider, and the maneuver sent Dax flying.

After a lifetime or two of being airborne, he landed on his ass.

The pain shot through him, from ass to head, and he

could have sworn he actually heard his teeth rattle. It took every bit of his willpower to get up, but he had plenty of motivation to do that. Because Hell Raiser was coming for him. Even over the roaring in his ears, Dax could hear the thunder of hooves, coming closer. And closer.

This was slam of pure adrenaline number two, and Dax had learned he needed to save his own now-sore butt.

Mike and the other two trainers jumped into action as well to distract Hell Raiser, but the bull wasn't buying it. He went straight for Dax who was already running for the fence. Not an especially pretty exit because he was limping and possibly whimpering with every movement, but he made it to the fence and scrambled over it right before Hell Raiser could stomp him into the ground.

Man, he felt good.

He could thank the adrenaline for that as well, but the bad was already making itself known. Because there was the pain. Lots of it. The sore ass, too. Hell Raiser had passed the test.

The trainers all scrambled out of the arena, saving their own butts. Not much for them to do now except wait for Hell Raiser to settle down so they could move him out and give him a nice feed reward. The trainers were also celebrating and giving each other high fives because all of them knew they had a winner here.

"Did Hell Raiser get your ribs?" Mike asked, going to Dax.

Since so many parts of him were hurting, it took Dax a couple of seconds to realize that his ribs were, indeed, aching more than the rest of him. Not from a kick. Hell Raiser hadn't managed to get one of those in, thank goodness. This had likely come from some part of the bull's body ramming against that particular part of Dax's.

Trying to level his breathing, Dax unbuttoned his shirt and looked down at the already-forming bruise. He'd need a soak in the hot tub and a whole bunch of ibuprofen, but nothing was broken.

"It's okay," he assured Mike.

Mike muttered, "Good," and looked back over at the bull that was still bucking. "Hell Raiser might not be a good fit for the Last Ride Charity Rodeo. He might have too much hell in him for a less experienced rider. Maybe even experienced ones."

Even with everything else going on, Dax certainly hadn't forgotten about that. It was still about six weeks away, but it always took a lot of prep since Sunset Creek Ranch and therefore Dax hosted the event. Something he'd done for the past three years. It was a good way to raise money for the various local charities. A good way, too, to showcase the ranch itself, and it gave him a chance to invite his rodeo buddies in for a fun day.

This year, though, wouldn't be fun.

Because Dax figured it'd be his last as a rider. Correction—his last as the star rider that folks came to watch. He could certainly do rides for show in years to come, but he wasn't sure how long his body would allow even that. Besides, once he was no longer a pro, his audience would dwindle down to family and those wanting to shoot the breeze about his good old days.

Yeah, this year wouldn't be much fun at all with that weighing on him.

"I hear what you're saying," Dax told Mike. "Hell Raiser might be too much for my old rodeo buddies, but I can ride him myself."

Mike made an immediate sound of disapproval. "Wouldn't you rather go out in like a blaze of glory?"

He would, indeed, and he wouldn't get that on a lesser bull. The only way to make any of this retirement feel like a triumph was to try to win with a bull where his chances of winning were slim. Then, if the slim happened, he'd truly have something to celebrate before it all ended.

Dax thankfully got to push that aside when he heard his phone ring. As usual, he'd left it and all other items from his pocket on a shelf rigged on the outside wall of the barn.

For the short time it'd taken for Dax to get ready for and actually do the ride, he hadn't thought about the other things in his life. The personal, messy things that had caused him not to get much sleep, but the sound of the ringing phone brought it all back. This might have something to do with Stellie, Lorelei or the custody crap.

And he was right.

The caller was Curt Dayton, his lawyer, so while Dax tried to walk off the pain, or rather limp it off, he took the call.

"Give me good news," Dax greeted.

Curt's response was silence. Probably not something that qualified as good. "I came up with a plan," Curt finally said. "Some parts you'll like. Others you won't. And one of the suggestions will probably make you curse and fire me."

Dax cursed at the idea of something else making him curse. "How bad?" Dax pressed.

"Bad," Curt verified.

And his lawyer began to lay things out. Oh, yeah, there was definite cursing involved.

LORELEI PLACED THE glass birds on the display shelf in the front of the store. A bluebird was front and center since it was her favorite of the one dozen pieces that Nola had recently blown. Then, she adjusted the others, trying out the cardinal in the prime front and center spot. Sighing, she adjusted again with a sparrow. And again with a hummingbird. Trying out all twelve of them in various spots.

She knew she was going through the motions of pretending everything was normal, and that was the reason she'd stuck to her routine. She'd left Stellie with Hilda and come into the shop before opening time to do the new bird display. Lorelei knew, too, that she was failing at those motions, but she didn't stop. She had to hope that the routine of her life would help her get through the next couple of days. Heck, or even get her through the next minute.

It'd been a little over three days since Aaron and the Fords had arrived in Last Ride. Three days that'd started with their visit to her house and had continued. Unfortunately, it would almost certainly continue until the legalities played out.

Lorelei had taken Dax's advice and talked to her lawyer, and now Sophia Parkman was the liaison between Aaron and her. That was the best way for Lorelei to handle it because it meant she didn't have to personally deal with the bully and that he wouldn't be able to just show up at her house because of the ground rules Sophia had set. But it was bad news, too, because Sophia had warned her that Aaron would get the court order for a paternity test, and it might take two weeks or more to get back the results. More because Sophia had insisted such a test be administered as defense of the custody suit that Aaron had already filed.

Yes, already filed.

Ditto for the Fords. They'd also petitioned for their claim to Stellie.

The paternity test for Aaron and the repeat one for Dax were being processed, and once they had the results, Aaron might finally back off.

Might.

Lorelei's fingers started to tremble. Because it was possible the test Dax had taken was wrong. There was only a very slim chance of that, but the chance was still there. The only way she could stay sane was to try not to think about it.

Of course, that wasn't the only item on her "don't dwell on it" list. There was Dax himself. Since she now truly believed he was Stellie's father, that meant he was also a threat. Not just to her keeping custody of the baby, though that was a huge worry. But even if he didn't fight the adoption, he still might want to play a part in Stellie's life. He could end up being around. A lot. And Lorelei didn't like the different kind of worry that gave her.

She might not approve of Dax's lifestyle or past, but simply put, he was hot. And for reasons she didn't want to explore, her body wasn't going to let her forget that. It was that hotness and urgings of her body that had prompted her to do some internet searches on him.

Talk about an eyeful.

The man looked born to wear chaps and bull-riding gear. Since she'd seen him in only his boxers, she knew that his birthday suit was equally impressive as well. No, her body wasn't going to let her forget that.

Lorelei looked up from the display when she heard the tapping on the door, and since it, too, was made of glass, she had no trouble spotting the tapper. Not Dax, the Fords or Aaron, thank goodness. She didn't want to see any of them just yet. It was one of her best friends, Millie Parkman McCann. Millie wasn't alone. She had her three-month-old son, Nathan, in a front-facing carrier pouch.

Managing a smile, Lorelei went to the door to let them in, and Millie immediately pulled her into a hug. That meant Nathan got in on the action, too, and he batted at

Lorelei with his tiny fists. Lorelei gave the baby a kiss on his head before she looked up at Millie. The worry was right there in the woman's blue eyes.

Millie and she were cousins, but they looked more like sisters. They both had the trademark Parkman blue eyes and blond hair. Both were five-eight and had similar curvy builds. The similarities didn't end there, though. They both had businesses on Main Street with Millie's antique shop, Once Upon a Time, only two blocks away. Before they'd become parents, they'd shared many, many lunches together.

"I'm sorry," Millie said when she pulled back from the hug.

"How much do you know about what's going on?" Lorelei asked, leading her toward her office so they could sit.

Millie sighed. "Gossip," was all she said, and that was enough to let Lorelei know that the gossips had not only gotten hold of this situation, but they'd also run with it.

Of course they had. Gossip was like tasty treats in a small town, and while most would sympathize with Dax and her, with the Fords as well, that wouldn't stop folks from talking about it.

"What's the gist of the talk?" Lorelei asked while Millie took a seat in the office.

"That you're a victim and should be pitied," Millie readily provided.

Pity. Something that wasn't exactly new for her. Before she'd adopted Stellie, Lorelei had heard the talk about her hitting her mid-thirties without ever having been married or even engaged. The gossip consensus was that since she wasn't butt-ugly and was a Parkman, that something must be wrong with her.

And there was.

But few people knew about that. Millie did but not Lorelei's own sisters or mother. Lorelei had held that back from them because she hadn't wanted the worry or that pity. Millie wasn't a fan of that particular reaction, either, since she'd been widowed in her twenties, but thankfully the sympathy had finally tapered off significantly after Millie had gotten remarried to hot rancher Joe McCann.

"Many people are saying they're surprised Dax didn't knock up someone sooner than this," Millie added.

So, no chatter that Dax wasn't the bio dad. "And the talk about Aaron?" Lorelei asked as she poured Millie and her cups of the black coffee that they both preferred.

"That's he's an—" Millie stopped, covered Nathan's ears with her hands "—asshole."

"He is," Lorelei agreed, and after gusting out her own sigh, she took the chair next to Millie.

"Well, if I can help in any way, just let me know. Not just about that but the Last Ride Society research. As someone who's been there, done that, I know it can be tough."

True. Millie had firsthand knowledge of that toughness since the year before she'd drawn the name of her husband's late wife and had had to dig into her past.

"So far, there hasn't been much to find on Dana Smith, AKA Valerie Ford. You met her," Lorelei reminded her. Sheriff Corbin had already gone over this with Millie when he'd been trying to find Valerie's next of kin, but Lorelei was hoping that her question would jog something in Millie's memory. "Did she say anything about...well, anything?"

"Not really. I only met with her twice. Once when she first came to the shop to talk to me about me buying some jewelry she'd made. Several necklaces, bracelets and two rings. I snapped them up because they were beautiful, and she'd pieced them together with antique settings and stones.

They sold right away so I called her and asked if she had any more. She brought in a second group that sold fast, too. I was trying to contact her for more, but then I heard she'd died."

Yes, all of this meshed with what Millie had told the sheriff nearly a year ago. Still, Lorelei pushed a little more.

"Did Valerie seem desperate for money?" Lorelei wanted to know.

Millie immediately shook her head. "No, not at all. She just seemed like an artist who wanted to get her work out there. Since she was mega-pregnant, I asked her about the baby. Due date, gender, that sort of thing, but she was vague. She said she was due in late spring and hadn't wanted to know the sex of the baby."

Lorelei didn't want to read too much into that. After all, Valerie wouldn't have known Millie, and maybe the woman had just been shy. Except she clearly hadn't been that way to have a one-off with Dax.

"Sorry I can't be of more help," Millie muttered, and when Nathan started to stir, she began to gently rock him.

"It's okay. I plan on talking more to her parents. Not just for the Last Ride Society report, but I should probably collect family medical history and such for Stellie."

Millie's eyes met hers. Eyes filled with worry and sympathy. "Just how much trouble can these people cause for you?"

"Plenty," Lorelei admitted and just saying it caused that crushing feeling in her chest. As if someone had grabbed hold of her heart and was squeezing hard. "I had to force myself to keep the routine of Stellie being with Hilda."

But that was the tip of the iceberg. Lorelei had also had to force herself not to grab Stellie and run. To get as far away from Aaron and the Fords as she could manage. Sophia's lawyerly advice had put a stop to that, though, because she'd reminded Lorelei that doing something like that could give Aaron ammunition he could then use to convince a judge that Lorelei wasn't a trustworthy, responsible parent.

Nathan squirmed again, adding some fussing this time, and Millie stood up. "It's not time for him to nurse, but I should still be getting back to the shop." She gave Lorelei another hug. "Oh, I nearly forgot. I'm supposed to tell you that Frankie's having a First Date Party at her shop the last Saturday of the month, and she wants you to come."

Lorelei shook her head. "First Date Party?"

"Yes, you're supposed to dress up like you did for your first date with your significant other. I know Alan and you keep things casual, but it might be fun."

Millie was so right about Alan Sandoval not qualifying as a significant other. In fact, Lorelei hadn't been out with him since she'd gotten Stellie. Alan had visited her to bring a baby gift, but that had been nearly a year ago.

"Tell Frankie that I'll think about it," Lorelei said.

"Which is code for no." Millie gave her a commiserating smile. "I understand. You're probably not in a party mood..." Her words drifted off when there was movement outside the window, and they watched as Dax got out of his truck.

Oh, mercy.

What a sight to behold. His shirt was partially unbuttoned, and he had on a pair of well-worn jeans that fit him exactly the way jeans were meant to fit. He looked rumpled and hot. Emphasis on the hot.

"Holy moly," Millie muttered. "When you see him like that, it's not hard to figure out why he's had so many women. That's the walking, talking definition of panty-dropping."

"You're married," Lorelei reminded her.

"Yes, and I have my own panty-dropping man, but since I'm not blind, I can look. Besides, Joe will benefit from this. I can easily get him to re-create that 'sweaty cowboy' look." And with a gleam in her eyes, Millie said her good-bye and headed for the front door.

Just as Dax came in through it.

"Oh, hey," he said to Millie.

His attention quickly slid, though, from Millie to Lorelei, and he seemed to be looking for any signs that they'd been in the middle of a private conversation. Not the middle but the tail end of it had certainly been private. No way would Lorelei ever want Dax to know her reaction to him when she'd seen him get out of his truck.

"Sorry," he added. "For the possible smell and for interrupting. I know the shop isn't open yet, but I saw Lorelei's car in the parking lot."

"Not interrupting," Millie assured him. "Nathan and I were just heading out." She sniffed at Dax. "Been riding bulls?"

"Yeah," he verified, muttering another apology under his breath. "For the past three days, I've been testing out the newly trained bulls, trying to clear my head." His gaze met Lorelei's, and she could tell this visit had something to do with the paternity/custody.

"Riding bulls clears your head?" Lorelei asked.

He nodded. "It does. It gets my mind off my troubles when I'm riding and getting slung around, and that usually leads to a head clearing."

And there was a prime example of just how different they were. Lorelei didn't think she could even watch a bull ride without cringing at the thought of being in danger like that.

Apparently, neither could Millie because she shook her head. She had also figured out that Dax was eager to tell her something because Millie repeated her goodbye and added, "Give some thought about that First Date Party," as she walked out.

"Sorry," Dax said again, watching from the storefront windows.

"It's all right." Lorelei went to the front door and locked it, though, so Dax and she wouldn't be interrupted.

The shop wasn't due to open for another half hour, and Misty would be in by then. Good thing, too, because Lorelei was rethinking that whole notion about having come in to work today.

"I got another call from Curt Dayton," he explained, referring to his lawyer. "He called me yesterday and laid out some possibilities for me to think about. Well, I have thought about them, was still thinking about them," he amended, "when Curt called me again to say I should get moving on this."

Lorelei had been bracing herself to hear bad news, like more of Aaron's awful antics, so she felt some of the tightening in her chest ease up. As she'd done with Millie, she poured him a cup of coffee since it was obvious they both had that particular addiction.

"First step is me getting what's called a paternity order," Dax explained. "Since Valerie isn't alive to agree to this or verify my paternity, Curt will use the current DNA test results and my sworn statement that I did sleep with Valerie to try to get a judge to issue one. That will be the legal proof that I'm Stellie's biological father."

The tightening returned. Lorelei couldn't see how this

would help anything. Especially not help her to keep custody of Stellie.

"Aaron's lawyer would no doubt fight something like that," Lorelei pointed out. "The Fords might, too."

"Probably, but Curt believes we'll eventually get that order even before Stellie and I have to do another round of testing, this time by an independent verified source. After that, then we'll need to start prepping for any challenges to my paternal rights. That includes blocking custody claims from others like the Fords."

Lorelei had to force herself to try to relax just so she could draw in enough air to stop the light-headedness that was causing her vision to be spotty. This conversation definitely wasn't soothing any of her raw nerves.

"But what about my custody claim?" she came out and asked. "I adopted Stellie. She's my daughter."

Dax looked at her. "She is," he verified without a drop of hesitation. "And I'm guessing from the way you're staring at me, you think one of those custody claims will come from me. It won't."

Lorelei latched on to those two words—*it won't*—as if they were lifelines, desperately needed breaths and silver linings all in one.

Dax wasn't going to try to take Stellie from her.

She made a sound of relief as said relief washed over her. A very loud sound that made her feelings and fears about this situation very clear.

"Hell," Dax muttered. "I'm not an asshole. I wouldn't try to take Stellie from the only mother she's ever known."

Lorelei felt the blasted tears burning her eyes again, but for the first time in three days, these were of the happy variety. Or rather the thankful variety that she wasn't going to be faced with a third custody threat from Dax. No, he wasn't an asshole.

"FYI, I didn't know if you'd be in the shop today so I went by your house first," he added a moment later.

There didn't seem to be any judgment in his tone or comment. No questioning accusation of why she was at work and not with Stellie. Of course, Lorelei was questioning it now and decided she'd ditch work as soon as Misty got in and go home to her baby.

"Hilda didn't answer the door right off," Dax went on. "She probably figured it was the Fords or Aaron, but when I called out to her, she let me in and told me you were here."

She tried to figure out why he'd just spelled all of that out. "Uh, you saw Stellie?" she asked.

He nodded in an "of course, no big deal" kind of way, but she thought maybe it had, indeed, been a big deal. After all, part of that clearer head would be coming to terms with being a bio father. Heaven knew how long it would take for that process to happen for him. Maybe years. Maybe never.

"I saw Stellie," he verified several moments later. "And seeing her got me thinking about something else Curt said. A suggestion for this plan of action that he has to fight Aaron and the Fords. An extreme one that I discounted right off the bat, but I figured I'd make the offer and then you could decide for yourself if it was something you wanted to consider."

"Extreme?" she repeated, definitely not liking the sound of that.

He nodded. "Yeah," he said. Then, Dax paused, gathered his breath and didn't appear to like the sound of what he was about to say, either. "Lorelei, do you and Stellie want to move in with me?"

CHAPTER TEN

DAX WATCHED AS Lorelei opened her mouth. Closed it. And she went through that process a couple more times without managing to make a sound. Probably because she was having trouble forming words. He certainly had when Curt had first mentioned it as a possible fix.

Actually, when Curt had brought this up to him, Dax's stomach had dropped to his balls. Not an especially long drop distance wise, but when it came to internal organs, it wasn't about the distance but the actual "jab in the gut" feeling he'd experienced. It'd been a bad kind of jab.

Once Dax had gotten past the initial shock, he'd laughed, then dismissed it. Then, reconsidered it after he'd realized they might need every available tool to fight, well, the tool Aaron. Even if Dax hadn't fathered Stellie, there was no way in hell he'd want asshole Aaron to get his hands on her.

Lorelei must have finally gotten her mouth working because as he'd done, she laughed. Not a "funny haha" kind of deal over a good joke. This was more of a burst of air from a mix of shock and *no possible way*. He saw the dismissal soon follow but figured it would be a while, or never, before she reached the stage where she might actually consider his pretense of a proposal.

"Curt suggested that?" Lorelei finally managed to say. She made it sound as if the lawyer had asked them to move to Pluto.

"He mentioned it," Dax clarified.

Curt had delivered it under the pretext of many things that could happen to put a speedier end to this challenge to Lorelei's and his custodial rights. Other possibilities had included hiring PIs to dig for dirt on Aaron to prove the ass that he was. Digging dirt on the Fords, too. Curt was all in favor, too, of Lorelei and him joining legal forces to fight the custody threat. Added to that last suggestion had been the mention of a possible arrangement or relationship between Lorelei and him that would present a united front.

Dax had interpreted that as them living together.

And because he'd already worked his way through his own shock over considering it, he could easily spell out his lawyer's rationale for the suggestion. Perhaps a rationale that sucked, but Dax didn't want to toss the possible sucky idea before running it past Lorelei.

"Curt said expressing our commitment to a long-term relationship might get the Fords to back off and throw their support behind you. Behind us," he amended. "Bio father, adoptive mother raising their granddaughter along with giving them the normal kind of visiting rights and privileges that grandparents get. Curt also thought it'd put a big dent in any claim Aaron might try to assert since he was legally married to Valerie at the time she gave birth."

Dax didn't believe for a second that Aaron was Stellie's father, but that the man only wanted his hands on the kid so he could then control Valerie's estate. But Aaron could still make a bunch of waves by dragging out the whole legal process. That delay had already started with Aaron demanding his own paternity test, and when the results didn't come back in his favor, he could still play the husband card along with keeping up the legal delays.

There was no need for Dax to spell all of that out to Lorelei, but clearly Curt's suggestion/mention wasn't one they could just dismiss.

Even if that's exactly what they wanted to do.

Dax certainly didn't want to have someone move in with him even if it was for a worthy cause. But hey, there were a lot of things he didn't want in his life right now. Unexpected fatherhood. Knowing he'd failed Valerie big-time by not being there for her when she was pregnant with his kid.

Not being there when she died as well.

Added to that, all of this was coming at a bad time for other things. The earlier rides had given him dings and bruises that'd hurt like hell. Both mentally and physically. Unless you were a teenage pop star, most people didn't have to face retirement when they were barely thirty.

"You can't think that us living together will solve anything," Lorelei said, drawing his attention back to her.

"I don't think it would hurt," he countered. That was a lie, and looking at her now, he knew just how much of a lie that was.

Because of the heat.

It was there all right. He might not be top-notch in a lot of things, but one thing he knew when he saw it was lust. When he felt it for a woman. And when a woman felt it for him. Lorelei was definitely attracted to him. She didn't want to be. He could sense that, too. She didn't want to feel one bit of tugging in her body, but it was there, and worse, it wasn't one-sided.

Dax was feeling some heat for her as well. Understandable because she was flat-out beautiful. Not understandable, though, since she wasn't his usual type. And there lay the potential to make things worse. Because Lorelei was a big part of Stellie's life. If he messed up with Lorelei, then it could screw up things with his daughter. It would definitely be a fine line to walk, but Dax had seen Curt's logic on this. Two were better than one when it came to a fight like this.

Lorelei shook her head, and he wasn't sure what to make of the emotions he saw in her eyes. "No," she said. "I can't move in with you."

All right, so that was the emotion. She was feeling bad about nixing this portion of the plan. Maybe because she'd been hoping he would have come up with something a whole lot better. He'd tried. That's why he'd spent most of the last three nights tossing, turning and thinking. But nothing had come to mind that would stand a chance of making this custody threat go away.

Dax nodded as well because he'd expected her to turn him down. Heck, he had hoped for it on more than one level. But he hadn't wanted to hold back on an offer that could have helped her keep Stellie.

"I get it," he agreed. "But I think Curt has a point about us sticking together on this."

"Yes," she said after a long pause. "Now that I know you're not going to try to take Stellie from me, we should definitely stick together."

She practically froze, and her eyes widened. Probably because that last part had sounded a little sexual. Then again, it could be just the way his idiot body was interpreting it. It was probably his body urging him to say what he said next, but underneath the heat, there was some logic.

"If you bring Stellie to the ranch for a while," he offered, "it'll prevent Aaron from just showing up and trying to barge his way in. I'm not always around, but I have ranch hands and trainers who live in a bunkhouse just a stone's throw from the main house. They keep a close eye on the place because every now and then, I'll have a fan who shows up there looking for me. That hasn't happened in a while. A year or more. And I can also close the gate so that no one can just drive up."

Her eyes widened even more. "You think Aaron would try to take Stellie or something?"

Dax mentally cursed, hating that he'd put that fresh worry on her face. "Probably not, but he might try to bully you into handing her over to him. I know you wouldn't do that," he quickly added, "but Aaron could cause a scene that might upset Stellie."

It would sure as hell upset Lorelei, and he watched her process that. Watched as it sank in that bullying her was no doubt something Aaron might try.

"I could also stay here for another night or two," he offered.

Dax didn't have to guess that she was uncomfortable with either of those options. He wasn't exactly comfortable with them, either, but this was important, and he was going to do the right, responsible thing.

"I'll give it some thought," she finally said. "But it's a definite no to moving in with you."

Good on her giving it some thought and not out-and-out nixing the idea. And since he wasn't into bullying, Dax was ready to say a quick goodbye when Lorelei's office phone rang.

"The Glass Hatter," she automatically answered. "This is Lorelei Parkman. How may I help you?"

Dax mouthed his goodbye, but he stopped again when Lorelei's shoulders snapped back so fast that he actually heard the movement.

"What do you want?" she asked the caller, and there was no smidge of friendliness in her tone or body language.

He couldn't hear what the caller said and didn't have a

clue what had caused Lorelei to have this reaction, but he decided to wait around and find out.

"The adoption is final," she said, "and there was nothing illegal about it."

Hell. This was about Stellie. Of course it was. The baby was definitely someone who could get this kind of reaction from Lorelei.

"I won't agree to that," Lorelei told the caller. "You can't make me agree to that," she amended.

Dax didn't know what the caller had said to make Lorelei respond like that, but her words didn't match her expression. She seemed to be feeling that this person could and would make her agree to whatever was being asked.

"I did nothing wrong," Lorelei stated a moment later, "and anything else you have to say to me should go through my lawyer, Sophia Parkman." With that, she hung up.

Dax didn't push on what had caused the color to drain from her face. He just stood and waited for her to spill while he tried to keep his temper in check. But, oh, his temper was brewing, and he wanted to have a chat with whoever had caused Lorelei to react this way.

"That was the attorney Aaron just hired. Julian Martin," she finally said. "He's with a firm in San Antonio."

Okay. So, Aaron hadn't gone with anyone from his neck of the woods. That made sense, though, since he'd want someone who knew Texas law and was licensed to practice in the state.

"This guy threatened you?" Dax asked.

She nodded, swallowed hard. "He said Aaron will be able to prove that I didn't go through all the necessary steps to find Valerie's next of kin. That the so-called proof will be the basis for challenging the adoption."

Well, hell. Dax figured the proof would turn out to be a

crock since Matt had been the one taking those steps. He was a good cop and would have exhausted all avenues. But Aaron could use this to drag things out.

"The lawyer also said Aaron and he would get visitation rights with Stellie," Lorelei went on. "He insisted that Aaron has a right to be with his daughter and that I can't stop him. He said as soon as he got a court order, that he'd be accompanying Aaron here to make sure I comply."

Dax groaned and cursed. He wanted to dismiss that as another crock, especially since he wasn't certain that a judge would give visitations to a man who couldn't prove paternity.

Lorelei gathered her breath, and that worry in her eyes had gone up some significant notches. "If the offer still stands, can Stellie and I stay at Sunset Creek for a night or two?"

"It stands," he assured her. "And it's not limited to a night or two. Stellie and you can stay as long as you need."

Lorelei's nod lacked all confidence and conviction. "I'll bring her over after work."

Dax's nod was lacking in those departments as well. No way, though, would he back out of doing this, not after what that lawyer had just threatened. But he walked out of her shop with just one question on his mind.

What the hell had he just done?

CHAPTER ELEVEN

"Uh, are you sure this is a good idea?" Hilda asked Lorelei.

Lorelei wasn't at all certain that going to Sunset Creek was a good idea. In fact, she had reservations the size of Texas about it.

The nanny was on the floor of the nursery, stacking up plastic blocks for Stellie to knock down. With each build up and knocking down, Stellie giggled. Giggles that Lorelei very much needed to hear right now. They were like an audio lifeline, a reminder that she couldn't just give in to the panic, and the reason she couldn't was because of the giggling baby.

"I mean, Sunset Creek is big and all," Hilda went on, "but do you even get along well enough with Dax to be with him in his house?"

That last part fell firmly in the "to be determined" category. "I believe Dax wants what's best for Stellie," Lorelei settled for saying, knowing full well that she felt that way because Dax had said he wouldn't challenge her for custody. That he would, in fact, help her keep the baby.

But there was an even bigger reason she was going to the ranch.

And it was a reason she would no doubt have to share with Dax. With others, too. For now, though, she just kept packing, kept moving.

"Yes," Hilda agreed, "he does seem to want what's best." She paused. "But he is Dax Buchanan."

There was no need for Hilda to spell out exactly what she meant by that. Lorelei knew. This was about that "hot rodeo star" reputation. And looks. And body. This was about the fact that she'd be in the house with a man that few women had ever resisted.

She would resist, of course, but Lorelei wasn't stupid. It would be like someone fasting having to walk through bakery after bakery of wonderful delights. Definitely tempting, but the price for giving in wouldn't be just extra pounds on her thighs, it would put a serious monkey wrench in this tentative "no wonderful delights" arrangement she'd worked out with Dax.

"It'll be okay," Lorelei assured the woman, hoping that by saying the words aloud, she'd reassure herself.

It didn't work.

Lorelei knew she had to give herself some thinking time. But her mind was racing with so many questions, with so much fear. Yes, the fear. There were huge mountains of it coursing through her, and she knew it was driving her to hurry, hurry, hurry.

Even if hurrying could be a huge mistake.

Still, she didn't think this hurry to take Stellie to Dax's ranch would be as much of a mistake as staying put in her house and having Aaron and his slimy, bullying lawyer show up with a court order and yank Stellie from her. Of course, they could still do that if she was at Sunset Creek, but at least Dax would be there to help stop it. She hoped so, anyway. Because she couldn't let Aaron get his hands on her baby.

While Hilda and Stellie continued to play, Lorelei didn't exactly throw Stellie's clothes and things into a suitcase, but it was close. *Hurry, hurry, hurry.* Outrun the fear. The panic. And once she had Stellie safe, then maybe she could think straight. Of course, one of the big things she'd need to come to terms with was that even if she was at the ranch, that wouldn't stop Aaron.

"I don't want to risk Aaron or his lawyer coming here," Lorelei told Hilda, and she left it at that. She could have said more, so much more, but there was no need to ramp up Hilda's concerns since she was already clearly concerned enough.

"All right, then," Hilda finally said, "if you're on board with this, then I am, too. Just let me know if you need me to watch Stellie, and I'll drive out there."

"Thank you," Lorelei told her and the thanks was heartfelt. She might need Hilda to get through these next couple of days. And she assured herself it would only be that. A couple of days. Just long enough for Sophia to figure out a way to keep Aaron at bay.

Lorelei finished packing Stellie's stuff, and she scooped up the baby to take her into the main bedroom so she could do the same with her own things. Of course, Hilda followed, bringing some of the blocks with her so that Stellie and she could resume their game.

Grabbing another suitcase from her closet, Lorelei began to pack, but had barely gotten started when her phone rang. She jolted, silently cursing the reaction and the fact it made her want to add an extra *hurry* to her already rushed movements. But when she saw the name on the screen, she relaxed. Then, she silently cursed some more.

Alan Sandoval.

Her friend who was also an occasional boyfriend in a "general, noncommittal, loosey-goosey" sort of way. And while she didn't especially want to talk to him at the moment, she thought just hearing the sound of his voice might help with these jangled nerves. Besides, he'd perhaps heard about the trouble she was facing, and he might be calling to make sure she was okay. She wasn't, but she could do her friend duty just by taking his call.

"Alan," she greeted, sandwiching the phone between her shoulder and ear so she could continue to pack.

"Lorelei." And with just that one word, she heard the emotion in his voice. Oh, yes. He'd heard about her troubles. "Is there anything I can do to help?"

This was why she'd taken the call. Because Alan's offer wasn't just lip service. If there was something he could do, he'd figure out a way to get it done. "Thank you for the offer. I appreciate it, but everything is in the hands of the lawyers now."

She nearly stuttered on the word, *lawyers*, and tried to tamp down the fresh wave of emotion.

"I understand both the grandparents and the birth mother's husband are challenging you for custody?" Alan pressed. "And that the local rodeo rider is the baby's biological father?"

"That's right." She nearly stuttered again and gave up on tamping down the emotion. "I'm going to fight this. Dax Buchanan is going to help."

She didn't clarify that Dax was the rodeo rider. Alan had other friends in Last Ride so by now he had all or most of the details. Well, not the detail about her staying on Dax's ranch for a couple of days, but Lorelei was going to keep that to herself. Not because she thought she owed Alan an explanation about whose roof she'd be staying under, but because she didn't want to get into it with him. Soon, though, he would hear. Soon, everyone would.

"Let me make some calls and see what I can find out

about the grandparents and the husband," Alan added a moment later. "It doesn't hurt to know every detail you can get about who you're dealing with."

No, it didn't hurt, and Lorelei wasn't going to turn down any help that would allow her to keep her child. Alan wasn't a lawyer, but he owned an investment company and had a lot of connections.

"Thank you, Alan."

"Anytime." He paused. "I know the last thing you probably want to do is go out and about, but Frankie Parkman invited me to her First Date Party, and I wondered if we'd be going together?"

Lorelei silently groaned. She so wished Frankie hadn't done that. Of course, Frankie would have assumed it was the polite thing to do since over the years Lorelei had gone to other parties with Alan.

"I won't be going," Lorelei assured him.

"I understand." There was no disappointment in his voice. Nor had she expected any. Alan was a "low temperature, no heat" kind of guy. "I'll call you if I find anything you can use to keep Stellie."

Lorelei thanked him, ended the call and was just finishing up the packing when there was a knock at the door. She froze again, then relaxed when she heard her mother say, "It's me."

She'd been expecting either a call or visit from Evangeline, who also knew all about the custody threat, and this would give her a chance to tell her mom in person that she'd be staying at Sunset Creek for a couple of days. It was also possible that Evangeline would give her a valid, reasonable explanation as to why that shouldn't happen.

Lorelei wasn't exactly looking for excuses as to why staying with Dax was a bad idea, but at the moment she wasn't trusting her own thought process. She was harried, afraid and sick to her stomach with worry.

She picked up Stellie and was heading to the front door but came to a quick stop when her mother added, "Miriam Ford is with me."

Great day in the morning. What kind of crappery was this? Miriam wasn't the absolute last person in Last Ride she wanted to see—Aaron and his lawyer were—but the woman was a close third. Added to that, Miriam and her mother might not be alone, though if Aaron had been with them, Lorelei felt that Evangeline would have led with that nasty little tidbit when she'd called out.

"You want me to take Stellie to the nursery?" Hilda asked.

Lorelei was already handing the baby off before Hilda had even finished her question. Miriam likely wanted to see her granddaughter, and Lorelei would allow that, but she did want to make it clear first that she didn't just want the woman showing up on her doorstep like this. She threw open the door, her lecture fading away, when she saw the tears spilling down Miriam's face.

Evangeline had her arm around the woman and was clearly trying to comfort her. Was clearly failing, too, since Miriam was out-and-out sobbing. However, if anyone could do any comforting right now, it would be Evangeline since she was a counselor. A good one according to those who'd used her services.

"Bright blessings," Evangeline said, giving Lorelei her usual greeting. Lorelei didn't know how the woman managed to stay so rosy-eyed even when things were crap. "I came over for a quick visit and found Miriam on your porch. I think she needs to come in and sit for a moment."

Lorelei wanted to refuse. But couldn't. So she stepped

back, allowing Evangeline to lead in the crying woman. She took her to the kitchen, had Miriam sit at the counter, and she got her a glass of water.

"It all just hit me so hard," Miriam said. "My daughter is dead. I'll never see her again."

Lorelei pinched her eyes shut a moment, trying to pinch away the emotion with it. But she failed at that, too. Miriam was a grieving mother, and Lorelei wasn't immune to the pain the woman was feeling. That's why she got a pot of tea started while her mother sank down next to Miriam and continued with her soothing "there, there" murmurs. Evangeline also put an envelope on the countertop.

"Some help on the research for the Last Ride Society," her mother said, tapping the envelope. "I went ahead and pulled some info from social media you can use. I know this is a very low priority right now, and I didn't want you to have to think about it."

Fat chance of that. Lorelei was thinking about it. Well, in a roundabout way because the person she was researching was Valerie.

"Thank you," she told Evangeline, and Lorelei turned back to Miriam.

"That's about Valerie," Miriam said, her voice catching. "I heard that you drew her name for some tombstone research."

Lorelei nodded. "The Last Ride Society does quarterly drawings for local history reports. Maybe when things settle down for both of us, you can tell me some stories about her that I can include."

Miriam didn't dismiss that, but it was obvious the research and storytelling wasn't a priority for her, either. "I told Greg I needed some fresh air, and I started walking,"

Miriam went on. "I ended up here. I thought if I just could see Stellie for a minute or two, that it might help."

Lorelei thought of how Stellie's giggling had leveled her out a bit. It would probably work for Miriam, too, but Lorelei wanted to push the pause button on the visit until the woman had at least stopped crying. Stellie was just a baby, but she could pick up on the emotions. Besides, there were some things that Lorelei needed to tell Miriam.

"Aaron's lawyer called me," Lorelei said, "and he made threats."

Miriam looked at her with those tear-reddened eyes. "Yes. He threatened us as well. He wants us to join forces with Aaron to fight Mr. Buchanan and you."

Since Dax had wanted Lorelei to go for a similar arrangement between him and her, she knew she shouldn't have been surprised that Aaron would try to do the same thing.

"Are you joining forces?" Lorelei came out and asked.

"No." Miriam's voice was barely a whisper. "But Aaron says you and Mr. Buchanan will play dirty, that you'll do whatever it takes to keep Stellie."

Lorelei couldn't deny that. She had always thought of herself as a good person, but she was afraid she just might play dirty to keep her baby. And that led her to what she had to tell Miriam before she heard it from anyone else.

"Now that Dax has proof he's Stellie's father, I'm going to take her to his ranch for a couple of days so they can spend some time together." That was the sanitized version, anyway.

Miriam's tears didn't dry up completely, but alarm went through her eyes. "Are you trying to hide Stellie from us?"

"No," Lorelei tried to assure her. "In fact, I'll let you

see her in a just a couple of minutes. I wanted you to hear it from me that I was taking her to Sunset Creek Ranch."

Miriam kept her gaze pinned to Lorelei, studying her as if trying to suss out if Lorelei did, indeed, have hiding on her mind. She did, sort of, but it wasn't because of the Fords.

"Greg and I can't and won't drop our custody suit," Miriam finally said. She wiped away the tears with quick hard strokes all the while keeping her attention on Lorelei. "If it turns out that Mr. Buchanan is truly Stellie's father and that he wants to raise her, then we'll reevaluate our position."

Even though Miriam probably hadn't meant that as a threat, it felt like one to Lorelei. Of course, it would have felt that way with pretty much anything the woman said. But it stung that Miriam was seemingly discounting that Lorelei had adopted the baby. Apparently, that didn't count as much as DNA. And Lorelei was afraid the legal system might feel the same way.

Was that the real reason she was going to Sunset Creek Ranch?

To appease Dax so he wouldn't try to swoop in and take Stellie from her? Maybe. In part, anyway. It worried her that Dax had come to such a quick acceptance of fatherhood. Then again, maybe he hadn't. Maybe he was struggling just as much as she was right now.

"Stellie's in the nursery," Lorelei said, motioning for Miriam and her mother to follow her.

"Thank you," Miriam murmured. "I won't stay long."

Lorelei opened the nursery door, stepping to the side so that Miriam could go in. Stellie and Hilda were on the floor again, but this time they had a stash of books. Stellie was on Hilda's lap, clearly enjoying the reading time, and the baby stayed in her cheery mood even when Miriam came in and sat down beside them.

"How are you holding up?" Evangeline whispered to Lorelei.

Lorelei doubted her mom would approve of the response that she obviously wasn't holding up well. "I'm okay." It was a lie, and they both knew it. That's likely why Evangeline sighed and gave her arm a pat.

"Is there anything I can do?"

"You're doing it," Lorelei assured her mother while she kept her attention on a suddenly shy Stellie and Miriam, who was trying to read to her.

"You could bring Stellie to stay with me if you don't want to be here with her alone," Evangeline pointed out.

Lorelei's headshake was fast because she'd already mentally gone through this. "Your house is small, and I'm trying to prevent Aaron from just showing up anytime he wants to throw his weight around."

No need to add the way Miriam had just done. Being at the ranch probably wouldn't stop Miriam and Greg from visiting. Heck, it might not even stop Aaron and his lawyer, but at least with the gate locked, she'd have some advance warning.

And Dax would be there.

Lorelei didn't want to explore the reason that was a biggie on her mental list of why she'd agreed to stay with him. But it was.

"I didn't want to go to Wyatt and Nola's because they're dealing with getting ready for their own baby," Lorelei went on. "And I ruled out going to Lily's because spring is such a busy time for her on her ranch." Added to that, there was no gate or Dax there.

Evangeline made a sound of understanding. Paused. "I

hate to even bring this up, but should I cancel the party for the adoption and Stellie's first birthday?"

Lorelei didn't have to think about this, either. "Yes." It crushed her to think of not being able to celebrate such a joyous event, but Aaron and the Fords might not be ready for any kind of party, not when they were reeling from the death of their daughter. And as for the adoption part of the celebrations, the Fords might see that as rubbing her custody in their faces. She didn't want to antagonize them any more than they already were.

"All right, I'll cancel," Evangeline said and did more pausing. "Are you sure you'll be okay staying with Dax? I mean, he's not the sort who usually has babies for houseguests."

No, he wasn't. But this wasn't just any ordinary baby. It was his child. Well, probably his.

"Dax asked Stellie and me to move in with him," Lorelei said, keeping her voice a murmur.

Evangeline's gaze flew to hers. "And?"

"I said no."

"But you didn't say no to staying at his ranch," Evangeline pointed out.

"I didn't." Lorelei stopped, gathered her breath. "Look, Aaron's lawyer shook me up."

"Lorelei—" her mother started. But Lorelei nipped the maternal concern—which could be enormous—in the bud.

"Everything will be okay. I just need some time away." Which was why she'd already arranged for two cashiers she employed during the holidays. They'd assist Misty, and if any problems arose, Misty could just call her. "I need some time to think."

Thankfully, Evangeline didn't point out that Sunset Creek might not be an ideal thinking place. Not with a dreamy cowboy who happened to be the father of her adoptive daughter. And not pointing out the obvious made Lorelei love her mother even more. That's why she kissed Evangeline's cheek.

Miriam gave a now-fussy Stellie a kiss, too, and got up from the floor. "Thank you for letting me see her," she said. "May I call you about setting up another visit? I'm sure Greg will want to see her as well."

"Of course." Lorelei sighed when she saw the fresh tears in Miriam's eyes. "And I'm sorry you're having such a tough day."

Miriam nodded, and wiping away those tears, she headed toward the door.

"I'll go, too," Evangeline said. "I can walk back with her to the inn."

Lorelei locked up as soon as they left, and with Hilda occupying Stellie with another book, she went ahead and put the suitcases and the diaper bag in the car with the things she'd already carried out. Stellie's portable playpen that would double as a crib and a booster seat that would serve as a makeshift high chair. She looked at all the stuff and sighed again. So much for what could turn out to be a bad experiment.

She tried not to dwell on the bad possibility. Mainly because she was disgusted with herself for the way she was handling this stress. Instead, Lorelei just focused on getting Stellie into the car and reminding Hilda to lock up before she started the drive to Sunset Creek.

Just as she'd done on her first trip to show Dax that photo, Lorelei drove through town, and while she was still berating herself and her reaction to the call from Aaron's lawyer, her heart skipped a couple of beats when she saw Aaron coming out of the inn. Thankfully, he didn't recognize her vehicle. Didn't even spare a glance in her direction. He was on his phone, his face tight with anger, and he headed in the direction of her house.

Of course, there were plenty of other things in that particular direction, but she knew in her gut that he was on the way to see her. Or rather to see Stellie.

Lorelei drove straight to the ranch, checking her rearview mirror to make sure Aaron wasn't following her. And that caused her to mentally curse again. She had a spine, and she needed to steel it up.

At the end of the tense drive, she breathed a little easier when she saw that Dax had left the gates open for her. The moment she pulled into the driveway, the gates whispered shut behind her. Glancing around, she soon spotted Dax on the porch, and he'd obviously pressed something on his phone to close them.

In addition to a functioning spine, she also had eyes. Eyes that landed on her host. His shirt was buttoned today, and he was wearing another pair of those jeans that had clearly been made to emphasize parts of him that she shouldn't be noticing.

"The gate texted me when you drove through," he said, and he flashed her a welcoming smile. She was betting both that smile and those jeans would qualify as foreplay.

"I hope we're not too early...or late," she muttered, checking the time. It was a little past four o'clock. She'd told him she would come after work, but she'd left work before the shop had even closed. Lorelei had spent all her normal working hours just pacing and worrying.

"Nope. Right on time." He came down the steps, stopping in front of her, looking at her as if to make sure she was okay. Lorelei did some looking at him as well. And coming clean.

"I'm here because I'm a coward," she said.

His eyebrow winged up. Not foreplay but he still managed to make the gesture look hot. "Let's get your things inside, and you can tell me all about that. Do you prefer wine, beer, coffee or soft drinks with your confessions?"

"Wine," she confirmed, sighing.

"Coming up." He took her keys from her, inadvertently touching her fingers in the process, and he popped the trunk. "I've got red, white or champagne. If I were you, I'd go for the champagne because it looks as if you've had a crappy day."

She had, indeed, and yes, she nodded to let him know that the champagne would be great.

Dax hauled everything into the foyer, but when Lorelei stepped in, she saw the high chair in the dining room and the play mat and toys in the living room.

"I might have gone a little overboard," Dax admitted, tipping his head toward the hall. "This way."

He led her into a bedroom where Lorelei could see that overboard had certainly happened. Along with a king-sized bed that looked more suited to a high-end hotel, there was a crib, a comfy-looking rocking chair and more toys.

"How did you get all of this stuff so fast?" she asked.

"I called in a few favors." He set the suitcases on the floor. "The bathroom's through there," he said, pointing to the en suite. "If you need office space, you can use the room across the hall. There's another guest room next to it if you don't want to sleep here in the nursery."

It was very nice. All of it. And very overwhelming. All of it, including Dax himself.

"You really keep champagne on hand?" she asked.

"I do. You never know when you'll need to celebrate something or use it to lighten a crappy mood. I'll be right back," he said, walking away, and a few minutes later, she heard the popping of a champagne cork. A few minutes after that, he returned with a glass of bubbly for her and a beer for himself.

He moved closer to her again, giving Stellie a grin and jiggling her toes. Her baby's fussiness instantly disappeared, and she began to babble her new favorite word. *Gak.* She also began to squirm to get down on the floor so she could play with all those new toys. Before she let Stellie get her hands on them, Lorelei did a quick check to make sure they were safe. They were. Apparently, Dax's called-in favors had taken child safety and age appropriateness into consideration.

"So, why do you think you're a coward?" Dax asked. Sipping his beer, he sank down on the floor next to Stellie. "And FYI, I know you're not. Along with running a business, you're a single parent. That takes ball…" He stopped, obviously rethought using that in front of Stellie. "Balance," he amended. "Balance in a non-cowardly way."

Sighing, Lorelei sank down beside him and had some of the champagne. Not just sparkling wine, she realized, but the real deal.

She so didn't want to get into this with Dax, but he'd have to know. Well, know bits and pieces of it, anyway. And at the end of those sad bits and pieces, he'd agree with her coward label.

"Lots of people, especially my mom, want to know why I've never married or been engaged," she started while Stellie played with a toy dump truck. "Well, it goes back to a relationship I had in college. Things were great with him, until they weren't great. Lots of jealousy and accusations if I even looked at another guy. Lots of attempts to control me."

Probably very much like Aaron had done to Valerie. And that was probably one of the reasons all of this had gotten to her. One of the reasons, anyway.

"Anyway," Lorelei went on, "when I finally found the *balance* to end things, he stalked me, vandalized my car, spread ugly rumors about me." She paused, had to, and she downed some more of the champagne. "And he assaulted me."

Oh, the flashbacks came. Of course they did. They were like bloodsucking leeches that latched on to her and just wouldn't let go. Some people probably would have been able to just let go of something like that. Especially since it'd happened thirteen years ago. But Lorelei could still feel the sharp pain when his hand smacked against her face. She could still taste her own blood. Could still be terrified that she'd been involved with someone who could physically hurt her like that.

Dax groaned, mouthed the F-word. Groaned again. "Please tell me that d-i-c-k paid and paid hard for doing that to you."

Lorelei did some silent cursing as well. "No."

The muscles in Dax's jaw turned to iron. "What's the d-i-c-k doing now?"

She drank more champagne to clear her throat. "Helping Aaron fight us to get custody of Stellie," she answered. "He's Aaron's lawyer."

"What the f...udge?" Dax demanded. "How can he be a lawyer if he assaulted and stalked you?"

"Because I didn't report it. And that's what makes me a coward." She hushed, giving him some time to let that sink in before she continued. "It's the reason I agreed to come here to the ranch. With everything else going on, I just don't have the energy to face Aaron and him right now."

Dax didn't touch her, maybe because he now thought she fell into the "wounded bird/treat her with kid gloves" category. Lorelei hated that. Hated that it might be true.

"That's BS. You have the energy," Dax argued. "That doesn't mean I want you to leave," he quickly added. "It means I want you to dig down deep and find your mad. Because I know it's there. Mad for the jerk and for what Aaron's trying to pull. This just knocked you off-kilter for a little while, but it won't last."

Surprised with the pep talk, Lorelei looked at him. The man clearly had too much faith in her, considering he didn't know her that well. But his words got through, and she felt just a little spark that hadn't been there minutes earlier. Not the spark of heat. No, that had been there. But this was something else. A reminder that she wasn't a wuss. It wasn't *finding her mad*, but it was a start, and that meant she needed to come up with a plan for this fight.

"His name is Julian Martin," she explained. Maybe if she gave him the details, Dax would be able to help with this plan to fight Aaron and him. "Old money, powerful family. Lots of judges and politicians in his family tree. I don't know how Aaron found or chose him, but unless Julian has let bygones be bygones, then he'll be especially aggressive in trying to nullify the adoption."

Aggressive and mean. It was the flashbacks from the pain of him hitting her that had sent her in a bad spiral. But Lorelei reminded herself that she wouldn't give Julian the chance to do that to her again. She certainly wouldn't let him anywhere near her child. Being here behind closed gates was a start, but she couldn't just stay put.

"I'm so sorry, Dax," she told him. Not in a mutter or whisper. She wanted him to hear every word of this apology. "My past could end up hurting us."

He lifted his shoulder, but there was nothing casual about his shrug. The muscles in his jaw were still tight. His eyes, though, seemed to be offering comfort. But not sympathy exactly.

"We all have pasts," he said. "Well, maybe not Stellie here." He ruffled her curls, causing her to flash him a grin. "But I've done some things that could come back to bite us." He paused. "Things that would give you a really good clue as to why I've never married or been engaged."

"Yet you asked Stellie and me to move in with you," she pointed out.

Another shrug. "All for a good cause." His eyes met hers, and like Stellie, he grinned. A grin that seemed more automatic than the real deal.

Their gazes stayed locked, and Lorelei could feel a different flood of emotion. The blasted heat. And he seemed to be moving in. Maybe for a kiss. One that would almost certainly be a mistake since it would get all balled up with the other things going on. But he didn't kiss her. Not with his mouth, anyway. He just lowered those hot "let me take you now" eyes to her mouth and let his attention linger and slide there. Considering there was no physical contact whatsoever, the visual kiss packed a punch.

The moment seemed to freeze. Then heat up even more, and Lorelei figured she needed to say something before she ended up kissing him.

"So, what's the reason for you never being married or engaged?" she asked to get her mind off that kissing threat.

Dax didn't jump to answer. "One day I'll tell you all about it. For now, let's just say it's not a pretty story. No happy fairy-tale ending, that's for sure."

That should have put a lid on her curiosity about him. It didn't. Just the opposite, and she had to wonder if the non-pretty story had involved a fan who'd turned stalker. Lorelei recalled him saying that sometimes such fans got onto the ranch.

Lorelei's phone rang, the sound slicing through the silence, and she saw Sophia's name on the screen. At the same moment, Dax's phone rang. A call from his lawyer, Curt Dayton.

She groaned because this couldn't be good. Lorelei waited for Dax to answer his first, and because he was right next to her, she heard what Curt said.

"I want you to know that Sophia and I will do everything possible to stop it, but the gloves are off, and round two has apparently started."

"Started? How?" Dax demanded.

Curt's sigh was loud and long. "Aaron and his attorney just filed for a court order, demanding that you and Lorelei hand over Stellie."

CHAPTER TWELVE

Dax dashed off his signature for the bulls that were being prepped for transport to a rodeo in Austin. Not a long trip for them, and normally he would have gone with them. Even if he wasn't competing in an event, he still liked to see how his bulls performed. But it was best if he stayed close to home.

Normally, that whole "staying close to home" deal would have put the fear of God in him. Or rather the fear of... something. Sometimes, staying put just made everything close in around him. It brought the old bad memories too close to the surface. Bull riding and even watching them could tamp that down some. But as bad as staying put was, leaving would make him feel even worse. Because it would mean leaving Lorelei to face Aaron and his dick of a lawyer alone.

He couldn't do that.

And didn't want to dwell on the fact that her problems were now his. Not just the problem of custody, either, but her having to face what had to be her own round of memories when it came to Julian Martin. The son of a bitch had hurt Lorelei and had gotten away with it, but he sure as hell wasn't going to get away with trying to take Stellie from her.

The problem would be stopping him and stopping him hard.

Sophia and Curt were doing their legal things, and that included pushing to get Dax's paternity order. It was the reason the lawyers had arranged for an independent lab tech to come out to the ranch that morning to take another round of DNA samples from both Stellie and him. Curt had already warned him that getting these results wouldn't be nearly as fast as the other test because these had to be able to be entered as evidence in court.

The results had to hold up.

The test had to prove he was Stellie's father so that Aaron couldn't take the child. But Aaron and his slimeball lawyer were almost certainly trying to come up with their own proof that would get them what they wanted.

With that weighing down on him, Dax made his way back toward the house. It was warm but not hot, which made it a good day to spend some time with the bulls. He might be able to take Lorelei and Stellie out to do that, especially since he was betting that Lorelei could use a distraction or two.

He had no doubts, none, that she'd had as restless of a night as he had. Not only because she was in a new place— with him—but also because of the threat of that court order. So far, Curt and Sophia were fighting it, and Dax had to believe they would win.

Had to believe.

Because he didn't want to think of how this would crush Lorelei if Aaron and the dick managed to find a judge who'd do something this reckless. No way should a man like Aaron get his hands on a baby.

Then again, there were probably plenty of people who were saying the same thing about him.

He wasn't a dick like Julian and Aaron, but other than bull riding, he hadn't had a lot of stellar moments in life.

In fact, he'd had some downright crap ones. Crap ones that he'd nearly spilled to Lorelei when she'd told him about Julian. Dax had never hit a woman, never stalked or bullied anyone, but he had more than his share of screwups and scars.

Yeah, there were reasons all right as to why he'd never married or gotten engaged.

Dax went into the house through the kitchen, washing up in the half bath just off the mudroom, and he went in search of Lorelei and Stellie. They'd had breakfast together. A rather messy affair with Stellie slinging oatmeal in various directions. Dax didn't mind, especially since it'd made her giggle. But it was all cleaned up now, something Lorelei had likely done after he'd told her he had some paperwork to do for the bulls. She'd cleaned and was now nowhere in sight.

For one heartbeat-skipping moment, he thought maybe she'd left. Maybe had gone on the run with Stellie, but he heard the sound of her voice coming from the office he'd set up for her, and Dax headed in that direction.

He spotted her sitting at the desk, the phone pressed to her ear while she typed something on her laptop. Multitasking. While barefoot. He wasn't sure why that snagged his attention, but it did. So did the way the loose pale yellow cotton dress slid against her body when she moved her hands with the typing.

Definitely no polished look for her today. Her hair was down, loose and unstyled on her shoulders, and she was using her bare toes of her left foot to scratch her right calf. That did some attention-snagging, too, which meant he was one sick puppy to get a cheap thrill out of something like that. This was probably how fetishes started.

"So, why do you think Valerie didn't tell Dax she was pregnant?" he heard her ask.

That caused him to stop daydreaming about her clothes, hair and feet, and he glanced around the room. No Stellie, but when he looked in the open door of the nursery, he saw her napping in her crib.

Dax didn't know who Lorelei was talking to, and he couldn't hear the response to her question, but Lorelei continued to type on her laptop.

"All right," Lorelei said several moments later. "I can add that, and I'll be glad to write up any others you might have. Thank you, Miriam."

Miriam? What the heck was she doing talking to Valerie's mother?

Since he didn't want to eavesdrop any more than he already had, Dax cleared his throat, but he immediately cursed himself because it had Lorelei nearly tumbling out of the chair. Clearly, she was on edge.

"We'll talk soon," she quickly said to Miriam, and she ended the call. Lorelei also tried to steady herself. "That was Miriam," she told him. "She gave me some stories about Valerie's childhood that I can use for the Last Ride Society research."

It surprised him that she could even think of something like that at a time like this, but maybe for her the research was like the bulls for him. A welcome distraction.

"Anyway, I thought that one day Stellie might want to read the report," Lorelei went on. Then, she stopped, muttered under her breath something that he didn't catch. "All right, I'm trying to keep things civil with Greg and her. I don't want to have to fight both them and Aaron."

"Same here," Dax said, causing Lorelei to release a breath that he thought might be of immense relief. Maybe because she thought he might be pissed at her chatting up someone who could turn out to be the enemy.

"How did Miriam answer your question as to why Valerie hadn't told me she was pregnant?" he asked.

Lorelei swallowed hard. "Well, remember Miriam told us that Valerie had called her once and texted a few times. Valerie didn't say anything about being pregnant, but she did mention that something hadn't worked out."

Dax had no trouble connecting the dots on this. "And Miriam thought that meant Valerie's relationship with me?"

Lorelei's confirming nod was pretty shaky. Spelling it out like that made Dax feel more than a little shaky, too.

"I was seeing someone right about the time Valerie would have arrived here," he explained. "Shari Dayton. No need to tell you it wasn't serious. But I was also out of town around that time for a couple of days as well. I was actually at a rodeo the day Valerie died."

So, it could have played out one of two ways. Either Valerie had seen him with Shari and figured he was involved, or Valerie could have realized her baby's daddy was basically a rolling stone who made a habit of rolling in and out of women's beds. If she'd been looking for any kind of commitment, she probably would have thought he was a bad risk in that particular department.

But Valerie would have been wrong.

"If she'd come to me and told me, I would have done the right thing," Dax insisted. "Maybe not marriage or a commitment, but I sure as hell would have made a commitment to the baby. I know what it's like to feel abandoned, and I—" He stopped, cursed himself and waved that off. "Sorry, venting now."

Lorelei didn't push for more of that vent, but she did give him a questioning look. One that he ignored, and Dax went closer to the desk and looked at the notes she'd typed on the laptop. It was general stuff like Valerie's date and place of birth, milestones like when she walked and talked. He skimmed what appeared to be an account of Valerie's first day of school, and a Halloween costume where she'd dressed like a dentist because a family friend had been one.

And that jogged something in Dax's memory.

"I had a missing toothbrush," he blurted out. In hindsight, though, he should have better explained the buildup to that. "About a year ago, I came home from a trip, and my toothbrush was missing. I just assumed the cleaning service tossed it for some reason, but when I asked, they said no. Then I thought about one of the hands telling me that a fan had sneaked onto the ranch when I wasn't here. It was that same time the toothbrush went missing."

"And you think Valerie took it." Lorelei shook her head. "But why would she do something…" The question trailed off. "You think it's possible that Valerie didn't know who her baby's father was so she took your toothbrush to do a DNA test?"

It did sound far-fetched, but maybe there was a way to prove that's what had happened. Dax motioned toward her phone. "Do you still have that picture of Valerie outside Once Upon a Time?"

She nodded and scrolled through until she found it.

"Send me a copy," Dax instructed, and the moment she did that, he forwarded it to his head ranch hand, Mike Espinoza, since Mike had been the one who'd told him about the trespassing fan that he'd run off.

Have you ever seen this woman on the ranch? Dax texted Mike.

As expected, it didn't take Mike long to answer, but the

moments seemed to crawl by. Yeah, I think she's the one who hurried off when I spotted her.

Dax frowned at the word *hurried*. She would have been pregnant. Mega pregnant, Dax emphasized.

Again, Mike's response was quick.

She might have been. Couldn't tell. She was wearing a bulky raincoat, and I didn't get an up-close look at her. I spotted her on the porch, coming out of the house. She spotted me, too, and took off in a blue car.

"Valerie's car was blue?" Dax asked Lorelei, and she nodded.

Dax thanked Mike for the info and didn't bother to ask if she'd had a toothbrush with her since Valerie probably wouldn't have held that in plain sight. Bulky raincoats usually had pockets.

"So, she likely did come here," Lorelei concluded. Her forehead bunched up as she gave that some thought. "But maybe it wasn't because she didn't know you were the father. It could have been because she wanted proof in case Aaron found her. I mean, it's obvious she was hiding, and it's my guess he was the reason she was doing that."

That was Dax's guess, too. It still didn't explain why Valerie hadn't come out and told him she was pregnant, but perhaps this new info gave him a different angle on that, too.

"Maybe Valerie thought I wouldn't believe the baby was mine," he muttered, groaning. "And she would have done that because of my reputation. She could have believed I get hit with claims of paternity all the time. I don't," Dax assured her. "Never have."

"I know," Lorelei said, sighing.

There was something in her tone. Not solely an acknowledgment of what he'd just said, but it seemed to be some kind of acceptance that he wasn't the run-and-gun womanizer that most people thought he was.

"Thanks for that," Dax told her.

She gave him a little smile that should have been just that. A smile. But when her gaze landed on him, there was the blasted heat in her eyes. Heat that he shouldn't want to see, but since it was already there, Dax considered testing the waters by kissing her. Of course, it was the worst idea in the history of bad ideas, but the thought was firmly in his head. He might have done something about it, too.

If his phone hadn't rung.

Dax yanked himself out of the lust trance, not an especially hard thing to do when he got a jolt of a different kind after he saw Matt's name on the screen. Hell. He hoped Aaron wasn't pushing Matt to try to take Stellie.

"You're on speaker," Dax told Matt when he answered. "Lorelei is here with me."

Matt did hesitate for a couple of seconds. "This stays with just us for now," he finally said, "but I got some info on the flag I told you I found when I did a deep background check on Valerie. St. Louis PD didn't give me a lot, but apparently Valerie was assisting them with an investigation that involved embezzling."

"Embezzling?" Lorelei and Dax said in unison.

"Yeah," Matt verified. "It's still an active investigation so I'm not going to get much more than she was helping. I don't know how, and I don't know who the cops there suspect of the embezzling."

"Aaron." Again, Lorelei and Dax said that at the same time.

"Maybe. He'd be my guess, too. Anyway, like I said,

this stays with just us. I'll keep digging, and it might lead us to some dirt on Aaron."

Dax could practically see Lorelei latch on to that like a lifeline. He latched, too, but he wanted more. "What can we do to speed this up? And can we use it if Aaron manages to get that court order to take Stellie?"

"Nothing and no," Matt quickly answered. "Let me work this cop to cop. If St. Louis PD is building a case against Aaron, I don't want to do anything to blow it. If he gets wind that he's under investigation, he might be able to hide incriminating evidence. And as for the court order, let Sophia and Curt fight that. They sent someone out to get DNA from Stellie and you?"

"Yes," Dax verified. "And they're working to have the same lab do a test on Aaron. To rule him out. He's fighting that, claiming we will try to falsify his results so he's not a match. Of course, the real reason he's fighting it is because he's not Stellie's father."

Matt paused again. "You're positive of that?"

Dax nearly gave a resounding yes, but he throttled back a bit. "According to the test I am, and it's supposed to be 99.9 percent accurate."

That was pretty damn accurate. But the doubt came. Of that tiny fraction of tests that came back with false positives. Doubts, too, created now that he suspected Valerie had sneaked into his house to get his DNA sample so she could do her own paternity test on the baby.

What had happened with that?

Had Valerie had time to run it? Or how would a test like that even be carried out while she was still pregnant? Maybe she'd planned on waiting until the baby was born, but if she'd started the testing process, then there might be a record of it.

"I just found out that about a year ago Valerie likely sneaked into my house when I wasn't here," Dax explained to Matt. "She might have done that to try to get a DNA sample from me. Do you still have Valerie's laptop?" Because there might be something on there about internet searches for such things.

"Yes, but there was no email account. None that we could find, anyway." Matt paused again. "After Valerie died, I sent the laptop to the crime lab, just so they could search to see if there was anything on it we could use to locate her next of kin. I can send it to them again, this time for a deeper search that might give us some answers. Deleted browsing history or sites or accounts she might have bookmarked."

"Do that," Dax insisted.

Because he had a bad feeling that Lorelei and he were going to need a whole lot of those answers to fight Aaron. Heck, he personally wanted answers, too. Needed them, he amended. Because if that 99.9 was a false positive, he had to know.

"We also need to consider that Aaron might be dangerous," Dax went on. "Valerie could have been on the run from him because he found out she was helping with the police investigation."

"Already considered that," Matt assured. "I can't use the investigation, though, to get a restraining order against him." The breath he took was long, loud and heavy with frustration. "But I can and will talk to the Fords again. I won't just come out and ask about the investigation, but I will fish around and try to find out if they know anything about it."

Dax thanked him and ended the call with Matt. Then, he realized he felt even more unsettled than he had before the somewhat promising conversation. After all, the computer techs at the lab might be able to find something, but he was hoping it was something that worked in Lorelei's and his favor. The Fords might be able to give some insight as well. That said, if they'd known Aaron was doing something illegal, they probably would have already shared that with Matt.

Lorelei turned to him, their gazes instantly connecting. "Thank you for pushing on this. I know you're doing it for Stellie, but that means you're doing it for me, too."

Yeah, he was, and Lorelei must have thought he'd done it because of this simmering heat between them. But it wasn't that. Couldn't be that. Because heat cooled, and he didn't want any cooling playing into future visits with Stellie. Keeping his hands off Lorelei was the way to go here.

And that's why Dax shocked the heck out of himself when he leaned in and kissed her.

He expected her to push him away or at least go stiff. She didn't. Lorelei sighed again, and her mouth sort of melted against his. She didn't make a sound of "what the heck are you doing" outrage. Nope. The sound was more of a silky moan, one that slammed into his body like a lust heat wave.

No way should a "closed mouth, no-foreplay" kiss have hit him like that. No way should Lorelei be making silky moans. She was the sensible one. And it didn't take long for the sensibility to kick in.

She pulled back, and he saw that her eyes were wide. Her breath was gusting, and her face was flushed. "Oh, that really shouldn't have happened," she insisted, but her voice was all dreamy and hot, and he could practically feel her body revving.

"You're right," he murmured back, and yeah, his body was still in the rev mode, and a certain stupid part of him thought it hadn't been a mistake at all. But rather a stellar idea. And that he should do it again.

"You can't actually be attracted to me," Lorelei complained.

That caused him to frown. "And why not?"

"Opposites," she readily supplied.

"Can and do attract," he supplied just as readily. "Besides, we're not that opposite."

The corner of her mouth quivered a little as if threatening to smile. "Oh, yes we are."

He was about to play with fire, run with scissors and stick his wet finger in a light socket. Because he flashed her a grin that had been darn effective in getting women to grin back. He'd learned that smiling women were a lot more open to a kiss. And that's what Dax was about to test. He'd already started moving his hand in the direction of the back of her neck so he could ease Lorelei to him.

When her phone rang.

The relief that flashed in her eyes let him know this was a "saved by the bell" kind of moment for her. It should have felt that way for him, too, but it just seemed like an annoying interruption. Then again, that was dick-thinking, and he knew for certain that thinking with that particular body part could screw things up big-time.

"It's Millie," Lorelei said when she took out her phone. "It's probably about Frankie's party," she added in a murmur.

Dax had heard about that. Small town, lots of talk. Frankie had even sent him a text invite, but she'd added, So many first date options for you to choose from.

There were, indeed, options. None that he wanted, though, and it occurred to Dax the one person he might like to go with was Lorelei. Then again, since they'd never been on a date, first or otherwise, that probably wouldn't qualify. Well, unless he bent the party rules and made that their first date.

Dick-thinking again.

There should be no dates with Lorelei. No kissing Lorelei. No fantasizing about just how warm she could get if he put his mouth on her...

"Valerie asked you that?" Lorelei said, and it yanked Dax's attention off Lorelei and on to that question. A question and/or subject that had caused Lorelei's forehead to bunch up with worry.

Since she hadn't put the call on speaker, Dax had no idea what the question was. Or the answer. But he could hear the slight murmur of Millie's voice.

"And Valerie didn't say why?" Lorelei pressed. She stayed quiet, listening to Millie's response. "No. I'll have a talk with him. Thanks so much," she added as she ended the call.

With her phone still clutched in her hand, Lorelei turned to him. "Millie remembered something about the day that Valerie came by Once Upon a Time. She asked Millie if there were any lawyers in town."

"A lawyer," Dax repeated, latching right on to that. "Did she tell Millie why she needed one?" Because it could have been so she could start divorce proceedings against Aaron.

Lorelei shook her head. "No, but Millie told her that her father, Asher Parkman, was a lawyer."

"Valerie could have gone to see him," Dax immediately said, causing Lorelei to nod again.

She did an internet search to come up with the number to Asher's law firm. "I'll call him right now and find out."

CHAPTER THIRTEEN

As far as Lorelei was concerned, the past five days had been a big fat bust. Along with the legal wranglings being at a standstill while paperwork was being filed and blocked, she'd struck out with getting answers from Asher Parkman because the man was on a romantic getaway with his wife and wasn't taking business calls.

The Fords hadn't been able to help, either, when Lorelei had talked to them when they came out to visit Stellie. Neither had had a clue as to why their daughter would have wanted to contact a lawyer.

So, that meant Dax and she were at a standstill on that particular question.

A standstill that might just stay that way if Asher pulled some kind of "client-attorney privilege" card and wouldn't talk to them. Lorelei was hoping those rules might not apply since Valerie was dead, but until she actually spoke to Asher, she wouldn't know if he could help them.

Work had been pretty much a bust, too, despite Hilda coming over to watch Stellie while Lorelei took care of some paperwork and orders for the shop. She just hadn't been able to concentrate enough to get it done well. Added to that, it'd felt like, well, work. Probably because she wasn't doing it at the shop where she would have been surrounded by all the beautiful glass.

And it was the reminder of the glass, of being in the

shop, of the days and hours just crawling by, that made her realize that hiding out here at Dax's ranch was only adding to her downer of a mood. This wasn't like her. She faced things head-on. Always had. That meant she'd have to face Aaron, Julian and the threats to the adoption, and she'd do that by getting on with her life. She couldn't live with fears and what-ifs any longer.

After having a pep talk with herself, Lorelei checked on Stellie who was chowing down on the lunch Hilda had made for her. She gave the baby a kiss and went in search of Dax.

In the five days since she'd been at Sunset Creek, Lorelei had noticed his routine was to get some work done in his office for a couple of hours in the morning and then he'd head out to the barn or pastures. Since she'd never followed him out of the house, she wasn't sure what he did there, but he always stayed away long enough that she never felt he was underfoot.

Probably because she was the one underfoot.

Dax no doubt regretted that kiss. Regretted, too, that there'd been enough heat between them in the first place to generate thoughts of kissing. So, he was keeping his distance. That was good, she assured herself, since kissing only complicated things. Wanting him did as well, but Lorelei figured once she didn't have to see Dax on a daily basis, the wanting would level out and eventually go away.

She threaded her way through the back hall to his office. Which she found empty. She considered just texting him to let him know she had to run an errand, but she thought this was better handled face-to-face. So, she went out the patio doors and started toward the barn nearest to the house. Lorelei was still yards away when Dax's ranch hand, Mike, called out to her.

"Dax is in the east barn," he said, and then he motioned to the smaller one.

Thanking him, she headed in that direction, figuring that Mike and the other hands she saw working with the bulls were wondering why she was there. Of course, there'd been gossip so they likely knew at least some of the legal wranglings going on. For certain, they had heard about the paternity results for the test Dax had done.

Lorelei stepped into the barn and immediately caught the scent of the bulls. Not the most pleasant odor, but it was somewhat toned down with the smell of the feed and fresh pine shavings.

This wasn't just some slapped together outbuilding. It resembled more of an upscale stable with stalls and automatic feeding and watering systems. Everything looked neat and organized, including the bulls themselves. There were three of them, and while Lorelei knew diddly about livestock, she thought these were young, maybe recently brought in for training.

She glanced around, but when she didn't spot Dax, she kept walking through the large area that ran like a wide hall between the rows of stalls, and she finally heard Dax. With his back to her, he was to the side of the open barn door, leaning against the jamb while he talked on the phone.

"Miranda, we've been through this before," she heard him say, and dang it, her feet seemed to stop of their own accord. Seemed to freeze in place, too. But her ears were certainly working just fine and were latching on to this conversation she shouldn't be hearing.

Miranda. One of his lovers no doubt. And Lorelei silently cursed the whip of jealousy she felt. The jealousy didn't last, though, because it was soon replaced by some concern.

"I can't get involved in this. Can't," Dax emphasized.

He scrubbed his hand over his face, muttered something under his breath and hit the end call button. Dax stood there for several moments just looking at his phone before he turned his attention back to the pasture. He was obviously staring out at what some would consider breathtaking views, but judging from his body language, he wasn't in a breathtaking kind of mood right now.

This was so different from his usually cocky, grinning self, and she could practically feel the unhappiness coming off him in thick hot waves. What the heck had caused this, and who was this Miranda who could twist him up like this?

Something must have alerted him that he wasn't alone because he turned and looked at her. For just a split second, she saw that unhappiness before he closed it down and dashed off one of those grins.

"You look like one of those photography subjects," he said. "A study in contrasts. The lady and the bulls."

She glanced down at her pale blue skirt, cobalt top and ice-gray heels. A work outfit that she'd purposely put on to trick her brain into thinking she was actually at the shop while she tried to tackle doing all the invoices and such. It was the reason she'd done her makeup and hair. Well, partly the reason, anyway. She realized Dax had played into that decision because the makeup and clothes created, hopefully, the impression that she had her act together.

Which was a crock, of course.

But for a long time now she'd lived by the "fake it until you make it" rule. And she wondered if that's what Dax had been doing as well. Because he certainly didn't live up to his carefree persona right now.

"Is everything okay?" she came out and asked.

He must have considered that she'd overheard at least

some of his conversation, but Dax didn't waver. "Lots of calls from Curt today," he said. "Sophia and he are still blocking whatever crap Aaron and his lawyer try to throw at us. Added to that, Aaron's still trying to muddy the waters by saying he doesn't trust the lab that's currently running the paternity test."

None of that was a surprise to her since she'd been getting lots of calls from Sophia. Aaron was trying to force them to use a lab in St. Louis. A lab where he likely knew someone who might try to influence the results. It was the reason Sophia and Curt had insisted multiple labs do the test. It would delay things, but this way they could negate any false results that Aaron managed to finagle.

Of course, there might not be any finagling needed if more than one of the tests proved he was Stellie's father. And if that happened… Lorelei decided not to "worst-case scenario" it right now since she was barely hanging on by her fingernails.

"I'm pushing Matt to get us anything he can on the criminal investigation Valerie was helping with," Dax went on. "He's made a request to St. Louis PD so something might come of it."

Hopefully, something that would work in their favor. She mentally paused again, wondering when Dax and she had collectively become "their."

"What about you?" he asked. "How's your day going?"

She started to get into all the "busts" since it appeared he'd already had a bust or two of his own with that phone call from Miranda.

"Hilda's with Stellie for the rest of the afternoon so I need to go to the cemetery to get a photo of Valerie's grave," she explained. "Of course, the name is wrong on the tombstone, but it's part of the research I need to finish." And it was something she'd been putting off for worry about running into Aaron and Julian.

Yes, the hiding out ended now. In all areas of her life.

"Mind if I go with you?" Dax asked.

For a moment, she wasn't sure how to respond to that. "If Aaron and Julian show up there, I'll be okay."

"No, it's not that. All right, maybe it's a little bit that," he amended. "But I'd like to see her grave. It could be argued that out of everyone in Last Ride, I knew Valerie best."

True, but with Dax already being down from that phone call, a trip like this wouldn't help. Still, Lorelei nodded because she couldn't think of an argument against it unless she brought up what she'd overheard.

"What cemetery?" he asked.

"Ophelia's Peaceful Gardens," she supplied.

She mentally winced at the name. Last Ride had lots of cemeteries, some with oddish names. But in this case the near wince was because this particular cemetery had been set up by a rich spinster, Ophelia Dayton, about a century ago, and Ophelia had stipulated that only women could be buried there. Since Ophelia had set up a trust to pay for burial costs for future occupants, that's where the town council had decided to bury Valerie. Over the decades, obviously others had elected to be buried there as well, and now there were about a hundred graves and mausoleums.

Dax looked at her. "Is that the cemetery just past the chalk bluff?"

She nodded, and it hit her then. The reason for that slight hesitation she saw in his eyes. His brother had died there when he'd driven his car off that bluff. His brother Griff had been nineteen then, which would have made Dax sixteen.

Losing a sibling was almost always hard, but it had to have been especially difficult at that age. Added to that, he'd already lost both of his parents several years before and was living with a relative that everyone agreed fit the textbook definition of mean and crotchety.

"I can go alone," she assured him. "It's just to take a picture so I won't be there long."

But he just shook his head and started walking. "We'll use my truck. It's better on those steep curves than your car will be."

She didn't turn down this offer, either. Now that she'd remembered that he was right about the driving conditions. Like spring weather, Last Ride didn't have actual mountains, but the chalk bluffs were, indeed, steep.

They stopped by the house to say a quick goodbye to Stellie, and on the way to his truck, Dax texted Mike to let him know that no one should be allowed through the gates while they were gone. It was a security measure that made her feel a little sick. Sick but necessary. She didn't want Aaron or Julian showing up while they were gone.

Thankfully, the weather wasn't a bust for this particular trip. It was a perfect spring day, somewhat rare for this part of Texas since Mother Nature often just skipped right over spring and went straight into summer heat. But today it was in the low seventies, and the sun was shining.

They drove in silence on the road that would thread them through the other side of town. Not a bad time for the quiet, though, since the trip gave another picture-postcard view with the pastures and woods filled with spring wildflowers. The bluebonnets, Indian paintbrush and firewheels, all blending together to create the landscape that drew thousands of tourists every year. Along the way, they passed several vehicles that had pulled off on the side of the road to snap some pictures.

Lorelei tried to keep watch on Dax from the corner of

her eye when they reached the bluff. Yet another breathtaking view, but she doubted Dax could appreciate it. Still, it was a lot safer now than it had been all those years ago. Nola and Wyatt were responsible for that. They'd donated a lot of money to improve the road, and soon there would even be a memorial park nearby that would commemorate Griff's short life.

"I had an argument with Griff right before he died," Dax said, breaking the silence. "That sort of thing stays with you."

"Yes," she agreed and hoped what she was about to say didn't make the memories worse for him. "So did I."

He whipped toward her for a quick glance before nailing his attention back to the curvy road. "You argued with Griff?"

"More or less. I yelled at him because he'd broken up with my sister Lily and she was an emotional mess. I took it upon myself to tell Griff that I didn't care for the way he handled things, especially since Lily and he had dated for years. I thought she deserved better from him."

"And how'd Griff take that?" Dax asked.

"He agreed with me, said he was sorry and left. The next day, I heard he'd died." She had to pause. "So, yes, that sort of thing stays with you."

"Griff didn't end his life because of anything you said to him," Dax quickly pointed out.

That was kind of him to say. And she supposed it was the truth. Only recently everyone had learned that Griff had died because he hadn't been able to cope with the ALS diagnosis he'd recently gotten. That had probably been the reason he'd ended things with Lily and driven off that cliff. Still, it had felt as if she'd played a part in what had happened to him. Dax was so right about that staying with you.

They both seemed to hold their breaths until they got past the deadly spot on the bluff, and Dax continued to drive on the country road. She could already see signs of the land being cleared and prepped for the park.

"About that phone call you overheard, in the barn," Dax volunteered several moments later, "that's sort of a 'hornet's nest' deal for me."

Lorelei definitely hadn't expected him to bring up the subject since it obviously bothered him, and she wasn't sure if by bringing it up that meant he wanted to talk about it. She decided to settle for saying what sounded like a supportive but no pressure, "I see."

"Miranda's not a lover," he continued, obviously answering one question she had when she'd heard him say the woman's name. "She's the grown daughter of someone I was once involved with."

Lorelei stared at him, mentally doing the math. Dax was barely thirty so if this ex had a grown daughter, she must have been older than him.

"Miranda's mother, Joy Jackson, has some mental health issues," he explained, and Lorelei didn't think it was her imagination that he was picking and choosing his words. Leaving things out as well. "When Joy's having a bad day, she often wants to see me so Miranda tries to intervene and make that happen so that she doesn't have to do the bad days solo with her mom."

I can't get involved in this. Can't. That's what Dax had told Miranda, and even now with his words echoing in Lorelei's head, she could still hear the pain in his voice.

"Joy was important to you?" she asked, carefully choosing her own words.

He stayed quiet a long time, the somber mood in the truck clashing with the scenery speeding past outside the window, and Lorelei was so sorry she'd pushed for any additional info.

"She made herself important to me," Dax finally said. "Then, she tried to take over my life."

The last word had barely left his mouth when Lorelei saw the shift in his expression and body language. He was back to being the rodeo star, and she suspected that role covered up a multitude of truths. Heck, she'd done the same for many years when she'd tried to forget what Julian had done to her. How frightened and beaten down he'd made her feel. Maybe it was the same for Dax with Joy.

Dax drove through the pearl-colored gates of the cemetery. Yes, pearl. It was yet something else Ophelia Dayton had insisted on so it would be a reminder of the heavenly pearly gates where she firmly believed her fellow deceased would be accompanying her.

Apparently, Ophelia had also believed those deceased would get many visitors since the parking lot was huge. And empty. She was thankful for that and definitely hadn't wanted to interrupt any time the Fords were spending here.

"It's there." Lorelei pointed to the right side of the cemetery, and then she silently cursed when she looked down at her shoes. When she'd dressed to get herself into the mood for work, she hadn't taken into account that she'd be trekking through a dirt and gravel path.

"Here," Dax said, taking hold of her arm when she took the first wobbling step. "Never been out here before. In fact, I've never been to a cemetery."

"Never?" She hadn't meant to blurt that out.

"Never," he verified, tightening his grip on her when she teetered again on the blasted heels. "I was seven when my folks died, but they were cremated so no burial. I had strep throat and a high fever for Griff's burial. Added to that, I was pissed off at the world, Griff included, so even if I hadn't been sick, I probably would have just gone off somewhere and sulked."

Lorelei had been at that particular funeral, mainly to give some support to Lily who was beyond broken. Of course, her sister had recovered, more or less. Less since Lily had gotten married shortly thereafter in what even Lily agreed was a rebound thing. More because Lily had divorced the rebound guy, bought a horse ranch and was raising her daughter there. Life went on.

Well, except for those here and all the other cemeteries of Last Ride.

"My father died when I was two," Lorelei said as they took the final path toward Valerie's tombstone. "I obviously don't remember him, but I do try to get out to his grave every month. I visit Griff's grave, too."

"What? Why?" Dax had the same blurting tone that she'd had with her *never?*

Lorelei shrugged. "Guilt."

"It's the guilt that keeps me away," Dax muttered, causing her to look at him again. "Seeing his name on the tombstone would be like rubbing it in that I hadn't seen what was going on in Griff's life. If I had, if I'd known about his ALS diagnosis, I could have talked him out of doing what he did."

"You couldn't have," she assured him. "From everything that's come out recently, Griff had made up his mind."

Dax made a sound to indicate he didn't quite buy that, and Lorelei didn't have a chance to convince him otherwise because he stopped. That's when she realized they were right in front of Valerie's grave. It hadn't been that hard to pick out since it was the most recent one in the cemetery, and it still looked new.

"Nice headstone," he commented. He let go of her and slid his hands into his pockets.

Lorelei had upgraded it since Ophelia's fund only paid for the basics, but she'd wanted Stellie's birth mother to have something much better than basic. That's why Lorelei had chosen one in bronze, and she'd had the image of a mother holding a baby engraved on it.

"I hope to hell someone went to her funeral," he added.

"There were about thirty people. We waited until Stellie was six weeks old to hold the graveside service because I thought she should be here. I know she was too young to be aware of what was going on," Lorelei quickly tacked on to that. "But I kept thinking if Dana's…Valerie's and my situations had been reversed, I would want my daughter there for my farewell."

"Yeah," was all he said, and because that sounded as if he was climbing deeper and deeper into this guilt pool, Lorelei went ahead and took out her phone so she could take a couple of photos.

Lorelei didn't even have time to put her phone away before it rang, and she saw the Unknown Caller on the screen. "Probably spam," she muttered, not answering it. Seconds later, though, she saw that the caller had left a voice mail. She clicked on it to listen.

And it felt as if a truck had slammed into her.

Because the message was from Julian.

"Hi, Lorelei," he greeted.

His voice had a sickening sweet tone that brought back an avalanche of flashbacks.

"Just a heads-up," the message said. "Some photos of you have surfaced, and my client will definitely be using them in his petition for custody of his daughter. I guess it's true what they say about nothing ever being lost or deleted from the internet. Good luck keeping your squeaky-clean image when people get a look at these."

CHAPTER FOURTEEN

DAX HAD OFTEN thought that squeaky-clean images were way overrated. After all, why the hell care what people thought, especially people who made it a habit of gobbling up dirty gossip as if it were premium chocolate? He still pretty much felt that way, but it was obvious that Lorelei didn't.

Obvious, too, that her dick of an ex, Julian, was an even bigger dick than Dax had thought he was. A surprise. Since Dax had already assumed Aaron's dickhood was monumental and unmatched. But being a dick didn't necessarily mean you were stupid, and Julian had certainly known how to send an arrow straight to Lorelei's heart by locating those pictures of when she'd been in college.

Julian hadn't stopped with just locating them, though. Nope. As more proof of his dickhood, he'd not only sent them to all the lawyers involved in this custody battle, he had also made sure they were posted on social media. By now, everyone in Last Ride, and possibly the world, had seen photos of a drunk Lorelei, wearing just her skimpy bra and panties while dancing on a table.

Dax hadn't asked her anything about the photos, and she hadn't volunteered anything other than a dozen or so variations of "I'm so sorry." But this violation was no doubt eating away at her and had played big-time into Stellie and her leaving. They were now back at Lorelei's house where he hoped like the devil that she was getting the emotional support she needed from her mom and sisters. Dax had called Evangeline to make sure Lorelei wouldn't be alone, and the woman had assured him she wouldn't be, that she'd be staying with her daughter.

That was good.

What wasn't good was that Lorelei wasn't taking his calls and only responding to his texts with emoji. Whenever he'd messaged, asking how she was, she'd sent him a thumbs-up. He had no choice but to take that for now and give her the space that she clearly needed. But he'd also advised Sophia to file a harassment suit against Aaron and Julian for posting those photos.

Figuring he needed his own space to think this through, Dax climbed into the chute to test drive the ranch's newest trained bull, Thunder. A simple handle, but Mike had assured him that Thunder lived up to his name with the deep rumbling snorts he made.

And he did.

Even before Dax's butt landed on the bull's back, Thunder was making plenty of noise with those protesting snorts. Dax went through the hand-wrap routine but not the "bull rub" steadying because he wanted to see just how solid and high this agitated big boy could kick.

The answer was very solid and very high.

Like all rodeo bulls, Thunder obviously didn't approve of his current situation, and he twisted, kicked, snorted and bucked. Because one particularly rough buck rattled Dax's brain a bit, he lost count of the time, but he thought he lasted about six seconds before Thunder sent him flying. Then, crashing. He hit hard and fast, emphasis on hard. The impact jolted through every part of his body.

Every part.

And that made it difficult to scramble out of the way when Thunder turned and came after him. Thankfully, Mike and the other trainers were right there to distract the bull and give Dax a chance to do a limping run to the fence. He scrambled over it as fast as he could. Which wasn't especially fast.

"Three seconds," Mike called out to him.

Three? That was it? Three measly seconds? Yeah, his brain had obviously been rattled for him to be that far off. Of course, so few seconds was great for rodeo competition because it meant Thunder would give any rider a run for his money. But Dax had always been better than just "any" rider. Even with Thunder's superior moves, he should have lasted at least five or six seconds.

Using his hat to knock off the dust from his clothes, Dax glanced at Mike as the trainer approached. "Please tell me you're not thinking about riding Thunder or Hell Raiser for the Last Ride Charity Rodeo?"

Well, it would be a challenge, and Dax liked challenges. Added to that, Sunset Creek didn't use easy bulls for rodeo events. If the bull's temperament wasn't suited, he was moved on to other ranches for breed stock.

"Still deciding about that," Dax let him know, causing Mike to groan. Since Mike knew him well, he knew that Thunder or Hell Raiser was exactly the sort of bull that Dax would choose for that particular event.

Dax was about to shuck off the chaps before trying to walk off the pain, but he spotted the sleek silver car pulling to a stop in front of the house. The vehicle didn't belong to anyone he knew, and he wasn't expecting company. However, with Stellie and Lorelei gone from the ranch, the gate was open so whoever the heck this was could have just driven through.

Dax left on the chaps and made his way toward their visitor just as the guy got out of his car. One look at him and Dax cursed.

Julian.

He recognized the dick from the photos he'd seen when he'd done internet searches on him. Julian was wearing a pale gray suit over his bulky "football star" build. Bulk that hadn't turned to fat so that meant he probably worked out. All those muscles twisted at Dax because Julian had used that strength when he'd hit Lorelei.

Dax wanted to tear off his arms and shove them up the guy's ass.

"You're trespassing," Dax informed him.

Julian flashed him a smile even though there was clearly nothing to smile about. "I'm here just to give you an update on the legal proceedings. I thought you'd want to know since you've made the erroneous paternity claim."

Dax wanted to tear off his legs, too, maybe his ears as well, and he had to fight to hang on to a temper that rarely bubbled up for him. But it was sure as hell bubbling up now.

"You're trespassing," Dax repeated, and he kept his hard, narrowed eyes nailed to the idiot as he stalked toward him. Dax made sure to look as menacing as he could. Which wasn't hard to do. Because he felt a whole of lot menacing when it came to this piece of shit.

Julian lifted his hands, probably in some sort of "suit yourself, I come in peace" gesture. "I thought you'd want to know that my client and I are trying to speed things along now that we've uncovered some financial irregularities on the Fords."

Dax hadn't known about that, but when his phone dinged with a text and he saw it was from Matt, he figured the message was to let him know of this latest development.

A development that Julian obviously had rushed right over to gloat about. This was likely an attempt to mark his territory, too. Like a dog pissing on a tree. But Dax had already marked this territory for himself.

"The Fords' petition for custody will obviously be harmed with these irregularities," Julian went on.

Dax went on, too. He kept walking straight toward the man, and when he was only a few feet away, Julian backed up and lifted his hands even higher.

"Physical violence won't help your case," Julian pointed out, adding a nervous laugh.

Julian tried to keep up his cocky tone, but Dax caught that flash of fear in his eyes. So, the dick was a coward, too, especially since he outweighed Dax by a good forty pounds and was a couple of inches taller.

"You're trespassing," Dax growled.

Oh, yeah. It was a growl all right that would have given Thunder a run for his money. Again, not hard to do because Dax was feeling a whole lot of hatred and really pissed-off anger for his visitor.

"I'm here to talk to you in a reasonable, calm way," Julian argued, but he got back in his car and lowered his window to say the rest of what he'd apparently come here to say. "I'm advising you to drop the harassment charges against my client for releasing the photographs of the woman who's illegally keeping his child from him."

There were so many things wrong with that statement. Lorelei wasn't doing anything illegal. Until someone proved the adoption was fraudulent—which Dax believed they wouldn't—Stellie was hers. She had a right to refuse to let Aaron see the baby because the man hadn't and couldn't prove he was the father. However, Aaron had proved he could be a belligerent, bullying ass, and that was the reason Lorelei had opted to keep the man away from the baby.

"You're trespassing," Dax repeated, not even bothering to address all the crap that Julian had just slung around. "I can either escort you to jail or have the cops come out. Choose wisely," he warned him, kicking his scowl up a couple of notches.

Dax saw a flash of anger go through Julian's icy blue eyes. Anger that he quickly reined in as he started the engine. "Just because Valerie cheated on her husband, it doesn't mean her husband didn't father her baby."

True, but the reverse was also true. Being married to someone didn't mean you'd been the one to get her pregnant.

"You didn't even know Valerie," Julian went on, and there was disgust in his tone now. He was clearly trying to get a rise out of Dax. Not very smart, though, since Dax was already plenty riled up. "A one-night stand. That's all you had with her. Heck, I'll bet you didn't even know that she didn't want children, that she was terrified of being pregnant."

Dax studied him a moment, trying to suss out if that was the truth. Hell. It was. He could see that from the smug-ass look in the man's eyes.

"Terrified," Julian emphasized, "because when she was a child, her favorite aunt died in childbirth." He rearranged his expression, no doubt to try to convey how tragic that was. "Imagine how horrified she must have been when she died alone here in Last Ride."

Well, hell. That arrow hit its mark. Right in Dax's guilt-ridden heart. Because Valerie must have, indeed, been scared. Still, she hadn't tried to contact him. She'd just stolen his toothbrush and kept away from him, not giving him the chance to make things right.

And that was another level of guilt.

Because Dax wasn't sure how he could have made this situation right. If Valerie had simply wanted child support, she could have just told him. Ditto for telling him if she wanted him to be part of Stellie's life. But he'd gotten nothing from her. Nothing but the guilt and regret, anyway.

"From everything I've read, you're at the tail end of your so-called career," Julian said, yanking Dax's attention back to him. "Whatever will you do?"

Seriously? The asshole had now gone smirking third grade on him. Oh, well. Dax threw third grade right back at him.

"What do rich young cowboys do? Oh, yeah," Dax said before the idiot could take it as a real question. "We go on to do other things. Non-slimy things where we don't try to dick people over. You've got five seconds to get off my property, and that's your final warning."

Julian's already hard jaw went even harder, but he tamped down his "elementary school" attitude enough to get his butt out of there. Dax stood, watching him leave while he took out his phone to press Matt's number.

"I just got a visit from Julian Martin," Dax said the moment Matt answered.

"Yeah, I texted you about him. Well, about Aaron and him. They claim to have discovered that Valerie's parents made some questionable payments that might be illegal."

Dax drew in a long breath. "Is it true?"

"To be determined, but Julian and Aaron are pressing it to try to get the Fords to back off with their custody claim."

"Too bad they aren't pressing to get the DNA results that would prove Aaron's not the father," Dax pointed out.

Matt made a quick sound of agreement. "They'll do a whole lot of stalling on that, which tells me they know the results won't work in their favor."

"So, why do it?" Dax countered.

"My guess is to try to wear Lorelei, the Fords and you down. Maybe they believe if they create enough stink that everyone will back off, and he'll get the baby. The Fords might even try to offer him some kind of settlement to get him to go away."

The wearing down was definitely happening. It was a pain in the ass to have to deal with this sort of thing. But Dax had no intention of giving in to Aaron, and he knew for a fact that Lorelei felt the same way.

"Speaking of Lorelei," Matt continued a moment later. "How is she?"

"You've seen the pictures?" he asked, and when Matt made a sound of agreement, Dax added, "She's back at her place, laying low and probably trying to figure out how to show her face again in town. If I knew it wouldn't screw around with any of the custody stuff, I'd post naked pictures of myself just to get the gossips off her back."

Matt chuckled. "Best to hold off doing something like that but don't be surprised if Aaron and Julian don't already have some R- or X-rated pictures of you. They might be holding back on those so they can use them when the paternity test doesn't come back in their favor."

True enough, and Dax figured with his past, there could be plenty of such photo options out there. But that got him thinking about what there might be for Julian. Dax had a quick debate with himself as to how much to tell Matt, and he decided to go for broke.

"Lorelei won't care for me spilling this so keep it quiet,

but the asshole Julian assaulted and stalked her when she was in college," Dax explained.

Silence. Then, some cursing. "Please tell me she filed charges."

"No. But it shook her, Matt. You should have seen how pale she got when she found out Julian was repping Aaron. And FYI, I don't think that's a coincidence. I think Aaron dug around until he found out Lorelei's past connection to Julian, and that's why he hired him."

"Agreed," Matt quickly said. "He probably thought by rattling her, she wouldn't be able to stay on top of this, that she might even back down."

Dax made his own hasty agreement to that. "Here's a thought. Since Julian did that to Lorelei, I'm betting she wasn't the first or the last woman he hit and stalked. Any chance you can poke around and find something like that?"

Or better yet, this might be something he could hand over to Derwin Parkman and the Snoops. Dax wouldn't have to tell Derwin about Julian assaulting Lorelei. He could just frame it that Julian might have had a connection—a bad one—to Valerie and the Last Ride Society tombstone research.

With all the free time Derwin and his club had on their hands, they could possibly find some dirt on the piece of shit lawyer. Added to that, Derwin might be an oddball, but Dax could aim the man in the direction he wanted this pseudo investigation to go. A direction where if anything came up about Lorelei, Dax would insist Derwin keep it to himself. Since Derwin owed him a couple of favors for getting him rodeo tickets, Dax figured he'd play by those rules.

In addition, Dax could ask Derwin to make noise while he looked for the dirt on Julian. That would get back to Julian and rattle his cage some along with giving him a little payback as to how it felt to have his privacy invaded. It was a win-win as far as Dax was concerned.

"Let me see if I can find anything," Matt suggested. He paused again. "You're sure you want to get in the mud and muck with Aaron and his lawyer?"

"Positive." Dax couldn't say that fast enough. He didn't mind playing dirty. Anything to make them pay for what they were trying to do to Lorelei.

He mentally stopped. Cursed. Well, hell. Since when had Lorelei become his top priority? Apparently, right now. Because no way was he going to let the two dickheads get away with going after her.

CHAPTER FIFTEEN

LORELEI KEPT TRYING to envision the metaphorical "big girl" panties she was wearing while she worked in her office at the Glass Hatter. It was better than envisioning the real "barely there" panties she'd had on in those photos that Julian had found.

Of course, he likely hadn't had to look far to find them since he'd almost certainly been the one to take them. Lorelei had no proof of that, of course, but she was positive the shots had been done when Julian and she had still been together. Pictures taken at a party where she had indeed gotten drunk. She couldn't blame that part on Julian, but she recalled him encouraging her to strip to her undies when everyone at the party had decided to go for a swim in the frat house pool.

It didn't matter that the party debauchery had been limited to drinking, dancing and swimming. The photos had been taken, and they made her look like the partying wild child she wasn't.

The sound of Stellie's giggling shoved away some of her dismal thoughts, and Lorelei glanced up to see her daughter laughing over a book about talking horses that Hilda was reading to her in the playroom Lorelei had converted from the storage room next to her office. Her little girl could always lighten her mood. Always.

When Stellie was just a newborn, Lorelei had brought

her to work with her every day so she'd set up the playroom with a crib and rocking chair. Those items were still there, but over the months, she'd added lots of toys and books to occupy Stellie and Hilda on the days that the nanny accompanied her as well. Lorelei had also taken out part of the wall between the two rooms and added barn doors so that when the doors were open, she'd have an unobstructed view of Stellie. She closed them only when she was on the phone or having a meeting.

Today, she wanted the doors wide-open so she could keep an eye on her baby. She doubted that Aaron or Julian would just burst in and try to take her, but it certainly felt as if she were under siege, and she wanted her baby close. That's why Lorelei had asked Hilda to bring Stellie into the shop for the day.

Her first day back at work in the shop in a week and a half.

She was done hiding out both at Sunset Creek and her house. Done with the regrets over having kissed Dax. But that was yet something else she wouldn't be dwelling on since it seemed way too "wild child" for her. That's why she'd put on those "big girl" panties, straightened her spine and gone home. Now, she had taken the next step and was at work. The sooner people saw her, the sooner they'd get past those looks she was getting. Some judgmental. Some pity. And a couple of guys had winked at her.

Three had called her for dates.

She'd turned them down, of course, but it was obviously going to be a while before her reputation was restored. Maybe more than a while before she pushed aside the memory of Dax's kiss that she had to remind herself, again, not to dwell on.

Lorelei forced her attention back on the supply orders

and listened to the chatter of customers in the shop. Business was booming, but she suspected that was because people were coming in to get a look at her now that they'd seen her nearly in the buff. Apparently, those would-be gawkers felt guilty enough that they'd made purchases. If this kept up, she would need to hire another assistant and double up on the inventory.

Her phone dinged with a text, and before she even looked at the screen, she knew it would be from Dax. Since she'd left the ranch, he'd made a habit of texting her two or three times a day just to see how Stellie and she were doing. She kept her replies short, mainly because she didn't want to get into a discussion about how things were definitely not okay. No need to spell that out for Dax or anyone else who knew her.

Got a sore butt from a bull ride, Dax texted. The bull won this time. How about you? You winning today?

Lorelei nearly sent another thumbs-up reply, but this time she opted for an actual response. Absolutely, she lied.

She was winning at some things, anyway. Having a wonderful daughter, a supportive family and increased sales revenue. Everything else about her life was up in the air.

Including this annoying ache in her body for Dax.

Lorelei was about to put her phone away, but Dax texted again. How are your visits going with the Fords?

It didn't surprise her that he would know about the daily visits the couple had made to see Stellie. Added to that, the couple had visited the baby here in the shop just an hour or so earlier.

News of that shop visit had no doubt hit the gossip mill within seconds after Greg and Miriam had come in. Nosy people who'd timed the visit would have passed along the info that they'd stayed about a half hour. And during that time, the Fords hadn't mentioned Aaron or the custody fight. Lorelei hadn't brought it up, either. She'd just let the pair spend some time with their granddaughter and agreed they could come back that afternoon to bring Stellie some new books.

They go well enough, she replied to Dax. No lie there at least. The Fords had been cordial and, like her, riding on the shame train because of what Aaron and Julian had uncovered about them.

Lorelei didn't know all the details as to exactly what had been uncovered, but it apparently had to do with accusations of paying employees under the table. Yes, that was a crime, but Lorelei hated that Aaron would try to use it to prove they weren't fit grandparents, all so it would bolster—in his mind, anyway—his chances of getting his hands on Stellie.

This time Dax was the one to send her a thumbs-up emoji, but she had to wonder if he was moping as much as she was right now. Probably. After all, he'd said he wanted the adoption to hold, that she should be the one raising Stellie. So, everything Aaron and Julian were doing was putting Dax's wishes in jeopardy.

Once again, Lorelei went to put her phone away, but this time it rang, and she saw Asher Parkman's name on the screen. Finally! It had been nearly a week since she'd tried to reach him.

"Mr. Parkman," she said the moment she answered. "Thank you for returning my call."

"Of course, and I'm sorry it's taken me this long to get back to you. I've been on vacation."

Lorelei wanted to start hitting him with a bunch of questions, but she went the polite route instead. "I hope you had a good time."

"I did. Now, what did you want to talk to me about?" Obviously, Asher was ready to cut to the chase, and that suited her just fine.

"Millie mentioned that Dana Smith, AKA Valerie Ford Marcel, asked her about a lawyer here in Last Ride and that Millie referred her to you." Lorelei paused, gathered her thoughts. "Anyway, I was wondering if you could tell me why she wanted to see a lawyer."

Of course, Asher didn't jump to answer that, and Lorelei heard him sigh. "The woman I knew as Dana Smith was a client so I can't or won't discuss anything about her that comes under client-attorney privilege."

"But she's dead," Lorelei pointed out.

"And that doesn't change things for me. Now, if she'd tried to use my legal services for the purpose of committing a crime or fraud, then the privilege could be broken. That wasn't the case."

She'd worried this would be his response, but since this could be important, she pressed harder. "Look, if Dana went to you for something like a will, then it could be important for her daughter's inheritance."

Lorelei didn't care squat about an inheritance, but if Valerie had, indeed, left a will, she might have spelled out her wishes. Specifically, she might have said she didn't want Aaron to have the child. Or she might have named Dax as Stellie's father. If so, Dax and she could use that to fight Aaron.

Again, Asher stayed quiet for a long time. "I won't get into specifics, but I can tell you that my client had questions about custodial rights for her then unborn child. If you want more, then have your lawyer file a request, and I'll take it under consideration after I've spoken with my client's next of kin. It's my understanding they're staying in Last Ride."

"Yes, her parents are at the inn." Lorelei didn't push for more because this was at least an opening. Asher might turn down the request for more info, but if the Fords pushed, they might soon learn what plans Valerie had for Stellie.

And that caused an icy chill to go through Lorelei.

Because what if Valerie had wanted Stellie to go to her parents? What if that had been Valerie's life backup plan?

Sweet heaven.

This was a Pandora's box that she maybe should have kept closed. But it was like that blasted butt photo. She'd had to know then, and whether she wanted to face it or not, she needed to know about Valerie's last wishes, too.

"And my client's husband?" Asher pressed. "He's at the inn as well?"

Crap. Lorelei certainly hadn't forgotten that Aaron fell into that "next of kin" category as well. "Yes, but Valerie was estranged from her husband. When you speak to her parents, they'll tell you that the marriage wasn't a happy one."

"That may very well be, but unless my client divorced him, he was still her spouse. He'd have to approve of any and all information I release."

Lorelei mentally repeated that crap. Because there was no way Aaron would share any info unless it benefited him.

Sighing, she managed to mutter a thank-you to Asher before she ended the call, and then Lorelei sat at her desk, forcing herself to slow her breathing and not panic. Hearing Stellie's babbling helped, and she focused on it. After she'd settled herself, she'd go into the playroom and hold her. That would help more than anything, but she didn't want Stellie to see her like this.

She thought of texting Dax. Or calling him. For reasons she didn't want to dive into, she thought maybe hearing his voice would help with her nerves. Then again, that was only because of the lust. Lust could leap right to the front of thoughts and cancel out everything else. But lust had a price, too, since it didn't necessarily just go away when it was no longer useful.

After a few minutes and some signatures on the orders she'd been working on, Lorelei texted Sophia to get her started on that request to Asher. As usual, Sophia responded right away to let her know she'd get right on it.

Lorelei refused to dwell on the possibility that such a request would give her bad news. Instead, she got up from her desk so she could go into the playroom. But she stopped when she heard a voice. Not Dax and his lust-inducing drawl.

Julian.

"Hi, I need to speak to Lorelei," she heard him say to Misty.

All conversation stopped in the shop, and that was because everyone in there knew who this man was. Or rather they knew he was Aaron's slimy lawyer who was trying to screw Dax and her over. They didn't know about her past with said slimeball.

Lorelei didn't wait for Misty to have to come up with a response. It was "big girl panty" time again, and even if she felt as if she might throw up, she intended to face Julian head-on. She'd given herself that cowering time at the ranch and her house, but that was over, even if she had to stuff down her fears and plaster on a fake "I'm just fine" facade.

Misty was still hemming and hawing on how to answer Julian. And more. Misty looked shell-shocked and terrified. Maybe because she thought Julian might be there with a court order to try to take Stellie. But if Julian and Aaron had managed to get such an order, Sophia would have given Lorelei a heads-up.

While every eye in the room watched her, Lorelei strode toward the front. She was glad she'd put on one of her favorite tops and a skirt. A rich turquoise color that she'd paired with cobalt heels. It made her look professional, cool and sleek, and right now appearances were the best thing she had going for her. That, and knowing if she buckled or fell apart, it would only add to the gossip about her. That was a strong motivation to stay, well, strong.

"Julian," she greeted, going for a tone that hit between detached and downright chilly. She sometimes had to use that when dealing with rude suppliers.

"Lorelei," he greeted back, obviously going for a tone that hit between snake oil salesman and butthole. He succeeded, and just in case she hadn't known he was a butthole, he flashed her an oily grin and slid his gaze over her in an "undressing you" gesture.

She slid her gaze over him as if he were particularly smelly cow dung. She succeeded, too, because he pulled back on that fake grin.

It was the first time she'd seen him since college days, thirteen years ago, and she wasn't sure if the years had been kind to him or if he had paid for all that body and face maintenance.

"I was hoping we could talk," he said. "Maybe I can buy you a cup of coffee."

She paused, as if giving that some thought and then said, "No." With that message delivered, Lorelei turned and headed back toward her office.

Of course, Julian was right on her heels, and because she hadn't closed the door to the playroom, she stopped when she was still several yards away from her office and eased back around to face him.

"No," she repeated, and because that ignited his temper, Lorelei leaned in and lowered her voice to a whisper. "If you try to hit me again, I will ram my knee straight into your balls. It'll be so hard that you won't be able to sit for a month. Understand?" She had to ask that last part once she got her teeth unclenched.

"I understand you're the same bitch you were way back when," he whispered back.

Oh, yes. She had gotten to him all right, and it caused some of those heart cracks to mend just a little. "Good. Then, there's no reason for you to hang around and try to talk to a bitch."

He reached for her when she started to move. Big mistake, and Lorelei was already positioning her knee for some ball-busting when the front door flew open and Dax came in. Not especially hurrying. It was more of a purposeful moseying, and when his narrowed eyes landed on Julian, he moseyed in their direction.

Lorelei silently groaned because she didn't need two men duking it out in a glass shop. The ball-busting wouldn't have caused much damage because it would have dropped Julian to his knees. Flying fists, though, could break a lot of stuff, and that was just the tip of the iceberg of concerns. A fight might upset Stellie and cause Dax to be arrested.

In fact, Aaron might have sent Julian here to pick a fight, hoping he could get Dax or her in some kind of legal hot water. Because even if Julian deserved ball kicks and punches, it wouldn't look good to a custody judge if Dax and she were involved in a nasty altercation. Aaron, on the other hand, would come out smelling like the proverbial rose since he wasn't anywhere near this.

"I'm glad you're here," Lorelei said to Dax after she did some quick thinking. Unfortunately, it wasn't smart thinking.

Because she kissed him.

Not a "steamy open-mouth" kind of kiss, but, hey, this was Dax, so there was plenty of hotness. So much hotness in fact that her heartbeat kicked up, drumming in her ears so she couldn't hear the reactions of Julian or anybody else in the shop. She couldn't see them, either, because her eyelids had drifted down, obviously cooperating with this whole distraction that didn't feel much like a distraction at all. It felt like the real deal.

Dax didn't go stiff with surprise. Didn't back off. As if it were second nature to him to get unexpected kisses, he slipped his arm around her waist, drew her closer in an ever so slick and gentle move that she hadn't even known it was coming.

But, mercy, she felt it.

No way could she tamp down the response of having his body do that dirty, slippery slide against hers. Except maybe this wasn't even dirty to him. Maybe this was just the norm for someone who clearly knew exactly what to do with his mouth.

Lorelei finally came to her senses—not easily—and she eased back from him. There was heat in his sizzling green eyes, but she detected some questions there, too. Or rather one question.

What the heck?

Then, he slid his gaze from her to Julian and got his answer. All in all, it had been a hugely successful distraction. Neither Julian nor Dax looked ready to throw punches, but Julian's stunned expression made it seem as if he'd been on the receiving end of a couple of particularly hard right hooks.

"I'm glad I'm here, too," Dax said in his "cocky rodeo star" voice.

If it hadn't been for the tense set of his jaw and the tightened muscles in his arms, she might have thought he'd gotten totally lost in the heat of that kiss. But no. He was still braced to do some butt-kicking if it came down to that.

"You were just leaving," Dax told Julian. It wasn't a question or a request.

Julian huffed, put his hands on his hips. "I see what's going on here. You two are pretending to be together to help with the custody fight."

Dax smiled, leaned in closer to Julian and whispered, "Lorelei and I don't have to pretend. Feel that?" He circled his index finger in the air. "That's heat. Can't be faked, can't be all for show."

Julian opened his mouth, no doubt to argue that it was BS, but he closed his mouth after volleying some glances at them. Apparently, Julian didn't believe it was BS, after all, because every muscle in his face turned to iron. The expression of a man who'd just gotten a nonviolent butt-kicking.

With the anger shooting off Julian in hot waves, one of his fiery glances landed over her shoulder, and when she followed his gaze, Lorelei realized he had seen Stellie, who was playing on the floor with Hilda. Hilda must have seen it, too, because she quickly got up and shut the door.

"So, that's the baby," Julian said, his arrogance and venom returning in spades. "She looks like Aaron."

"Think so?" Dax said. In contrast, there wasn't a trace of venom in his tone. Oh, but there was some cockiness. He took out his phone and pulled up a side by side photo on his phone. "That's me as a baby," he explained, tapping the picture on the left. "That's Stellie." He tapped the right one.

The resemblance was, well, striking. Sweet heaven, seeing that left no doubt in her mind that he was Stellie's father.

Dax put away his phone and met Julian eye to eye. "Why don't you peddle your mind games and bullshit elsewhere." Again, it wasn't a question. "I've heard the town council is looking to hire someone to clean the public toilets on the fairgrounds."

With that, Dax slid his arm around her waist again, and without the least bit of hurrying, he led her into her office. He shut the door in Julian's face.

Lorelei held her breath, waiting for a belligerent Julian to crash through the door. Or crash into something else in the shop. But he didn't. Several crawling moments later, she heard his footsteps heading out of the shop. A few seconds after that, the gasps and urgent gossipy whispers started. Soon, very soon, it would be all over town that Aaron's lawyer was a hothead jerk.

And that Dax and she had kissed.

Of course, some of that gossip would be speculation as to how much those kisses had been for show, but Lorelei figured Dax had made his point about it being impossible to totally fake that kind of heat.

It couldn't be faked.

That meant she was going to have to figure out how to deal with it. Either way she went could be a mistake. If she just kept pretending it wasn't there and fought it tooth and nail, then she was going to have to live in a state of high frustration. But if she gave in to it, things would lead to its natural course.

Sex.

Then, there would be consequences for that, too. And

no, she wasn't solely thinking "incredible orgasm" consequences but rather how this would affect them down the
road.

"You okay?" Dax asked.

That's when she realized she'd been staring at him. Not
staring in an "I'm upset" kind of way. But looking at him
with what was almost certainly a firestorm of heat in her
eyes.

She nodded and then swallowed hard so she could clear
the obstruction from her throat and speak. "How did you
know Julian was here?"

He studied her a moment longer as if he were trying to
figure out if that was truly what was on her mind. It wasn't.
But it was something she wanted to know.

"I was just up the street at the feedstore and saw his car,"
Dax explained. "And I knew it was his car because he paid
me a visit at the ranch. Nothing happened," he quickly assured her. "He was just giving me a firsthand display of
how much of a jackass he can be."

Dax made it seem as if that'd been nothing, but she was
learning the subtle nuances of his expression, and something was bothering him. She didn't have to wait long to
find out what that was because he groaned and then bit off
what would no doubt have been some profanity. Profanity
he'd held back because Stellie was nearby in the playroom.

"The SOB told me that Valerie didn't want children and
was afraid of being pregnant," Dax explained. "I checked
with the Fords, and they verified that. Valerie's aunt died
in childbirth, and it rightfully spooked her."

Lorelei mentally went through every word of that, and
she heard the guilt in Dax's voice. Saw it on his face. She
didn't bother to remind him that Valerie had chosen to carry

her baby because Stellie was proof of that. However, she could make one point clear.

"You didn't even know Valerie was pregnant, and there's nothing you could have done to stop her from dying."

"I could have stopped her from getting pregnant by not having sex with her in the first place," he blurted out, and then he groaned, moved away from her.

Lorelei countered his moving away by stepping in front of him and taking hold of his face to force eye contact. "The sex was consensual." She had zero doubts about that. "And since neither Valerie nor you have crystal balls, you couldn't have known what would happen. Playing what-ifs changes nothing, and what's done is done."

She hoped that sank in. Because it was the truth. It was also a reminder that sometimes heat and attraction often made it very hard to do the sensible thing. She was facing that big-time right now with Dax. Facing, too, that there was another whammy of not so good news that he needed to hear.

"Asher Parkman finally got back to me, and he verified that Valerie did see him shortly before she died." She quickly added the rest when she saw some hope spring to Dax's eyes. "However, he wouldn't say what kind of legal service she wanted from him."

The hope vanished, and he looked as if he wanted to spout the curse words he was no doubt thinking.

"Asher played the 'client-attorney privilege' card," Lorelei went on, "but said he'd consider a formal request from Sophia. She's working on it, and I'd planned on contacting the Fords to see if they could give Asher a nudge."

His expression changed again, and this time there was concern. Concern for her, she realized.

"No matter what Valerie said to a lawyer, it doesn't

change what happened," he said, using some of her own words that she'd doled out to comfort him.

Their gazes locked. Held. And the corner of his mouth lifted into that blasted smile that made her feel wobbly.

"No looking back," Dax added. His smile kicked up a notch. "Well, you can look back on that kiss if you want. Do I need to apologize for that?"

She shook her head, maybe a little too fast. "Only if I need to apologize for kissing you first."

His headshake was fast as well, and it made her feel gooey on top of the wobbliness.

"I've never kissed a man I haven't even dated," she grumbled, frustrated with herself. She had way too many important things on her plate without adding lip-lock confessions.

"Hey, I can do something about that," Dax threw out there.

And for some heartbeat-skipping moments, she thought he was going to kiss her again. He didn't.

"Lorelei, will you go out on a date with me?" he asked.

She felt relief that he hadn't fogged her head with that incredible mouth, but she also felt that knee-jerk of worry that this could be a Texas-sized mistake. Apparently, though, it was a mistake she was going to make.

Because Lorelei heard herself say "Yes."

CHAPTER SIXTEEN

DAX KNEW IF he weren't careful, this date with Lorelei could turn into a post-party night of sex. The heat was that high between them. No denying that, but even with the often stupid part of his body urging him that sex would be a stellar idea, Dax intended to take things slow.

Maybe even to a standstill.

Work schedules had helped with that since it'd taken a while for Lorelei and him to figure out a date night that didn't clash with everything else going on in their lives. In Dax's case, it was a one-day rodeo competition in Austin. He'd considered not going to that, but since this was supposed to be his farewell year, he wanted to do the scheduled events so he could go out with a bang.

But work hadn't been the only stalling point to this date. So had all the legal crap that Julian and Aaron kept throwing at them. One stall tactic after another, but Curt had assured Dax that Aaron couldn't stall forever, especially since the delays wouldn't get him what he wanted.

Custody of Stellie.

Sooner or later, Aaron was going to have to concede that he wasn't the child's father and then move on to the next phase of the legal battle. Curt had warned him, though, that Aaron could still press for custody since he'd been married to Valerie at the time she'd given birth. It was a fight that

Aaron would almost certainly lose. However, he could drag it out for a long time, all the while disrupting their lives.

Dax had considered just trying to pay Aaron off. Considered and dismissed it since it wouldn't put an end to the battle. Nope. Aaron would no doubt just keep returning for more cash, using the threat of going after Stellie. It was best just to put a legal end to the threat so they could be rid of Aaron for good.

Gossip was still going strong about Lorelei's college photos, but Dax was certain there'd be something else that would come along to replace it. Something low-down and dirty that Julian would dig up to try to smear anyone who was challenging his client. That could mean more dirt on the Fords who'd been forced to return home to battle Aaron's claims about their illegal business practices. It could mean more dirt on Lorelei, something dredged up from her past. Or something about him. Plenty to dredge up there.

In the meantime, Dax was getting ready for a date.

Yep, he was taking Lorelei to Frankie's First Date Party, and yes, he'd asked her out when their emotions and lust had been running high. But lust and sex had screwed up plenty of things for him in the past, and he couldn't let it screw up his future with Lorelei. Because that in turn could mess up things with Stellie.

Sometime in the past month since he'd found out he was a father, he had come to terms that he would be, well, a father. That would include all the daddy stuff of spending time with Stellie—something he'd already been doing. He'd be there for all the milestone celebrations that used to make him shake his head when he'd heard parents gush about them. Now, he was the one gushing, and he'd be damned if he let Aaron or his asshole lawyer take that away from him.

Or add to the pile of doubts that didn't seem to be diminishing much.

During bad moments, he believed all the gossip about himself. Heck, he admitted plenty of it was true, and it was all those truths that made him wonder just how much he was going to suck at this whole fatherhood deal. Probably a lot.

But during good moments, he could shove aside the gossip and hang on to one simple truth. He didn't have to do the "daddy deal" alone. Lorelei was like his safety net, there to make sure he did the right thing at the right time. There was some peace in that, and he needed to latch on to it to get him through the bad moments.

His phone dinged with the reminder that it was time for him to leave for his date. Not that he would have forgotten it, but he'd set the reminder because he hadn't wanted to leave anything to chance, like getting caught up with a ranch problem or being neck-deep in another legal conversation with his lawyer. It'd been a long time since he'd looked forward this much to a date, and he sure as heck didn't want to be late.

When Dax stepped out of his house to go to his truck, the sky opened up. Not just rain, but there was thunder and lightning, too. The pastures could use it, but Dax had to wonder if Mother Nature was trying to give him a warning to rethink this. Or it could be some kind of reminder to at least keep his jeans zipped. He would. He was certain of that.

Well, almost certain.

With the rain battering his windshield, he drove to Lorelei's, pulling into her driveway as close to the house as he could get. He fished around behind the seat to come up with an umbrella, but before he could even pick it up, the garage door opened, and he saw Lorelei.

Oh, man. He was toast.

Lorelei was wearing "sex against the wall" heels and a snug dress that was nearly the same color as her eyes. That perfect crystal blue. And instead of pulling her blond hair back as she often did, it was now tumbling onto her shoulders.

She held up her finger in a wait gesture and popped open an umbrella she was holding. When he realized she intended to make a dash for the truck, Dax leaned over to open the door for her.

Somehow, she did manage to dash in those heels, and she looked damn graceful while doing it, too. She scrambled inside the truck, bringing in the scent of the rain and something that had clearly been designed to make him notice her. Of course, he'd already noticed her without the addition of whatever perfume or lotion she'd chosen.

"Stellie's already at Wyatt and Nola's for her sleepover," she said, "but since she'll still be awake, we could pop over there for a few minutes if you'd like."

He considered it but then shook his head. "Maybe I can come over tomorrow. Maybe even help you do the nighttime routine and put her to bed."

Dax winced a little because that sounded as if he'd just invited himself into her house. When Lorelei and he would be alone in the house with a sleeping Stellie.

"Of course," Lorelei agreed, though she was probably doing some mental wincing, too.

When the time came for that visit, he wouldn't stay after Stellie had fallen asleep. Best not to serve up that kind of temptation to himself.

"I thought you might cancel," they said in unison.

She smiled, showing some nerves, but even with her obvious uncertainty, that smile was something to see. He nearly told her that he'd like for her to do that more often, but instead he just stayed quiet and enjoyed the view.

"I thought I might cancel," she amended a few seconds later, "but I decided this could be a good thing. Us, spending some time together. And it doesn't have to be a real date. It can be…" She stopped. "Sorry, I babble when I'm nervous."

"Then, it balances out because I usually get quiet when I'm dealing with nerves." He followed that with an obvious silence to let her know they were on the same nerve-filled page. But it was an interesting page, too.

A month ago, before the Stellie bombshell, if someone had told him he'd be lusting over a woman he'd considered an ice princess, he wouldn't have believed it. But he sure as heck believed it now that he'd seen her like this.

Now that he'd kissed her.

So that he wouldn't be tempted to kiss her again, Dax started driving toward Ink, Etc. It wasn't far, only a few blocks away, but he took his time because of the storm and because he wanted this time with Lorelei.

"I thought having Wyatt and Nola keep Stellie for the night," she said, the nerves still in her voice, "would give them good practice since their baby is due next month."

He made a sound of approval, but Dax already knew about the babysitting arrangements because Wyatt had called him to tell him that he'd make sure Aaron or Julian didn't get anywhere near Stellie. He trusted his brother, and yes, it would be good experience for them even though it seemed they were plenty ready for the big event.

Dax was lucky enough to find a parking spot on the street just outside the shop, and because of the pair of large storefront windows, he could see that plenty of guests had already arrived despite the raging storm. He spotted Joe and Millie. Frankie and her husband, Tanner Parkman. Matt and his bride-to-be, Emory, and a local rancher friend, Brody Harrell and his wife, Janessa. Since the theme was to wear the attire of first dates, there was a wide variety of clothes, including 1960s outfits on Alma and Devon Parkman who were in their late seventies.

Frankie had cranked up the music loud enough for the sound of it to make it to the truck. A Rolling Stones song, maybe to go along with Alma and her husband. Mick Jagger was belting out a warning about playing with fire. Good advice. Too bad Dax knew he stood a snowball's chance in hell of listening to that advice and keeping his hands off Lorelei.

"Just how much gossip do you think this will stir up?" she muttered.

"Plenty," he answered honestly.

"Good," she said, surprising him, "because people might finally stop talking about those pictures Julian posted of me."

Again, he stayed honest. "It won't stop that, and I can't tell you how sorry I am about that. If there was something I could do to fix it, I would, but I figure pictures like that have a longer shelf life than say pictures of me. I mean, everybody expects me to be dancing in my underwear."

"Because I'm supposedly squeaky-clean," she muttered, sounding disgusted with herself. "Well, except for getting involved with the wrong man in college and letting him get away with hitting me. Not very squeaky of me."

Dax didn't like hearing Lorelei get down on herself like this. Especially didn't like hearing her take on even a sliver of the blame for what the jerk Julian had done to her.

"Want to hear a story about my non-squeaky past while we wait for a break in the rain?" he threw out there.

That obviously got her attention, and she turned toward him. "A story about Valerie?"

He shook his head. "I've already told you everything there is to know about me and her." Because he'd only been with Valerie a handful of hours. His non-squeaky past story had lasted a hell of a lot longer.

"Does your story have anything to do with your therapy appointments with my mom?" she came out and asked.

It didn't surprise him that she knew about those. Even though Evangeline wouldn't have spilled anything about their sessions, people weren't blind so someone would have seen him coming and going from her office. Even when the comings and goings had been well after duty hours. All it would have taken was one glimpse of him being anywhere around Evangeline's office, and the gossips would have taken it and run with it.

"Some," Dax admitted. "I've heard gossip about my appointments with your mom, and most think it's because of my parents' death. I lost them both when I was seven."

"Yes, I'm sorry," she muttered.

Coming from many, that would have sounded like lip service. It sounded like the real deal from Lorelei. Probably because she'd lost her own father when she hadn't been much older than Stellie, so she knew what it was like to go through life with some seriously important missing pieces.

"Thanks," he said, then paused to figure out how much to say, how much to leave out. He'd leave out plenty, he decided. "After my folks died, my brothers and I had to move here to Last Ride to live with our cousin."

"Maude Muldoon," she provided. "She had a reputation for being a mean woman."

"Oh, she was that and plenty more."

On good days, her abuse was just neglect or the verbal crap. On bad days, the abuse turned to slaps and kicks. He'd definitely leave that out since it might be a trigger for Lorelei's own assault.

"Sometimes, I could soothe Maude," he went on. "Not the 'bull rub' stuff. I didn't know about that then. But just by talking to her and listening to her gripe about whatever had put her in the pissed-off mood. When that didn't work, I dealt with her by not dealing with her. As soon as I was old enough, I stayed out of the house as much as possible and started to run with what many would call a wild crowd. I did plenty of things I'm not proud of. Things that gave me the reputation I have now."

Dax stopped and decided he should have just found a bucket of rocks and bashed it against his head rather than put himself, or Lorelei, through this crappy childhood tale.

"Sorry," he muttered. "All of this was meant to explain that the parts of your non-squeaky past are nothing you should feel guilty about. Because what Julian did to you wasn't your fault." Dax paused, sighed. "But I clearly got off course, and instead of trying to make you feel better, I'm bringing you down."

"No," she assured him. She did some pausing and sighing of her own. "It's good for us to go beneath the surface. It's good to bring up things that we wish we hadn't done or wish hadn't happened to us. After all, that's what people do on dates when they're getting to know each other."

Lorelei smiled, no doubt to ease the tension he was feeling over spoiling this night. And it worked. Tension eased. Plus, he liked that she actually thought there was something more of him beneath the surface. Most people believed what they saw with him was what they got.

"You admitted you were in therapy with my mother," she went on. "And you saw the photos of me dancing in my underwear. That's a tit for tat." She winced, blushed. "I probably should have thought of a different way of putting that."

Dax laughed, because, hey, those images of her in her underwear were memorable. Tits had definitely been involved. But it ate away at him that Julian and Aaron had used them against her like this.

Outside the truck, the storm was still raging and had even kicked up a notch or two. The rain was coming down so hard now that he couldn't see inside the windows of the shop, but he could still hear the music. It'd switched to My Chemical Romance, a song that probably would have been a hit when Frankie and Tanner had had their first date.

"I like it when you laugh," she said, causing Dax to look at her again. Lorelei certainly wasn't joining him in that laugh. She looked worried about him.

"But?" he questioned.

"But," she repeated after she gathered her breath, "I don't want you to feel you have to do bull rubs or talks to pull me out of my low moods. I appreciate it, really appreciate it," Lorelei emphasized, "but you're going through a lot now, too, and you should focus more on yourself."

Crap. This was about therapy. Since she didn't know the reason for those sessions with Evangeline, Lorelei was probably thinking the worst. That maybe he was suicidal or depressed. That maybe his childhood had left him with scars that couldn't be fixed. He didn't want Lorelei to believe any of that.

"I see your mom about sex," he said. In hindsight, he really should have chosen a different way to say it than that. "I don't have sex with your mom," he tried again. "But I saw her for about a year to work on my attitude toward sex."

In another bout of hindsight, Dax wished he had that bucket of rocks for some head-hitting. He cursed, mentally regrouped.

"It's better now," he insisted. "In fact, I don't have any future appointments with Evangeline."

There. Now maybe Lorelei wouldn't think he couldn't get it up. Or that he had a fetish like being aroused at the sight of cardboard. He'd sought out counseling because he'd wanted to understand why he slept his way from one to the next without making a lick of commitment or connection along the way.

Not a lick.

In fact, he'd made more of a connection on this first date with Lorelei than he'd made in any and all of his past relationships. No way could he tell her that, though, because it would make her think this was getting more serious than she could handle. Correction—more serious than *they* could handle. Because it was obvious that both of them had been handed platters of crap when it'd come to relationships.

"You don't have to answer, but did your therapy have anything to do with Miranda's mom, Joy?" Lorelei asked.

Dax was sure he looked surprised. Because he was. He damn sure hadn't expected Lorelei to home in on that. Just what the hell had she overheard him say when he'd been talking to Miranda that had made her connect the pieces like that?

The right connection.

Since Mother Nature was continuing to dump three months' worth of rain on them at once, Dax decided to confirm what Lorelei had obviously already sussed out for herself.

"Yes," he verified. Best just to go ahead and say it fast. "When I was fifteen, Joy was a promoter in the junior rodeo

competitions that I'd started riding in. She was my first."
He paused to give Lorelei some time for that to sink in.

"How old was she?" she immediately asked, obviously
not needing much sinking-in time.

"Thirty-two. It was a little like *Fifty Shades of Grey*
except I wasn't a rich teenager," he added to try to keep
things light.

Lorelei's mouth dropped open. "A grown woman molested you?"

Going with another light attempt, he shrugged. "Trust
me, at the time I thought I was damn lucky to be able to
have sex anytime I wanted."

"You were molested," she insisted, the outrage and anger
in her voice.

Yeah, that was the correct word all right, and it wasn't
the worst of it. "It went on for two years, and when I tried
to end things with her, she threatened to kill herself. Then,
she threatened to kill me and my brothers."

There, it was all out with that quick pull of a bandage so
he could now put it aside and do something to help Lorelei
get back in the date/party mood. Because, after all, that's
why they were here, not to rehash his past.

"Please tell me she's in jail," Lorelei said.

"She was. Not for what she did to me," he quickly added.
"There were others, a few younger than me. She served her
time, but she still has a lot of issues so she's in and out of
mental health places."

And that was all he intended to say about that so he
swiveled in the seat, turning to Lorelei. "I'm okay, really.
I just didn't want you to think I was so messed up that it
wouldn't be safe for me to be a father to Stellie."

"I don't think you're messed up," Lorelei assured him.
"I wouldn't be here if I believed that."

Since he'd never felt he needed validation and such, he wasn't sure why that felt so darn good, but it did, and it made him smile.

"I'm here because I can't get you out of my head," she went on. "Because I can't get that kiss out of my head. And because I've been dreaming about you."

Well, hell. He hadn't expected all of that, either, and it only added another layer to his feeling good. Lorelei, on the other hand, looked stunned by what she'd just confessed, and she was probably wishing she could take it all back.

Dax did something about that.

He leaned in and kissed her. He just put his mouth on hers and hoped it washed away any regrets over her spilling that she was attracted to him.

Oh, yeah.

The kiss seemed to do just that. No regrets, no more digging up the past. Just two people kissing each other as if there were no tomorrow. Of course, there was a tomorrow, and Lorelei might add this to her regret pool, too, but for now he was just going to savor the moment by savoring her.

Like the other kisses, he felt her holding back. Barely. The woman definitely had a good leash on her libido. But beneath that holding-back, he could also feel the simmering fire, and it was both humbling and damn arousing that he was the cause of that fire.

So, he took on that fire, sliding his tongue over her bottom lip, tasting her. Deepening the kiss, moving his hand to her waist so he could touch her. All was going amazingly well until he realized they were parked on Main Street where someone could see them. His reputation wouldn't take a ding for making out in broad daylight, but Lorelei likely wouldn't care to have yet more gossip piled onto her.

As if pulling himself out of a trace, Dax eased back, met her equally tranced-looking eyes, and he smiled.

Lorelei blushed again and shook her head. Maybe because she couldn't believe what was happening between them or she could have just been trying to clear her thoughts. He was trying to do the same thing, and he had to wonder who was more surprised by these turns of events. Him or Lorelei? At the moment, he thought she might be the winner of that particular contest.

Still enjoying the slide of heat Lorelei had sent through him, Dax looked out the windshield and saw that the rain was finally tapering off. Not only that, Frankie was at the shop window and had obviously noticed them because she was motioning for them to come in.

Dax sighed since the woman had no doubt seen the kiss as well. Frankie wouldn't blab, but Dax figured he should expect a lecture about not dicking around with Lorelei's heart. He'd accept that lecture because he knew he was dicking around with his own heart as well. He'd never given his heart the chance to be broken, not with his run-and-gun approach to women, but he wouldn't be able to do that with Lorelei. Nope. So, the risks were pretty damn high for both of them.

"Wait here," Dax told Lorelei, and opening his umbrella, he got out and went to her side of the truck.

By the time they made it into the shop, all the other guests had stopped whatever they'd been doing and had turned toward them. Maybe because they, too, had seen the kiss. If so, there were some smiles of approval. Tanner gave him a thumbs-up. Frankie didn't dole out any hints of a lecture, but she took aim with her phone and snapped a photo of them.

"The tables are set up with the most popular party food

and drink the year of the first date," Frankie explained while she snapped another picture and then started tapping in something on her phone. "So, since this is your first, I went with trendy fusion stuff and hard seltzers."

Within seconds, Frankie had the two photos of Lorelei and him scrolling on a wall screen where there were pictures of the other couples. Pictures of some famous historical ones, too. Apparently, Frankie had taken this "first date" theme and run with it.

Millie went straight to Lorelei, pulling her into a hug and murmuring something in her ear that had her responding with an uncertain smile. When Millie pulled back from the whispers, she handed Lorelei a glass of white wine.

Dax steered away from the seltzer and helped himself to a beer from the "Frankie and Tanner's first date" table just as the music kicked up in a current country music hit. Apparently, this was his and Lorelei's first date song.

While Lorelei chatted with Millie and Frankie, Dax made his way to Matt, who was watching the photos scroll by. Dax caught one of Matt when he'd been a star on the high school football team. Obviously not a "first date" photo, but Emory was there in the background.

"Well?" Matt said, turning to Dax and lifting his eyebrow.

"I was going to say the same thing to you. Except my *well* was going to be about Julian. Have you found anything on him?"

"Not yet. As a lawyer, he might have been able to have any previous accusations of stalking expunged from his record. I'll keep digging."

"Thanks," Dax told him. "I asked Derwin to look, too, and he's come up empty so far."

Matt frowned. "Derwin? Why the hell would you involve

him…" But he trailed off, no doubt recalling that it'd been Derwin and the Snoops who'd come up with a key piece of info that had allowed them to figure out why Griff had driven his car off that cliff.

"I asked Derwin not to keep the search to himself," Dax added, and he grinned. "Julian's gotten wind of it, and he called Curt to demand I back off. That just tells me there's something to find." Something other than what Julian had done to Lorelei.

Matt drank some of his beer and smiled at his fiancée when their gazes met from across the room. "Are you going to answer my *well*?" he asked Dax.

Dax didn't need any clarification of what Matt wanted to know. This was about Lorelei and him. About whether or not he was getting in too deep because he wasn't thinking straight. The answer to that was possibly. And it wasn't an answer Dax much cared for. He truly didn't want Lorelei getting hurt from anything he did, but he was positive this heat between them wouldn't be denied. It would build until it led to sex. Or build and send the sensible Lorelei running. Either way, this was going to lead to some changes, and tension, between them.

"There's a lot going on right now," Dax settled for saying. "Lorelei's making things a little easier for me."

In fact, he couldn't imagine anyone else better suited to raising a child. Especially not him. No way could he do that on his own because he'd just screw it up. And Stellie was too important for that.

Conversation stopped again when the front door of the shop opened, and a woman hurried in out of the rain. No umbrella, but she had on a raincoat that was drenched.

"I'm so sorry, but the shop's closed for a private party," Frankie immediately called out, and she headed in the direction of the door, no doubt to usher the woman out and lock up.

The woman pushed back her hood to reveal a mop of curly red hair, and she spared Frankie only a glance before her gaze skirted around the room. And landed on Dax.

"Dax Buchanan," she said on a rise of breath. "I'm Chloe Franklin."

Dax thumbed back through his past one-nighters and knew this woman wasn't one of them. She didn't seem to be a fan, either, since she didn't have that "fan girl" glee in her eyes. However, it was obvious she knew him. Obvious, too, that she wasn't leaving because of what Frankie had said about this being a private party.

So that Frankie wouldn't have to deal with this, Dax went closer. "Do we know each other?" he came out and asked.

"No," she readily admitted, her breath hitching up again. "But Valerie Ford and I were friends, and you and I need to talk. I have some things you'll want to hear."

CHAPTER SEVENTEEN

EVEN THOUGH LORELEI was across the room and the music was still playing, she still heard what the auburn-haired woman had just said about being Valerie's friend. About needing to talk to Dax.

And Lorelei's stomach sank.

Because nothing about that sounded good. Maybe this was someone Aaron and Julian had found and were planning on using to hurt Dax's and her custody fight. Frankie must have decided it didn't sound good, either, because she motioned toward the back of the shop.

"If you want, you can use my office," she offered.

Dax muttered a thank-you under his breath and looked at Lorelei. He didn't verbally invite her to join in on this conversation, but the invitation was there in his eyes.

"This is Lorelei Parkman," Dax said to Chloe. "She'll want to hear what you have to say, too."

Chloe didn't ask who she was, but Lorelei didn't think it was her imagination that the woman dodged her gaze. Definitely not a good sign, and that's why she took another glass of wine when she followed Dax and Chloe back to Frankie's office.

Not a conventional office, Lorelei quickly realized, but then Frankie wasn't a conventional person. There were life-sized cardboard figures from *The Avengers* paired with framed photos of elaborate tats. All very Frankie, and even at a troublesome time like this, the photos made her think of the longhorn on Dax's butt. Frankie had been the one to ink him and there was a long story behind it.

She wished he could share that story now. Wished that he could do something to ease this horrible tension building inside her.

And he did.

Dax took hold of her hand, giving it a reassuring squeeze and easing her onto the atomic-green loveseat. Chloe took the purple chair across from them after she tugged off her raincoat. Now that Lorelei could see her face up close, she noticed the woman was just as tense as she was, and that's why Lorelei handed her the glass of wine.

"Thank you." The relief gushed out in her voice, and Chloe took a large gulp of it before she said anything else. "I'm sorry about barging in on your party, but I have an Uber waiting to take me back to the airport in San Antonio. I have a lot going on at home, and I plan on getting the first available flight back to St. Louis," she added a heartbeat later.

"St. Louis," Dax repeated. That's where Valerie had been born and raised. Where she'd lived, too, with the exception of the last year of her life. "How did you know I'd be here?"

"I called your ranch, and the man who answered told me you were at a party here in town. He wouldn't give me more specifics than that. Maybe because he thought I'd come to stir up some kind of trouble for you. But I had the Uber driver stop at the diner, and several people told me you'd be here."

So, that meant the gossips had likely seen all the kissing, too. But that kind of talk seemed minor now in the grand scheme of things.

"You knew Valerie well?" Lorelei asked the woman.

She nodded. "I'd known her most of my life." Chloe pulled up some pictures on her phone. Photos of Valerie and her at various ages. "We went to school together and were best buds for a long time, but we drifted apart when she married Aaron. We reconnected after she left St. Louis."

So, Chloe had perhaps had contact with Valerie when she was pregnant. Oh, yes. This conversation was important, but rather than pepper Chloe with questions, Lorelei just waited for her to continue. Beside her, Dax was obviously doing the same thing, but he did tighten the grip on her hand.

Chloe had another sip of wine and shifted her attention to Lorelei. "Aaron's attorney, Julian Martin, contacted me. He said he was talking to all of Valerie's friends and former friends because he was trying to stop a travesty of justice."

"A travesty of justice?" Lorelei whipped out. "It's not—"

"I know," Chloe interrupted, "and it's the reason I'm here. The travesty would be if this lawyer succeeds and manages to give custody of an innocent little baby to a man like Aaron. Simply put, Aaron's a jackass. A smothering, overbearing jackass, and he's a big reason why Valerie left and tried to start a new life."

It was good to have Chloe confirm that jackass label. Of course, Dax and Lorelei had already figured that out for themselves. Chloe had confirmed something else as well. That Aaron and especially Julian were digging for any and everything so they could win this custody fight. They apparently thought they'd find dirt by going to Valerie's friends.

"Let me fill you in on how my reconnect with Valerie played out," Chloe went on, "and then I'll try to answer any questions you have. The day after Valerie left Aaron, she called me out of the blue and asked if I'd meet her at a café on the other side of town from where she'd lived. She had some jewelry she wanted me to try to sell for her. She knew that pawnshops and such had surveillance cameras, and she didn't want anyone trying to track her down that way."

Dax shook his head. "Valerie was scared?"

"Yes, I think so," Chloe readily agreed, "but she insisted Aaron had never gotten violent with her."

As Dax well knew, there were other forms of abuse, and Aaron had probably used plenty of those other forms on Valerie. After all, things had been bad enough with him that it'd caused her to uproot her whole life. That included breaking ties with her parents except for those few texts and a phone call she'd made.

"Anyway, Valerie said she needed the money," Chloe explained, "that she wanted cash to start a new life. There was a lot of jewelry, including some old family pieces, so it took me a couple of days to sell them all, and I met her again to give her the money. That's when she told she was leaving St. Louis but that she'd be in touch with me. She gave me a prepaid phone and said that was the only way I should contact her."

Valerie wouldn't have been pregnant by then. Well, she wouldn't have been if Chloe's timeline of events were accurate. When Dax and she had worked through the timing of events, Valerie hadn't gone to the rodeo in Fort Worth until a week after she'd left home.

"You stayed in touch with Valerie?" Lorelei prompted when Chloe fell silent. She couldn't be sure, but Lorelei thought the woman got trapped in the memories of the past for a couple of moments.

"Yes. She'd call about once a week, but she changed out her own prepaid cell often, and of course, she swore me to secrecy because she didn't want me to tell anyone that she had been in contact with me." Chloe shifted her attention back to Dax. "She told me about you. Her dad is a big rodeo fan so she knew who you were, and she went to the rodeo, hoping to see you."

"Hoping for a one-nighter?" he asked.

Chloe shrugged. "Maybe," she admitted. "You have to remember that Aaron kept her on a tight leash. She didn't realize it was happening at the time, but one by one, he cut her off from her friends. Me included. He was working to cut her off from her parents, too. So, once Valerie had a taste of freedom, she might have decided to take that freedom for a spin with you."

Dax sighed, and Lorelei thought she knew why. He wasn't proud of his one-offs with any woman, but part of him was probably glad Valerie had gotten a taste of that freedom Aaron had tried to take from her.

"Why didn't the Fords do anything to stop Aaron?" Lorelei asked.

"I don't think they knew a lot of what was going on in her marriage. I mean, they knew Aaron was a jackass. He didn't show that side of himself before Valerie and he married, but he certainly showed it afterward, and her parents would have seen at least a little of that. They probably didn't know things had gotten so bad for Valerie."

That was the sense that Lorelei got from them as well. Despite what Julian and Aaron had uncovered about them, Lorelei thought the Fords were good people.

"You knew Valerie was pregnant?" Dax asked.

"Oh, yes." Her answer came fast after another gulp of wine. "She called me the day she took the at-home pregnancy test." Chloe stopped, smiled just a little. "Actually, she'd taken thirteen tests. All positive."

"I'm so sorry," Dax muttered, and Lorelei could feel

him replaying the guilt over that. Valerie would have been alone and probably scared.

Or not.

Lorelei had to amend that thought when Chloe blinked and pulled back her shoulders. "No need to be sorry. Valerie was thrilled. Well, she was once she got past the initial shock of seeing the plus signs on those thirteen tests."

Dax made a sound of surprise. "Valerie was happy about being pregnant?"

Chloe nodded. "Yes." Then, she volleyed puzzled glances at them before realization dawned in her eyes. "Oh, you heard about her being afraid of childbirth. She was because of her aunt dying. But Valerie wanted a baby. It was Aaron who didn't. He kept putting her off, telling her they should both focus on their careers, and they could have a baby in a couple of years. Then, things got bad between them, and the baby plan was completely off the table."

Lorelei was certain she was doling out some puzzled looks of her own before it sank in. And the breath of relief she took was long and fast. Thank God Valerie hadn't had to go through a pregnancy she was dreading. That had to ease some of Dax's guilty conscience.

"Valerie said the baby was mine?" Dax pressed.

This time Chloe wasn't so quick to respond. "I asked, but she simply said the baby was hers. You should have a paternity test done, though, because she didn't call me about those pregnancy tests until she'd been gone from St. Louis for about a month."

"I've done the test, and it proves Stellie is mine," Dax let her know. "Aaron and his lawyer are challenging it, though, and putting up roadblocks to the truth. That's why I was hoping you could confirm that Valerie knew I'm Stellie's father."

Chloe shook her head. "Sorry, but she dodged that question when I asked her about it." She paused, sighed. "For what it's worth, I don't believe Valerie was pregnant when she was still in St. Louis. When she asked me to meet her in that café right after she left Aaron, she had a glass of wine. If she'd even suspected she'd been pregnant, I doubt she would have done that."

True, but again it wasn't any kind of proof that would help Dax and her fight Aaron. Added to that and assuming Dax's paternity test was wrong, Valerie could have possibly been pregnant but might not have known yet.

"I know you're going to ask so I'll just get it out of the way," Chloe continued a moment later. "I don't know why Valerie came here to Last Ride. In fact, I didn't know she had until Aaron's lawyer contacted me and told me she died here."

Well, that was something Lorelei had been hoping Chloe could fill in for them. "Did you have any phone conversations with Valerie in the month before she passed away?"

"Yes," Chloe verified. "But again, she didn't say where she was. She did talk about the baby, how excited she was that she'd be born soon. She knew she was having a girl," she slipped in there. "And she was making jewelry again so she seemed pleased about that. I asked her for an address so I could send her a baby gift, but she said it was best that I not know her location because she didn't want to be found."

Lorelei tried to take that all in. If she hadn't wanted to be found, then why hadn't Valerie gone to a place where no one had known her? Why come to Last Ride? Because if Dax had seen her, he would have known who she was. Or rather he would have known her by the name she'd given him in Fort Worth.

And that brought Lorelei back to the toothbrush.

If Valerie had come here for the sole purpose of confirming Dax was Stellie's father, then maybe she had been just lying low until she got back the results. Results she wouldn't have shared with Chloe or else the woman would have already volunteered that.

Lorelei didn't doubt anything the woman was telling them, but first chance she got, she'd have Matt run a background check on her. She could ask the Fords about her as well so she could make sure Chloe didn't have any ulterior motives for being here. After all, Julian and Aaron could be using her in some way so it would help their case.

"Did Valerie happen to mention that she spoke with a lawyer here in Last Ride shortly before her death?" Lorelei asked.

Chloe's forehead bunched up a moment. "Yes. She wanted to know what she'd need to divorce Aaron. She wasn't actually going to start that process just yet. She only wanted to know what kind of paperwork and such she'd need."

Well, that would have been the right step for Valerie to take, but Lorelei was betting Aaron wouldn't have just agreed to a divorce without a fight. Not unless Valerie had given him a huge settlement. But maybe that's what Valerie had talked to Asher about. Of course, there was another possibility as well. One that Valerie might not have mentioned to Chloe.

Lorelei took a moment and chose her words. Best not to spill details that Valerie might have been helping the cops investigate a case that was still ongoing. "Did Valerie ever mention anything about the St. Louis PD?"

This time Chloe did more than just pause. It was a full-stop hesitation. "You know about that?"

Bingo. So Valerie had talked to Chloe about it. "Some," Lorelei verified. "What did she tell you?"

Chloe shook her head, hesitated again. "I didn't hear about the investigation from Valerie. I heard about it from St. Louis PD."

Now Lorelei was the one who hesitated, and she exchanged a glance with Dax before he asked, "The cops there talked to you about Valerie?"

"Yes," Chloe said on a sigh. "They paid me a visit right before she left St. Louis. I tried to call her then, so she could help clear it up, but she didn't answer." She downed the rest of her wine. "And I don't believe it for a minute. I think whatever was going on is something that Aaron cooked up to try to get his hand on her trust fund, and that's exactly what I told the cops."

Along with another hesitation, Lorelei was just downright confused.

"What was going on?" Dax asked. "Why did the cops want to talk to you about Valerie?"

Chloe stared at him a long time and then belted out, "Oh, crap. You didn't know. I thought you knew and that's why you'd asked."

"You thought I knew what?" Dax insisted.

Another sigh, followed by some muttered profanity. "That St. Louis PD was investigating Valerie for embezzling and theft of funds. The cops were looking for Valerie so they could arrest her."

CHAPTER EIGHTEEN

DAX WANTED TO PACE, but Frankie's office wasn't big enough for two pacers, and Matt had already claimed that particular moving space. He'd started the antsy walking back and forth shortly after Dax had asked him to come in and hear what Chloe had just told them about Valerie, the jewelry and the possible investigation. That had prompted Matt to make a phone call to St. Louis PD, and while he chatted with someone there, he paced.

In contrast, Lorelei had gone so still that Dax couldn't even hear her breathing.

Like him, she was probably thinking and rethinking everything they'd learned about Valerie over the past weeks. It put a different spin on things if Valerie was actually a fugitive from justice, but Dax refused to believe the worst about her. She'd certainly had opportunity to steal more than a toothbrush from him, and she hadn't. Added to that, she hadn't come to him and asked for a dime to pay for her medical expenses and such. Heck, even if she hadn't been carrying his child, he would have helped her cover those costs.

After some very long moments, Matt finally ended the call and dragged in a long breath. "It's true," he said. "Valerie was under investigation. It's not tied to what her parents did," Matt added. "It has to do with missing money. Valerie took the maximum withdrawal, a hundred-thousand dollars, from her trust fund. Nothing illegal about that. But Aaron claims she took funds from their joint accounts by forging his signature."

Lorelei and Dax groaned in unison. Because anything, absolutely anything, that Aaron said and did was suspect. In this case, it was likely plain old bullshit.

"Was this investigation the reason you found that flag on Valerie when you were running a background check on her?" Dax asked.

Matt nodded. "St. Louis PD just came clean about that. According to Aaron, Valerie syphoned off about three-hundred-thousand dollars from those joint accounts."

"A lot," Lorelei muttered, "but Aaron could have been the one who did the syphoning."

Chloe made a sound of agreement. "If Valerie had had that much money, four-hundred grand, why would she have asked me to sell jewelry for her?"

Good question, and since the answers seemed to be pointing back to Aaron, Dax decided to push on that a bit. "Any chance you can get St. Louis PD to take a look at Aaron for those missing funds? Maybe check and see, too, if he's the one who took money from her trust fund."

"They already are looking into it," Matt verified. "If he has the money, then he's hidden it well. But I'll speak to the Fords again. According to the detective I just had a chat with, he says Aaron told him that the Fords were in on it, that they would cover for their daughter. That's why the cops there kept details about this investigation close to the vest. Aaron even alleged that they knew where she was and were helping her hide from the cops."

Since Miriam had, indeed, covered for her by not telling Aaron about the texts and phone call Valerie had made to her, Dax couldn't dispute that. But something wasn't adding up.

"Since Valerie was under investigation, the St. Louis cops must have known she was missing," Dax spelled out. "Why didn't they reach out to cops nationwide to try to find her?"

"They did," Matt assured him. "Heck, I might have even glanced at the APB, but I wouldn't have automatically connected the picture to Dana Smith. Remember, Valerie changed her appearance."

Again, Dax couldn't dispute that, but that left them with the problem of the missing money. Potentially a lot of it. Where was it? And was it playing into the reason that Aaron was fighting so hard to get Stellie?

"I have to leave for the airport," Chloe said, getting to her feet. She took out a business card from her purse and handed it to Lorelei. "That's my number if you need to get in touch with me."

Lorelei thanked her and gave Chloe her number as well. Dax did the same.

"Both of you need to watch out for Aaron," Chloe warned them as she put their numbers in her phone. "He's bad news, and he won't stop until he gets what he wants."

Oh, he'd stop all right because Dax wasn't going to let him try to steamroll over Lorelei. Now he just needed to figure out a way to make sure the steamrolling came to a quick stop.

Lorelei and he walked to the door to show Chloe out and thanked the woman again. The party was still going on, though much quieter than it had been before Chloe's arrival.

"Everything's okay," Dax told everyone, knowing it wasn't even close to being a good answer, but no one here would press him on it. Ditto for not pressing if Lorelei wanted to head out early.

"Want to call it a night?" Dax murmured to Lorelei.

"God, yes," she murmured back, and he saw that Chloe's visit had taken a toll on Lorelei. Not because the news of the investigation was scandalous as the underwear photos of her had been, but because each new bit of info seemed to give them yet more questions and no new answers.

Lorelei and he said their goodbyes and darted back out into the rain to get in his truck. Dax hadn't even started driving yet when his phone rang with a call, and he saw the name on the screen. Calvin Walters, a rodeo pal. Since Dax didn't want to have a conversation with Calvin tonight, he let it go to voice mail, and then he played the message while he made the drive to Lorelei's.

"Hey, Dax, it's me, Calvin. Just wanted you to know that I'll have to pull out of Houston. One of your bulls messed up my shoulder. My balls, too." Calvin chuckled. "You've got a real mean ballbuster with Thunder. Anyway, my shoulder and balls should be recovered in time for the Last Ride Charity Rodeo. Wouldn't want to miss your farewell ass-busting." Calvin chuckled again before he ended the call.

"A friend," Dax explained, though Lorelei had no doubt already figured that out.

"Your farewell ass-busting?" she repeated.

Of course, she would latch on to that, and it wasn't exactly a secret. Dax just hadn't talked about it much. "Yeah, I've got a competition coming up in Houston and then the one in Last Ride."

She shook her head. "I didn't know you were retiring so soon."

Again, it was because he hadn't talked about it. Correction, he didn't like talking about it. Or thinking about it.

Or doing it.

But he realized if he whined about it to anyone, it should be to Lorelei. After all, this would affect his future, which in turn would affect Stellie's. Not in a bad way for the baby since he'd be able to spend more time with her. But it'd sure as hell be in a bad way for Dax.

"I wanted to go out when I was still on top," he said, and then realized that wasn't the truth. He owed Lorelei the truth, though he didn't want to get into why he felt that way.

"Over the past twenty-one months, I've had some injuries," he continued. Concussions, broken bones, sprains and too many deep bruises, cuts and scrapes to count. "I got a really serious head and back injury right before I met Valerie and was in the hospital for a while."

She made a soft sound of sympathy. "Is that when you got the scar on your knee?"

"No, that was another time." Same for the scars on both his elbows where he'd needed stitches. "But being in the hospital for that long made me realize things had to change, that I was going to have to think about retiring."

"Twenty-one months ago," she pointed out. "That's a long time to think about stopping something."

"It is." And the way she'd put that made him smile. The smile vanished, though, before he spilled the rest of it. "The hospital stay changed things. Changed me," he amended. "Valerie played into that, too. When she didn't return my call, it hit home that I was being as reckless with my personal life as I was my choice of professions. That's when I started doing therapy with your mom and decided retirement was in my near future."

She stayed quiet a moment. "That was brave of you."

He snorted with dry laughter. "Well, let's just say the

bravery wasn't optional. I consulted eight doctors about my previous injuries. All eight told me to retire then and there."

"Eight?" She huffed because it was obviously hitting her what lengths he'd gone to before he'd even started accepting the idea of retirement. "Why so many?"

"It was like all those pregnancy tests Chloe told us that Valerie took. I knew what the outcome would be, but I had to be sure."

"And you're sure?" she asked when he pulled into her driveway.

Not even close, but he didn't want to dump any more of his baggage onto Lorelei. Not when she had enough of her own. Instead, he unhooked his seat belt and moved in to kiss her.

Even though their last kiss had been less than an hour ago, it still felt as if he were starved for her, and Lorelei certainly knew how to dish up something to fill the hunger clawing away at him. She tasted like all the good things he'd ever had in his life. A flawless eight-second championship ride, that last Christmas morning with his folks and all the best of his birthdays.

Man, he wanted her.

Too much. And it didn't seem to matter that he shouldn't be feeling this way about her. Especially since he wasn't absolutely sure that this wasn't part of his old pattern. When facing something tough, or celebrating something good, or just when a woman was right there in front of him, the old pattern was to take what was offered and not question the consequences. Well, he was questioning those consequences now, but the need for her was overriding everything.

Including common sense.

Thankfully, Lorelei was the queen of common sense,

and he figured she'd just give in to the kiss for a little while and then issue a goodbye so she could hurry in and mentally scold herself for doing this.

But that didn't happen.

She broke the kiss all right, long enough to mutter, "My neighbors might be watching." Which wasn't a goodbye at all. Especially wasn't one when she added, "Let's take this inside."

Lorelei pulled back, meeting his gaze, and he saw the concern flash in her eyes. "Unless you don't want to."

"Oh, I want to. Trust me." But he held back on taking her hand and placing it on the front of his jeans where there was hard proof of how much he wanted this.

Again, he expected her to hesitate, think and rethink, but she only nodded. "Inside, then," she said, and she gave him a kiss that might have been quick, but it made up for it in sheer scalding heat.

She used her remote app to open the garage door, but the rain didn't cooperate with their hasty exit from his truck. The sky unzipped once again, making them plenty wet by the time they reached cover. Lorelei immediately hit the app again, and the moment the garage door was closed, she kissed him again.

He wasn't sure how she managed it but each kiss from her felt even better and hotter than the last one. Of course, this time they had the added advantage of being body to body. He could feel her breasts and all those curves pressed in all his right places.

"Don't ask me if I'm sure," she insisted, breaking the kiss only long enough to speak. She picked it right back up again while she took hold of him and led him out of the garage, into the mudroom and then into the house.

Clearly, they'd skipped right over just mere kissing and

had dived right into foreplay waters. Familiar waters to him, but again, somehow Lorelei managed to make it seem as if this were all foreign territory to him. Maybe because beneath the hard-on and the heat, he knew the stakes were sky-high with her.

She finally stopped when they reached the kitchen, and she stepped back. "You must think I've lost my mind."

"Nope. In fact, that wasn't anywhere on my radar." He met her eyes and didn't bother to take out the heat that he knew was there. "I was just thinking that you must have been doing a lot of, well, thinking about this."

Oh, that pretty blush came, and it turned his mind to mush. Even though Dax knew he should be giving her a little breathing room, he took hold of her fingers, eased her back to him and brushed his mouth over hers.

"Yes," she verified. "I've been thinking about you for days."

He smiled. "Right back at you." But he had to add some disclaimers here. "I don't want you to kiss and regret."

Lorelei kept her gaze on him. Locked to his, actually. And she nodded. It was slow and sensual and meshed perfectly with the other sensual vibes she was throwing at him.

Hell, he was toast.

Using just his grip on her fingers, Dax moved her closer, and closer and closer until they were breast to chest again. He clearly came out on top with that position since her breasts were far more interesting than his chest.

"I don't want you to kiss and regret, either," she murmured, and her breath hit against his mouth like the dirtiest of tongue kisses.

Neither did he, and that's why he took a moment. Then, two. Then, three. Before he accepted that no regret was going to be worse than the regret of not taking this to the next level. The next level was turning these little breath kisses into something long, deep and French.

So, that's what he did.

He kissed as if there'd never be a regret or consequence. As if this was the best, and last, kiss he'd ever be given. Lorelei seemed to take that same approach because she amped up the touching that went along with the kissing. She hooked her arm around him, anchoring him against her while her back landed against the wall.

The kiss raged on, and Dax added some touching of his own. He slid his hand between them to cup one of her breasts. Man, she was built, and he couldn't stop himself from ducking down and kissing her erect nipple through the top of her dress. He wished he could make her clothes vanish. Wished he could take her on one wild ride to burn off some of this fire so he could settle down and have sex with her the right way.

Slow, easy and something that would last a whole lot longer than this "fire burning" pace.

Unfortunately, though, Lorelei was in the "burning up" stage, too, so yeah, this first round was going to be fast. Well, maybe it would be.

"I don't have a condom," she said as she went after his neck. "Please tell me you do."

Shit. He repeated that several times and shook his head. "I used to carry one in my wallet but it was too much temptation." Her mom had suggested it, but he had no intentions of mentioning Evangeline's name, or really lousy advice right now.

Lorelei's lips sort of froze on his neck for a moment before her head whipped up, and she looked at him.

Dax did a mental shrug. "I haven't had sex since Valerie," he admitted.

"Really?" She cursed, groaned and squeezed her eyes shut for a moment. "I haven't had sex since before I got Stellie."

Their situation wasn't funny. It truly wasn't. But Dax imagined that somewhere in the universe, fate was laughing her ass off that he of all people would be caught without a condom when he was with a beautiful woman he wanted more than his left kidney.

"Think we've forgotten how it's done," he teased and ran his index finger over her damp mouth.

"Probably." She groaned again and bopped the back of her head against the wall. "Well, we can't go running out to the store to buy condoms right now. The idea of starting that much gossip puts a chill on the mood."

Yeah, it did, but Dax knew of a "safe sex" way to heat things right back up, and it started with another kiss. Lorelei slipped right into it, too, obviously hoping the kiss would take care of this hunger she had building, building, building inside her. A kiss wouldn't do that. Well, not a kiss on the mouth, anyway. But there were other kinds of kisses tailor-made for this.

Dax kissed his way down her body until he made it to the hem of her dress. He caught onto it and pulled it up and off. She made a sound of surprise that he trapped with his mouth. Tongues were good for that, and the next sound she made was exactly what he wanted to hear.

A silky purr of pleasure.

Kissing her breasts probably wouldn't lead to an orgasm and release, either, but Dax tested out the theory just in case. He pushed down the cups of her bra and rolled his tongue over her right nipple before tugging it into his mouth. Of course, that was mainly for his own pleasure, but Lorelei seemed to enjoy it just fine. She caught onto his hair and called him a dirty name.

Yeah, she liked it just fine.

Vowing to go back to her breasts when the urgency wasn't so damn urgent, he kissed his way down her stomach and to her panties. They were white lace and covered up pretty much nothing, but Dax treated them with the gentleness they deserved. While he occupied Lorelei's belly, he slid down her panties as he slid down his mouth. Lower. Then lower. Until that silky purr of hers took on a needy demand.

Dax caught onto the back of her knee, lifting it to ease it onto his shoulder. And he went lower.

Since Lorelei still had her hand fisted in his hair, she controlled some of the movement of his head, but Dax put his tongue and mouth to good use. He flicked, tasted, applied some pressure and did a repeat until he heard and felt Lorelei's reaction.

Her silky purr was a groan now. A long, slow sound of pleasure that went right along with the fast, hard orgasm that slammed through her. Dax still didn't pull back. Didn't stop. He kept it up, drawing out every last bit of the pleasure.

Oh, yeah. There were kisses made for this.

CHAPTER NINETEEN

LORELEI FIGURED IT was wrong for her to be daydreaming about sex with Dax when she was in the same room as Stellie, her sister Lily, and her fourteen-year-old niece, Hayden. Still, she couldn't stop herself. Couldn't stop that floating post-sex glow that had somehow managed to last for two days.

Two days of glow. Of wanting another round with a man who clearly understood how to draw the maximum amount of pleasure from her body.

Because of that notion of future pleasure from him, she'd bought condoms. Not in town but rather at a convenience store out by the interstate. It hadn't felt presumptuous for her to do that, not when Dax had given her such a needy kiss when he'd left her house after giving her that amazing orgasm. He'd also left with an erection, which had told her he might have also purchased condoms. If so, they'd be doubly prepared the next time they got together.

"You're blushing," Lily whispered to her while she set their glasses of iced tea on the table.

Yes, Lorelei could feel the heat on her cheeks. Heat that she tried to cool down by watching Stellie play with the new blocks that Lily had gotten for her. The baby was on the kitchen floor with Hayden who was off from school because it was the weekend, and Hayden had asked if she could babysit Stellie. Lorelei had debated the request. Not because Hayden wasn't a good sitter. She was. But because with Hayden babysitting, it was yet one more temptation for Lorelei to go to Sunset Creek to see Dax.

Where sex would happen.

Well, maybe it would. Because Dax and she had had many text conversations over the past forty-eight hours, she knew he was working at the ranch today, and he'd invited Stellie and her over. He'd kept it casual, maybe because he'd thought it would be awkward between them, but Lorelei wasn't feeling any awkwardness. She was only feeling the need.

Apparently, Dax was feeling some of that himself because in one of the texts, he added, I had a good time after the party. Would like to see you. Very much.

She looked at Lily, their gazes connecting, and Lorelei hoped she silently conveyed the reason for her blush, and it was a reason she didn't want to discuss in front of Hayden. Lily got it. She smiled in that "all knowing" way of hers, but it was possible Hayden got it, too, because she stood from the floor and scooped up Stellie in her arms.

"Is it all right if I take Stellie to the family room?" the girl asked. "Don't worry. Mom and me made it kid-safe, and there are more toys and books in there."

"Of course," Lorelei agreed, giving Stellie a quick kiss.

There were, indeed, more toys and books. Ditto on it being kid-safe. Both of her sisters had set up play areas for Stellie, something that Lorelei hadn't fully appreciated until now. That's because she hadn't made much use of Hayden's babysitting offers, but she would today. She'd still feel a little guilty about leaving Stellie to go see Dax, but Lorelei also knew her baby would have a blast.

And would be safe.

Lily's ranch didn't have a gate like Dax's, but Jonas had

assured her that he'd be around. Added to that, Aaron and Julian likely wouldn't know that Stellie was even here because Lorelei had kept that to herself.

"Well?" Lily asked after Hayden and Stellie were out of earshot.

Lorelei blushed again. Smiled. Mercy, it'd been a long time since she'd felt anything like this. "I didn't actually have sex with Dax," she settled for saying.

If this had been Nola, there would have been some gleeful squealing, maybe even some jumping around. From Lily, she got a raised eyebrow and a very logical question.

"Are you sure that's the right path to go with Dax?" Lily asked.

"No, I'm not sure at all," Lorelei readily admitted. "In fact, what's going on with him would definitely qualify as one of those 'it's complicated' labels on social media."

Lily stared at her from over the rim of her iced tea glass. "But you're not holding back."

Even though this wasn't something Lorelei wanted to hear, she knew she needed this. She had to go to Dax with both eyes open and not just pretend there'd be no consequences.

"Something happened after the First Date Party," Lorelei tried to explain. "It wasn't actual sex, but it was a point of no return in some ways." She stopped, got another wave of that postorgasmic glow. "I'm not ready to dive headfirst into a relationship with him where I lose my heart and my head, but I am ready to spend more time with him."

Lily made a sound that seemed to be a warning. "And what is Dax ready for?"

Lorelei just didn't know, and that was the reason she had to do some heart-guarding. She'd been shocked when he had told her he hadn't been with another woman since

Valerie. So, obviously he'd made some changes in his life. Maybe because of the counseling he'd gotten. Maybe because he'd finally just reached an age where he'd wanted something less shallow than a one-off.

But that didn't mean Dax wanted less shallow with her.

It also didn't mean he was going back and forth on this "it's complicated" start to a possible relationship. With his history, he'd be cautious. So would she. And after the caution…well, the back and forth might continue for a while until both of them had sorted out their feelings. In the meantime, Lorelei wanted sex from him.

"If I have a fling with Dax," Lorelei admitted, "I know it could end badly. But like I said, we've reached a point of no return." She paused. "I bought condoms."

She braced herself for another one of Lily's disapproving looks, but her sister just sighed, leaned over and kissed Lorelei's cheek. "It's occurred to you that if you'd wanted someone to cheer you on and tell you to run not walk to Dax's bed, you would have gone to Nola."

Lorelei smiled, confirming that.

"But it's also occurred to you," Lily went on, "that you've made up your mind about this."

Lorelei smiled again, confirming that.

After another sigh, Lily smiled a little, too. "Then, run don't walk to Dax's bed. Have fun. Have a fling. Give him a test drive because he's hot and dreamy. Just guard your heart some as well."

"I will," Lorelei assured her, and with this truce worked out with her sister, she stood. "How long do you think Hayden will want this babysitting gig to last?"

"Hours and hours," Lily quickly assured her. "Go. Run. Have some fun."

The glow came again and it just kept coming while she

kissed Stellie goodbye, thanked both Hayden and Lily, and made the drive to Sunset Creek. It was on that drive, however, that she realized that midafternoon weekend sex might not be something Dax was up for. But at least she'd be able to see him and feel him out. She'd be able to tell if he truly meant what he'd texted.

Would like to see you. Very much.

When Lorelei drove through the ranch gates, she immediately spotted several of the hands and trainers around the corral that she knew was set up like a rodeo competition arena. It took her a moment to pick out Dax. He was sitting on a railing at the top of a chute, and since there was already a bull in the chute, he was obviously getting ready for a ride.

She got out of her car and walked to the corral to stand next to the head trainer, Mike. "Just in time," he said, giving her a surprised look to go along with his friendly smile. He glanced around as if checking to see if she'd brought the baby. "Dax is about to test drive Lightning, one of our newest trainees."

"Lightning," she muttered. She couldn't see much of the bull because of the chute slats, but he was snorting and moving around in there.

"Yeah. He's Thunder's brother. One of our other bulls," he added. "Lightning doesn't seem to have the ornery streak like his brother so he might not be ready for competition."

Lorelei was thankful for that lack of an ornery streak. She didn't especially want to see Dax slung around like a rag doll, but she reminded herself that this was part of what he did for a living. Part of who he was.

"Dax tests all the bulls?" she asked Mike.

"All of them," he verified. "And he'll be plenty busy because we're adding more bulls to the inventory. Dax'll have more time to spend with the training and such once he stops competing."

Lorelei watched as Dax climbed down onto the bull's back. "How's he dealing with that? The not competing," she clarified.

The corner of Mike's mouth lifted in what was probably a wry smile. "Best to get that answer from Dax." He paused, though, and studied his boss. "It'll be an adjustment for him."

Yes, and that was yet something else added to all the other adjustments he was having to make. Learning that he was a father. Dealing with the barrage of attacks from Julian and Aaron.

Dealing with her.

Lorelei couldn't blow off that sex would be easy for Dax. Not the mechanics of sex. He no doubt had that down pat. But the emotional part, and that had her rethinking this trip here. She might have turned around, gone home and done more of that rethinking had the chute not opened, and the bull came charging out.

Mike hit the stopwatch he'd been holding, starting the countdown to that handful of seconds that had to be a mix of adrenaline and fear. For her, the fear would have won out big-time but apparently not for Dax. She could see the focus and sheer determination on his face. Could see the way his body moved and reacted to the attempts from the bull to toss him. It was like a graceful, choreographed dance.

One that ended with Mike calling out, "Eight seconds," and Dax sliding off the side of the bull with all the ease of an able-bodied person getting out of a chair. Dax glanced at the bull, probably to see its intentions, which were obviously to charge at him, so he ran to the corral fence and climbed over. In the same motion of the climbing, he glanced over at her.

And smiled.

There it came again. The heat and glow. The memories of how he'd used that magic mouth on her. All notions of heading home and rethinking vanished. Just disappeared with his flash of a smile, and she made her way to him.

"A great ride," she said, hoping that was the right compliment.

He shrugged, went to her, and in a move that was as fluid and easy as him getting off the bull, Dax brushed a kiss on her mouth. Oh, the heat came in a fiery hot wave.

"An easy bull," he clarified. "Which means he's nowhere near ready for competition. Might never be," he added in a mumble.

There wasn't disappointment but rather sadness in his voice. Maybe some sadness in his eyes, too. "What will happen to him if he's never ready?" she asked.

"He'll get to go to a ranch and have lots of cow sex. So, not a bad deal for him except that I can tell he wants to compete." Dax hooked his arm around her waist and got her walking into the barn. "And, no, that's not a metaphor for my life."

Maybe not. But there were some similarities. Dax maybe still wanted to compete. Maybe wanted that lots of sex, too. Possibly with her.

Definitely with her, she amended, when he kissed her again.

"Where's Stellie?" he asked.

"At Lily's. Hayden is babysitting. I can bring her over later, though, if you want to see her."

"I do. Later," he verified. Once they were in the barn, he

started shucking off his chaps. Too bad about that because they were revving up some fantasies for her.

Dax must have noticed the fantasy gleam in her eyes because he smiled. "I can leave them on," he said, flashing that bad boy grin. "But they smell like sweat and bull. Me, too. If you're game, though, I can shower and find some clean ones."

She was game all right but no props or costumes were needed. Ditto for showers. He smelled just fine as far as she was concerned, and she would have sunk right into the kiss he brushed on her mouth if she hadn't heard the chatter of the trainers. They were obviously nearby, and it was probably best if Dax and she didn't put on a show for them.

"I was thinking about bringing Stellie to see you ride," she said while he continued to take off his protective vest. "Maybe to the event in Houston?"

He stayed quiet a moment. "That's a long drive for just a couple of seconds. But the Last Ride Charity Rodeo is only a week after that one."

Yes, and it'd be his last as a professional rider. Lorelei had thought—no, she knew—that would be a tough day for him. But maybe the Houston one would be as well. Still, he was right about the long drive. She hadn't done one of those with Stellie yet, and if the baby got fussy, it might only add to Dax's stress. Might distract him, too, and after he'd described some of his injuries, she didn't want him getting hurt because of a distraction.

"The Last Ride Charity Rodeo, then," she agreed, though she might keep Stellie and herself out of sight for that one as well.

He nodded, made a sound of agreement and flashed her another grin. "How do you feel about playing around in the shower with me?"

This time it wasn't just a wave of heat but an avalanche. She was ready to jump right on that invitation when Mike called out.

"You've got company, boss."

She cursed. Dax groaned. And Lorelei braced herself in case this was a visit from Aaron or Julian. But it wasn't. When Dax and she came out of the barn, she saw the man step from his car.

Derwin Parkman.

This time, she groaned. "If he's here to offer help for the Last Ride Society research, then I'll get rid of him fast." Derwin didn't call out a greeting to her, though.

"Dax," the man said. "I found something on that matter we discussed."

Dax muttered some profanity as Derwin walked toward them. "I asked Derwin to try to find dirt on Julian. Specifically find out if Julian had any other abusive relationships. I didn't tell Derwin about Julian and you," he added in a whisper.

That definitely cooled the heat. Not because she was pissed off at Dax for going to such lengths but because even if Derwin hadn't known about her past with Julian, that didn't mean the head of the Snoops wouldn't have unearthed it.

"I found something," Derwin repeated, but again he didn't direct that at her but rather Dax. "Julian Martin is a nasty sort of fellow, and while he was never arrested, I had discreet chats with some of his old acquaintances. I learned that about thirteen years ago, he assaulted a woman."

Oh, God. So, Derwin had found out about her. She was certain of that when Derwin finally turned to her, and she saw the sympathy in his eyes.

But she was wrong.

"When they were both still in college, Julian assaulted a woman who lives right here in Last Ride," Derwin added. "She's waiting in the car and wants to talk to you."

Lorelei's neck popped because she moved so fast to look in the direction of the car, and when she did that, the car door opened.

And her assistant, Misty Bennington, stepped out.

Lorelei's annoyance over Derwin's untimely arrival vanished, and it was replaced by a boatload of concern for Misty, who apparently had plenty to tell them. Probably so that the plenty wouldn't be overheard by the trainers and hands, Dax got them all moving into the house.

Obviously, that shower was going to have to wait. The potential for shower sex, too, since it wouldn't likely be a short conversation with Misty. The woman had clearly been crying so Lorelei would need to do some soothing once this was all out in the open.

"Lorelei, I'm so sorry I didn't tell you about this," Misty muttered with more tears spilling down her cheeks.

"It's okay," she assured her, and slipping her arm around Misty's waist, she led the woman inside and helped her to the sofa.

Dax took a minute to play host by bringing out some bottles of water and a box of tissues before he sat across from them. Derwin stayed standing, obviously waiting for Misty to fill them in.

Misty had a long drink of water first. "You might remember introducing me to Julian when I came to the campus for one of the parties."

Lorelei nodded. Unfortunately, she'd spent way too much time going over every minute she'd spent with the man. "Julian and I had just started dating then." She paused, debated how much to say and went with, "We had a difficult breakup."

"He mentioned something about that when I saw him at a bar in San Antonio a few months later. He didn't badmouth you," Misty quickly added. "If he had, I would have told him to get lost. But he just said it didn't work out with you and he'd been sorry it'd ended the way it had."

Lorelei's stomach tightened because she was almost certain what the woman was about to say. Derwin wouldn't have brought her here otherwise.

"Anyway, Julian and I started dating," Misty went on. "I'm sorry about that. He was your ex, and he should have been hands-off."

"It's okay." Lorelei slid her hand over Misty's. "Julian hit you?"

A dam of emotions seemed to give way inside the woman, and she managed a shaky nod before she started to sob. "Yes," she verified in between the crying. "He hit me and said very ugly things to me. He said I was just like you, but…" Misty stopped, glancing first at Derwin and Dax before turning back to Lorelei. "He hit you, too?"

Lorelei could deny it and continue to hide it as she usually did, but what would be the point? Other than the bad judgment of getting involved with Julian and keeping the consequences of that bad judgment to herself, she'd done nothing wrong. The worst of it was all on Julian.

"Yes," Lorelei said. "And I think that's why Aaron hired him. Because Aaron knew Julian would be able to tap into some old memories." She hugged Misty. "I'm so sorry Julian did those things to you."

Misty's breath broke and another sob rolled in right behind it. Dax and the others just stayed quiet until she regained some of her composure. "I never heard anything about Julian hitting you," Misty assured Lorelei. "I mean, you really kept that to yourself."

She had, and that's why Lorelei said what she had to say. "I'm so sorry about that. If I'd gone to the cops, this might not have happened to you. Even if the cops hadn't believed me, at least you would have heard about it and steered clear of him."

Misty was shaking her head before Lorelei even finished. "I did the same thing. I kept it private because I didn't want anyone to know it'd happened to me." She squared her shoulders. "But I won't keep it to myself now. I'll shout it from the rooftops if you think it'll make Julian back off. I mean, I know he has to be the one who released those photos of you."

"Yes, he was the one." But she had to stop before agreeing to any of the rest. The problem with shouting from the rooftops was that Lorelei would have to join in on that shouting. And honestly what good would it do?

"It's too late for us to file charges against Julian," Lorelei pointed out. "At this point, I can't see this harming him."

"It will if other women come forward," Dax pointed out. "Women who can file charges because the assaults were more recent."

Sweet heaven. He was right. God, he was right. Added to that, her silence had already led to Misty being hurt, and it could have done the same to others. Speaking up now might stop Julian from doing this again to someone else.

Before Lorelei could say any of that to Misty, her phone rang, and because she had Julian on her mind and was worried he'd gone to Lily's, she whipped out her phone. And relaxed a little when she saw Sophia's name on the screen.

Dax's phone rang, too, and when he muttered, "It's Curt," Lorelei figured this had to be important.

Lorelei stood. "Could you please excuse us for a minute or two?" she said and looked at Derwin. "You'll stay with Misty?"

"Of course," the man quickly agreed.

Dax and she both answered their calls while they made their way to his office. "Is it bad news?" Lorelei immediately asked Sophia.

"Both good and bad," Sophia admitted. "Dax is probably getting the bad news right about now."

Lorelei heard him mutter some profanity to confirm that. "What did Aaron and Julian do now?"

"They put out the word that Dax has been seeing a therapist for years, that he might be suicidal like his brother Griff. And if that isn't bad enough, they managed to dig up that Dax had a sexual relationship with his teacher when he was a teenager."

Now Lorelei did her own cursing. She went to Dax and even though he was still talking to Curt, Lorelei pulled him into a hug.

"Who told Aaron and Julian about Dax?" Lorelei demanded and then she moved away from Dax so she could finish this call. Then, she obviously needed to try to lend him a shoulder before she went back into the living room to do the same to Misty. She hated every inch of Julian and Aaron for dumping all this misery on them.

"No way of knowing for sure how they found out," Sophia explained. "And even if it's not true, it's out there and will have to be addressed if there are any future custody hearings."

Despite the ball of anger in the pit of her stomach, Lorelei heard something in Sophia's tone. Optimism, maybe. "If?" Lorelei repeated.

"If," the woman verified. Yes, definitely optimism,

something she hadn't heard from Sophia in a long time. "The judge finally ordered Aaron and the labs to release the results of the paternity test. It's not a match, Lorelei. Aaron's not Stellie's father."

Well, that sure as heck helped with the anger, and the relief washed through her so fast that Lorelei had to sit on the edge of Dax's desk. "Does this put an end to his custody claim?"

"Oh, Aaron will continue to fan the flames by playing the husband card, but this puts a serious dent in his case. This means Dax and you need to push forward. As soon as you can, Curt and I are advising you both to come into my office so the two of you can make a joint petition for custody of Stellie."

Lorelei had no trouble latching on to one of those words. And it caused her heart to skip a couple of beats. "Joint?"

"Yes." Sophia paused, then sighed. "Look, I know you wanted sole custody, that you wanted a judge to uphold the adoption, and that you're willing to give Dax and the Fords visitation rights—"

"That's exactly what I want," Lorelei interrupted, and while she figured Dax would be fair about all of this, she'd always thought of Stellie as hers. Added to that, the adoption had been legal. She hadn't cut corners, hadn't done anything wrong.

"This must probably feel like some sort of punishment," Sophia went on. "But if you want to get Aaron and Julian out of the picture fast, then joint custody with Dax is the way to go."

CHAPTER TWENTY

DAX DASHED OFF his signature on the paperwork for the purchase of two new bulls that Mike had left for him to sign, and then he got back to packing. He still had a couple of hours before he had to leave for the rodeo in Houston, but he wanted to finish any other paperwork and packing so he could go over and see Lorelei.

Hilda had brought Stellie by earlier so the baby could babble her "Gak" and make him feel like a million bucks with her smile. But he felt like pond scum when he thought of Lorelei.

In the two days since they'd learned about Aaron's paternity results and Julian had leaked the info about his therapy, Lorelei and he hadn't had any alone time. He needed to fix that.

Not so they could finally have sex, either.

Though Dax was hoping that would still eventually happen. But first he needed to try to soothe away the hurt he'd seen in her eyes when they'd gone to Sophia's office to sign the joint custody petition. Dax had told her that the paperwork meant nothing. Well, nothing other than a means to put a stop to Aaron. Other than that, Dax had spelled out that she was and always would be Stellie's mom and that he would be there for both of them.

But, oh, it had hurt Lorelei for them to sign those documents that spelled out his paternal rights. Worse, the documents listed Dax as the primary custodian since he was her father, and the legalese stated that it would be up to him to decide how to share custody with Lorelei and visitations with the Fords. The document had basically bucked up against what he had told her he wouldn't do.

That he wouldn't challenge her for custody.

He still wasn't doing that. Wouldn't. But it must have felt that way to her, and he could tell that in her text responses to him. She hadn't been cold or mean, had simply said she needed a little time to deal with it. He'd given her that time, two days, but he didn't want to go to Houston until he'd at least tried to make things better with her.

There was a little wiggle room with the Houston trip. His event wasn't until tomorrow, but he had to arrive there tonight in order to do the promo for not just the rodeo but for the one in Last Ride as well. He wouldn't be riding one of his own bulls in this, but others would be, and it was always a good plug for the ranch for Dax to point that out to the reporters doing the preliminary interviews.

Dax put the paperwork in his office so that Mike could process it, and then he shoved the rest of his stuff in his suitcase. He was carrying the suitcase out to his truck with plans to load it and then head to Lorelei's. That's when he saw Lorelei's car pull into the driveway.

He could have sworn his heart did a little happy dance. The rest of his body was in on that, too, and the happy dance got even better when she stepped from her car. She was probably wearing that "body hugging" outfit for work, but Dax figured she knew such things hiked up the heat in him.

"I wanted to catch you before you left for Houston," she said, making a beeline toward him. She barely paused when she reached him and then she put her arms around him and kissed him.

The relief came. Followed by a punch of lust that was so potent that he wanted to haul her off to bed then and there. First, there were those things he had to say. He waited, though, because Lorelei apparently had a message she wanted to get across, too, and that message involved the scalding kiss she was laying on him. A kiss that frazzled his brain and fired up every inch of him.

Every inch.

She finally pulled back, met his eyes, and Dax got that chance to speak.

"Would it screw things up if we fell hard for each other?" he asked.

All right. So, that hadn't been what he'd intended to say. *Shit*. He'd figured to start with an apology and go from there. He sure as heck hadn't meant to blurt that out.

She blinked, clearly not expecting him to let his mushy mind do the talking for him. And rather than wait for her to come up with how to respond to that, Dax kissed her.

He played dirty with it, too, by hooking his arm around her and hauling her to him so nearly every part of them was pressed together. Dax didn't stop kissing her until they had no choice but to break for air.

"Don't answer that question," he advised her, and because she looked as if she might ignore that advice, he kissed her again.

This time when he pulled back, he didn't see any answers to any spoken questions. However, he did see a whole lot of heat, which pleased him to no end.

"I have about two hours before I have to leave," he told her. "Want to see how we can use that time?"

She paused only a heartbeat, and then a slow smile

curved her beautiful mouth. "Yes," she said, her voice already silk and breath.

Dax did a loud and long mental, *Whew*. He'd dodged a bullet by her not focusing on his question. A question he didn't want answered until he was absolutely certain that her answer would be no, that it wouldn't screw things up if he fell for her.

Even if it might.

He wasn't in the mood for logic and consequences. He was in the mood for sex with Lorelei, and any and all discussions about future things that didn't involve sex could wait.

Or not.

The "or not" thought came when he both heard and saw the blue car speeding toward the house. It wasn't Julian's normal vehicle, but just in case it was Aaron or him, Dax automatically stepped in front of Lorelei as the car's tires squealed to a stop.

Dax looked inside, ground out, "Shit," and watched as the woman barreled out.

"Who is that?" Lorelei asked.

Dax needed to take a long breath first. "It's Joy."

No need for him to spell out exactly who that was. He'd mentioned the woman's name when he'd done his tell-all to Lorelei about his early sexual experiences. That was probably why he felt the muscles tense in Lorelei's body.

Joy strode toward them in her tight red dress and sky-high heels. Her usual attire. Ditto for her thick makeup and big hair that made her look a little like a country music star from the '60s. Joy wasn't old enough though for that era. She was forty-seven now and looked every one of those years and more.

"Why?" Joy demanded, and with just that one-word

question, Dax knew what she meant. She'd obviously gotten wind of what Aaron and Julian had leaked.

"I wasn't the one who leaked it," he said, purposely keeping his voice calm. He could tell Joy had been crying, and every nerve in her body seemed to be right beneath her skin. Not a good combo. He didn't want her to have a meltdown, especially in front of Lorelei.

After hearing his answer, Joy pulled back her shoulders and studied his face. Maybe rethinking, well, whatever the hell it was she'd come here to do. Yell, cry, cause a scene, threaten any multitude of things.

"Then who did it?" she pressed with her voice shaking from the anger.

Dax had no intention, none, of protecting the idiots who'd tried to dick around with him about this. "Aaron Marcel and Julian Martin. The first is a jackass businessman from St. Louis, and the second is his jackass of a lawyer who lives in San Antonio."

Joy made a sound of outrage and then burst into her usual tears, all the while sobbing, "Why? Why? Why?"

"They leaked it to hurt Dax because he's fighting them for custody of his daughter," Lorelei muttered.

Even over her sobs, Joy obviously heard that, and her head whipped up. "They did this to hurt Dax," she paraphrased. "But I'm the one who got hurt. This got back to my family. To my friends."

Dax doubted any of them were surprised by the news that she'd initiated a sexual relationship with a minor, but maybe those friends and family preferred not to have Joy's activities spelled out in a public way.

Welcome to the club.

Then again, Dax would have preferred if Joy had kept her hands off him when he'd been in high school. They couldn't go back and put this particular cat back in the bag. And he wouldn't undo this leaked info about him even if he could. There was something liberating about having his life an open book, and with this particular revelation, it meant the two dickheads didn't have any more ammunition they could use against him.

"They ruined my life to hurt you," Joy sobbed out.

Dax could have counted off the seconds to measure out just how long the crying would last. About the same amount of time as a successful bull ride. Eight seconds. And then, bam, she realized the tears weren't going to fix this so the anger came. He'd dealt with Joy enough over the years to know her pattern. Lash out, cry, lash out.

"I'm going to make the son of a bitches pay," Joy spat out. "I'm going to sue them for every penny and then make them issue a written apology. Then, I'll castrate both of them in public."

Good luck with that. The dickheads hadn't lied, and if anyone had a claim of wrongdoing in this, it would be him. After all, the leak had been things that had happened to him when he was a minor, and the courts frowned on that kind of stuff being used as gossip bait and name-smearing.

Dax wouldn't sue them, though, wouldn't demand any apologies and wouldn't schedule any castrations, public or otherwise. He just wanted Aaron, Julian and their particular brand of dog and pony show to disappear.

"I'll get payback," Joy vowed. "For me, for you." She stabbed her index finger at him, got back in her car and sped away.

ONCE LORELEI HAD Dax inside his house, she dropped her purse on the coffee table and had him sit on the sofa. She then located a bottle of whiskey so she could pour him a small shot. Small because she didn't want him buzzed. She just thought he needed something to take the edge off, and right now there seemed to be a lot of *edge*.

She briefly considered that a kiss might work as well, but after what had just happened, she wasn't sure the timing was right. Dax might be dealing with the mother lode of bad memories that Joy had caused him.

"Shit," he grumbled. Not his first time, either, to belt out that particular word of profanity. Groaning, he scrubbed his hand over his face. "I need to cancel going to Houston."

"No, you don't." Lorelei handed him the whiskey and knelt down in front of him so they were eye to eye. "You aren't letting Joy, Julian or Aaron take this rodeo event from you. If you're worried about Joy coming to my house, then Stellie and I can stay with Wyatt and Nola."

"She won't go to your house. Jealousy isn't her go-to response. It's anger, sex and hysterics." He paused, though. "Still, stay with Wyatt and Nola. If Joy stirs up Aaron and Julian, they might try to see you."

If so, it'd be the first time since Julian had shown up at the Glass Hatter. Dax and she could thank Curt and Sophia for that. They'd threatened legal action if Julian and/or Aaron continued to harass them. The threat had been enough to get them to back off. Well, back off from visits, anyway. They were obviously still working behind the scenes to cause trouble.

"Are you okay?" Lorelei asked. She touched her fingers to his right temple, on the vein that throbbed there, and she rubbed gently.

"Yeah," he said, but she figured he would have told her that whether or not it was true. "How about you?"

"It's a yes for me," she said. "But I'm so sorry you had to deal with this now."

He stared at her and set the untouched glass of whiskey on the side table. "Joy doesn't have any power or control over me anymore." He paused again. "You do, though."

Well, that was a confession she hadn't expected to hear, and she certainly hadn't expected to see that heat in his eyes. Heat for her. So, maybe he wasn't dealing with bad memories but rather just the frustration of having this encounter. And maybe the notion of that kiss wasn't a bad idea, after all.

Slowly, so he'd have time to decide if he wanted to back away or not, Lorelei stayed on her knees and leaned in to touch her mouth to his. But Dax didn't back away. Nope. He made a rumbling sound deep in this throat, and he slid his hand around the back of her neck to draw her even closer. Slow and easy. Inch by inch.

Until the kiss was much more than a touch.

He made another of those sounds before the slow-and-easy approach seemed to snap. And Lorelei welcomed that. Mercy, did she. Because Dax didn't hesitate or hold back one bit when he pulled her to him.

They angled their bodies toward each other, their mouths taking advantage of that new closeness, and Dax immediately deepened the kiss. She welcomed that, too, and did some deepening of her own. She did that by climbing onto his lap and kissing him as if nothing bad had ever happened to either of them.

All in all, it was the right approach.

Because it was hard to think of bad things, of the past or pretty much anything else when he made her feel all this want. This need. This heat.

Dax shifted, sliding his arm around her butt and standing. He managed that without breaking the kiss, and for a moment she thought he was taking her to his bedroom. But no. He headed for the front door, fumbled around and then locked it. With this sudden firestorm of heat, she'd forgotten that someone could just walk in on them.

The realization of anyone walking in on them, or of anyone else, period, vanished when he just kept kissing her, and he took her back to the sofa. He dropped back down into a sitting position with her anchored on his lap.

And he kicked things up a significant notch.

Dax went after her top, pulled it off her and sent it flying. In the same motion, he shoved down the cups of her bra and tongue-kissed her breasts. The man was certainly good at this so it was hard for her to be jealous of all the practice he'd clearly had to perfect this particular skill. He used his tongue to send the need inside her soaring.

Lorelei wanted to give in to that soaring. To that urgent building heat. But first she wanted her hands on Dax, and that started with getting off his shirt. Not easy to do since she had to work around all those kisses he was using to torment her breasts and neck.

When she finally got the buttons undone, she shoved the shirt off his shoulders and started some tormenting of her own. She finally got her mouth, and her tongue, on his chest. On all those incredible muscles that before today she'd only managed to get glimpses of. Well, this was no glimpse now, and despite her body urging her to hurry, hurry, hurry, she slowed down enough to draw out a long groan of pleasure and some curses from him.

Obviously, his body was urging him to hurry as well because he went after her skirt and somehow managed to make it a heat-charged striptease. He didn't just unzip her skirt and slide it down. He pressed his hands against her, giving her a quick thrill from the pressure. Not a bull rub meant to relax. This was clearly meant to arouse.

And it was mission accomplished.

Lorelei heard her own groan of need. She cursed him, too, when he managed to get off her panties while she was still struggling with his darn belt. Dax wasn't helping with that, either. That's because he was tongue-kissing every erogenous point on her body. Oh, yes. He managed to locate every last one of them.

If she hadn't been so worked up and ready to climax, she would have cheered when she finally got off his belt and his jeans unzipped.

"I have a condom in my purse," she managed to say.

"I've got some, too." He took out his wallet, retrieved one and then stood long enough to shove off his jeans and boxers.

Oh, my.

The man definitely exceeded any and all expectations, and she promised herself that she'd have a better look at him and all those expectations once they'd burned off some of this heat. Now wasn't the time for lazy admiring and exploring. Now was the time for sex.

Dax must have agreed with her on that because he got the condom on in no time flat, and he dropped back down onto the sofa. Not on top of her but rather pulling her back into his lap.

"Easier to kiss you this way," he drawled.

Yes, it was. He took her mouth while he took the rest of her. He entered her in a hard but slow thrust that nearly caused her to lose the grip she had on staving off that climax. She wanted this to last. Of course, it could never last as long as she wanted, which was a day or two. No, this soaring heat wouldn't be denied.

Dax used the grip he had on her hips to continue the thrusts. One after another. Each one going deeper. Each one harder. Each one faster. And true to his word, he did all of that while he kissed her.

With his mouth taking hers, Dax gave her that one final thrust. The one that snapped her restraint. The one that sent her flying.

Lorelei made sure that Dax flew right along with her.

CHAPTER TWENTY-ONE

DAX FIGURED THIS side trip was going to screw up his getting to Houston in time to do some of the promos for the ranch, but it couldn't be helped. He needed to get some things straight, and once Lorelei and he had said their farewells—and kissed a whole bunch—he'd headed not to Houston but rather to San Antonio.

To see Joy.

He knew she was home because he'd texted her after all that farewell kissing with Lorelei, and Dax had told Joy he was on his way over. He hadn't told Lorelei, though, because he didn't want her to worry while he was away on this trip. But he would tell her when he got back. See her, tell her, kiss her and hopefully have sex with her again.

There'd been times in his life when sex had felt wrong. Not because it'd been bad but because it'd left him feeling empty and frustrated. That hadn't happened with Lorelei. It'd been, well, the best, and while it didn't fix everything about their current situations, it sure as hell didn't hurt anything, either.

He hoped.

Just in case, though, Lorelei had some reservations and doubts, he'd owe her that long chat when he got back. Thinking about her and that chat just might make him forget, too, that this was his next to last ride before he officially retired. Since that definitely didn't improve his mood, he put it aside, parked in front of Joy's and went to the door.

He'd known her address because Joy had a habit of sending him letters. She couldn't text him because she no longer had his number. Something that Dax had made sure of. No way had he wanted to hear from her when she was in the middle of one of her rants. He'd stopped her as well from just showing up at the ranch by threatening her with a restraining order. An order that would violate the terms of her probation and send her back to jail.

The probation wasn't for what she'd done to him but rather what she'd done to another teenage boy. That arrest had landed her in jail, given her the label of a sex offender, but now she was out on probation. Any violation of that would mean she'd have to serve out the remaining five years of her sentence.

Joy threw open the door before he even had a chance to ring the bell so that let him know she'd been watching for him. And she'd obviously used the short lead time to fix herself up. She'd changed out of the red dress and gone for an equally snug blue one.

"I'm glad you came," she said, her words breathy and rushed. "I'm sorry I caused such a scene earlier. I was upset."

"Yeah, I got that. I was upset, too, when word got out about it. I'm not here for that," he told her right off when she reached for him.

Joy pulled back her hand, tried a mock playful pout that made him wish there was a cure for whatever had made her this way.

"I'm not staying long," he added, and Dax didn't go in despite her stepping back and motioning for him to do that. "I just wanted to say some things to you."

She pulled back her shoulders and obviously didn't care much for his serious tone. But it was a tone she should have expected since they hadn't been lovers in a very long time.

"What happened between us shouldn't have happened," he stated, "but I won't let it mess me up. I won't let it define who I am. This is goodbye, Joy."

Joy grabbed his arm when he went to turn. "You can't mean that." Tears sprang to her eyes, and he didn't think these were of the fake variety. Still, he had no intention of being affected by them. In fact, he had no intentions of being affected by anything she ever did again.

"Do I have to show you the tat to remind you of what you mean to me?" she threw out there. "Or maybe you could look at yours and remember?"

Dax sighed and eased her grip off him. That tat reminder wasn't going to work, either. He could have told her to have the tat removed. Or fixed. But if Joy wanted to hang on to that long gone stuff, then that was her choice. His choice was to never deal with her again.

"I'm going to ruin Aaron Marcel and Julian Martin," she snarled when he backed away from her. "I'm going to make them pay."

He nodded. "Whatever you do won't involve me," he stated. "Nothing you ever do again will involve me. Understand?"

She frantically shook her head. "We have a history together. I'll always be part of your life—"

"No," he interrupted. "The part you had in my life is over. Goodbye, Joy." He heard the cool tone of his own voice. Felt the cease-fire settle inside him.

Maybe Joy heard it as well because she didn't argue, didn't threaten, didn't cry. "Goodbye, Dax," she murmured.

And he realized that was the first time she'd ever said

that to him. The first time, too, in a very long time that he felt this cool wash of peace go through him. It was too bad he wasn't feeling so peaceful about the rest of his life, but for now, it was a start.

He got back in his truck and headed for Houston.

LORELEI FELT THE nerves zing through her. Excitement, too. Unfortunately, there was also more than a smidge of doubt as to whether or not she was doing the right thing.

It felt right, coming here to Houston to watch Dax ride, but it had occurred to her on the drive, and now, that this might not be a moment to celebrate. He might not want anyone he knew around to see the almost certain sadness that this was the near-end of his career.

Of course, he had another career with the bulls on Sunset Creek Ranch, but since he'd been juggling both that and the riding for years, it might not feel enough for him. Stellie might not fill that void for him.

She might not, either.

Great sex, and it had been great, didn't mean any kind of commitment, and Lorelei hadn't wanted to put strings on whatever Dax and she ended up doing together. Both of them had been burned with relationships so anything more than sex might not be in the cards for them.

Except for that question he'd asked.

Would it screw things up if we fell hard for each other?

That definitely sounded as if he might want more than just sex. Might. And that might dropped to only a slim possibility, considering he'd practically waved off that question by telling her not to answer it. So, he'd had second and maybe even third thoughts about even bringing it up.

But even with all those doubts, she'd still come.

After she'd arranged for Stellie and Hilda to stay with

Lily and Hayden, that is. Even though Aaron and Julian hadn't made any new threats in the past twenty-fours, she hadn't wanted Hilda to be alone with Stellie at the house if trouble came their way. Since Dax's brother Jonas was also at Lily's ranch, he wouldn't let trouble get anywhere near Stellie.

This wasn't Lorelei's first rodeo, but it was the first big one she'd ever attended. And it was *big* along with being popular. She'd had to pay an outrageous price through a third-party seller to get a ticket to the already sold-out event, and then had had to work her way through the crowd to get to the main arena where Dax would be riding.

At least her seat had a good view of the arena, and once the event started, Lorelei bought a beer and some popcorn and sat back to watch the other riders. It was different seeing it like this rather than in a corral at Dax's ranch. The energy of the crowd and the cheers. It was impossible not to get caught up in it, and the catching-up hit her especially hard when Dax came on the huge screens in the center of the arena. The camera had zoomed in on him as he was prepping for his ride.

"The man's a walking, talking orgasm," the perky young woman next to Lorelei declared. She and her equally perky companion giggled and speculated as to whether or not he was as good in bed as he looked.

"Yes," Lorelei answered before she even realized she was going to say anything.

The women both looked at her, giving her a bit of the stink eye mixed with some suspicion that she might not be telling the truth. But Lorelei just smiled and kept eating her popcorn.

Her smug munching didn't last, though, when she saw the size of the bull. According to the announcer, its name was Crusher, and she prayed the bull didn't manage to do some of that to Dax.

She sucked in a hard breath when Crusher and Dax bolted out of the chute. Yes, definitely different from watching him at the ranch, but in that exciting, terrifying and awe-filled moment, she understood why there were some who were seriously attracted to this. Watching a hot guy ride had its pluses.

Lorelei continued to hold her breath. Continued to wince, too, when she watched Dax being slung around, and she could honestly say it was the longest eight seconds of her life. It must have seemed like a lifetime or two to Dax. But at the end of it and with the crowd shouting out his name, he eased off the bull. Not on his butt, either, but his feet. And since the rodeo clowns hurried in to distract the bull, Dax gave his fans a wave and a wide grin while he made his way out of the arena.

"Come on," one of the perky women said. "I know where to go to get his autograph. I'm going to see if he'll sign my boobs."

Lorelei didn't want a boob autograph, but she followed the women. Her plan had been to wait until the ride was over and text Dax to let him know she was here, but this way she could maybe get a peek of him and see what his mood was.

The women did, indeed, seem to know where they were going, and they threaded their way around clusters of people, some of them still talking about Dax's ride. They went past the concessions and to an area at the back of the arena where Dax was talking with several reporters.

Along with the TV cameras, there were plenty of others snapping pictures and calling out to him. Dax handled it all with the same skill and agility that he handled sex. He doled out plenty of cockiness and charm even when one of the reporters asked how he felt about his recent personal troubles and retirement.

Lorelei's heart sank.

Of course that would come up. The things that Aaron and Julian had released about him being in therapy wouldn't just stay confined to Last Ride gossips.

"I'm a firm believer that if folks need counseling, they should get it," he said. "I did, and it helped. As for the retiring, well, that's not happening just yet." Dax paused, chuckled. "If folks want to see one ride more, then they need to show up at the Last Ride Charity Rodeo next weekend."

With his easy grin still in place, Dax stepped back and waved in a way that signaled the end of the press interviews. Still waving, he turned in the directions of those calling out to him. And then froze when he spotted Lorelei. Her own chuckle was solely from nerves as she watched the surprise freeze his face for oh, about eight seconds. Then, his smile returned, and he made a beeline toward her. The perky women must have thought he was heading to see them because their giggling and jumping up and down skyrocketed.

"Ladies," Dax said to them, but he kept his attention nailed to Lorelei.

Even though there was a fence between them, he leaned in and kissed her. Her legs dissolved. Her brain turned to mush. But she still heard the disappointed huffs of the perky pair. Lorelei wasn't disappointed one little bit.

"I watched you ride," Lorelei gushed out, realizing that she sounded very much like a total fan girl. "You were amazing."

"I drew an easy bull," he said with that same easiness as his smile.

"We wanted you to sign our boobs," one of the perks said, and she started to lift her top.

Dax stopped her, and while he kept on smiling, he took the permanent marker she offered him and dashed off his autograph on her arm. He did the same for the other woman, and then reached out to pick up Lorelei.

"It's all right," Dax called out to several men in security uniforms who started toward them.

Dax's maneuver caused some cheers. Some grumbles. And he set Lorelei on her feet inside the arena. He gave his fans a final wave before he slid his arm around her and got her moving.

"Where's Stellie?" he asked.

"Staying the night with Hilda, Hayden and Lily."

That brought on a fresh grin. "Want to have some dinner and then see my hotel room?" He touched his mouth to hers.

Everything inside her relaxed. The nerves vanished, and it felt as if everything had fallen into place. "Yes, to both."

The day before he'd asked her what was the worst that could happen if he fell for her? But that question was like closing the barn door after the horse had bolted.

Because it had already happened on her part.

Lorelei knew with absolute certainty that she had already fallen and fallen hard for Dax.

CHAPTER TWENTY-TWO

DAX HAD PLENTY of work to do, but none of it seemed as important as walking with Stellie so she could see the new bulls.

Well, that was *walking* in the general sense of the word.

Sometime in the past four days since he'd gotten back from the Houston rodeo and an amazing night with Lorelei, Stellie had taken her first steps. Except it hadn't been just steps. While in the playroom he'd set up for her, she had taken off in a toddling run that made her look like an out-of-control bumblebee. Butt waddling, arms waving, giggling like a loon and falling every third or fourth step.

Still, the falls didn't make her slow down or stop so Dax just did his best to keep up with her while Lorelei finished a work call on the back porch. A call she'd gotten right after Stellie and she had arrived. From the gist of what he'd heard, the call wasn't to put out any new or existing custody fires but rather from a new glass artist who would be supplying pieces to the shop while Nola was on maternity leave.

Lorelei was no doubt keeping an eye on Stellie and him, making sure he didn't let the baby do anything dangerous, but the whole notion of toddler mobility seemed on the dangerous side to him. Heck, the notion of toddlerhood and fatherhood, period, still seemed scary as hell, but as he watched Stellie run, and fall, as she hurried toward the pasture fence, he saw the fun in it, too.

Maybe that was DNA's doing. Making a parent feel that deep connection to their child. Then again, Stellie was an interesting, cute kid. So even if she hadn't been his, she would have been fun to be around.

Thankfully, she was around a lot.

Lorelei had seen to that by bringing her over nearly every day in between Stellie's early dinner and before it was time to get her back for the whole bedtime routine. In turn, Dax had gone to Lorelei's to help with that routine. And so he could spend some time afterward exploring Lorelei and her body. Tonight, Stellie and she would be staying, which meant more time with both of them.

All in all, it was working out well.

Or well-ish, anyway.

Dax certainly wasn't going to forget his looming retirement in three days. Or the work he still had to do to get ready for the Last Ride Charity Rodeo that he sponsored. He also wasn't going to forget, either, that Aaron and Julian just weren't giving the hell up and were still making legal motion after motion to try to stake some kind of claim on "his wife's child" so Aaron could no doubt in turn stake some kind of claim on Valerie's money.

All annoyances and stuff to do on his already piled high proverbial plate. But there were some sweet spots in his life, and Lorelei and Stellie were responsible for that.

"Mama," Stellie babbled, pointing to the bulls. She did a decent job imitating a snort that the Brahman mix made, but Dax was reasonably sure that Lorelei wouldn't care much for her mama label being shared with the bull.

"That's Thunder," he said.

Stellie attempted that, too, and then grinned, sporting

those four tiny teeth. Her pause lasted mere seconds before she wanted to keep toddling down the fence line, all the while pointing out the bulls. Despite the animals' size, they didn't seem to frighten her.

He glanced back at the house and saw Lorelei had finished her call and was making her way toward them. She stopped to have a short conversation with Mike, who was carrying some paperwork he'd just gotten from Dax's office. Insurance forms and such that Dax had already signed for the rodeo since the Last Ride town council had yet to go paperless.

Lorelei had some paperwork of her own. A large thick envelope that he hoped had nothing to do with the custody fight. But maybe it did. As she got closer, he could see some worry on her face.

"Sorry about that," Lorelei said, walking toward them. She tipped her head toward Mike, who was heading to the bunkhouse where he had his office. "Mike says I'm to try to talk you out of riding Thunder at the Last Ride rodeo."

It didn't surprise Dax that Mike had gone to Lorelei for that. Mike had already broached the subject with him, and Dax hadn't been receptive to opting for an easy bull for his farewell ride.

"Yeah," Dax said, and he left it at that.

Lorelei, though, didn't leave it. "What if I said I didn't want you to ride him, either?"

"You don't have faith in my riding skills?" He added a grin to that so she'd know he wasn't pissed for her bringing it up.

She shook her head. "I have complete faith in you. But you have nothing to prove, Dax."

He kept up the grin for the first part of that. He liked Lorelei having faith in him. The grin faded, though, on the second part because he didn't want to gloss over the important stuff. Definitely didn't want to shove it back down the way he used to do.

"It sort of feels as if I do have something to prove," he admitted.

Lorelei studied him for several moments before she leaned in and kissed him. "You don't," she assured him.

Dax might have drawn her back to him to add to that kiss, but Stellie banged on his leg with one hand while she pointed to the bulls with the other. Whatever she babbled wasn't Mama or Gak but something that sounded more like a snorting belch.

"I've been trying to teach her to say Dada," Lorelei explained. "She still has a way to go."

Yeah, she did, but it pleased him that Lorelei was trying to take the kid's vocabulary in that direction even if the word *Dada* tapped into that whole boatload of fear and worry he was still dealing with.

"FYI," Lorelei continued, "what we're doing here doesn't have to become your new norm. You can pause, hit the snooze button, slow down or whatever it is you need to do."

Now he studied her, and he was reasonably sure she'd just offered him an out. Part of him, that part being pecked to death with worry, wanted to cling to it, but hell, if he could ride a mean bull that wanted to make hoof grit of him, then he could do this.

Or rather attempt it, anyway.

He only hoped he didn't go down his usual path of screwing up something. Because Lorelei and Stellie were too important to him for that.

"The speed is just fine," he assured her. "No snooze button required." He didn't verbally add, not at the moment, but it seemed to be there, hanging in the air between them.

Rather than dwell on it or spell it out, he tipped his head to the large envelope she was carrying. "What's that?"

When she didn't give him a quick answer, Dax sighed. Hell, was this another legal ploy by the dick duo?

"It's the Last Ride Society report on Valerie," she finally said. "I finished it a couple of hours ago." Then, she paused. "Miriam managed to find a photo of you and Valerie together."

Dax nearly cursed. "Please tell me it wasn't another naked butt shot."

"No." She gave a nervous laugh. "It's one Miriam got from one of the newspapers that covered the rodeo."

He had to shake his head. He'd been interviewed after his ride, that was the norm, but Dax couldn't recall any photos being taken.

Dax was about to look in the envelope to see the photo for himself, but his phone rang, and he groaned when he saw Curt's name on the screen. *Hell. What now?*

"It's Curt," he relayed to Lorelei, and he shifted so that she could take Stellie's hand while he answered the call. "How bad?" he immediately asked.

"A judge is going to review Aaron's petition for visitation rights since he was married to Valerie when she gave birth to Stellie," Curt explained.

Even though he hadn't put the call on speaker—just in case there was some cursing involved—Lorelei obviously heard what the lawyer said because she groaned.

"Visitation rights?" Dax questioned. "Why would he want that? Better yet, why would a judge even consider giving him such rights when it's already been proven that he's not Stellie's father?"

"My guess is Aaron will give the judge a sob story about

how much he loved his wife and that Stellie is the last piece he has of her."

It was hard, but Dax kept his curse words in his head and didn't snarl them aloud for Stellie to hear. "What's your guess as to why Aaron would even want this because I'm not buying that 'love for his wife' bit."

"Neither am I. A judge might, though."

Again, it was damn hard to hold back the profanity, and Lorelei looked ready to implode. "Why would Aaron really want this?" Dax pressed.

"Probably so he can use the visits to get money from the Fords, Valeric's trust fund or even you or Lorelei. Money that he could claim he needs to set up a nursery for Stellie, buy her toys, food, etc. It's a long shot that it'll even work—"

"I'm not letting that—" Dax had to stop and come up with a name that would be kid-appropriate and wouldn't blister Curt's ears "—*person* have visitation rights with Stellie."

"Agreed," Curt readily said, "and that's why I think Aaron's looking for some kind of settlement or a negotiation that'll put money in his pockets. After all, if a judge did grant even limited visitations, the Fords, Lorelei and you would no doubt be willing to deal to make it all go away."

Dax despised the notion of giving that dickhead one cent. But Curt was right. There were at least four people who'd be willing to do pretty much anything to keep Aaron from getting his hands on Stellie even for a short visit.

"I'll keep you posted," Curt added a moment later. "And have Lorelei call Sophia if she wants to discuss this. We figured there was no need for both of us to call with the news since you two are probably discussing all aspects of the case."

That was a lawyerly way of saying there was likely pil-
low talk. Which there was. But Dax didn't want to spend
his time with Lorelei going over all this bullshit. He just
wanted Aaron to go away so maybe it was, indeed, time to
consider paying off the SOB.

Since the mosquitos were starting to buzz around them,
Dax scooped up Stellie so they could start back to the
house. Sunset was still an hour off, and he made a mental
note to go out onto the porch with Stellie and Lorelei to
watch it. He could fire up the various bug-repellant candles
and such to stave off the mosquitos long enough to watch
because the view didn't get any better than sunset on the
ranch. It just might improve his now sour mood over what
Curt had just told him. Then again, that was asking a lot
from a mere sunset and bug repellant.

They went inside to one of the spare bedrooms that Dax
had turned into a playroom so that Stellie could have some
time with her new toys before her bath and then that sunset-
viewing.

Lorelei handed him the envelope and then went to the
kitchen. A few minutes later, she came back with a beer
for him and a glass of wine for herself. Dax didn't open
the report, though, until they were both sitting on the floor
with Stellie. He had a long drink of the beer that he figured
he'd need, and he pulled out the contents of the envelope.
The report and the photo.

Since he knew he hadn't posed for such a shot, Dax had
expected a grainy photo. It wasn't. The photographer had
likely been trying to capture the huge banner that sported
the name and date of the event, but Valerie and he had been
standing directly beneath it. He was still wearing his chaps
and riding gear and facing Valerie with her looking up at
him as he was looking down at her.

Thankfully, they didn't look like a couple who had the one-off hots for each other. No groping or other PDA. Just them looking at each other, which had a G-rated sort of intimacy about it.

"Are you okay?" Lorelei asked.

"Yeah," he answered without even thinking if it was true. It was, he decided. But he glanced at Lorelei to see how she was handling it. "Are you okay with it?"

Unlike him, she wasn't so quick to answer. "Yes." She sipped some wine, gathered her breath. "This way, Stellie will have a photo of her birth parents together. Not that you're only a birth parent. Clearly, you're more." She fanned her hand around the room as proof of that.

Dax made a sound of agreement. Yes, if he had his way about it, he would continue to be more than just a bio dad.

"I made a copy of the report for the Fords," Lorelei went on. "Most of the stories and other photos came from them, but I thought they'd like it as a keepsake. I have a copy for Stellie, too."

There seemed to be a question at the end of that. Did he want one as well? He didn't, but he would read through it. Maybe he'd finally get to know the woman he got pregnant.

"How are the Fords doing?" he asked.

Lorelei shrugged. "As well as can be expected. I suspect this latest antic by Aaron will set them back a bit."

Yeah, and whether Dax liked it or not, it was setting back Lorelei and him, too. Hard to think about the future when you were still dealing with the present. At least he'd closed the door on one thing from his past.

"I went to see Joy before I left for the rodeo in Houston," Dax told her and waited for her gaze to come to his. Oh, it came all right, and he hated that he'd put some fresh worry in her eyes. "It's okay," he assured her, and that was the truth. "I just had to make sure she didn't have any kind of pull on me. Not sexual," he quickly clarified.

Then glanced at Stellie to make sure she wasn't tuning in to this conversation. She wasn't. She was playing with some toy horses.

"Definitely not sexual," Dax went on. "That hasn't been there for more than a decade, but over that decade, she's pulled the 'damsel in distress' act on me. Maybe not a total act," he admitted, "but I can't fix what's wrong with her, and I don't want to try. That's why I went to see her, and I told her goodbye and that she was no longer part of my life."

"How did Joy take that?" Lorelei asked, still studying him.

Now it was his turn to shrug. "Well, she said goodbye back, but time will tell if she means it. Right before that goodbye, she brought up the tats, I guess her way of saying she'd marked me for life or something."

Because he was studying her, too, he saw the surprise flash through her eyes. Only then did Dax remember he hadn't explained the tats.

"Oh, yeah," he said, mentally backing up a bit. "That."

"You don't have to tell me if it'll bring up bad memories," she quickly offered.

It would bring up some bad, some good, but he didn't want Lorelei thinking of anything bad when she looked at his ass. And he was hoping she'd have many opportunities to check out his ass in the future.

"When I was sixteen," he started, "Joy took me to a tat studio where a friend of hers broke the law and inked me even though I was underage. He inked her initials on me and put mine on her."

Lorelei's mouth dropped open. "She branded you."

"Yep," he readily agreed. "I guess she thought it would

always make me think of her, and it did, but not in a good way. So, when I turned twenty-one, my brothers threw me a party at Three Sheets to the Wind, and Frankie was there. After I'd had too much to drink, I told her about a tat I wanted removed."

That, of course, had involved him actually showing her the tat. Thankfully, though, that night he hadn't bared his ass to anyone else that would have asked questions about who the hell JJ was.

"Frankie didn't own Ink, Etc. back then, but she was working at another place in San Antonio, and she said it'd be easier to make the initials into something else. So she took me then and there to the shop. Needless to say, large quantities of alcohol and selecting a tat don't always mix, and I nearly agreed to a cute wart-speckled frog before Tanner showed up and steered us in the direction of livestock."

"And you went with the longhorn," she concluded, sounding relieved that this hadn't been an incident from hell. More like covering up an incident from hell.

He nodded. "The initials are still there," he admitted. "I guess like a metaphor for the past. But I put something new over it for a fresh start."

Lorelei stayed quiet a moment. Then, she smiled. And some of the tightness eased up in his chest. He was okay with his tat metaphor do-over, but he hadn't wanted it to stir up any memories of Joy for Lorelei.

"It's ironic that the tat was how I found out you were Stellie's father," she said. Not with the worry and fear she'd first had that day when she'd come to him with that photo.

"So, something good came out of it," he concluded.

Their gazes locked and held, and he could feel the heat stirring between them. Maybe something deeper than the heat, but it blinked away when someone rang his doorbell.

Since he wasn't expecting company and family would have called or texted first, he figured this would put a fast end to the moment he was having with Lorelei.

"Wait here with Stellie," he advised in case it was Aaron or Julian. Dax didn't know if Lorelei had shut the gate after she'd driven in, but if she hadn't, then one of the two idiots might have taken it upon themselves to risk that restraining order Curt had threatened them with.

Ready to snap and snarl, Dax went to the front door, threw it open and saw his visitor. Not Julian or Aaron but rather Derwin Parkman. He wasn't alone, either. He had Mildred Schwartz and Frank Dayton with him, and while Dax wasn't positive, he thought they were members of Sherlock's Snoops.

"The game is afoot, and we found something," all three of them said at once.

Dax didn't invite them in, didn't say anything, but that didn't stop Derwin from whipping out a piece of paper. "We did some more digging on that lawyer fella, Julian Martin, but when we didn't find anything else on him, we had a little look-see at his current client, Aaron Marcel." Derwin leaned in and gave a smug nod. "We're dealing with a liar, liar pants on fire here."

That got Dax's attention and so did the paper he took from Derwin. It was a marriage license from Kansas City, and his gaze skirted over the names. Aaron Marcel and Katie Miller.

"Look at the date," Derwin prompted.

Dax was already moving in that direction and he saw the marriage had taken place nearly thirteen years ago when Aaron had been barely twenty. The bride had been just nineteen.

"So, Aaron was married before Valerie," Dax murmured,

and there was plenty of disappointment in his voice. Clearly, he'd gotten his hopes up too high that the Snoops had actually found something important.

"Yes," Derwin verified. Then, he smiled as if there was actually something to smile about. "Mildred here is a whiz at going through hatch, match, scratch and dispatch records."

Dax stared at the woman. "And what does that mean? Better yet, what does it have to do with Aaron Marcel?"

Mildred smiled, too. "Hatch, match, scratch and dispatch," she repeated. "Birth, marriage, divorce and death records. There's not a scratch record in any of the fifty states for Aaron Marcel and Katie Miller. Even more, Katie Miller Marcel is alive and well and living in Topeka, Kansas."

"Aaron never divorced Katie," Dax muttered.

"Bingo," Derwin happily agreed. "There is a marriage license on file for Aaron and Valerie, and Aaron states on it that this is his first marriage." He wagged his index finger in a no-no gesture. "Liar, liar pants on fire."

Oh, yeah. Those lying pants were on fire all right, and because of that lying, things had just gotten a lot easier for Lorelei and him. Because Aaron had not only broken the law, this meant his marriage to Valerie wasn't even legal.

CHAPTER TWENTY-THREE

FOR THE FIRST time since this whole custody ordeal had begun, Lorelei was actually looking forward to seeing Aaron. Of course, that meant she'd be seeing Julian, too, since the man had insisted he wouldn't meet with Dax, the Fords and her unless his lawyer was present. But in this case, she thought it would be fun to watch Julian taken down a notch or two.

Fun to see Aaron go down even more notches.

Lorelei wasn't ready to sing "Ding-Dong the Witch Is Dead" just yet, but she might just do this after the meeting. It might be fun to sing it when she went to pick up Stellie, who was spending the day at home with Evangeline.

"I never thought I'd actually say this, but I'm glad Derwin has too much time on his hands," Dax remarked.

Lorelei made a quick sound of agreement. So did Miriam, Greg, Sophia and Curt. They were all assembled in Curt's large meeting room, waiting for Julian and Aaron to arrive. Thanks to Curt and Sophia's quick work, they now had official copies of Aaron's marriage licenses and a sworn statement from Katie Miller that Aaron and she had never divorced.

According to Katie, she'd simply never gotten around to filing for a divorce from the *scumbag, control freak*, and since she'd yet to find someone to remarry, she hadn't felt the need to do the paperwork. However, the woman had been none too pleased to learn that Aaron had married someone else and was more than willing to give any testimony needed to make him pay for what he'd done.

"Any chance Aaron could end up getting jail time?" Miriam asked the lawyers.

Curt shrugged. "Maybe. That depends on how far you want to push it. Since he committed the act of bigamy in the state of Missouri, I checked the laws there. It's only a misdemeanor, punishable up to a year in jail. He's unlikely to get jail time, though, only probation since he doesn't have a criminal record." He motioned for Sophia to continue the explanation.

"You could perhaps prove that Aaron married your daughter for the purpose of defrauding her," Sophia said. "That'd likely mean a long legal battle where you'd have to come up with proof that he tapped into her accounts without her knowing."

Miriam sighed. "And since we know that Valerie was under investigation for removing funds, we probably wouldn't be able to prove that Aaron was the one to do that, not her."

"As Curt said, you'd have to push," Sophia agreed, and then she paused. "Curt and I have discussed this, and it's our advice for you to consult your lawyer there in St. Louis. Which brings me to something else we can discuss while we're waiting on Aaron and his lawyer. Stellie was born before Valerie died. In absence of a will, that means she's Valerie's next of kin."

"Unless Mr. Ford and you challenge that," Curt added, "then Stellie will inherit Valerie's estate."

Miriam and Greg exchanged a quick glance. "We have no intentions of challenging it. We want her to inherit," Greg insisted, and he shifted his attention to Dax. "We have no intentions of challenging your claim to paternity, either, or the adoption. We would like in writing, though, that we have visitation rights."

Lorelei hadn't known just how much tension she was carrying in her body until she felt her muscles relax. So much weight dropped from her shoulders. She heard Dax take in a quick breath. Probably of relief, and he reached over, took hold of her hand and gave it a gentle squeeze.

"You can definitely have visitation rights," Lorelei assured them. "And I hope you'll be a big part of your granddaughter's life."

Tears shimmered in Miriam's eyes. "Of course, we will." She glanced at her husband again, and he gave a confirming nod. "Once Greg and I have settled our own legal problems, we intend to buy a second house here in Last Ride. Not so we can take over Stellie's life," the woman quickly added. "But so it'll make it easier for us to be here for her birthdays, milestones and such."

More weight lifted from Lorelei's shoulders. Since her father and Dax's parents were both dead, that meant Stellie might have missed out on the whole grandparent deal. Now, she'd have the Fords along with Evangeline. Things were definitely falling into place.

Well, maybe they were.

Dax seemed perfectly fine with her being the primary custodial parent to Stellie and with him being a hands-on father. Added to that, her own personal relationship was, well, satisfying. He was a great dad, a good man and an awesome lover.

But both the "satisfying relationship" and "awesome lover" part might go away.

Maybe because of his damaged past he'd never be able to take that leap of faith and hand over his heart to anyone.

She would just have to accept that. And so what if they never managed to make it past the "just being lovers" stage? What they had now was much better than what some had.

Lorelei looked at Dax when he squeezed her hand again. Just a gentle little nudge of pressure because maybe he'd seen the fresh worry on her face.

"Once we're done here, we'll celebrate," he whispered to her while the Fords were discussing possible legal action against Aaron.

Dax added one of his smiles, and just like that, she was snapped right back into the heat. Snapped into a moment where at least her body believed that all would be perfect.

The sound of shouting stopped the perfection, though.

Lorelei recognized Julian's and Aaron's voices, both of them yelling a mishmash of words she couldn't make out. There was a woman shouting as well, but her voice wasn't familiar. Not to her, anyway. Apparently, it was to Dax.

"Joy," he spat out, automatically getting to his feet.

Lorelei and the rest got up as well, and the shouts got a lot closer. Now she was able to make out what was being said.

"Back off," Julian shouted over Joy's wails of, "You'll pay for what you've done."

Oh, mercy. Was Joy attacking Julian and Aaron? Dax must have thought it was possible because he muttered for her to, "Stay put," and he rushed to the door to throw it open.

Since there was a large reception area just outside the meeting room, Lorelei could see both Julian and Aaron, and they appeared to be jockeying for position while they tried to cower behind each other. Definitely no one rushing to be the hero here.

No one except Dax.

"Joy," Dax said, lifting his hands in a "stay calm" gesture.

She was on the other side of the receptionist's desk and wielding a knife, slashing it through the air while she spewed a litany of profanity. The terrified receptionist, Christine Dayton, was huddled on the floor in the corner with her phone pressed to her ear. She was no doubt calling the cops.

Lorelei's heart dropped when she realized Dax's intentions. He walked into reception, moving in between Joy and the two men.

"They have to pay for what they did to me," Joy shouted, sounding like the ultimate victim. Tears were streaming down her cheeks, and her face was red and splotchy, no doubt from the crying and the rage of temper.

Lorelei had no sympathy whatsoever for Julian spilling the woman's secrets. All sympathy she had was for Dax and what Joy had put him through. What she apparently was still putting him through since he was smack in the middle of this.

"Joy, you need to put down the knife," Dax said. His voice was as calm as a lake, and she thought of him telling her that he'd had to soothe the woman before. Mercy, had those times involved weapons as well?

"I need to make them pay," Joy argued, and she jabbed the knife at the air again.

"You can't make them pay this way." Again, Dax stayed calm, and he caused Lorelei's heart to skip a couple of beats when he took a step closer to Joy. "File a complaint to have Julian disbarred."

"That's right," Curt said from the doorway. "You can file a complaint with the CLD, the Commission for Lawyer Discipline. Your attorney can assist you with the paperwork."

That caused Julian to shoot Curt a glare, but his attention quickly fired back to Joy when her breath broke in a loud sob. Outside the window, Lorelei saw Matt and Deputy Azzie Parkman approaching with weapons drawn. Dax, however, motioned for them to stay put.

"Drop the knife, Joy," Dax said, his tone still even, but it wasn't a request. "If you don't, things are about to get even uglier than they already are. Just put down the knife, deal with the consequences of this, and then you can work on getting Julian here disbarred. Aaron's already screwed over six ways to Sunday so you don't have to worry about him."

"What the hell are you talking about?" Aaron demanded.

"You weren't legally married to Valerie," Curt promptly informed him. "Oh, and I think both your wife, Katie Miller, and the state of Missouri are going to have lots and lots of questions for you."

Aaron hadn't had much color in his face. Probably because of being threatened by a knife-wielding woman, but hearing that blanched him out even more.

"That son of a bitch is going to jail?" Joy asked.

"Looks that way," Dax said. He didn't mention that it was a slim possibility. Still, it might happen. "Now, put down the knife."

The seconds crawled by, and Lorelei could see the fierce debate Joy was having with herself. Her voice broke again, her breath rushing out.

And she dropped the knife.

It clattered onto the floor, and Matt and Azzie rushed in. Matt took hold of Joy while Azzie kicked the knife away so that Joy wouldn't be able to scoop it up again. Matt had the handcuffs on the woman in no time flat.

Lorelei hurried to Dax, but thankfully he was already heading in her direction. He immediately pulled her into his arms and brushed a kiss on her cheek. She was shaking, she realized, and the mother lode of adrenaline was spiking through her. But Dax stayed calm. He even managed to work up a reassuring smile for Lorelei while Matt and Azzie hauled a sobbing Joy out of the building.

Aaron and Julian started talking at once, their voices and words tangled together, but Lorelei caught the gist of it. Julian wanted to know who to blame for the lax security. Aaron was snarling about that whole bombshell of not being legally married to Valerie.

Lorelei ignored both of them and tuned out Sophia's and Curt's attempts to calm things down. She just held on to Dax and waited for the storm inside her to pass. Some of it did. Thanks to the soft murmured assurances Dax was giving her.

However, a new storm came. One that whipped through her and flashed like neon in her head. A realization that had the worst timing possible. Because that realization was something that would change everything.

She was in love with Dax.

DAX WAS GLAD Lorelei hadn't had any objections to him taking her to Sunset Creek after they'd given their statements of the "incident" to Matt. He'd thought she might insist on going to get Stellie from her mom's place, but apparently Lorelei realized she needed to steady her nerves before seeing the baby.

He was dealing with his own nerves and the blasted guilt that came with hindsight. He should have anticipated Joy would do something this stupid. Should have done a better job of making sure Lorelei stayed safe.

"You'd better not be beating yourself up about this," Lorelei muttered when he pulled to a stop in front of his house.

He glanced over at her and saw that she was staring at him. Clearly, he must have had a guilty face for her to pick up on his thoughts. Or maybe she just knew him. Knew how he'd be handling all of this.

"Nobody else to mentally beat up but myself," he pointed out.

"Yes, there is. This is solely on Joy," she pointed out just as fast. "You aren't responsible for what she does."

Maybe not. But it certainly felt that way. Lorelei or someone else could have been hurt had he not been able to talk Joy out of dropping that knife.

Yeah, he was dealing with jangled nerves all right.

The silver lining in this was Joy's probation would be revoked, and she'd be going back to a state psychiatric hospital to serve out her previous sentence along with years added for this new incident. Dax was betting Julian would make sure the woman got the maximum time for that. Not necessarily a bad thing since Joy had shown over and over again that she needed every bit of psychiatric help available to her.

And that was all the attention he intended to give the woman right now.

He turned his focus back on Lorelei, on soothing her nerves, so when he slipped his arm around her to lead her into the house, he was already figuring out how to handle that.

"I'll pour you a glass of wine," he suggested. "And if you want, you could take a long soak in the tub."

Lorelei made a sound of agreement, but the moment they stepped inside, she turned to him and kissed him. It wasn't a quick reassuring peck, either, but a long deep one.

Well, hell.

He certainly hadn't seen this kind of need in her. Then

again, kissing could cure all sorts of things, jangled nerves included. Especially this kiss. It was long, deep, and since Lorelei was the kisser, it was prime. He sank into it, pulling her against him and letting the heat of her body slide through his.

Oh, yeah. This was the cure all right.

Dax was smiling when he finally eased back from her. "Better than wine and a soak," he murmured.

Her eyes locked with his, and she stared at him a long time. Dax got the feeling that she was about to confess something, but if so, she must have changed her mind because she shook her head and went in for another kiss. This was even longer, and she pressed even harder against him. Clearly, she had something more than kissing in mind for whatever was bothering her.

"Are you okay?" he had to ask the next time they came up for air.

"Yes." Her breath was gusting now, and her cheeks were flushed with arousal. "Are you?"

"Well, I'm a whole lot better now that you've kissed me."

He expected her to smile about that. Or maybe talk about the ordeal they'd just gone through. But nope. Apparently, she was aiming for even more soothing by giving him a scorcher of a kiss. This one skyrocketed the heat and let him know that the kissing was soothing foreplay and that she wanted a whole lot more from him.

Dax gave her more.

Later, once they'd burned off some of this fire, he could try to work out what had caused this urgency. For now, though, he just took. And gave. He made sure he gave Lorelei all the fire and heat right back.

Kissing her, he hooked his arm around her waist, turning her and anchoring her against the door. That freed up his hands so he could touch. Specifically so he could use his thumb to torment her nipple that was already hard and tight beneath her thin silk top. He also went with some torment in another place, too. He wedged his leg between hers, easing his thigh against her center. Then, not easing. He added some pressure right on the front of her panties.

When she cursed him, he knew he'd hit pay dirt. When she started pulling at his shirt, he knew he had to speed things up a little. He wouldn't have minded all the playing around lasting a while longer, but he quickly had to amend that when Lorelei played dirty and slid her hand over the front of his jeans.

Okay, so he was definitely speeding this up.

Lorelei began an all-out war with his clothes, but Dax didn't mind since he was battling hers as well. Still, he wanted to add some cheap thrills to getting her naked so he kissed her stomach and breasts as he lifted her top and pulled it off over her head. He kissed her breasts and stomach again on his way down as he shimmied off her skirt and panties.

Lorelei moaned in pleasure, cursed him again, but she didn't let him finish her off with his tongue and mouth. Nope. She managed to get down his zipper, and she got her hand in his boxers. He had one thought. Just one.

She was really good at this.

However, a second thought quickly followed. He didn't want to be finished off this way, either, and it would lead that way if he didn't put a stop to it.

Kissing her again and keeping her face-to-face with him, he scooped her up. It was the right move because she finally got her nimble fingers off his dick when she hooked her arms and legs around him.

Dax considered just taking her there on the floor, but

since he was hoping this would be only the first round, he opted for the bedroom. Opted, too, for locking the door in case any of his brothers dropped by to check on him.

He kissed her all the way to his bedroom, but Lorelei wasn't passive about kissing him back. She obviously had a very hungry mouth, and she thankfully thought he was the cure for that hunger.

Somehow, after banging into multiple things, he got her to the bed, and Dax lowered her back onto the mattress. He kept his weight off her, knowing that some women didn't care for that. Apparently, though, Lorelei did because she took hold of the front of his shirt and hauled him down to her. All in all, it was a great way to land with her soft, silky naked body already sliding against his.

Dax wanted even more sliding, though, so he rolled to the side to get rid of his boots, jeans and boxers while Lorelei managed to get off his shirt. And, oh, the kissing began again. Even hotter this time. Needier.

"Now," she insisted.

Even without that demand, he would have known it had to be now, and unfortunately, that meant he had to break the kiss long enough to reach into his nightstand and come up with a condom. Lorelei tried to help get it on him, nearly giving him a hand job in the process. But he finally managed to suit up, and in that instant, Lorelei dragged him back to her.

Into her.

Then, she rolled him so she was on top of him. She was neither slow nor easy. Which suited him and his overly aroused dick just fine. Lorelei was clearly on a mission to make sure they both got off so Dax just let her carry on.

While he watched her.

She moved like a naked siren. A damn beautiful one.

The kind of beauty that could take away a man's breath. That's what she was doing to him now. Working him and robbing him of his breath. Dax didn't mind one bit. Didn't mind when she kicked up the pace even more. When she pumped her hips to take him in and out of her. In and out. Until he felt the climax spasm through her.

Dax kept on watching her as she threw back her head. As she let out a long moan of pleasure. Watched her peak and then start the slide back down.

That's when he gathered her to him and let himself go.

CHAPTER TWENTY-FOUR

LORELEI CLAMPED HER teeth over her bottom lip to stop herself from blurting out those three words that she knew Dax wasn't ready to hear.

I love you.

In fact, it was possible he'd never be ready to hear them, but her mind wasn't going to let her get all down about that. Not when her body was still humming from not one round of great sex but two. That first frantic one, followed by slow wet shower set. It was a toss-up as to which one had been the best; but since both had been stellar, it didn't matter.

She got another stellar moment by watching Dax dry off from the shower. Thankfully, it wasn't one of those huge towels that cover up all the interesting parts of him. Then again, all his parts were interesting.

"That look on your face tells me you might want round three," he remarked, tossing her a grin.

"Tempting. Very tempting," she emphasized as she pulled on her skirt. Then, she kissed him because, hey, he was the very definition of temptation. "But I need to get back to Stellie since Evangeline might have plans for the evening. You also need to have that meeting with Mike you mentioned."

A meeting that she knew was important because Dax had gotten several texts about it during the shower sex. Unfortunately, the meeting left her with a logistics problem.

"Mind if I use your truck?" she asked. She'd left her car

at home because Dax and she had driven to the meeting with the lawyers together, and then he'd brought her back here.

"Go ahead. There's a spare set of keys on the foyer table by the front door." He paused, his expression turning a little serious. "No need for you to worry about Joy. She's locked up, and Matt's not letting her out. She'll be transferred tomorrow to a jail in San Antonio."

Apparently, that was info he'd gotten from one of those texts, and it didn't surprise her that Joy would be kept in custody. Even if the woman had been out, her beef had been with Julian and Aaron. They should be the ones worried if and when Joy was released. At the moment, though, the two of them were probably off somewhere trying to figure out how to keep Aaron from ending up behind bars as well.

"Thanks for the reassurance, but I'm not worried," she told him. In fact, she had a nice floating feeling thanks to the sex. She winced, though, when she checked the time and realized it was almost four thirty. "I'll make arrangements for someone to bring back your truck, but I'll also need to fix Stellie dinner soon."

"I can have one of the hands get my truck. And why don't you bring Stellie back here for dinner?" Dax immediately said. "Once I'm dressed, I have that meeting with Mike, but I can also have the diner deliver something we can all eat. Maybe roasted chicken, mashed potatoes, biscuits and some veggies?"

"Sounds great." And this way, she could spend time with Stellie and Dax rather than cook. Added to that, Stellie loved mashed potatoes, and she could shred tiny bits of the chicken for her. "I won't be long."

Lorelei gave him another kiss and slid her hand under the towel to give them both a cheap thrill. A quick one because she really did need to get Stellie. She hurried out, snagging the keys along the way, and she went to his truck. The floating feeling returned, and she smiled all the way to her house. She probably should be worrying about guarding her heart and such, but she just couldn't bring herself to do that.

Her smiled faded fast, though, when she pulled into her driveway and saw the man pacing in front of her garage.

Julian.

She groaned. Apparently, she'd been wrong about Aaron and him being holed up somewhere together since Julian was alone.

Lorelei parked the truck on the side of the driveway so she could get out of her car, and she glanced around to make sure Evangeline and Stellie weren't outside and anywhere near Julian. They weren't, but she spotted her mother peering out the sidelight window of the front door.

"Go away, Julian," Lorelei snarled the moment she got out of the truck.

"Not until you've heard what I have to say. Your mother wouldn't let me in," he snarled right back.

He'd barely finished that when Evangeline opened the door and glared out at Julian. That was an extreme reaction for her mom since she wasn't a glarer.

"You want me to call the sheriff?" Evangeline asked her.

"No need. If he tries to land one hand on me, I'll knee him in the balls." She said it plenty loud enough for neighbors to hear. Neighbors that were no doubt already watching and would be prepared to do all manner of things to help her if things got out of hand. "Where's Stellie?"

"In the playpen in the nursery." Evangeline held up the baby monitor she was holding.

Lorelei nodded. "All right. Go back with her. I'll be in soon."

Evangeline nodded as well. Then, hesitated. "If he

touches you, I'll knee him in the balls," her mother muttered, and she eased the door shut.

"I can see where you get your charm," Julian snapped, probably thinking that was an insult. It wasn't. Then again, there wasn't anything he could say to her that would cause her to feel insulted. He no longer had that kind of power over her.

"What do you want?" she demanded. "And speak fast because I'm in a hurry."

"What do I want?" Julian howled. "I want your ass on a platter, that's what. Yours and that idiot assistant of yours."

"Misty?" Lorelei questioned.

"The little bitch posted photos on social media of a black eye she says I gave her. Three more women jumped on that bandwagon to say I'd done the same to them. They're trying to smear my good name."

Lorelei rolled her eyes. "I hate to break it to you, but you don't have a good name, Julian. You're basically a dirtbag bully who likes to hit women. If there are any other victims of yours, I hope they come forward."

"Yes, you'd like that, wouldn't you? Well, how are you going to feel when I file defamation of character suits against you and all those women?"

She stared at him, wondering why the heck she'd ever been afraid of him, why she'd let him control her all these years. "File away. That might bring even more women forward. Witnesses, too, since I'm certain someone saw you hit me. All the tongues you'd get wagging about this. Might take, oh, forever for the gossip to die down."

Julian pulled back his shoulders, and she saw the concern spread over his face. If he stirred this particular pot, he'd be facing a lot of fallout. She saw the concern deepen when he realized he was screwed. Still, it didn't take him long to regroup, and he must have believed he could get in one last jab at her by smiling.

Lorelei smiled back. Then, laughed. "Thank God I don't have your initials tattooed on my butt."

Which, of course, he didn't understand. But she did. There were no more repairs or fixes necessary to rid herself of this scab. She went past him, onto the porch, and opened her front door.

Apparently, though, Julian thought he needed to get in yet another jab. "If you think you're going to prattle on to your friends about what you claim I did to you—"

"I'm not going to prattle to anyone or anything about you, Julian," she interrupted as she stepped into her foyer. "Because, you see, when I shut this door, I will never give you another thought."

She shut the door and locked it.

All right, so maybe she would think about him every now and then when he popped into her head. But she refused to feel even a drop more of shame for what he'd done to her.

"Are you okay?" Lorelei heard her mother ask.

Evangeline was standing guard at the nursery door, and because it looked as if she could use it, Lorelei went to her mother and gave her a hug and a kiss on the cheek.

"I'm fine," Lorelei assured her and then paused. "How about you? Are you okay? Because I know you must have heard what I said about Julian hitting me."

"I heard." Evangeline sighed, and she shook her head. "And I already knew the gist of it. Knew that was probably the reason you hadn't trusted your heart with another man."

Oh, she'd trusted her heart all right. Was still trusting it. To Dax. That didn't mean it wouldn't get broken, but she wasn't going to live her life based on the possibility of something bad happening.

When Stellie giggled, they both went into the nursery, and Lorelei saw her daughter having a blast with the new board books that Evangeline had brought over for her as an early first birthday present. A birthday that was only two days away. A reminder for her to put together a celebration now that Aaron and his threats were out of the picture. A reminder, too, of just how fast things had moved with her falling in love with Dax.

Lorelei picked up the baby and gave her a kiss. In the same motion, she picked up the diaper bag. "Stellie and I are having dinner with Dax tonight, but why don't you and I plan for lunch tomorrow?"

Evangeline smiled. "I'd love that." She stared at Lorelei. "You look happy."

"I am," Lorelei assured her, and she intended for that happiness to continue at the ranch. "You want me to drop you off at your house?"

"No. I'd rather walk. Then, I can stop by the bakery and get me some cookies for a midnight snack."

They said their goodbyes, and after Lorelei got Stellie loaded into her car, she pulled out of her garage, glanced around. And smiled some more. No more Julian. She listened to the chorus of Stellie's "Gak, Gak, Gak," all the way back to Sunset Creek.

Lorelei's happy mood waned a bit when she arrived at Dax's and saw the car coming to a stop in front of his house. Not Julian, thank goodness, but rather Asher Parkman. And she immediately got a tight feeling in the pit of her stomach. Heck, had Julian already managed to contact Asher about that defamation lawsuit he'd tried to use as a threat?

Asher looked over at her as she was taking Stellie out of the car, and her stomach tightened even more. "Are you here to see me?" she came out and asked.

"Dax." He gave a weary sigh. "But it applies to you, too."

She didn't launch into a spiel about how Julian had no case against them. Lorelei just carried Stellie toward the porch. Dax was on the phone, but he opened the door, aiming a smile at Stellie, and he managed to keep the smile in place despite the uneasy glance he gave Asher.

"I'll get back to you on that," Dax told the person he'd been talking with before he ended the call. He went out to take the diaper bag from Lorelei and gave Stellie a quick kiss on the head before turning his attention to Asher. "Bad news?" he asked.

Asher drew in a long breath. "We should go inside," he said, clearly dodging the question. "We need to talk."

Oh, mercy. So, definitely bad news.

Asher didn't say anything else. He just waited until they were all inside, and since Lorelei wasn't sure how long, or how bad, this conversation would be, she put Stellie in the playpen that Dax had set up for her in the living room, and Lorelei gave her a teething cracker that she took from the diaper bag.

"Just say it," Dax insisted after they'd all taken seats. Lorelei took the chair nearest the playpen so she could keep a close eye on Stellie.

"The Fords made a formal request through their lawyer to release any info about the appointment I had with their daughter," Asher started. He kept his gaze on Dax. "I'm about to do that, but I thought I should go over it with you first. Valerie came to me with several legal questions and requests. She admitted to me that you were her baby's father, and she came to Last Ride for a visit to figure out if she should tell you."

"If?" Dax questioned on a huff. "She didn't think I had a right to know she was carrying my child?"

Asher lifted his shoulders. "She seemed more concerned about what type of father you'd be." He paused, groaned. "And she evidently didn't like what she heard about your reputation. Your past. She didn't think you had a good track record with women or relationships."

"I don't," he readily admitted, "but that doesn't mean she should have kept the pregnancy from me."

Asher made a sound of agreement. "For what it's worth, I did advise her to tell you. I also advised her she should spell out what if anything she wanted from you. Child support, visitations and such." Another pause. "She didn't want any of those."

Dax groaned, scrubbed his hand over his face. "Why did she wait so late in the pregnancy to come here and *assess* me? Where was she all those months?"

"I can't answer the first part of that, but from what she told me, she'd been living and working in Dallas. By the time she came to me, she had already decided to leave Last Ride and return to her house that she owned there."

"Dallas?" Dax and she repeated in unison.

Asher nodded. "She indicated she'd purchased a house and planned on continuing to live there after the baby arrived."

Dax opened his mouth, then closed it. Maybe because he'd changed his mind as to what he'd been about to say. Or maybe because there was nothing to say. Lorelei saw the hurt in his eyes. Saw it wash over him all the way to the bone.

"Valerie was just going to leave and never tell me I had a child," Dax finally managed to say. There was an angry snap to his words.

Even though it wasn't a question, Asher made a sound of agreement. "Since Valerie indicated she had plans to divorce her husband, she asked me to draw up estate documents in case anything happened to her. She didn't have a lawyer in Dallas and wasn't sure she'd be able to find one since the baby was due in a month." Asher paused again. "She wanted her parents to have custody of the baby she was carrying."

Oh, God. Lorelei took hold of Dax's hand to try to steady him.

Asher cleared his throat. "I'm sorry, Dax, but Valerie made one thing clear. She didn't want you to be the one to raise your daughter."

DAX WAS CERTAIN he was feeling a lot of things at the moment. Shock, anger, hurt. But it was hard to sort through that tornado of emotions because his entire body just felt numb.

Because of his past, Valerie hadn't wanted him to raise Stellie.

She had essentially wanted to erase him from Stellie's and her lives by never telling him she was pregnant and moving to a city hours away from Last Ride.

Oh, yeah. Shock, anger, hurt. And once again his damn past had come back to haunt him. He couldn't even put any of this on Joy. He'd been the one who'd slept around, and creating a stable homelife hadn't even been on his radar. Valerie had obviously seen that when she'd "observed" him in Last Ride and had decided that while he'd been suitable for a one-off, he wasn't fit to raise their child.

"Dax," Lorelei murmured. She was clearly going through her own tornado of emotions, and she tried to comfort him when she put her arms around him.

But this wasn't a comforting situation. Hell, it wasn't even a "staying put" situation. He needed to get out of there. Needed some place private for the meltdown he was about to have.

"I'm going for a drive," he heard himself say and cursed the extra worry that put in Lorelei's eyes. "I'll be okay."

That was a big-assed lie but a necessary one. It might cut down on her worrying about him while he found that privacy. Privacy that wasn't an option right now.

"You'll be able to see yourself out?" Dax said to Asher, but he didn't wait for a response. He turned to Lorelei. "Dinner should be here in about a half hour. I'll call you before then."

A call he'd make to tell her that he was going to need a hell of a lot more than thirty minutes. That wasn't fair to Lorelei, but at the moment he couldn't deal with fair, either. Dax just gave Stellie and her quick kisses and hurried out to one of his trucks.

Dax didn't look back. Didn't want to see Lorelei shaken to the core. As he was. He'd need to do something to help her get through this, but again, that couldn't happen now.

He started driving and just kept going. Out of town and past the newly restored drive-in theater, a place he'd intended to take Stellie and Lorelei. Definitely not something he wanted to remember right now, but he couldn't push it aside. Because he might not have those kinds of opportunities to spend time with Stellie.

Or Lorelei for that matter.

He wasn't sure how she'd feel about spending time with him when Stellie's birth mother had insisted he not be part of the baby's life.

His phone rang, and Dax saw Curt's name pop up on the dash. He ignored the call. Ignored the next two as well. Then, cursing, he answered the fourth one.

"I'll call you back later," Dax snarled before Curt could even say anything.

"Good. In fact, you should come on by my office now so we can talk."

Dax had no trouble hearing the concern in his lawyer's voice. "Lorelei called you?"

"Asher," Curt provided. "We need to work out how to address this."

"There's nothing to address. Valerie didn't want me near Stellie." He groaned, cursing himself and this shitty situation.

"There's plenty to address," Curt assured him. "Even if Valerie had gone through with that in her will, that doesn't mean you wouldn't have gotten custody of Stellie. She's your daughter, and you should have a big say in what happens to her. Especially since her birth mother is no longer in the picture."

Dax wanted to hold on to any hope he was hearing. But it wouldn't change the truth. He wasn't father material. He'd always known that, and it hadn't taken Valerie long to figure it out.

Something else, though, popped into his head. "Does this mean the Fords will have some legal clout to try to nullify the adoption?" Dax asked.

"They could try."

Hell. "I'll go talk to them. Not now, though. I need a little while." Who was he kidding? He was going to need a long while, maybe forever, to get over this gut punch.

"Let me talk to them first," Curt insisted. "Now that they've gotten to know you, they might decide to go with not challenging the adoption and recognizing your paternity claim."

Yeah, and they might just go for broke and try to get full custody of their granddaughter. That would completely crush Lorelei. Would crush the hell out of him, too.

"Let me talk to them," Curt repeated. "And I'll get back to you. Are you home?"

"No." Dax had to glance around to figure out where he was, and that caused him to curse again. He was at the cemetery where his brother Griff was buried. "Do me a favor and call Lorelei to explain everything you just told me."

Curt didn't jump to agree to that. "Any reason you don't want to tell her yourself?"

"Yeah. I'm not in any shape to do that right now," he admitted. "Call her, explain things and tell her I'll be in touch soon."

Dax ended the call before Curt could give him any reason whatsoever why that wasn't a good idea. He knew it wasn't good. But it was the best he could manage.

He parked his truck, silenced his phone and did something he'd never done before. He went to visit Griff's grave. Well, that's what he did after he wandered around the cemetery until he found the tombstone. He had no idea what qualified as a good resting place, but it seemed peaceful enough. Well-kept, too, right down to some fresh flowers.

The sunlight glinted off something on top of the tombstone, and Dax went closer to see the plain gold ring. He'd heard about it. A sort of mystery that folks still gossiped about. That's because no one knew for certain who'd put it there.

"I'm guessing you know who left it for you," Dax muttered and figured it wasn't a good sign that he'd meant that comment for a brother who'd been dead for nearly fifteen years.

He ran his finger over the ring, and despite the heat, the gold was cool. So was the marble tombstone that stood silent as, well, a tomb. He wasn't sure why he'd come here, because he certainly wouldn't be getting answers from a dead man. Then again, there weren't actual answers, only truths, and Valerie had spelled out that truth for him with what she'd told Asher.

Since there was a shade tree nearby, Dax sank down onto the ground so he was eye level with the tombstone and continued the chat that only the mosquitos and he would ever hear.

"I still think you're a son of a bitch for leaving without telling me goodbye," he muttered. And he just kept on muttering. "Between you and me, I believe Lily's daughter, Hayden, is your kid."

There. That was something he'd sure as hell never said aloud. Neither had anyone else in his side of the family or Lorelei's, despite Griff and Lily having been an item since early high school. Of course, that item label had ended when Griff and she broke up, and Dax had always figured they could have had one last hookup that resulted in Lily getting pregnant.

"Maybe knowing you were going to be a father played into what you did," Dax went on. "I wouldn't have understood it way back when, but I understand it now."

Dax wouldn't do a repeat of what Griff had done, though. No. Even if the Fords took away everything from him, he couldn't do that. And that left him with one big question.

What the hell was he going to do?

No immediate answers came, and he had the sickening feeling that it might stay that way. That he might have already lost…everything.

Dax sat there and let the grief and the past tear him to pieces.

CHAPTER TWENTY-FIVE

LORELEI FIGURED THIS visit could backfire on her, but she was desperate enough to risk backfire or plenty of other things to make sure Dax was okay. Well, as okay as he could be considering he'd had multiple rugs pulled out from beneath him. There wasn't much she could do about that, but she had to try to soothe him in any way she could.

Of course, that meant soothing herself, too, because Dax's rugs were now hers. And her heart was breaking for him.

"Thank you," Lorelei muttered when she got to the security gate at Sunset Creek Ranch and saw that it was open.

It wasn't her first thanks of the night. She'd given a huge one to her mom when she'd called Evangeline and asked her to come over and stay with Stellie. Not only had her mother quickly agreed, she hadn't asked where her daughter was going at this time of night.

Since it was going on midnight, all the lights in the house were off, but her headlights might alert someone. Maybe not Dax since his bedroom was at the back of the house, but if one of the ranch hands in the bunkhouse saw them, they'd soon recognize her vehicle and know they didn't have a trespasser.

Lorelei parked and grabbed the bag of goodies that she'd picked up from the gas station. Hardly bakery quality and definitely not an appetizing combination, but she hadn't wanted to come empty-handed, and the pickings at the Quik Stop hadn't been stellar.

She considered ringing the doorbell but instead went around the house to the patio doors off Dax's bedroom. The curtain was drawn so Lorelei couldn't see inside so she tapped on the glass. Waited. Tapped some more. Waited. And cursed.

Because it occurred to her that Dax might not even be there.

His truck was out front, but he could have used one of the ranch's vehicles. He could be somewhere right now, crushed and hurting, and the thought of that gave her a jolt of panic. Panic that dissolved when someone eased back a side of the curtain, and she came face-to-face with Dax.

Like the first time she'd come here, he was wearing just a pair of black boxers. Also like that morning, his hair was rumpled, his eyes a little sleepy, and there was a puzzled expression on his amazing face.

"Lorelei," he said, hitting some switch that caused the curtain to fully open, and he unlocked the glass door. The sleep quickly vanished. "Is Stellie okay?"

"She is," Lorelei assured him. "My mom is with her."

With that explanation, she stepped in and didn't rush to kiss him. Though that's what she wanted to do. She wanted to kiss him, hold him and try to make this sadness all go away. Sadness she could practically feel coming off him.

"I brought late-night snacks," she said, opening the bag to show him the six-pack of beer, two bottles of water and a twin pack of Moon Pies.

He eyed her selections and managed a smile. Not his usual dazzling grin, but at least he tried. And that crushed her some, too. Because he had tried for her.

"You don't have to say anything about, well, anything," Lorelei added.

Since she was hoping to re-create his visit to her house, she glanced around the bedroom and located a spot where she led him. It was on the floor by the door that led into his bathroom. She had him sit while she took out the stash.

"Stellie learned how to throw toys," Lorelei went on, hoping that her voice was soothing. Hoping that Dax wouldn't feel any pressure whatsoever to bare his heart and soul to her. "She managed to whack my knee with a plastic block."

That caused the corner of his mouth to lift, and he kept his eyes on her while she opened him a beer. "You're hurting, and I'm sorry."

She definitely didn't want him doling out fixes for her. Not when he was clearly in need of fixes himself. So, she brushed a soft kiss on his mouth to stop him from adding anything else.

"Drink," she insisted. "Eat sugary carbs and let me try this."

Lorelei reached behind him, her hand sliding against his bare back, and she gave him her version of the bull rub. Dax chuckled. Not a "laughing out loud, rolling on the floor" kind of deal, but she'd take it.

"I was thinking today about a time I saw you at Three Sheets Bar," she continued. "This was about three years ago, and I'd gone there with Lily and Nola to celebrate their birthdays. Someone had set up one of those mechanical bulls. Everyone was egging you on to try it, but I figured you knew it was a no-win situation for you. If you stayed on, people would have just said you were showing off. If you'd fallen, those same people would have said your rodeo rankings were all luck."

He made a sound of agreement and another sound to indicate he was pulling up that particular memory. The third sound he made might have been because she moved her bull-rubbing hand lower down his back where she kept up the massage.

"Anyway, you resisted getting on the bull," she went on, "until Nola decided to give it a go. You decided to get on with her."

"Because she was drunk, and I was afraid she'd break her neck," Dax explained. He closed his eyes, made a sound of pleasure when she moved her hand even lower. Right in the general vicinity of his tat.

"Yes." She smiled now because that proved the point she'd been about to make. "That's the kind of man you are. You're thoughtful and caring." Lorelei hoped he understood the unspoken part of what she was saying.

That Valerie had been wrong about him.

Valerie had only seen the facade. The hot bull rider who'd had more than his fair share of lovers. But the woman had missed the bigger picture of the man who'd gotten her pregnant.

Lorelei had missed it, too, until she'd gotten to know him, and she knew in her heart that if he gave himself the chance, he'd make a thoughtful and caring father. If Valerie's conversation with Asher hadn't crushed him, then maybe Dax would give himself that chance.

Maybe.

She refused to dwell on that right now, though. Refused to look back or forward. She wanted these moments with him and could only hope that it helped both of them. That's why she moved her hand lower, sliding her fingers into his boxers and turning him so she could kiss him.

The heat came. Always did with Dax, and this time the fire hopefully soothed.

"You can have me or the Moon Pies," she muttered with her mouth still against him.

He didn't answer. Not with words, anyway. Dax pulled her onto his lap and continued the kiss.

The Moon Pies would obviously have to wait.

WITH HIS BOOT tucked on the lower rung on the corral fence, and his arms resting on the top, Dax stood and watched the trainers work with Thunder.

And that was "work" as in doing stuff that wasn't working.

The bull definitely had the right instincts for the rodeo, but the trainers were working on techniques to calm him down when there was no competition in progress. Like now. No matter what they seemed to do, Thunder was still operating at full throttle.

Sort of like Stellie.

Of course, her "full throttle" stuff was cute, and even though the Last Ride Charity Rodeo prep had kept him so busy he hadn't personally visited Lorelei and her, he'd FaceTimed with them enough to see that the kid seemed to have nonstop energy.

The thought of Lorelei and her made him smile. Then, not smile because the rest of the thoughts came, too. Hard to dismiss Valerie's last wishes. Hard not to let it feel like the punch to the gut that it was.

He glanced over his shoulder when he heard the sound of a vehicle, and for a moment he thought it might be Lorelei dropping by for another "Moon Pie and beer" visit. But no. It was Jonas.

When Jonas started making his way toward him, Dax

stayed put and tried to muster up enough energy to put on a fake face for his brother. Something to reassure Jonas that he was okay.

Even if he wasn't.

But Dax decided he couldn't manage even the slightest of pretenses. That's probably why Jonas took one look at him and sighed.

"I just left Wyatt's," Jonas said, joining Dax at the corral. "Nola had her checkup, and the doctor said the baby could come anytime now."

"That's good," Dax muttered. And he meant it. No one would ever say that Wyatt wasn't good enough to raise his own child. Nola and he were going to be amazing parents.

"Wyatt saw a dick on the ultrasound and doesn't want to tell Nola," Jonas added.

A dick? It took Dax a moment to flesh that out. Nola and he hadn't wanted to know the sex of the baby. Oh, well. Dax figured it'd still be a damn fine moment to see the kid being born even if you had prior knowledge about the dick.

"That's one hard-assed bull," Jonas muttered, his focus on Thunder.

"Yeah. I lasted three seconds the first time I rode him. Two seconds the next time."

Jonas glanced at him, frowned. "You're going in the wrong direction."

"Yeah," Dax repeated.

His brother stayed quiet a moment. "Ever thought of using those scented oils on him?" Jonas joked. "According to the ads, some of them have a calming effect."

So did Lorelei's "bull rub, beer, Moon Pies and sex" visit. Then again, it'd been the great sex that'd worked for him. Maybe it could be the same for Thunder. Except the whole idea of a rodeo bull wasn't to have him dozing off after getting off. It was best just to keep riding him until Thunder mellowed a bit or Dax just gave up. Right now, it was fifty-fifty as to which way that would go.

"I went to Griff's grave," Dax threw out there.

That caused Jonas to tear his attention from Thunder and give Dax another glance. "Did it help?"

Dax settled for a shrug. He'd never accept or understand why Griff had done what he'd done, but Dax felt as if he'd made some kind of peace with his sibling. Considering Griff had been dead for years, it was probably about time he'd done that.

"It's scary as hell when you consider fatherhood," Dax muttered, thinking about the possibility that Griff was Hayden's bio dad.

Jonas made a sound of agreement. "Want to know what's scarier?" He didn't wait for Dax to respond. "Loving a child and not being a father."

Dax opened his mouth. Closed it. Was Jonas talking about his own stepson now, or had that been directed at him? Either way, it was damn depressing.

What if Valerie was right?

What if he tried out being a father and he messed it up so much that it hurt Stellie? Hurt Lorelei, too.

"So, how are you going to handle the situation with Stellie?" Jonas finally came out and asked.

This was the reason Jonas had come. And depending on how Dax answered, his brother would do his best to offer sage advice and fix whatever he could.

But there was a huge problem with that.

There was nothing to fix because Dax didn't know what the hell he was going to do.

CHAPTER TWENTY-SIX

LORELEI COULDN'T MISS the cheerful sights and sounds going on around her. Impossible to tune them out since seemingly every resident of Last Ride was here on the fairgrounds for the charity rodeo.

There was excited chatter with folks moving from the amusement rides and to various booths that sported goods like corn dogs, cotton candy and funnel cakes. Those goods created a swirl of scents that clashed but also tapped into the childhood memories of fun times at an old-fashioned fair.

However, the "fun times" feeling just wasn't getting through to her.

Nothing here was lifting her mood. Well, nothing other than Stellie's occasional babble when something or someone caught her eye. The baby was in the stroller, the top protecting her from the late-afternoon sun, and since she'd yet to nap, Lorelei suspected she'd fall asleep any minute now.

"Glad you made it," Millie called out to her. She was with her own baby, husband and stepdaughter at a booth selling snow cones. "Want to join us?"

"Thanks, but I'm heading over there." Lorelei made a vague motion in the direction of the rodeo arena where she figured Dax would be since his ride was less than a half hour away.

Seeing Dax was the main thing on her mind right now, and she suspected there'd be no mood-lifting until she'd talked in person with him. Something she hadn't done for the past two days. Not since her late-night visit after Asher told him Valerie had intended to take legal steps to try to prevent him from raising Stellie.

She'd seen how hard that had hit him, and it'd tapped into all the old guilt of his past. And it had crushed her as much as it had him. That was the problem with being in love with someone. Their hurt became your own.

Thankfully, that hurt hadn't stopped Dax from Face-Timing with Stellie every night before her bedtime. Despite Valerie's intentions, he was still being a father to his daughter. Something she was sure he'd continue to do no matter how this all legally turned out.

Of course, Dax had talked with her during those Face-Time calls as well, but he kept the conversation focused on Stellie, on the events of her day. When Lorelei had asked him how he was, he'd just given her an *okay* or some other lukewarm response. He had pressed, though, to make sure she was okay. She wasn't. But Lorelei had given him the same white lie answers since he already had enough on his plate without her adding to it.

But, mercy, she was worried.

Lorelei hadn't personally spoken with the Fords because they had gone back to St. Louis to take care of some business and were due to return to Last Ride today. Maybe they were taking care of business involving whether or not to challenge the adoption. Sophia had assured Lorelei that even if they tried, they were likely to fail, but it would be a gut-wrenching fight on top of all the other gut-wrenching things she'd been going through.

She had to stop multiple times so that people could ooh and aah over Stellie, but Lorelei saw the pity in their eyes. Saw, too, the curiosity, but she didn't volunteer anything.

Mainly because there were so many things up in the air right now.

Lorelei finally made it to the arena, which was packed since there'd already been some rodeo events. She glanced around and didn't spot Dax, but she made her way to Mike when she saw him.

"He's riding Thunder," Mike said right off. Despite his obvious frustration, he kept his tone light, and he even reached down and gave Stellie's toes a playful jiggle. "Dax has ridden him three times now. The first, he lasted three seconds. The next, a second less than that. And the third time he barely made it out of the chute before he got tossed." He paused, shook his head. "Couldn't talk him into going with another bull."

Lorelei hadn't been able to do that, either, since it was one of the few things they'd actually discussed during Dax's calls. Part of her wanted to trust Dax's decision since he was a pro. The other part of her wondered why the heck he was risking so much on a ride. She understood his wanting to go out in a blaze of glory since this was his rodeo farewell, but she didn't want him hurt.

"How is Dax?" she wanted to know.

Mike shrugged. "I was about to ask you. Maybe you can find out. He's over there." Mike hiked his thumb to a waiting/prep area where she caught a glimpse of Dax talking with several other cowboys wearing chaps and protective gear.

Just as Dax did.

Despite the situation, the sight of him made Lorelei smile, and her heart revved up. Actually, all of her revved up, and she wondered if everyone around her could see the effect Dax had on her.

She pushed the stroller toward him, and even though

Lorelei didn't call out to him, it seemed as if Dax sensed she was there because he glanced over his shoulder at her. He said something she didn't catch to the other cowboys and headed in her direction.

Lorelei figured plenty of eyes were on them, and the gossips were no doubt gearing up to report anything and everything they might see. She decided to give them lots to talk about.

Wearing those chaps that framed the front of his jeans, Dax strode toward them, automatically stooping down so he could lean in and kiss Stellie's cheek. "She's asleep," he relayed to Lorelei.

She looked in the stroller and saw that he was right. Good. Because this probably wasn't something a baby should be witnessing. Lorelei slid her hand around the back of Dax's neck, pulled him to her and kissed him as if there were no tomorrow.

And as if they were doing this in private.

She made it long, deep and as scalding as possible. When she pulled back, she heard some whoops and whispers but ignored them and put all her attention on Dax. Even though he'd clearly participated in the kiss, she wasn't sure how he was going to react.

He grinned. "Well, hello to you, too," he said in that cocky drawl that had her taking in a breath of relief.

She lost that breath, though, when he hooked his arm around her, drew her back to him and gave her a kiss that was even hotter, longer and deeper than the one she'd given him. It lightened both her head and her heart.

"Are you okay?" he asked, taking the question right out of her mouth. But he didn't wait for her to answer. "I'm sorry I haven't been around much in the last couple of days. I needed to work out some things."

Because of that light-headedness from the kiss, it took her a moment to gather her thoughts and answer. "I'm better now that I've seen you." She paused, studied him. "Are you all right?"

His grin returned, and while it seemed genuine, she could tell he was still holding back. "I'm better now that I've seen you. And Stellie."

Good. Then, that was the right start to what she had to say to him. "I'm not turning stalker, but I'm also not going to let you shut me out until I've made sure you understand how important you are to me. To us."

His eyebrow winged up. "How important? And before you answer that, hear me out. When I saw you walking toward me, pushing Stellie in the stroller, I had an epiphany. Valerie didn't think I could do this. I didn't think I could do this." He looked her straight in the eyes. "But I can."

This time the relief came like an avalanche, and a giddy laugh rushed from her mouth. She threw her arms around Dax and kissed him again.

"Dax," someone called out. "You're riding in ten. You need to get in here."

"We'll talk when I'm done," he assured her.

Since he turned to walk away, or rather hurry away, Lorelei didn't have a chance to try to talk him out of his choice of bulls. "Come back to me in one piece," she settled for saying.

Apparently, it was the right thing to say since Dax flashed her a grin from over his shoulder. The heat from the kiss and that grin stayed with her. Until she heard the snorts from the bull, and she might have started praying had someone else not called out to her.

Greg and Miriam Ford.

The couple made a beeline toward her, and Lorelei nearly

groaned. She wanted to see them, wanted to have a long talk about what they were planning to do. But first she had to make sure Dax got through this ride.

Miriam surprised Lorelei by pulling her into a hug, and then the woman stooped down to have a look at Stellie. Greg said a quick hello to both of them but headed toward the arena fence, his attention on the prep that was being done for Dax.

"Oh, she's going to miss her daddy's ride," Miriam remarked while she was still hunched over with Stellie.

Lorelei didn't miss the woman's tone. Or the *daddy* part. It gave her hope as to how the rest of this conversation might go.

"Dax really is Stellie's father," Lorelei assured the woman. "In every possible way."

Miriam nodded and dragged in a long breath. "Greg and I aren't challenging him for custody. Because you're right. A father has a right to raise his child."

Lorelei had to do a mental double take to make sure she'd heard the woman right. She didn't dare say, *But what about Valerie's wishes?* Not because Valerie's wishes weren't important. They were. However, Dax wasn't the man that Valerie had believed him to be.

"Will you challenge the adoption?" Lorelei asked instead.

Miriam shook her head. "Dax told us that you're Stellie's mother, that you should continue to be her mother. Because you already are," she added with a catch in her throat.

Lorelei was certain there was a catch in her own throat. And maybe some tears watering her eyes. "Thank you for that."

Miriam hugged her again. "Thank you for being a wonderful mom to our granddaughter."

Heck, the tears didn't just water her eyes. A few of them spilled down her cheeks. But these were of the happy variety. Not just for herself but apparently for Miriam as well.

"By the way, Curt should be texting Dax right now to let him know our decision," Miriam went on. "We didn't want that hanging over him for his farewell ride."

Lorelei's gaze slashed across the arena, and she saw Dax looking at his phone. She saw the slow smile, too, and then he looked over at them. He gave them a grin and thumbs-up.

There was some hissy static over the intercom, followed by the announcement, "Ladies and gents, turn your attention to the arena for the farewell ride of our own local star, Dax Buchanan. Dax'll be hanging onto his hat and pretty much the rest of him while he gives us some chills and thrills when riding Thunder."

The announcer continued to talk about Dax's star-studded career, and with Miriam right by her side, Lorelei pushed the stroller closer to the fence so she could watch.

And hold her breath.

She didn't have to wait long before the chute gate opened, and Thunder came charging out. The bull immediately went into a buck, kicking up his back legs, obviously trying to toss Dax.

Her heart seemed to stop. Everything else stopped, too. Except for Dax and Thunder. The bull whipped around, muscles rippling while he made that ferocious snorting sound.

Since there was a huge timer at the front of the arena, no way could Lorelei miss the seconds ticking off. Seconds that each seemed to last a couple of lifetimes. The crowd cheered with each one, and the cheers got louder. Louder. Louder. Until the sound was deafening.

Six seconds flashed on the timer.

Six seconds, and the bull sent Dax flying.

There was a loud collective groan, and mutters of disappointment rippled through the crowd. But Lorelei couldn't respond. Her heart skipped some beats while her gaze stayed glued to an airborne Dax.

He landed hard on the ground, and as she'd seen him do on his other ride, he didn't stay there. He sprang right up and hurried to the fence. Good thing, too, because Thunder was already preparing to come after him. The bull pawed at the dirt. Snorted. And turned to charge in Dax's direction.

Dax was limping a little but definitely not dawdling, either, while the clowns and trainers distracted Thunder long enough for Dax to make his exit. He scrambled over the fence, dropping to his feet, and in the same motion, he pulled Lorelei into his arms. He didn't look hurt or disappointed. He just looked...hot.

The crowd's grumbles turned to cheers as he kissed her.

He was grinning when he pulled back to meet her eyes for a moment before he looked at the Fords. "Thank you," he said. Then, he shifted back to Lorelei. "All right. So, technically I didn't win—"

"But you more than doubled your best time on Thunder," Lorelei finished for him. "That's a win in my book."

"Mine, too," he assured her. "It's a good way for me to go out. Winning in my own way." He looked her straight in the eyes. "After that ride, you'd better be in love with me."

It took a moment for Lorelei to find the words but, oh, her heart was soaring. "I am." She had to practically shout it to be heard over the crowd.

"Good. Because that was the other part of the epiphany I had. I don't want to be just your lover, and I don't want to be just a part-time dad to Stellie. I want it all, Lorelei, and you're the person who can give it to me."

Even more heart soaring. At this rate, it might head to the moon. "Then, consider it given."

Both surprise and pleasure went through his eyes. "Just like that?"

"Hey, you aren't the only one who can have an epiphany. I'm in love with you, Dax Buchanan."

He grinned. And, oh, it was that grin that made her want to haul him straight off to bed. "H-e-l-l," he said, spelling it out even though Stellie was still asleep, "might just freeze over when I say this, but I'm in love with you, Lorelei Parkman." Dax paused a heartbeat and shook his head. "Nope, no freezing over."

Definitely not. The kiss he gave her made sure of that. It was scalding hot, deep and…perfect.

* * * * *

Now, turn the page for
Breaking Rules at Nightfall Ranch,
a bonus novella from USA TODAY
bestselling author Delores Fossen!

BREAKING RULES
AT NIGHTFALL RANCH

CHAPTER ONE

OF ALL THE things that Alana Parkman had figured could happen at the cemetery, she certainly hadn't expected running into her ex. An ex she hadn't seen in more than a decade. Yet, here he was.

Gray Russell.

Former rodeo champion, hot cowboy and all around breaker of hearts.

Well, breaker of her heart, anyway. In all fairness, that didn't mean he'd made a habit of it since he'd dumped her on the night of their high school graduation thirteen years ago. Gray had then hightailed it out of their hometown of Last Ride, Texas, and to the best of her knowledge, he hadn't returned except to go to his father's house for visits that didn't involve going anywhere else in or around town.

But he was sure as heck here now.

The years had been kind to him. *Unfairly* kind, she considered on a lust-filled sigh. His face had gotten even more character to go along with that cover-model jaw stubble, and he'd put on some muscle in all the right places on his once rangy body. The hair—oh, the storm-black hair that made you want to plunge your fingers into it—was thick and rumpled, making him forever and ever look as if he'd just climbed out of bed and over to the photo shoot for one of those calendars of dreamy guys.

Since her mouth seemed to have stopped working, and

her feet had as well, Alana just stayed put on the gravel path that led to the graves of Hilltop Cemetery. The place had dozens of graves with varying sizes of tombstones, but Gray wasn't actually standing in front or near any of them. Holding his Stetson by the side of his leg, he was under the shade of one of the massive oaks that dotted the final resting place for many of Last Ride's locals.

Even though it was going on 5:00 p.m., it was still hotter than Hades. Typical for Texas in early June. That was probably the reason for Gray being in the shady spot, but this time of year, most folks kept their outdoor visits short and sweet. Judging from the sweat beading on his bunched-up forehead, this had not been especially short and definitely not sweet.

"Uh, I'm sorry," Alana managed to say once she'd gathered enough breath to speak.

The apology was because she figured she'd interrupted him while he was visiting a loved one, but then she frowned. Because to the best of her knowledge, and her knowledge about Gray was pretty extensive, none of his relatives or friends were buried here. His mother had died from cancer when he'd been in high school, but she was buried in one of the town's other cemeteries.

None of Alana's friends or relatives had graves in this particular cemetery, either, though she did have a legit reason for being here. Well, legit-ish, anyway.

With his left hand crammed in the pocket of his great-fitting jeans, Gray slowly shifted his attention toward her in a way that made her think he'd already known she was there before she'd even spoken. Maybe he had, too. From his position under that tree, he had a good view of the parking area, and he likely would have seen and heard her car approach.

Since her Ford Focus and a shiny silver truck were the only vehicles in that parking area, it meant they were the only visitors at the moment. So, yes, he would have noticed her before she'd started the trek up the hill that'd given Hilltop Cemetery its name, and now he no longer had the place to himself.

Considering his somber expression, he'd likely needed that alone time.

"I'm sorry," she repeated. Obviously, there were some things about him she hadn't known, but this certainly wasn't the time to ask what the heck he was doing here.

Gray did some asking of his own, though. "Are you here to get a picture of Sadie Jo Walker's tombstone?"

That stopped Alana in her tracks, but she doubted that was a wild guess on his part. "Either you have ESP or you've been back in town long enough to hear gossip about the Last Ride Society."

"Gossip," he verified. "I dropped by the Quik Stop to fill up with gas, and in the span of the five minutes or so I was there, Melvin Ford tried to catch me up on the past thirteen years of things I'd missed." Gray leveled his brown eyes on her. Eyes that were just as dreamy as the rest of him.

Alana shook off the effect of having those dreamy eyes directed at her, and she groaned because Melvin, who was an attendant at the gas station, would have almost certainly focused that "catching Gray up" on things related to her. It wasn't exactly a grand secret in Last Ride that they'd been high school sweethearts. No secret, either, about that whole broken heart/his dumping her deal.

"So, you know I'm divorced and have had not one but two broken engagements," she laid out there. "Folks call me the Typhoid Mary of relationships. Melvin would have also told you that I was the winner of the Last Ride Society drawing." Balancing her phone and her purse in her hands, Alana managed to use her available fingers to put *winner* in air quotes.

Gray nodded, verifying that he had indeed been told that. "You drew Sadie Jo Walker's name."

Alana nodded as well, and was that a touch of disdain she'd heard in his voice? Maybe. Plenty of people didn't care much for the Parkmans, their silver spoon upbringings and their various legacies.

One such legacy, the Last Ride Society, was formed decades ago by the town's founder and Alana's ancestor, Hezzie Parkman. Hezzie had wanted her descendants to preserve the area's history by having a quarterly drawing so that one Parkman descendant would then in turn draw the name of a local tombstone to research.

And that was the reason Alana was here.

Research that required her to take a photo of the tombstone, dig into the deceased person's history and write a report for all the town to read. Well, for all the town who was interested in reading such things, anyway. She wasn't particularly interested in it, but family legacy meant family duty.

The Parkman name and the trust fund that had come with it had opened some doors for her. It didn't matter that she hadn't necessarily chosen to go through those doors. Alana felt as if she owed this to Hezzie for founding the town that Alana loved. Yes, *loved*. Despite Alana's overbearing, judgmental parents, this was and always would be her home.

"The drawing was actually last month, but I couldn't get started until school finished," she babbled to fill in the awkward silence that followed. And just in case Gray thought she'd procrastinated in getting this done.

"You teach theater arts at the high school," Gray supplied. "Melvin mentioned that."

"Yep," she verified. "And the end of the year stuff always keeps me busy. I couldn't get out here until after graduation." She paused. "In that five-minute conversation, Melvin probably told you my folks think I've sold myself way short in the career department."

"He mentioned it," Gray verified.

She didn't want to know the exact details of the spin that Melvin had put on it, but the gist had almost certainly been that her cattleman father and her socialite mother thought a job as a schoolteacher was way beneath her Parkman name. And that definitely wasn't something she wanted to get into with Gray. Besides, he'd dealt with plenty of her parents' disapproval when they'd been together.

"Anyway, taking a photo of Sadie Jo's tombstone is step one," Alana added in case Melvin had glossed over that part. If Melvin had, indeed, told Gray about the drawing and the tombstone picture, then was that the reason he was here?

Because Gray had expected to see her?

Alana stopped. Did some rethinking. No. If Gray had wanted to see her, he could have just gone to her house. Unlike when they'd been in high school, she didn't live with her parents any longer, thank God, but she owned a little cottage on the other side of town. Melvin and everyone else in town knew her address and could have given that info to Gray had he wanted it.

Maybe, though, Gray hadn't asked blabbermouth Melvin since it would have stirred up plenty of gossip.

Oh, that got her heart and body revving, and she got vivid sensations and images of their past make-out marathons that had gone on pretty much everywhere in Last

Ride. The revving and the tingling that followed were starting to eat away at her common sense.

And her memories.

Memories that ended when Gray had indeed stomped
on her heart. And she'd only endured more heart stomp-
ing since. It was one of the reasons Alana had sworn off
relationships. Not in a general "it's the wine talking" kind
of way, either. She'd made a pact not to get involved with
anyone for at least a year since her last breakup. She still
had five days to go.

"You knew Sadie Jo Walker?" Gray asked, snapping
her attention back to him. Not that it'd strayed too far. He
certainly had a way of latching on to her thoughts and not
letting go.

Alana shook her head. "I never met her. She only lived in
Last Ride for a few months before she died, and she mostly
kept to herself, not venturing into town much."

Maybe Sadie Jo had done that lack of venturing because
of her celebrity status. In her younger days, she'd been a
somewhat successful country music singer with a few songs
that had hit the charts. So wherever she went, people would
have noticed and might have asked for photos, autographs
and such. However, it was just as possible the woman hadn't
felt well enough to get out and about.

Even though Alana had barely scratched the surface on
the research she needed to do, she knew Sadie Jo had suffered from some form of leukemia that she'd battled for
years. A battle she'd lost shortly after moving to Last Ride.
What Alana didn't know was why Sadie Jo had moved here,
but she figured that would all come out when she dug into
the woman's life, and death.

Alana fluttered her fingers toward the general vicinity
of the west of town and shared something she did know.

"Sadie Jo owned Nightfall Ranch. She named it that after her first big song, called 'Nightfall Heartbreak.'"

She studied his face—no hardship for that particular task, either—and she looked past all the hotness, and the broken heart memories, to see that something was troubling him.

"Hey, I've heard some talk that someone is interested in buying Nightfall Ranch now that Sadie Jo's estate has been settled," she threw out there. "Is that why you're back in Last Ride, to buy it?"

That might explain why Gray was here at the cemetery. Well, it would explain it in a roundabout way if he'd wanted to pay his last respects to the ranch's former owner.

According to the rumor mill, Gray certainly had the funds to make a big purchase like that because he, too, was somewhat of a celebrity. He'd used his rodeo rankings and wins to land some endorsements, everything from jeans to manly scented aftershave, and those endorsements had given him the funds to build his cattle-broker business. Ironically, that hugely successful business was her father's main competition these days.

"Well?" she prompted. "Is that why you've come back?"

Gray made a sound that could have meant anything. He certainly didn't answer her question. He stared out at the headstones, the very same pose he'd been in when she'd first spotted him.

"I'm not sure why I'm back," he finally said.

There was a mountain of emotion in that short comment, and more emotion followed. He groaned, scrubbed his hand over his face and turned to her.

"You want to have a drink or get something to eat?" he asked.

Alana now understood the old adage of being so surprised you could be knocked over by a feather. A *yes* nearly flew right out of her surprised mouth before she recalled another old adage.

Think before you leap.

She hadn't done a whole lot of thinking when she'd been with Gray. That had been all about her feelings. About her wanting him. About her spinning a golden dream that they would get married and have their forever-after.

Obviously, that hadn't happened.

It hadn't happened with her marriage to Elliot Dayton, either. Nor with her two engagements. And that's why she couldn't do any more leaping without a bunch of thinking first.

"Uh," she started and then cleared her throat, trying to figure out the best way to say this. But Gray spoke before she could come up with anything.

"You're turning me down because of that support group you're in," Gray provided.

Of course, Melvin would have mentioned that, too. Not that it was a secret or anything. The support group run by her distant cousin and counselor, Evangeline Parkman, was held in one of the meeting rooms at the library so plenty of people would have seen her come and go from the weekly gathering of Positive Measures, Positive Lives.

Alana nodded. "Like I said, I have a track record of lousy relationships. Sorry," she added in a mutter when she realized that Gray was an early part of that track record. "After my last breakup, I went to counseling, and now I guess you could say I get weekly tune-ups from the support group."

Tune-ups that Alana thought would help her in doing more looking and less leaping. Dreaming of forever-afters would have to wait.

"You really took a vow of celibacy?" he asked.

Obviously, Melvin was a huge blabbermouth, but again, she shouldn't be surprised that the little tidbit was gossip fodder.

"Yes," Alana verified. "It was voluntary." She frowned when she heard what she'd said because the odds of it being involuntary were slim to none unless she'd joined a convent. "A way of clearing my head so I can think straighter about relationships."

Of course, a vow of celibacy hadn't actually been that hard since she hadn't wanted to get into a relationship and wasn't into one-offs. Never had been. For her, it had always been about the falling in love and the dreaming about the future. Sex had been more or less the icing on the cake.

She looked up at Gray when he made another of those could-mean-anything sounds, and Alana got another punch of lust. All right, so maybe sex would be more than just icing with Gray, a lot more, but she wasn't ready to dive back into heart-breaking waters with him.

"Anyway," she said to get herself moving so she wasn't just standing there lusting after him. "I should get that photo of the tombstone." She glanced around, though, and realized she didn't have a clue where it was.

"It's there." Gray pointed to a white marble tombstone toward the center of the cemetery.

She turned in that direction and noticed that the headstone wasn't as large as some of the others, but it did look new. Understandable, considering that Sadie Jo had only died about six months ago.

Alana took a couple of steps toward the grave and then turned back around to face him. "Did you come here to visit Sadie Jo's grave?" she came out and asked.

He paused, then nodded. That was his only response for a long time, and her mind began to whirl with some possibilities. Sadie Jo had been a big name when Gray had been in high school so maybe he was a fan.

Except it seemed like more than that.

"You weren't like involved with her, were you?" Alana asked, but then she immediately waved off the question. "Sorry, that's none of my business." Though she quickly did the math and tallied up the twenty-one-year age difference between Gray and Sadie Jo. Still, relationships like that happened, what with the woman being a celebrity.

"No," Gray answered. Then, he shook his head and cursed under his breath. "Not involved," he added a moment later, which didn't clarify much.

The moments crawled by. And just kept crawling.

On a huff, Gray turned to Alana, and his gaze locked with hers. "I found out today that the woman I thought was my mother, isn't." Gray tipped his head to the tombstone. "And that Sadie Jo Walker gave birth to me."

CHAPTER TWO

GRAY HADN'T PLANNED on telling Alana what he'd just told her. Hell, he hadn't planned on saying it aloud.

Sadie Jo Walker gave birth to me.

But there it was. All out in the open. Open to Alana, anyway, and judging from the way her jaw dropped, it had stunned her almost as much as it had him. Almost.

"Well, crap," Alana muttered.

Gray made a sound of agreement since that pretty much summed it up. Three hours ago, he'd learned his life had been a big-assed lie, and that his parents—yes, the very parents he'd loved and idolized—had been the ones to feed him that lie.

A lie that changed everything.

Because if he wasn't David and Mary Russell's son, then who the hell was he?

Gray had been trying to wrap his mind around that when Alana had arrived. In those first moments when he'd seen her step from her car and make her way to the cemetery, he'd groaned at the intrusion. Groaned, too, because even with the crap he was feeling right now, he still got that old punch of lust just by looking at her. But he wasn't groaning now. Well, he was about the lust part, but he was sort of glad she was here. If he was going to pour out his heart to anybody in Last Ride, then Alana would have been his first choice.

Before he'd learned about the big-assed lie, his father would have been choice number one. But no way could he go to his dad now. Or rather go to the man he'd been told was his dad. Eventually, he would have to face him, to demand some answers, but Gray had to steady himself first.

"Well, crap," Alana repeated. She opened her mouth, closed it and opened it again as if trying to figure out what to say.

Welcome to the club. Gray was still working on that himself. It was the reason he'd asked her out for a drink or dinner. That had seemed a more likely setting for breaking the news about Sadie Jo.

Likely setting, he silently muttered.

It was a sad day in a man's life when he tried to BS himself so Gray did a mental adjustment and admitted the truth. He'd wanted to get Alana away from here. Here where he was seemingly frozen in place while staring at Sadie Jo's headstone. Away from here so he could spill all and maybe have Alana help him make sense of things.

She'd always been good at that when they'd been together. Listening. Helping him put things in perspective. Allowing him to vent and grieve. Alana had done all of that when his mother had died fifteen years ago.

Or rather the woman he'd thought had been his mother.

Her death had shaken him to the bone, and Alana had helped him get through that.

"News about this hasn't made it to the gossips," Alana added a moment later.

"No," he agreed. "Her lawyer has apparently known for a while now, since Sadie Jo moved to Last Ride and asked him to handle her will and her estate."

"But neither her attorney nor Sadie Jo said anything about it to you?" she pressed.

"Not a word. Sadie Jo asked her lawyer to keep everything to himself until the estate was settled. That took a few months, and he managed to keep the details of the probate to himself."

The lawyer would continue to do that, but Gray knew word of this would get out. Well, it probably would. His parents obviously hadn't had trouble keeping his parentage a secret all this time.

"All right," Alana said after muttering something under her breath. Gray didn't catch all the words, but there was some profanity mixed in there. "You're sure Sadie Jo gave birth to you?"

He appreciated that Alana had phrased it that way rather than asking if he was sure the woman was his *mother*. Gray didn't want that label applied to her, especially since Sadie Jo had obviously been a big participant in the "let's lie our heads off to Gray" arrangement.

"I'm sure," Gray verified, and he dragged in a long breath, ready to spill the rest. That's when he saw the sweat popping out on Alana's face, and even though she'd scooped up her long blond hair into a ponytail and was wearing a loose cotton dress, she was obviously still hot. Rather than risk possible heatstroke, he motioned for her to follow him back to his truck.

"I would ask you if you're okay," she said when they got moving, "but I can see you're not. I'm so sorry, Gray."

And there it was. Sympathy that he wouldn't have wanted coming from anyone else. However, it seemed to be what he needed from Alana. It sure as hell didn't fix things, but Gray wasn't sure this was a fixable situation.

They climbed into his truck, and he immediately started the engine, cranking up the AC as high as it would go.

"Mind if I drive around while we talk? I can bring you back here later to get your car," he added.

"Drive," she agreed. "Last I checked, riding in a truck with a hot cowboy doesn't violate my vow of celibacy."

Despite his heavy heart, he smiled, which was no doubt her intention. That was something else he always admired about Alana. Even when he was in the darkest pit of despair, she could make him smile.

"This morning I got a call from Asher Parkman," Gray started as he pulled out of the parking lot and onto the road. "I was surprised since he's not my lawyer." But Asher was *a* lawyer, and was head of the most prominent law firm in town. "He said he needed to talk to me, that I was a beneficiary in a will."

That had given Gray a jolt because his first thought was that his father had made a will. That his father had needed a reason to do so. Such as having a fatal disease. But then Asher had clarified and said it was from the recently probated will of Sadie Jo Walker.

"Asher didn't want to get into the details over the phone," Gray went on, "so I drove from my place in San Antonio to his office, and he showed me a DNA report that proved Sadie Jo was my bio parent. She apparently had the test run when I was a kid and had given the results to Asher."

"When you were a kid?" Alana made a sound that seemed to be a mixture of surprise and outrage for him being kept out of the loop on this. "So, your folks would have known about the DNA test, or did Sadie Jo sneak around and do it?"

"My folks knew," he verified. He had to pause a couple of seconds to get over the gut punch of learning that. "Sadie Jo must have talked them into it because I remember doing the test when I was six or seven. I didn't know what it was because my parents lied and said it was because I'd been exposed to strep, but the dates match up on the report Sadie Jo gave to Asher."

Alana stayed quiet, obviously processing that. Maybe she'd have better luck with that than he had. Gray had spent the last three hours processing, and he couldn't get past the anger of all the lies.

"So, Sadie Jo would have been about twenty-one when you were born," Alana muttered. "Like I said, I haven't done a lot of research on her, but I don't believe she ever got married. Maybe she felt she was too young to raise a child, or maybe the guy who got her pregnant… I'm so sorry," she tacked on to that.

She'd no doubt been about to say the guy who'd gotten Sadie Jo pregnant hadn't wanted the kid. Or had run out on her. Either was possible.

"Sadie Jo didn't leave any DNA results for my bio father," Gray supplied. "She didn't leave any info about that either in her will or with Asher."

Alana went quiet, no doubt in the mulling mode again. "You don't remember your parents saying anything about any of this?"

"Not a word. I've seen my birth certificate, and it has their names on it, but Asher says that's the way it works in an adoption. The adoptive parents' names are listed as the birth parents."

Gray wanted to curse the words, *birth parents* and *adoption*, but that's exactly what had happened to him. He didn't know why, didn't have the details of why something so huge—his own parentage—had been kept from him.

"Have you talked to your father about this?" Alana asked.

"No." Gray wasn't ready to do that just yet, but if anyone alive had answers, it would likely be the man who'd raised him. And lied to him. No, Gray wasn't ready to talk to him just yet. "But I told Asher he could call him and tell him that I now know the truth."

"Sweet mercy," she grumbled. "That won't be a pleasant conversation."

No, and once it happened, Gray suspected he'd be getting a call from the man who'd raised him. Heck, maybe even a visit if he could find Gray.

Alana looked up when Gray turned off the road, and she sighed when she saw where they were.

Nightfall Ranch.

He hadn't actually planned on coming here today, but this was sort of like going to the cemetery. The places where Sadie Jo had lived and was buried. He seriously doubted something cosmic would happen, and he'd get answers for this crap situation he was in, but here he was hoping for that.

Gray stopped on the driveway of the ranch and looked around. No livestock but acres and acres of pastures surrounded by white fences. The posts were shaped like guitars, Sadie Jo's choice of musical instruments. According to what Asher had told him, the woman had never appeared on stage without one.

"The place makes a statement, doesn't it?" Alana murmured, her gaze combing over the unique fence posts. The same guitar image was on the roof tiles of the two-story ruby-red house. On the roof of the barn as well. The hedges leading to the house had been trimmed into guitar shapes. "Exactly what statement, though, I'm not sure."

Heaven help him, that made him smile, too, and Gray looked over, intending to thank her for helping to lift his mood. Alana looked at him, though, at the same moment, and their gazes locked.

That whole gaze-locking was something that had happened way too often. In class when they should have been paying attention to the teacher. At times when he'd run into her in town while she was out with her parents. Other times when he should have been paying more attention to where he was walking. Once, it'd caused him to run smack into one of the lampposts on Main Street. Right now, though, the gaze lock just felt comforting.

Like coming home for Christmas and those other warm and fuzzy things.

Unfortunately, though, there was another side to warm and fuzzy with Alana. The blasted heat. That was the problem with their being each other's first lovers. The memories and the heat stayed strong. At least it did on his part. Since he'd left Alana, and had therefore stomped on her heart, she might not have such sizzling feelings left for him.

Except she did.

Gray could see that heat in her eyes. Yeah, it was mixed with the sympathy and all, but it was still there. Worse, his stupid body was encouraging him to pick up where he'd left off years ago by kissing her. Maybe testing just how strong that vow of celibacy was. But that would be like playing with fire, running with scissors and a whole bunch of other reckless things. That's why Gray unlocked his gaze from hers and stared back out at the ranch.

"Did you want to say something to me?" Alana asked.

He frowned. "About what?" Because he had no intentions of getting into this sudden need he had to kiss her, to hold her and try to erase a good chunk of the past.

"About anything," she threw out there. "Maybe about

why I'm here. Or why you keep looking at me as if the last thirteen years didn't happen?"

The answer to this was easy. No, he didn't especially want to say anything about that at all. It'd probably been a mistake to drag Alana into this, but since he had, Gray needed to man up.

"No way would your parents have ever accepted me," Gray reminded her. "And you probably wouldn't have broken off things with me. That would have set us up for one miserable life, and I didn't want that for either of us."

She nodded as if that was exactly what she'd expected him to say and then added a *duh* sound when he lifted his eyebrow, questioning her reaction. "You always said you wanted what your parents had," she spelled out. "A perfect marriage."

He had, indeed, said that. Had believed it, too. Hell, maybe it had been perfect for them all the while they were lying to him.

"After you left, I looked for perfect," she added. "I obviously didn't find it."

That hurt, a quick deep cut. Because he had to take some responsibility on setting her on that self-proclaimed path of the Typhoid Mary of relationships.

"Don't blame yourself," she went on as if she'd developed that ESP she'd talked about at the cemetery. "My choices, my mistakes." She dragged in a quick breath. "Now, enough about me. What are you going to do about what you found out today?"

No easy answer this time. Gray didn't have a clue. Definitely no cosmic answers from seeing Nightfall Ranch. Added to that, seeing the place was a cue that he had yet something else to deal with.

"Sadie Jo left the ranch to me," Gray said.

"Wow," Alana muttered after another pause.

Sounding more than a little surprised, Alana repeated her *wow* a couple of times, and she was no doubt doing what he was doing—glancing around the acres and acres. Lots of land, a huge house, three ponds and a groundskeeper's cottage. Complete with the groundskeeper, Teddy Derrick.

In one of those ironic twists that kept popping up, Teddy was friends with Gray's father. Or rather the man who'd raised Gray. He recalled Teddy visiting many times when Gray had been a kid, but until Asher had told him, Gray hadn't known he was the groundskeeper at Nightfall. Then again, there were a lot of things he hadn't known.

Apparently, Sadie Jo had been satisfied with Teddy's work since she'd not only had the cottage built for him, she had included a provision in her will to pay his salary and the salaries of the seasonal helpers that Teddy hired for the next five years.

"What will you do with the place?" Alana asked.

His gut reaction was to say he wanted no part of it, but there was another irony going on here. Some might even say it was cosmic intervention.

"I've been working with a Realtor to find a place to expand my business," Gray explained. "This is one of the properties he recommended, and said since the owner had recently died, it would likely be coming on the market soon."

Nightfall Ranch was perfect for his cattle-broker needs and imperfect in every other way. He didn't mean the guitar decor, either. Nope. It was imperfect because it was a gift offered to him by a woman who hadn't wanted him and had given him away. Of course, she hadn't just left him on the streets. He'd been adopted by whom anyone would consider a stable, loving couple. Still, offering him Night-fall felt like some kind of bribe from the grave.

"Going with the rumor mill," Alana said, "the house hasn't been cleared out."

"It hasn't," he verified. "Asher said Sadie Jo had wanted me to be able to go through the things and keep anything I wanted." He paused. Had to. "There's nothing I want."

Except he rethought that. Hell, maybe there was something. A diary or written tell-all confession about why she'd given him up for adoption.

"There are apparently some outfits that Sadie Jo wore on stage," Gray added, looking at Alana again. "A couple of them she wanted to go to a friend of hers, but she told Asher that the rest of them should be offered to you in case you want to use them in the theater department."

Her blue eyes always seemed bright, like the sparkle of some rare jewel, but they brightened even more. "Yes," she said. Then, stopped what might have been some gushing over what she obviously considered happy news. "Sorry. I won't take them if you'd rather burn them or something."

Again, she'd made him smile. "No burning." Well, not outfits that Alana might use at school, but there were other possible pitfalls inside that massive house.

Alana must have seen the doom and gloom go over him because she reached out, took his hand and gave it a gentle squeeze. "We could play the 'name a place you've never been kissed' game, but that might not be wise and all, con-sidering where the game always led us in the past."

This time, he laughed. Couldn't help himself. Because, yeah, it'd been a fun game all right and it had, indeed, led to making out and eventually sex.

"My left earlobe," he provided.

She gave an exaggerated huff and rolled her eyes. "Since

I recall that being an especially sensitive hot spot for you, I'm sure that part of you has been kissed many, many times."

He frowned at the *many, many*. It was absolutely a hot spot for him, but he couldn't recall nudging his lovers in that direction. Alana had done her own nudging. When they'd been fifteen or so, she'd first located it with her mouth. Then, her tongue. After hearing and feeling his response, which had been an instant hard-on, she had often tortured him with it.

"You're making it difficult for me to honor your vow of celibacy," he muttered. "But then the kiss game wouldn't necessarily lead to sex."

She exaggerated a flat look to let him know that was total BS. A kiss, possibly just one, could land them in the most available spot for sex.

Gray's phone rang, the sound cutting off his foreplay chatter, and he cursed when he saw the name pop up on the dash screen. David Russell. Normally, he wouldn't have gotten "a punch to the gut" feeling by getting a call from his dad, but there wasn't anything normal about today.

Since the conversation wouldn't be private, Gray considered hitting decline, but he couldn't do that. His dad would no doubt be worried. In fact, Asher's call would have been a gut punch for him, too, and while Gray was pissed off to the bone about what his folks had done, there was no reason to shut off all communication, especially since this call might give him answers to a few of those questions he very much needed answered.

"Are you all right?" his father immediately asked.

Gray went with the truth. "Not especially. But Alana's with me," he added so that his dad would know he wasn't alone.

"Alana." His dad sounded relieved about that. Maybe because he thought Gray was wallowing in a pit of despair right now and might do something reckless or stupid?

Doing something reckless or stupid could, indeed, happen, but Gray had no intentions of harming himself. The reckless or stupid, however, might involve Alana. With her this close, it would be so easy to take any comfort she could possibly offer. Easy to have fun by playing the old games with her that would lead to kissing and such.

Easy but wrong.

After all, there was a reason she was in that support group. A reason she'd had all those failed relationships. He definitely didn't need to be adding to what she was going through.

"Where are you?" his father asked several moments later. "We should talk."

Yeah, they should talk, but Gray couldn't manage that face-to-face right now. "Why didn't you tell me about Sadie Jo being my bio mother?"

He heard his father's long weary sigh. "Because your mother didn't want you to know. She made me promise and made me promise her again when she was on her death-bed."

That felt like another gut punch. He had a lot of rough memories of his mother dying. Memories of her pain and the fight for her life that she ultimately lost. He'd had no idea that even during that pain and fight she'd wanted his father to keep a secret that shouldn't have been a secret in the first place.

"Why?" Gray pressed his father, figuring that one word would cover a multitude of things.

His father sighed again. "Sadie Jo didn't want anyone to know she'd had a child so it was a private adoption. She and your mom had known each other since high school, and Sadie Jo asked us not to tell a single soul. Then, as the years passed, your mom and I didn't want to tell you because it didn't matter to us. You were our son. You *are* our son."

Gray couldn't tamp down the anger that stirred in him. "It might not have mattered to you, but it sure as hell matters to me," he snapped.

And this was why he'd wanted to postpone this chat. His father was no doubt hurting, and everything Gray was saying would only add to that hurt. Still, there was one final thing he had to know, and once he had the facts, he could start dealing with it. Maybe.

"Who's my bio father?" Gray asked.

His dad paused for a long time. "Sadie Jo didn't want you to know that, either."

Gray nearly cursed again, but since it would fix absolutely nothing, he said a quick goodbye and ended the call. He did curse after that. Cursed Sadie Jo. The ranch. The whole damn situation.

Alana didn't attempt to cheer him up with the offer of a kissing game. She unhooked her seat belt, slid over and put her arms around him. For such a simple gesture, it packed a punch, and it yanked him back to the times she'd done this when he'd been grieving over the death of his mother.

Gray wanted to thank her, to tell her how important she was to him. How important she always had been. But that was a Pandora's box that should probably stay shut. The lust was already a big enough pitfall without adding heartfelt feelings to the mix. Because telling all would lead to him admitting why he hadn't been able to stay in Last Ride. Why he hadn't been able to allow her to buck up against her parents, who would have made her life a living hell. Gray hadn't wanted to put her through that year after year.

She eased back and looked him straight in the eyes. "You need the game," she muttered.

And that was all the warning he got before she leaned in and tongue-kissed his earlobe.

CHAPTER THREE

ALANA STOPPED OUTSIDE the meeting room for her support group. She didn't go in but kept mentally repeating to herself that she hadn't actually kissed Gray so she hadn't violated her vow.

All right, she'd put her mouth and perhaps the tip of her tongue on his earlobe so maybe in the strictest sense of the word, that was a kiss.

But she wasn't applying that interpretation.

In her mind, there hadn't been a kiss because there'd been no mouth-to-mouth contact. Just that little nibble to play the "name a place you've never been kissed" game. And to try to cheer him up. He'd looked so miserable that she hadn't been able to help herself, and she was pretty sure it helped.

Temporarily, anyway.

It'd made him moan in that oh, so delicious way of his that was an invitation to continue. But Alana hadn't tossed all common sense to the wind. She had eased back, savoring that hot look he got when he was, well, hot, and then she'd let him return to reality. Because old foreplay games and ear kisses couldn't replace what he had to do. And that was to come to terms with the fact that his life had been turned upside down and inside out.

That was the reason she hadn't gone to see him for the past two days, though she had gotten his number before he'd driven her back to the cemetery, and over the past forty-eight hours, she had sent him some brief texts to let him know she was thinking about him.

Which, of course, was a massive understatement.

She hadn't been able to get her mind off him. Heck, Gray had even haunted her dreams where he'd appeared stark naked and ready—

"Are you just going to stand there?" someone asked, the question slicing right through the vivid image Alana was having of a naked Gray.

Alana groaned, not in a good sexual way, either, but an annoyed one. Because it was a member of the support group, Mildred Crowley, who for some reason thought it was her place to police the group and make sure they stayed on track. Alana suspected Mildred did that because with her crotchety personality, she wasn't likely to end up in a relationship.

"Well?" Mildred prompted. "Are you going into the meeting?"

"Uh, I might skip it this week," Alana muttered.

Mildred's mouth pinched tight in disapproval. "Because of Gray? I heard he was back in town."

It didn't surprise Alana that folks knew that, but she waited to hear if Mildred was going to add anything about Sadie Jo being Gray's bio mom. She didn't.

"Not because of Gray," Alana insisted, and that was partly true. Partly because even before Gray's return, she'd started to wonder if being in the group was actually doing her any good. But, yes, that doubt had skyrocketed after she'd tongue-kissed Gray's ear.

Mildred clucked her tongue. Actually clucked. "You should keep your mind on the goal," the woman insisted. "According to my calculations, you have four more days to go on your vow not to have sex." Mildred lowered her voice to a secretive whisper for that last word. "Then, you can approach things with a clear head."

"I have three days left," Alana corrected.

She thought of the ear kiss. Of Gray's hot face. Of him naked in her dream, and she wasn't sure she could last three hours much less three days.

"Maybe clear heads are overrated," Alana grumbled under her breath. Oh, the illogical things a mind could come up with when it wanted what it wanted.

And what both her mind and her body wanted was Gray.

That brought on more clucking, more pinched lips from Mildred. "It's not overrated, and you need to put on your big-girl panties and do the right thing." She paused. "Especially since Gray will likely be around a lot more than usual. I've heard he's buying Nightfall Ranch and maybe plans to live there."

So, there was talk, incorrect talk, but Alana didn't set Mildred straight about Gray buying the ranch. But if Mildred and others thought that's what had happened, then word wasn't out yet about Sadie Jo being Gray's birth mother.

Alana's phone dinged with a text, and she could have sworn her heart did a little happy dance when she saw Gray's name on the screen.

Can you come to Nightfall Ranch? he'd messaged. I'm going through Sadie Jo's stuff, and I found some things.

Her heart quit dancing, and the worry returned full force. Alana couldn't imagine what *some things* would be, but it was possible that whatever Gray had found had sent him into another downward spiral.

I'll be there soon, she texted back.

Alana kept her farewell remarks to Mildred at a muttered

goodbye because anything she said to the woman would spur her disapproval. Heck, even the goodbye caused her to frown, but that didn't stop Alana from hurrying to her car.

Yes, hurrying.

She assured herself that this wasn't about the fire-hot heat between Gray and her. This was about comforting someone whom she clearly still had feelings for. It was true that he'd broken her heart, but she could rationalize that they'd been young and stupid then. They were no longer young, but the stupid label might still apply to her. Because she knew any comfort she could give Gray would automatically add more fire to the already-existing flames.

Alana was frowning at herself by the time she drove out of town and toward Nightfall, and she forced herself to remember there was a reason she'd needed the support group in the first place. Her frown deepened considerably, though, when her phone rang, and she saw her mother's name on the dash screen.

Like the support group meeting, Alana would have preferred to skip this chat, but she'd put it off long enough. She'd already dodged two other calls, and her mom would just keep calling until they'd spoken. Or worse, her mother would pay a visit to Gray or her.

"I just got off the phone with Mildred," her mother greeted when Alana answered.

Alana groaned though it really wasn't a surprise because Mildred was a tattletale. "Yes, I'm on my way to talk to Gray," Alana admitted. Over the years, she'd discovered it was best to tattletale on herself, but she chose her words carefully since she didn't want to spill about what wasn't hers to spill. "He asked to see me."

There. It was the truth. He had, indeed, asked, probably because he'd found something that had cut him to the bone again.

"You could have said no," her mother quickly pointed out. There was snobby disapproval coating all five of those words.

Over the years, Alana had also discovered that it was best to remind her mother of boundaries, and for that to happen, Alana had to use that spine she'd finally grown after years of dealing with her controlling parents. Of course, there was always a fine line between setting boundaries and being respectful, but she thought she'd gotten the right balance.

"I was in love with Gray," Alana stated. "That doesn't mean we owe each other anything, but I'm still going to find out why he wants to see me."

Her mother's sigh was loud enough to extinguish birthday candles. "You're not looking before you leap."

Her mother had obviously learned the motto of the support group. "I'm not leaping," Alana argued. Which might or might not be the truth since she'd kissed Gray's ear. "And before you continue, there's nothing you can say that will make me cancel this visit. Nothing," Alana emphasized, doling out some of that spine she'd grown.

Apparently, though, her mother did think there was something she could say. "You're risking your heart to a man who's already broken it once. Just remember how long it took you to get over Gray when he left. Remember all the nights you spent crying yourself to sleep and ask yourself if you can come back from that again. Because, Alana, I don't think you can."

Her mother didn't give her a chance to respond to that because she tacked on an "I love you" and ended the call.

Alana admitted there could be some truth in that whole

"not being able to come back from another broken heart." Admitted, too, that her mother did, indeed, love her and didn't want her to get hurt. But even that wasn't going to stop her, and that told Alana loads.

Like maybe her being in love with Gray wasn't a "past deal" sort of thing.

Maybe it never would be.

And with that utterly depressing thought, Alana turned into the driveway of Nightfall Ranch.

She spotted Teddy, the groundskeeper, tending to a flower bed that was bursting with colors along with being in the guitar shape. Alana also saw Gray's truck, not parked out front but rather on the side of the house. Maybe he'd done that so the truck couldn't be seen from the road and therefore start some gossip, but that ship had sailed.

"Afternoon," Teddy called out to her.

Alana waved, returned the greeting and went to the door. However, before she could knock, Gray opened it.

"Thanks for coming," he said, tipping his head to the box he had tucked under his arm.

She was about to ask him what was in that box, especially since it had likely been the reason he'd asked her to come over, but Gray stopped her by brushing a kiss on her mouth. Even though it was quick and barely qualified as a kiss, it still sent her pulse galloping.

"No, I didn't call you here for that," Gray told her. He must have seen the heat flare in her eyes. Of course, her quick breath and glassy look probably clued him in, too. "But I've been dreaming about you, and I wanted to see, well, I just wanted to see."

Alana smiled. "And what did you see?" she came out and asked.

"That I'm a jerk for jerking your feelings around like that."

That rid her of her smile, and she caught onto the front of his shirt, yanking him to her. She put her mouth on his.

And this one was definitely a kiss.

The flood of heat came. Mercy, did it. It raced through her all the way to her fingertips and toes. She thought that maybe it singed her eyelashes.

He tasted like everything her body had been craving. Like Gray. Like something sweet and forbidden.

Which he was.

Still, Alana lingered several moments longer so she could make her point. Because the heat made her mind all fuzzy, which she had to keep reminding herself of when she was around him. She eased back.

"All right," she managed. "We're equal because I just jerked you around, too."

Gray stared at her. "I didn't vow to stay out of a relationship. Since you did, I shouldn't have kissed you." He kept his gaze on her a moment longer and then shook his head as if trying to clear it. Then, he shifted the box so she could look at what was inside.

"Photo albums," she muttered. She shifted her attention back to him to try to figure out if this had caused his mood to sink, but she couldn't tell. "Pictures of Sadie Jo with your birth father?" Alana came out and asked.

"No. Pictures of me." He took hold of her hand, leading her toward the living room.

Alana practically stumbled over her own feet, though, when she noticed the decor. It was hard to put a label on the style, but over-the-top seemed to apply. There were guitar rugs on white hardwood floors, massive flower vases and a red sofa in that particular shape.

There were boxes sitting around the foyer and living room, and she spotted the clear plastic garment bags containing costumes that could also be considered over-the-top. Lots of red, beads and even some feathers.

"Wow," Alana muttered.

"Yeah," he agreed. "I had the same reaction." He motioned toward the costumes. "Those are the ones for you. There's another batch in one of the boxes in the foyer. Those are going to Sadie Jo's friend and backup singer, Callie Murdock. She's coming over later to pick them up." He paused. "Sadie Jo and Callie have been friends since they were teenagers, so I'm hoping she can, well, tell me who my birth father is."

Alana considered that a moment. "Your dad still won't say?"

He shook his head. "Things aren't good between him and me right now."

That gave her a surge of emotions of a different sort, and her heart ached for him. Gray had always been so close to his parents, and his dad and he had gotten even closer after his mother died. This had to be eating away at Gray. At his father, too.

Gray sat her next to him on the sofa and pulled out the first album. "It's pictures of me the first year of my life."

Again, she checked to see how he was handling this discovery, but Gray didn't seem depressed, just confused. Alana thumbed through the album and soon saw why. There were no photos of Sadie Jo but rather of a newborn Gray with his parents, David and Mary. Alana knew it was Gray because his name had been monogrammed on his blue swaddling blanket.

Alana continued to look through the pictures and saw that these were key moments of Gray's first year of life.

All the milestones were there. Sitting up, crawling, first solid foods and walking.

Gray patted the box. "There are albums that go through until age ten. Then, there are more boxes for the rest of my years. Graduation, rodeo events, pictures from parties and such where I was promoting my business." He paused. "There's one partially filled from late last year."

It wasn't easy to wrap her mind around that. Some of the photos had been staged shots. Family pictures with his parents beaming at the camera. So, clearly they hadn't been taken by someone sneaking around.

"You think your parents gave these to Sadie Jo?" Alana asked.

Gray shrugged, then nodded. "My mother had nearly identical albums of me, and after she died, my dad kept them up." He stopped and cursed. "Since Sadie Jo gave me up, why the hell did she want all of this?"

Alana didn't need to wrap her mind around anything this time. The answer seemed obvious. "Sadie Jo couldn't keep you for whatever reason, but she obviously wanted to stay connected to you so she allowed you to be adopted by people she knew and trusted. She must have loved you."

Gray certainly didn't jump to agree with that. In fact, he didn't jump to say or do anything. He just stayed quiet for a really long time before he finally groaned. "Yeah," was all he said.

She expected that response to be the calm before the storm. And in a way it sort of was. But instead of diving into the murky waters of his birth mother, Gray turned to her, his gaze combing over her face.

"I couldn't stay connected to you after I hurt you," he threw out there. "Because being around you or hearing about you latched on to my throat and wouldn't let go."

All right. So, she definitely hadn't expected a confession like that.

Alana nodded. "I understand."

Gray kept his gaze on her but cursed. "I don't want you to understand. I want you to yell at me and tell me I was wrong to hurt you."

Because this was obviously still latching on to his throat, Alana took hold of his chin and ran her thumb over his bottom lip. "No yelling required. I've been doing a lot of thinking since you've come back, and I understand why you left."

"You should yell at me," he repeated, his stare flat now.

She brushed a kiss on his mouth instead. "I understand why you left," she said, doing some repeating of her own. "And hindsight being twenty-twenty and all, I think you were right. I wasn't ready to stand up to my parents. Over the years, though, I've had a lot of practice with that, but in those days, they would have tried to plow right over both of us."

"I should have stood up to them," Gray insisted.

Alana shook her head. "You were too young and like me, didn't have the right skill set to deal with them."

The question was—did they have that skill set now? Alana was certain she did, and that's why she was willing to take the Texas-sized risk of kissing him.

Really kissing him.

No games, no hesitation. Alana slid her arm around the back of his neck and drew him closer. And closer. Sinking right into the kiss.

Gray made the sound that was so familiar. Part groan, part grunt. All pleasure. He acted on that pleasure, too. Gray shoved aside the photo albums and pulled her to him. Not just closer. Nope. He put them body to body, and it was exactly where her body wanted to be.

Alana heard herself make her own sound of pleasure. Easy to do since she was feeling a lot of that particular sensation at the moment. With one scalding kiss, Gray had caused the heat to skyrocket, and she instantly wanted more, more, more.

Gray gave her more. Without breaking the kiss, he hauled her onto his lap. Something he'd done quite often when they'd been teenagers, and he hadn't lost any of his smooth moves. He kissed her, touched her and aligned their centers in such a way that the more, more, more became an urgent need. A need she certainly would have given into had she not heard the ringing sound.

"Doorbell," Gray grumbled, adding some ripe profanity to that announcement.

Alana groaned and groaned even more when she heard the doorknob rattle and a woman call out.

"Yoo-hoo," she said, obviously already coming inside. "It's me, Callie Murdock."

Good grief. Talk about lousy timing for Sadie Jo's friend to arrive to pick up the costumes.

Gray and she untangled themselves, not easily and not without knocking into each other. They somehow managed, though, to get to their feet when the tall busty blonde came waltzing in.

Alana had never met the woman, but she recalled seeing her around town. Recalled, too, that folks had mentioned that Callie had been with Sadie Jo when she died.

"Oh, sorry," Callie said when she spotted them. Apparently, she realized what she interrupted. And what she interrupted was two people who'd been very close to having sex.

"I probably should have waited for you, but I'm just used to letting myself in," Callie explained. "After Sadie Jo got so sick, she gave me a key so I could come in and check on her without her having to get up and answer the door."

Callie crossed the room to shake hands first with Gray and then with Alana. Even though this was a textbook example of awkward, Alana introduced herself.

"Oh, I know who you are, sugar," Callie said. "I saw the photos of Gray and you way back when you were kids." The woman beamed a big smile with lips coated with neon pink gloss. "It's mighty good to finally meet both of you."

"So, you knew Sadie Jo had given birth to me?" Gray came out and asked.

"Oh, yeah," Callie readily admitted after a very long pause. "I was bunking with Sadie Jo when she was pregnant." Her forehead bunched up. "I'm not sure if you're ready to hear this, but, sugar, she loved you. She doted like a proud mama on all the pictures of you."

Because Alana's arm was touching Gray's, she felt him stiffen. She took hold of his hand and gave it a gentle squeeze.

Gray squeezed back, but he kept his attention pinned to Callie. "Sadie Jo loved me." There was plenty of skepticism in that short comment.

"Damn straight." No skepticism for Callie. "Never seen any woman love a kid as much as she loved you."

"Then why did she give me away?" Gray snapped.

Callie blinked and then sighed. "Oh, I just figured Sadie Jo had left you some kind of letter or something that explained everything."

"Nothing I can find, and she didn't leave anything like that with her lawyer." Gray paused a heartbeat. "If you were with Sadie Jo before I was born, then you know why she gave me up and who my father is."

Callie dropped back a step. "Yes, I do." She groaned. "I'm guessing nobody told you?"

"No." Gray didn't add more, didn't press the woman to confess all, but there was no doubt in his tone and body language that it was exactly what he wanted her to do.

"Gray deserves to know the truth," Alana insisted.

Callie stared at them both and made a sound of agreement. "You do deserve the truth, but it shouldn't come from me." She patted Gray's arm. "Call your dad, Gray. Anything about your father and your adoption should come from him."

CHAPTER FOUR

GRAY DIDN'T FIGURE he could groan loud enough to express his frustration over what Callie had just said. "I don't want to call my father," he informed her. "I want the truth, and you can give me that."

Callie sighed again and patted his arm. "I promised Sadie Jo that I'd keep a lid on what I knew. The lid's staying in place." She went to the costumes, gathering them up, and for a moment, Gray thought Callie would just head out without saying another word. But she stopped in front of him and looked him straight in the eyes.

"Sadie Jo loved you. Hang on to that." Callie glanced around the room. "Hang on to this place, too, because I know how much she wanted you to have it."

Gray followed her to the door, but he didn't press her to remove the lid that Sadie Jo had put into place by swearing Callie to secrecy. Part of him admired the woman's loyalty. Another part of him wanted to curse Sadie Jo, Callie and his parents for wanting to keep that secret in the first place.

He watched Callie leave, and this time he locked the door. Not because he thought Alana and he would dive back into another make-out session. Nope. She wasn't looking at him with lust but rather sympathy.

"I'm sorry," she said, pulling him into a hug. Not a heated one, either. This one was all comfort. "I'm sorry," she repeated when she pulled back to meet his gaze. "What are you going to do?"

Gray refused to say *the hell if I know*. He was a successful businessman and a former rodeo champion who'd worked hard to build what he had, and he hadn't achieved those things by waffling. He took out his phone and called his father. Or rather that's what he tried to do. But it went straight to voice mail.

"We need to talk," Gray said when he left his dad a message. "And you will tell me the truth."

There. That was one thing ticked off his to-do list. If his father refused to tell him anything, then Gray would consider it a done deal. Yes, it would eat away at him not to know, but it would eat away more if he didn't try to come to terms with this.

Nightfall Ranch was next on his to-do list, and he glanced around the foyer while he debated his options. "I've considered selling the place and donating the profits to various charities."

Alana glanced around, too. "You don't intend to own the ranch?" Thankfully, she didn't bring up what Callie had said about Sadie Jo wanting him to have the place. Gray didn't need that playing into this.

"I do want to own a ranch," Gray verified. "A place like this is what I had in mind for expanding my business. Minus the guitars, of course. The location is right. *Was right*," he amended, when he'd been thinking about living closer to his dad. "It has the right amount of acreage and water supplies for times when I'd need to pasture some livestock I'm brokering. Right number of outbuildings and a ready supply of help to keep the place running."

Alana nodded. "But?"

Oh, yeah. There were some *buts* for him owning the

place, and they weren't just limited to the possibility that things were so strained between him and his father that he might not want to live anywhere near him. But his father wasn't the only parental unit in this.

"My business already competes with your family's," he pointed out. "It might make things tough for you if I'm right here in the same town with them."

Alana smiled. Not the reaction he'd expected her to have. "It'll only make things tougher for me if I let it. Trust me, I won't let it."

Now, he smiled. This definitely wasn't the girl he'd left behind so that she wouldn't have to deal with the fallout. Alana was obviously a grown woman with enough confidence to deal with her parents.

Well, maybe.

Gray immediately rethought that notion. "Are you in that support group for them or for you?"

"For me," Alana readily answered, and then her forehead bunched up. "And despite that whole 'vow of celibacy' deal, I think talking out my feelings helped." She paused. "After you left, I wanted to stand my ground against my parents so I purposely got involved with men who wouldn't meet their standards. All those relationships failed."

"Because the men weren't right for you," he pointed out.

She gave a quick nod and looked him straight in the eyes. "But they failed because I never got over you."

Hell. Gray hadn't expected her to say that, and it slugged him with guilt.

"I know that look," Alana went on. "You're blaming yourself. You shouldn't. You shouldn't," she repeated in a much firmer voice. "It's not your fault that I had a really bad habit of calling out your name during...well, during times when I shouldn't have been calling it out."

Gray did another mental *Hell*. Said one aloud, too. "I'm sorry about that."

She smiled. "Yes, but not too sorry, I hope."

He fought a smile. Fought it hard, but the smile won. "Not too sorry," he confessed. "And that makes me a jerk because if you'd called out those other guys' names, you might not have had to end up in a support group."

"Yes, but I would have maybe been in relationships that wouldn't have made me happy." She stared at him. "I can take out the *maybe* in that. I would have been miserable with those guys. Miserable because I was with them all for the wrong reasons."

Gray was about to point out that she could easily end up being miserable with him, that he wasn't the fix for an ideal relationship. Then again, maybe no one had that. Once, he'd been certain his parents had, but now he wasn't so sure.

Well, not sure of relationships, anyway.

He was certain of one thing. That he wanted Alana. Wanted her more than answers, more than being guilt-free. More than his next breath.

That's why Gray slipped his arm around her, pulled her to him and kissed her.

ALANA HAD SEEN the kiss coming. Had felt the mountain of emotion that was behind it. But even with the heads-up, she hadn't braced herself nearly enough for the onslaught of heat and need.

Of course, she'd gotten a sneak peek of that heat and need during their kisses on the sofa, and while those had certainly packed a punch, this one had all the others beat. Maybe beating all the kisses they'd ever shared.

He immediately deepened the kiss, pulling her to him. Not that he had to put much of an effort into that since

Alana had already been moving in his direction. She landed against his body. Chest to breasts.

And the battle began.

The kiss wasn't gentle. Not this time. It was hard and hungry with the promise that it would only get a whole lot better. Gray got started with the better by putting her back against the wall, anchoring her in place with his body so he could touch her.

Every inch of her body shouted a yes as he slid his hand between them and over her breast. They'd played so many kissing games that he knew all her hot spots. Better yet, he knew what to do with those spots. He brushed his fingertips over her erect nipple and then lowered his mouth to kiss her there.

The pleasure raced through her, but the problem with really good pleasure was that the parts he was kissing wanted more, and it wanted it now. Even though her dress and bra were thin, it was way too much between his mouth and her skin. Alana started jockeying for position so she could do something about that.

Gray did something about it first.

He pulled her dress up and over her head, dropping it somewhere on the foyer floor. Her bra followed—obviously, he hadn't lost his touch when it came to the speedy removal of her undergarments. He hadn't lost his touch, either, when it came to tongue-kissing her breasts.

Oh, the sensations that whipped up inside her. The heat. The need. The urgency to go ahead and have him inside her. For that to happen, though, she had to get him naked. Much easier said than done since he clearly didn't want to stop the kissing and touching. Not only that, but he was also kissing and touching while he went lower. Lower. Lower. He slid off her panties and did what Gray could do best.

Alana jolted in a really good way when he kissed the center of her body. Jolted, moaned and just gave in to the pleasure for a couple of seconds. Unfortunately, it was way too good, and she knew if she didn't do something about it, his clever mouth and tongue would bring her to a too-fast end.

She slid lower, too, and because he didn't pull back on the kiss, Alana was on the receiving end of a trail of kisses that went back up her body. When she finally managed to drop down to her knees, she was well past the stage of being just worked up. She was ready.

"You'd better have a condom," she managed to say as she tackled his shirt.

"In my wallet," Gray answered, reaching in the back pocket of his jeans to retrieve it.

She let him deal with that while she unbuttoned his shirt, which took way too much time. She made a mental note to tell him to wear a T-shirt next time so it'd be easier to get it off him.

The *next time* thought made her pause, and she might have wondered if there would, indeed, be a next time, but the question flew right out of her head when Gray started kissing her again.

He could obviously multitask, because while he kept firing her up with his mouth, he managed to unhook his belt and unzip his jeans. Alana let him deal with that while she put her own mouth to good use on his chest.

Mercy, the man was built.

"You didn't have all these muscles way back when," she muttered.

He made a grunt of agreement, but he had to put the pause button on the chest kisses so he could rid himself of his boots and jeans. She helped with the boxers and had to mentally repeat what she'd thought seconds earlier.

The man was certainly built.

"I can probably find a bed," he offered.

But she shook her head. She didn't want to go searching through the house for a bed when her body was on fire. The floor would work just fine.

Gray got on the condom, and he reversed their positions so that his back was against the door. He hauled her onto his lap, giving Alana some amazing flashbacks of when they'd had sex in his truck. At least this time they wouldn't get bruises from banging into the gear stick.

He pushed inside her, and all thoughts of gear-stick bruises vanished. Everything vanished, maybe even the air itself, except for Gray and the pleasure he was giving her. He made sure that pleasure kept spiking, too, by moving inside her. By pushing her up, up, up to the peak.

Alana wanted to take hold of this urgent need. Wanted to grab it and make it last. But there was no way she could. Not with Gray hitting the best of her hot spots. Not with him making sure he was doing everything possible to send her flying.

And that's exactly what he did.

Taking her mouth in a hot hungry kiss, he pushed into her, and her body had no choice but to surrender. She went flying, and seconds later, Gray followed right along with her.

Alana felt the spasms of her own body blend with his. They certainly hadn't lost any steps in drawing out every ounce of pleasure there was to be had. Part of that pleasure was holding him. Of having their now-sweat-dampened bodies pressed against each other while their breaths gusted and they came back to earth.

She smiled at the slack, sated feeling that washed over her. Smiled, too, at all the other things she was feeling. Not feelings of guilt or doubt. Not worrying about what might happen next. Nope. Alana just wanted to hold on to this moment.

Gray held on as well. Making a sound that let her know he, too, was sated and slack, he dropped a soft kiss on the crook of her neck. He held her while their hearts and breathing leveled out.

"I'll be right back," he said, moving her off him. She groaned and was about to protest, but then he added, "Don't get dressed yet."

So, maybe he had seconds in mind, which suited her just fine. In fact, at the moment she would have probably agreed to pretty much anything.

She got an amazing peep show of his butt and back when he headed toward the bathroom. Yes, indeed. That was a sight for her memory banks.

The peep show continued after Gray returned from the bathroom, and this time Alana got a long, glorious look at his frontside. His amazing face, too. If he was having any regrets about what had just happened between them, he wasn't showing it. In fact, he was smiling.

He came back to her, kissed her, and Alana was pulling him against her again when his phone rang. Both of them cursed the interruption, and Alana cursed some more when the kissing stopped while Gray located his phone in the pile of clothes on the floor.

"It's my dad," he grumbled.

She saw the debate he was having, and after a few seconds, Gray finally answered. He opened his mouth to say something, but his father spoke first. Even though Gray hadn't put the call on speaker, Alana had no trouble hearing David since Gray was right next to her.

"I'm on my way now to Sadie Jo's so we can talk. You need to know the truth," the man said. "And that truth is I slept with Sadie Jo, and I'm your biological father."

CHAPTER FIVE

GRAY DIDN'T PACE while he waited for his dad to show up and explain what the hell he'd meant when he'd delivered the bombshell minutes earlier.

I slept with Sadie Jo, and I'm your biological father.

On the surface, that confession was self-explanatory, but as far as Gray was concerned, his dad owed him a whole bunch of explanations. Not just about why he'd lied to Gray all these years but why he'd betrayed his wife and had an affair. Why he'd convinced his wife that they should raise the child who would always be positive proof of that betrayal.

"It'd probably be better if I left," Alana muttered while she put on her shoes. Like him, she'd dressed as soon as Gray had ended the call to wait for his visitor.

"No." He couldn't say that fast enough, and while it wasn't especially fair that Alana would have to be privy to what could turn into a shouting match and an exchange of some mean words, Gray wanted her with him.

Even if with him was the last place she should be.

He'd gotten her to break that damn vow of chastity, had gotten her to open up herself and her heart to him. And that could turn out to be a big-assed mistake. He could end up hurting her all over again.

"All right," she said, and she went to him to give his hand a gentle squeeze. "Is there anything I can do to make this better?"

"No." He was quick with that answer, too, and he gave himself one last steeling up when he heard the vehicle approaching the house.

Not wanting to put this off for even a second, Gray went to the door, threw it open and spotted his father stepping from his truck. Judging from the man's expression and slumped shoulders, he was dreading this as much as Gray was.

"Alana," his father greeted as he stepped inside. He pulled off his Stetson and held it in front of him like a shield.

"I can go if you want to talk privately," she immediately offered.

His father shook his head. "If Gray wants you here, then stay."

Gray took hold of her hand to make sure she did just that. It would save him from having to repeat what was about to be said because Gray wouldn't have kept her in the dark about this.

Unlike what his parents had done all these years.

That was the real pisser in this. That his mother had lied to him as well. Of course, so had Sadie Jo. She'd lied simply by keeping quiet, but Gray didn't feel the anger toward her as he did for the man standing in front of him.

"I met Sadie Jo in a church in San Antonio," his father began.

"A church?" Gray questioned. He'd thought this was going to have a seedier start, such as a drunken encounter in a bar or after one of her shows.

His father nodded. "She was a guest at a wedding I'd attended. Your mom wasn't with me." He paused, swallowed hard. "We were going through a rough patch, and she had gone to stay with her sister in Austin."

Gray didn't repeat the words, *rough patch*, but he did lift an eyebrow. "Mom always said you had the perfect marriage. You let me believe it was perfect," he added in a snarl.

His father gave another nod. "By the time you were old enough to understand things like marriage, your mom and I did have a perfect one. Well, better than most, anyway."

Oh, that unleashed a whole storm of anger. "You had an affair with another woman. You got that woman pregnant."

"I did," his father readily admitted. "Like I said, I met Sadie Jo, and at the reception, we talked. Danced together. Laughed."

"And had sex with her." Gray didn't shout that, but the fury came through loud and clear in his tone.

"I did," he repeated. "We had sex, and we both agreed it was a mistake. A one-off that we wouldn't repeat. I went to your mother and told her what I'd done."

Gray flinched. "I'm betting she didn't take that well." And despite all the lies, he hurt for his mother, knowing how much that must have crushed her.

"No, not well at all," his father muttered in agreement. "But she wanted to work things out with me. She wanted to give our marriage a second chance." He paused again. "Things were going well enough until Sadie Jo called me and told me she was pregnant."

Again, Gray felt his mother's pain and hoped like hell that she'd had someone there to comfort her. Someone like Alana who was giving him that comfort now just by being here.

"It was a hard blow for your mom," his father went on, "because, you see, she'd been trying to get pregnant for years. That was the reason we were having that rough patch. She kept going through all these fertility treatments, and the doctor wanted her to stop. The meds were causing some serious health problems for her. But she didn't want to stop because she wanted a baby."

Oh, hell.

Alana looked up at him, silently questioning if he'd known any of this. He hadn't, so Gray shook his head. *I'm sorry*, she mouthed.

Yeah, so was he. Sorry for the crap his mother had gone through, and the hard slap it must have been when she'd learned her husband's one-off lover was pregnant with his child. A child she hadn't been able to conceive with him despite the fertility treatments.

"Anyway, Sadie Jo told me she wasn't ready to be a mom," his father explained. "Not just because she was so young but because she'd just signed this big record contract. She wanted to focus on that and figured she couldn't give a baby the attention he or she deserved."

"So, she offered me to Mom and you," Gray finished for him.

"She did." He stopped, shook his head and drew in a long breath before he continued. "Your mom said yes right off the bat, but it took a little longer to convince me. Not because I didn't already love and want you. I did. But because I wasn't sure your mom would ever be able to look at you and not see Sadie Jo."

Gray hadn't considered that, though it would have been a huge obstacle. He wasn't sure he wanted to hear the truth about that, but it was something he should know. It was the only way to get the big picture.

"Was Mom able to do that, to look at me and not see your lover's face?" Gray asked.

"Yes, she was. Of course, she was," he repeated like a plea. "She loved you. So did Sadie Jo. Over the years, your mom and she stayed in touch, and while I wouldn't say they got close or anything, Sadie Jo did confide in her that she was never able to get over the hurt of giving you up for adoption."

Gray knew he should try to see this through Sadie Jo's very young eyes, but he just couldn't. Not with the hurt and the emotions so fresh and raw; they were slicing him to pieces.

"When Sadie Jo found out she was sick with leukemia," his father went on, "she bought this ranch so she'd have something to leave to you. She knew it wouldn't make up for what she did, but she wanted you to have something from her."

"Something from her," Gray repeated, his voice flat now. "Even though I didn't live here."

"True, but Sadie Jo figured you'd eventually return since Last Ride is your home."

Gray had no idea if that last part was even true. It had been his home. *Had been.* But now it felt as if the past was closing in around him.

"I always figured the reason you left town was because you didn't want to cause trouble for Alana," his father continued. "I mean, what with the way her folks felt about you and all."

"It was the reason I left," Gray admitted. "And I broke Alana's heart in the process."

"Because you were trying to protect me," she quickly reminded him.

He looked at her, wanting to believe that was true. And maybe it was. But maybe he just hadn't wanted to deal with the flak with her folks. He couldn't blame it on his young age, either. Because if he made allowances for that, then he'd also have to make allowances for Sadie Jo, who would have only been three years older when she'd given him up for adoption.

"Did Sadie Jo and you pick up where you left off after that wedding reception?" Gray asked.

"No," he said, his father's voice a ragged whisper. "I was only with Sadie Jo that one time."

Gray cursed, and even though his father had opened his mouth to continue, Gray waved him off. He couldn't listen to any more of this. Couldn't take any more.

"I have to go," Gray managed to say despite the fist-sized lump in his throat.

He gave Alana's hand a quick squeeze and headed out the door. Gray had one question on his mind as he walked away. Just one.

What the hell was he going to do now?

CHAPTER SIX

WHAT WAS SHE going to do now?

That was the question going through Alana's mind while she drove to the Hilltop Cemetery to get that research photo of Sadie Jo's tombstone.

Actually, that specific question had been eating away at her for the past twenty-four hours. And even longer— since Gray had come back to Last Ride and had his world turned upside down.

Of course, her own world had tipped on its axis as well. Not in the horrible way that Gray's had, but the tipping wasn't much of a surprise since Gray was part of that world. At least he had been since his return. Before that, well, he'd been part of it, too. She understood that now. Just because Gray hadn't been physically there in her life and in Last Ride, it didn't mean he hadn't been with her.

Because she was in love with him.

Alana could see that. She had been in love with Gray since they were teenagers, and that love hadn't died when he left town. Nope. Her feelings for him had just stayed dormant until Gray returned. Maybe the great sex had caused them to resurface and come back even stronger, but she suspected they would have come back even if she'd stuck to that vow she'd made in the support group.

At the thought of the support group, she used her hands-free to send a text to the group leader to confess she'd broken that vow and would continue to break it with Gray if the opportunity arose.

She truly hoped the opportunity arose.

Alana added to the text that she'd still attend the tune-up meetings if she decided she needed them. Right now, that need was up in the air and would depend on how things played out with Gray.

It was possible Gray would dump her again. Equally possible that her heart would shatter again. But no way would she go back in time and change having sex with the man she loved all to avoid a possible broken heart.

With that somewhat dismal revelation running through her head, Alana pulled into the cemetery parking lot, and she had a déjà vu moment when she immediately spotted Gray's truck. Various parts of her body did those little happy leaps, but the happiness quickly bottomed out because he was probably here to try to work through what had happened.

Alana started to circle around the parking lot and leave when she spotted Gray. Looking exactly like the hot cowboy of her hottest dreams, he was coming down the path.

"Wait," he called out to her.

She did, of course. She needed to see him, to talk to him, to make sure he hadn't fallen apart.

Alana got out of her car, went to stand under one of the shade trees, and while he made his way to her, she studied his face. Not for the hotness, though it was impossible not to notice that, but to try to determine just how much all of this was eating away at him. It was eating away all right, and she wished she had a magic wand to make this better.

Gray came to her, and he kissed her. Not a scorcher lover's kiss but rather a brush of his mouth on her cheek. Maybe he'd done that because he, too, was wishing for something to make this better, and for them, a kiss—even a slightly chaste one—was a way to make that happen.

"Are you okay-ish?" she asked, knowing the *ish* was about the most she could hope for here.

He shrugged and leaned his back against the tree. "I've been having some conversations with my dad, and I visited my mom's grave before I came here," he said. "I think I get why it gives some people comfort to do that. Even though she's not actually there, seeing her name carved on the marble made it easier for me to talk to her." He shook his head. "She got a raw deal."

Alana wasn't sure if Gray was talking about her dying from cancer or her husband's cheating. "She got you. So not a total raw deal. A really good deal."

Gray made one of those sounds that could have meant anything. "I've been asking myself a lot of questions over the past couple of days," he said. "Like was my father lying when he said my mom was able to look at me and not see Sadie Jo?"

She jumped right on that. "Well, that's an easy one to answer. I saw the love in her eyes when your mom looked at you. She definitely wasn't seeing her husband's one-off. She was seeing her own son. *Her son*," Alana emphasized.

Gray shifted his attention to her, and the corner of his mouth lifted in a slight smile. "That's the conclusion I came to when I was talking to her at the cemetery. My mom loved me. I have no doubts about that. None. She loved me, and she was my mother in every way that mattered."

Alana smiled, too, because that was a darn good, and accurate, conclusion for him to reach. "What other questions have you been asking yourself?"

"The ranch," he quickly named off. "Isn't it like a bribe if Sadie Jo bought it for me?"

Alana considered that a moment. "Maybe, but Sadie Jo could have just done it out of love. It's not unheard-of for two women, Sadie Jo and your mom, to love the same guy."

Or in this case, three since she was in on that "loving Gray" club. However, she was *in love* with him so that was a big difference.

"Maybe," Gray repeated several moments later. "But I've considered that if I accept the ranch, then it might be some kind of acceptance of what went on between Sadie Jo and my father."

"No way," Alana disagreed. "Though I understand what you're saying. On the one hand, you hate the one-off they had, but on the other, if they hadn't gotten together, you wouldn't be here. Your mother wouldn't have gotten the son she'd always wanted."

He looked down at her and managed another of those thin smiles. "That's a pretty wise assessment."

She shrugged. "Must be all those weeks I spent in the support group."

"Yeah." He winced a little. "I caused you to break your vow."

"No." Alana stretched out that word. "I chose to break a vow that in hindsight I shouldn't have made in the first place. My relationships didn't fail because I leaped before I looked. They failed because they weren't what I needed or wanted. They weren't you."

There. Judging from his reaction, she'd spelled out something that Gray probably would have preferred she kept to herself because he groaned softly and scrubbed his hand over his face. Since talking about them seemed to only add to his worries, she went back to what had prompted that confession.

"So, will you keep the ranch and use it for your business?" she asked.

Again, he took his time answering. "Will you be all right with your parents' reaction to having me here right under their noses?"

Alana didn't even have to think about that. "Absolutely." She came up on her tiptoes and kissed his cheek. "It'll give them something other than my career choice to whine about."

Gray smiled, and this time it was a full-blown one. "Then, I'll keep Nightfall Ranch."

Alana did a mental happy dance and followed it up with a real one. She bobbled around and lifted her arms in celebration. And it was, indeed, a celebration all right.

Well, hopefully.

Gray was staying in Last Ride, but that didn't mean all was well with them. Or other things in his life. And one of those things was huge since it involved the only living member of his family.

"Going back to those questions you've been asking yourself," she said. "Will you be able to forgive your father?"

He nodded. "I'm already working on that. It might take a while to get past being lied to all these years, but being here, close to him, will be a start. Hard to mend fences with someone if I'm not around to do the mending."

She was glad about that. Yes, his father had screwed up big-time, and he'd been wrong not to tell Gray the truth, but Alana had no doubts that the man loved his son.

"I've been asking myself another question," Gray continued a moment later. He moved directly in front of her and looked down at her. "It's a tough one, and I don't know what the answer is."

She frowned. "What?"

His gaze locked with hers. "Can you fall in love with me again?"

The relief hit her so hard that Alana wobbled and might have lost her footing had Gray not taken hold of her. Her eyes watered with happy tears. Actually, the happiness caused other reactions, too. She suddenly felt giddy and light-headed.

And completely happy.

"Absolutely," she said. "Except I really don't have to fall. I'm already in love with you."

Now his smile was dazzling. And scorching. Because, hey, this was Gray. "Even better," he concluded, "since I'm in love with you."

Alana didn't gush out a *really?* or do a happy dance. That's because she had other things to occupy her mouth and her body. Gray pulled her to him and gave her his best hot cowboy kiss ever.

* * * * *